Family Reunion
By P. Mark DeBryan

A Novel by P. Mark DeBryan

Cover by: Justin McCormick

This book is dedicated to my mother. She gave me a love of reading that has taken me on many adventures.
Thanks Mom

Author's Note

Welcome to my debut novel. For those of you who have come to this story after reading "In for a Dollar In for a Dime" you will want to start at Chapter 2, as the first chapter is what you just finished reading.

Author John O'Brien reached out to his fan base a while back and asked for submissions of short stories set in his *A New World* series. He picked four of the stories to publish with several of his own in *Untold Stories*. Much to my surprise and excitement, my short story was one of those he selected. I had the pleasure of meeting John in Seattle, and he has permitted me to expand on that short story to create the novel you are about to read. Some minor changes were made to the short story "In for a Dollar-In for a Dime" to accommodate the full-length novel *Family Reunion*. I would like to thank John for his mentorship and friendship, both of which mean more to me than he can ever know.

I wrote this book almost a year ago and have been working with my editor Sara Jones and many beta readers to polish it into the great American novel. Alas, you may find an error somewhere in it and I take full responsibility for that.

One other thing I would like to mention. Some of my beta readers pointed out that there are a lot of characters in this book. It is due to the fact that it is about a large extended family. If you have a hard time keeping them straight go to my blog to see their profiles. Enjoy, and please visit my website and look me up on Facebook.

http://pmarkdebryan.com/marks-blog/

Chapter 1

The Trip

Ryan
11:48 p.m.
Cathlamet Ferry
Puget Sound, Washington
Day One of Outbreak

The screaming finally stopped, but that didn't make me feel any better about being jammed into a stinky janitorial closet. I continued to listen to those damn things banging around out in the passenger cabin, whatever they were. It seemed like the power to the ferry had been cut off and we were drifting—there was no vibration from the engines, none of the hum associated with being underway. It was the last ferry of the night, and as such, was nearly empty. There had been about ten or fifteen people in the seating area and snack bar when the crewman went nuts.

My name is Ryan Brant, and I've seen some violence in my fifty-four years, but nothing like what happened as I stepped off the stairs into the large passenger area. On the late-night rides, the lights are turned off in some sections to afford the luxury of semi-darkness to those who want to nap. At first, squinting through the dimmed lighting, I saw what I thought was just a fistfight and moved in to break it up. I am a big guy: 6′2″, 290 pounds, and most people respect my size. Even at my age, the shenanigans stop when I make my presence known. I grabbed the guy on top by the back of his coveralls and pulled. He wasn't that big, and I figured he would thank me once I disentangled him from the fight. As I yanked on him,

1

I was impressed that he didn't immediately lose his grip on the other guy.

Amidst the struggle, I caught a glance of the other guy and saw it wasn't a guy at all; it was a woman, albeit a rather large woman. My anger rose and I put my weight into pulling this punk off her. All of a sudden, there was blood—lots of blood. I quickly looked for the source.

Did he have a knife?

For a split second, I heard my wife's voice in my head. *"You had to make it your business, didn't you? Couldn't just turn around and go back to your car?"*

My next thought was, *I'm too old for this shit.*

I let go of the kid and took a step back to figure out the best course of action. Looking for his weapon and getting my bearings at the same time, I heard a scream from the dark corner to my left. Returning my attention to the melee before me, I almost lost my cookies. The kid was now gnawing on her. Her screams of terror and pain were the worst I've ever heard. He wasn't just biting her—he was eating her!

Something deep in my mind clicked. *This is off-the-charts weird. This is not something you can deal with. Get to a safe place, hide, and reevaluate.*

The only place I could see handy was the janitor's closet.

I hadn't been to the Pacific Northwest since Mom passed away in 2010. I was born in Everett, just north of Seattle... ten pounds two ounces, blue eyes, and a head full of blond hair that would eventually turn brownish. I have always been big boned, but that isn't a bad thing. When I was just a year old, my parents packed up the seven of us kids and moved to central California. Every summer of my childhood, we would all pile into the station wagon and take a vacation back to our old homestead on Whidbey Island in Langley. I'd always considered it home. Even after I left my parents' house at seventeen to join the Coast Guard, I would head back to the northwest to see the homestead and visit with family that had either gone back or never left. My dad died in the early 80s, and Mom ultimately moved from California to eastern Washington to live next to my sister Meg. From that time until my mom passed, I flew from West Virginia, where I now live, to Seattle to visit everyone living on the coast before heading over the Cascades to visit my mom and sister.

Our big family had spread out all across the country since then. We hadn't been together as a group since the reunion we had on Whidbey back in 1996. We have an e-mail group that we all use to keep in touch with each other. My brother, Max, suggested it was time for us to meet up again before we started dying off. I am the youngest of the seven. My oldest sister, Barb, is sixteen years older, so the dying off thing was a real possibility, and, I suppose, inevitable. I'd gone to visit her last year in San Diego, but hadn't seen any of the others for some time.

Max is my next-older brother who tormented me endlessly throughout childhood. I, of course, was a perfect angel and in no way deserved such treatment. We have since become much closer, and he'd worked hard at making up for being my nemesis in those early years. He was generous to a fault and actually paid the plane fare for my kids and me to go to the reunion in '96. My son was only seven then, my daughter five. The wife does not like big crowds, especially big crowds of my relatives, so she didn't go with us on that trip.

My kids are out of the house now, on their own and all grown up, so I was flying solo this time. A month before I left West Virginia, a flu virus broke out in South Africa. I kept an eye on it in the news, and as it spread, I started to wonder if I would end up having to cancel my trip. Three weeks before I was scheduled to fly out, the flu spread to Europe and the States. The government issued travel warnings and ordered the CDC to develop a vaccine. They were calling it *The South African Flu,* and although I was attentive, I wasn't overly

3

concerned. There had been so many pandemic scares in the last few years that turned out to be nothing. The Hong Kong flu, the avian flu, and the swine flu had all made their way to the US and never amounted to much. I decided I wasn't going to call off my trip over it.

The day before I left, my brother called and said that some of the family decided not to come because of the flu scare. He was disappointed and somewhat pissed! He'd already paid for the house we would be staying in, and now he would be stuck with the entire bill. I told him not to sweat it. I would still be coming, and he and I would have a great time. I also assured him that I would cover at least half the cost of the house.

"I don't care about the money," he said, but the offer seemed to mollify him to a degree. "I'll see you there. Call me if anything comes up."

His flight was scheduled to arrive earlier than mine, so I told him we would meet at the rental house. There was no point in him sitting around the airport all day waiting for me to arrive.

As I made a break for the closet, I heard more screams coming from the other side of the ferry, issuing from what used to be a man, but was now a meal. Draped over his body was a woman, covered in his blood with a hateful look in her eyes, shoving handfuls of the man's intestines into her mouth. She didn't seem to notice me and I quickly darted into the closet. Now, sitting in the dark, I could hear what sounded like loud panting, a few withering moans, and one or two god-awful shrieks. I checked my cell phone for bars.

Damn! I berated myself silently. I never took it out of airplane mode! I reset it to active mode, cussing myself the entire time. I always checked my phone.

How could I have gone hours without turning it back on?

It began to search for a signal. *Damn it! No service!*

4

I wasn't going to be able to call the wife and calmly ask her what the hell was going on.

I checked to see if I could connect to the Wi-Fi that was listed on the printout when I purchased my ticket. My phone saw the network SID, but it was asking for a password. I dug around for the printout, finally locating it in my cargo pants' lower front pocket. I turned my phone around and used the screen as a light to look for the password.

BINGO!

No, seriously, that was the password: "BINGO24," all caps. I joined the network and waited to see what kind of signal I would get. It came up as an "excellent" connection, but the speed depended on what kind of bandwidth the system supported. I opened up my browser and I headed to AOL. AOL was my e-mail provider. I've had it since the beginning of the World Wide Web, back when you still had to pay for your e-mail and log on with a 56K landline modem. It usually had pretty good news feeds. I still had not put it together that my current dilemma was related to the South African flu.

I'd flown into SeaTac around ten o'clock that evening, and while the airport didn't seem busy, there were a lot of guys in desert camo carrying M4 carbines around. Two people in lab coats and surgical masks stopped everyone as we got off the plane and asked where we had originated our travel. The couple in front of me said they had come from New York and were swiftly escorted by the gentlemen with the guns to another area to complete a "quick" health check.

I answered honestly that I'd come from West Virginia, had a layover in Dallas, and had no contact with anyone showing symptoms of the flu. They stared me down and asked why I was wearing a surgical mask and latex gloves. I was tempted to ask them why *they* were, but I told them I heard there was a bad flu bug going 'round and didn't want to chance catching it while traveling. They asked me a few more questions and then directed me to the baggage claim area. The thing was, I wasn't going to the baggage claim area. It was going to be a short trip and I only had my carry-on bag and my laptop in a backpack.

I'd considered checking a bag for one reason only. I could have brought my Smith & Wesson 9mm handgun. I have a conceal carry permit and almost always carried, but it was a hassle to check in at the counter with the weapon and go through the pat down at security, which came without fail because the girl at the front made the secret notation on your ticket that you had checked a firearm. So, for this trip, I decided not to carry my weapon. It would only enrage the liberals in my family anyhow, and besides, what could possibly happen... right?

I headed down the hall, then ducked out the terminal doors instead of continuing to the baggage claim area. I noticed there were two guardsmen, or DHS guys, or whatever they were, catching a smoke south of the exit, so I made a quick left toward the north part of the parking garage. I'd pre-booked my rental car, so I went straight to the garage, found the Enterprise self-check-in kiosk, swiped my credit card, signed the electronic form, and hit next. It hummed and buzzed and kicked out my keys and contract with the space number listed at the top. I walked down the line of cars and found my vehicle. My brother, Max, had no doubt rented a Corvette, Hummer, or something exotic. I, on the other hand, didn't care what they gave me. I ended up with a Nissan Altima, a nice little car that I could fit into without too much discomfort. I opened the trunk and threw my bags in. Just then, there was a scream, but it didn't sound human. It sounded more like a wounded animal.

I looked around. *Well, what the hell? I don't have my piece and I am kind of in a hurry.*

I jumped into the car and headed for the exit, feeling only

slightly guilty for not checking out a situation where I may have helped. There was heavy security of some kind present, however, so I filed the guilt away. I continued toward the booth where normally there was someone waiting to examine the rental agreement and check out the car, but no one was in sight. The booth light was on and I heard music playing, but nobody was home. I was already late and in danger of missing the ferry to Whidbey. I threw the car into park, opened my door, and stepped up to the booth. Reaching in, I hit the lift gate button. I got back into the car and tore out of there like a real criminal. All I had to do then was catch the last ferry to the island. I checked the time. I was okay; I could still make it. I set the car's GPS to the Mukilteo ferry terminal and merged onto the interstate.

I was feeling a bit claustrophobic in the closet. I took some deep breaths and concentrated on my iPhone. AOL had some deal with a news service, and that's where the first news link sent me. The headline read "South African Flu—A Full-Blown Pandemic." I scrolled to the body of the text and read on:

Reports today out of every major city in the US paint a grim picture. New York closed all transportation hubs at eight p.m. and the governor called the National Guard for help in quelling the spread of the infection. Los Angeles is suffering gridlock. The California Highway Patrol has been unable to open major freeways into or out of the city. Currently, the only method of travel is the surface streets. The governor of California has called for a dusk-to-dawn curfew.

Similar reports are coming in from all over the country. There are also reports of rioting, and that some of those infected with the South African Flu are becoming extremely violent and attacking anyone they see. If you have a family member with symptoms of the flu, monitor them closely and isolate them, or restrain them, in an effort to protect them and yourselves.

Holy Schmidt! I thought.

Whenever I travel, I usually tune out the rest of the world and focus on my destination and whatever book I am currently reading.

How could the situation have deteriorated so quickly?

I opened my e-mail, hoping to see something from my wife or kids. There was nothing from them; however, there was a message from Max. I opened it:

Hey Bro, the shit has hit the fan! I tried calling and texting you but you must still be in the air. Got my rental car and went back into the terminal to wait for Lisa. She wanted to surprise you, so I didn't tell you she was coming. She texted me when she landed and told me to pick her up outside the baggage claim. She called a few minutes later in a panic saying that the military was holding them in the baggage claim area and wouldn't let them leave! I beat feet to the loading zone and there were several troop carriers parked there, so I kept going and turned into the long-term parking lot. I stayed on the phone with her and told her to hold it together and that I would get her out of there. I am heading in now. I'll let you know more later! Max

I shot him a quick reply: *Max, meet me at Sarah's house if you can!* Sarah, our niece, lived in Seattle. I was pretty sure I was going to end up back on the mainland, where currents in the area would more than likely beach the drifting ferry. I wasn't sure if Max had made it to the island, but I doubted it. Sarah's was the only place that made sense right then.

Lisa is Max's stepdaughter from his second marriage. If it weren't for her raven-black hair, you would think she was cut straight from his genes, due to her piercing brown eyes and distinctly not-petite frame, with curves in all the right places. She thought of him as Dad and was one hundred percent his daughter.

Max's e-mail, sent at six o'clock, had me berating myself for not checking my phone earlier. But apparently, my decision not to check a bag had saved me from incarceration at the airport.

It was sheer luck that led me to escape the airport. I browsed Facebook, noticing that I didn't hear anything outside of my closet door. While Facebook was no longer the be-all end-all with the younger generations, it was still my "go-to" place to find out what was going on with the family. I hated using the app on my iPhone. It was too small to give me the experience I was used to on my laptop, but that was in the trunk of my car and I didn't plan on heading anywhere until I figured out what was going on.

There were no posts from my wife or our kids. That was not unusual. As I said, the kids didn't "hang out" on Facebook much anymore, and the wife never really did. There were posts from several others of my family on the west coast, though.

My heart caught in my throat, my pulse raced, and my eyes blurred. My niece, Carla, had married my best friend, Jacob, from high school. He and I joined the Coast Guard together, and right there in front of me was a post from Carla saying he'd gotten sick yesterday and died last night. She apologized for posting it, but she said she couldn't get through to anyone on the phone. The fact that Jake was gone was like a cold anvil lying on my chest. I closed the app and went to a search engine. I had to find out more about what was happening.

Article after article told of the devastation that the South African Flu was wreaking on the world. A story from early yesterday morning said that the vaccination the CDC had sent out all over the world was being recalled. It was apparently causing some people to become violent and attack anyone around them.

My god! How many people had rushed to their doctors and clinics to get that damn vaccination?

The government had actually made sure that all doctors,

nurses, paramedics, and servicemen were the first ones to get it.

Shit, oh dear! Leave it to the government to turn a pandemic into an epic horror movie.

The nut-jobs outside my closet were apparently people who had received the vaccine and now were some kind of freaks that ate people's faces off and gorged on their intestines.

Max
6:04 p.m.
SeaTac Long-Term Parking

Max closed his e-mail and unplugged the air card from his laptop. His brown eyes focused on nothing as he sat for a minute trying to come up with a plan to get Lisa out of quarantine. Knowing he wouldn't be able to break her out, the only other option was to do what he did best: bluff and bullshit his way through. Max had "the gift," as his brother called it. With it, he'd gained entrance to places and parties where they had no right to be. It had become a running joke over the years. Of course, it didn't always go his way, as his time spent in a Mexican jail would attest to.

Max drove out of the parking lot and squealed to a stop in front of the troop carriers. Exiting the Land Rover he rented that day, he put on his angry face. He eyeballed the guy who appeared to be in charge and marched straight toward him. When he was about ten feet away, he could see the rank of colonel velcroed to the front of the man's uniform.

"Listen, you fucking idiot. You have the goddamn attorney general's daughter in there! You might survive this flu, but your ass is going to be dead meat if you don't get her out here immediately!" Max stated.

The colonel looked up from a clipboard in his hand and took

in the picture of Max in all his outraged glory. He didn't bat an eyelash. He removed his M9 from its holster and pointed it right at Max's forehead. Max halted in his tracks, held up his hands, and started apologizing before the colonel had even cleared leather.

"Sir, I'm sorry as hell. I lost my cool! I'm the attorney general's brother-in-law, and I was supposed to pick her up. My sister will kill me if I don't get her home in one piece!"

"Son, I don't care if you are the Pope's daddy! No one is leaving the quarantine area until I get word from the governor," the colonel said, slowly lowering his handgun.

Max patted his pockets as if he was trying to find his cell phone, acting as if he'd left it in the Rover. He held up a finger and turned to go back. He made it a couple of steps before the colonel fired a round off into the air. Max threw his hands up again and asked the colonel not to shoot him, his voice several octaves higher than before.

Turning, Max observed the reaction of the soldiers to the colonel. To a person, they had their weapons aimed at Max, their expressions tense and fingers caressing their triggers. All except two of them; they were in mid-run and tackled Max, slamming him to the ground. Wrenching his hands behind his back, they proceeded to slap zip ties on his wrists and ankles.

The colonel walked over, crouched down, and politely stated, "You do know that I have the right to shoot anyone that doesn't comply with my orders, son?"

"Uhhh... sir, I uhhh," Max stammered his reply.

The colonel ordered his men to cut the ties and stand him up. He approached to within inches of Max's nose.

"If I were you, I would get back in that fancy SUV and depart the area before I decide to use my discretion and shoot your dumb ass!"

*****

After hanging up with Max, Lisa looked out the large windows in the front of the building. Knowing her dad, and knowing how he thought, she immediately scanned the room for a way out. She could see her dad showing up in an ambulance, a SWAT van, or something equally as outrageous in an attempt to free her with some kind of bullshit story. While her confidence in him was high, it was also realistic. She remembered the stories her Uncle Ryan always told about his antics. No matter what the story was, they all had the same ending. The success rate of his schemes was notoriously low.

"You can't steal a base if you're afraid to try!" her dad would say.

The meaning of that saying was, as he would go on to explain, that Ty Cobb held the record for stolen bases for many years not because he was fast, but because he was willing to try.

"Do you know who Brady Anderson is? No? Exactly. Brady Anderson has the highest percentage of stolen bases ever, but nobody knows who he is because he only stole a base when he was ninety-nine percent sure he would make it," he would continue.

With that in mind, she casually walked to the baggage conveyor and sat down next to the luggage chute. Keeping her attention focused outside, she wasn't surprised when, several minutes later, a black Land Rover squealed to a stop in front of the building and her dad jumped out. She watched as he started yelling at the guy in charge, making a whole big scene. She couldn't hear what was being said, but it was apparent he was trying to get her freed. Everyone in the quarantine area watched the display out front, including the young guardsmen who were supposed to be watching the detainees. With everyone's attention on her dad, she eased onto the carousel and positioned herself right below the conveyor belt, and waited.

BANG! A shot went off. She jumped to her feet to get a better view, fearing her dad had gone too far and got himself shot. She was relieved to see him still standing and apparently unharmed. Taking two steps back, she disappeared down the conveyor belt and out of view. She huddled at the bottom of the conveyor, listening for the yells that would indicate her escape attempt was known.

Ryan
3:00 a.m.
Cathlamet Ferry
Puget Sound, Washington

The Wi-Fi dropped. *Fricken great!* I thought. *Now I'm in the dark, both literally and figuratively.*

I turned off my phone to save the battery life, which was hovering around thirty percent. There was no use having it on without a signal or connection. I hadn't heard anything outside for about an hour. Did I mention that I have a problem with claustrophobia?

I had to get out of this damn storeroom and back to the car. I carried a few survival items in my laptop bag, my knife among them. I'd been surprised when I opened the pack earlier and saw it. I'd completely forgotten it was there when I packed and headed to the airport.

So much for the thorough searches of the TSA.

The survival knife was a small folding job with an LED flashlight, a whistle, and a fire starter all built into it. Thinking that I should probably find some kind of weapon before I tried the door, I found the light switch and flipped it... nothing. I guessed the power must be out; that would answer why the Wi-Fi dropped. I fumbled around the closet, feeling for something, anything, to use as a weapon. With a shake of my head, feeling a little stupid, I pulled out my phone and turned it back on. Using it as a flashlight, I examined the interior of my hideout. I'd been sitting on the edge of the janitor's sink this entire time. Across from me was a metal cabinet. I opened it, thankful it didn't squeak on its hinges. Inside was a bunch of toilet paper on the top shelf.

At least I won't die with a stinky ass! I thought, as I stifled a laugh that threatened to spill out.

On the second shelf were a few things that could come in handy: duct tape, a hammer, and a couple screwdrivers. The rest of the shelves were full of cleaning supplies. Staring at them, I wished that I had my bug-out bag. *Here I am. All the prep for an eventuality like this, and it's thousands of miles away,* I thought, shaking my head at the irony. I had a book in my bug-out bag that had instructions for making a bomb out of everyday household cleaners. I'd no clue how to make one without the book.

My dad's voice echoed in my head. *"If wishes were fishes, no one would go hungry!"* Yeah, thanks Dad.

I took a closer look at the cleaning supplies. On the bottom shelf was a bottle of bleach. I grabbed it, and it felt about half-full—what can I say? I'm a half-full kind of guy. While I didn't see an immediate use for it, bleach can be used to purify water. I'd been drinking from the sink in little sips throughout the night, but now the faucets would only give a dribble—another sign that the ferry's power plant was offline. My search of the closet turned up only one other item of use: a mop. While I was not about to swab the decks, the handle was made of thick wood with a rubber coating for a grip. I needed to break it, but hesitated to make that much noise. Weighing the pros and cons, I decided to risk it. I put it on the floor and propped the mop end up on the bottom shelf of the cabinet. I wanted it to break toward the end. I took a deep breath and put my weight on it.

CRACK! I held my breath, listening for any sign that I'd disturbed the freaks... *nothing. That's good.*

Turning off my phone, I returned it to my pocket. I was now armed with a four-foot spear in my hands, a hammer wedged in my belt, and a couple of screwdrivers in my back pocket. I couldn't figure a way to carry the bleach, so I placed it back on the shelf. The duct tape went into my North Face windbreaker. I was missing my 9mm, and my dad's voice threatened to invade my head again. I found the door handle and suddenly had the urge to relieve myself. Fortunately, I had the mop bucket handy.

That will lessen the chance of me peeing myself when one of those freaks jumps out at me from the dark... okay, here goes nothing.

As quietly as possible, I opened the door a crack. A stench assaulted my nose.

Oh jeez, smells like a mixture of crap and carrion!

The door opened outward so I couldn't immediately see very much of the interior. The main lighting was gone, but the emergency battery-operated lights bathed the area in a pool of lukewarm half-light. In reality, it was better than it had been when I went into the closet. It wasn't bright, but I could see fairly well. My heart was pounding as I nervously glanced around, expecting to be attacked at any moment. Nothing happened. I opened the door a few more inches and listened intently for any sign of the freaks.

The fact that I didn't hear anything was just about as bad as hearing something, anything... I stood there for what seemed like an hour, although I'm sure it was probably more like ten minutes. In all of the zombie books I'd read, this was the part where the zombies would grab the door, wrench it from the person's grip, and proceed to make him into an unhappy meal. My pulse climbed to about 180. Beads of sweat ran down my brow and I had to remind myself to breathe.

Zombies? When did I start to think of them as zombies?
I eased out of the door and stood still.

These things are not like the zombies I was told to expect. Focus, dammit, or you'll most certainly not get the chance to label the thing that eats you!

I was startled to see the remains of the woman that I'd tried to rescue. She was definitely no longer overweight. Lying in a wide pool of drying blood, there were only shreds of flesh left clinging to her arms, face, and ribcage. Thankfully, the rest of her was hidden by a row of seats. I felt bile rising in my throat and it was all I could do to not heave the remains of my dinner all over the place. After another hour—ten actual minutes—I decided that standing there wasn't going to accomplish much. Forcing my legs to move, I sidled down the wall, one slow step at a time. Every brush of my clothing, every crack of my joints sounded like a rock concert. The stairwell was about five feet away. In order to get to the car, I would have to go around the end of the wall and then head back down the steps toward the front of the ferry.

Although my car was on the main level, it was sternward. The only reason I chose this stairway to come up last night was because I'd spotted a military Humvee on the same deck toward the bow, and I wanted to check it out. When I'd walked up to the Humvee, I saw a couple of guys in fatigues slumped over, sleeping in the front seats. I decided I would be better off not bothering them.

I laughingly thought at the time, *they probably have my picture broadcast as the one guy that got away from SeaTac.*

The five feet to the stairs seemed like a mile. By the time I made it across, my panting breath and the sweat trickling down my sides made it feel like I'd sprinted the distance. I slowly worked my way down to the main deck, listening for any sounds. There was nothing but the creaking of the ferry riding the swells. Descending, I felt the rolling of the vessel.

I have to come up with a better name for these things. Zombies won't do. Hmmm... oh, for Pete's sake man, FOCUS!

I could feel the fear creep down to my very bones. Stairwells are scary enough, but with what I'd observed and the total hush that had fallen over the boat, the one I was currently descending took on a particularly sinister aspect. The swinging doors at the bottom of the stairs were like a mental brick wall. I couldn't force myself to go through them.

I could hear everyone in the theater shouting at me, "No! Don't go out there!"

Standing in the darkened stairwell, the faint green light from the exit sign above me barely illuminating the doors, I steeled myself and cracked the right side open an inch. The lighting on the other side was no better, no worse. Moonlight shone through the sides of the ferry, bathing everything in silver and deep shadow. Other than the moonbeams, a few emergency lights cast dim circles of light in places. Staring through the crack, I pictured a freak behind every car.

C'mon Ryan! Are you a man or a mouse?

Taking a deep breath, I crept through the door and scanned the area. I thought of the two National Guard guys in the Humvee. I slowly worked my way to the aisle of cars. WHUMP!

My heart jumped clean out of my chest and I damn near screamed. If it wasn't for the sharp intake of breath that I held, I would have. I whipped the mop handle around, hitting the car next to me. Inside, one of the freaks was trying to smash through the window to get at me. Its shrieks were muffled inside the Cadillac sedan. Even though I'd relieved myself earlier, I still felt a small trickle of warmth run down my leg.

So much for preventative measures, I thought, staring at the pale face, its hands hammering the glass.

I turned and ran toward the Humvee, hoping that the guys there could help me. I only took two steps past the Caddy when another freak emerged from between the cars ahead. I didn't think; I didn't slow down. I kept running, my makeshift spear out in front of me. The freak launched through the air, letting out a loud and unworldly shriek. My shoulders jarred with the impact of the spear sinking in at the base of its neck. The shriek ended with a gurgle as a shower of hot blood splashed across my face, drenching my jacket. I let go of the spear and did my best fullback impression. Tucking my shoulder down to my knee, I knocked the airborne freak ass-over-teakettle and continued running toward the bow.

Ahead on the right was a bulkhead door. It had a wheel in the middle to lock it down for a watertight seal. I slid to a stop in front of the door and grabbed the wheel. Quickly spinning it, I soon realized that it had already been unlocked and I'd just engaged the mechanism. I glanced up just in time to see another freak bearing down on me from the other direction. As it ran through a pool of light, I saw that it was wearing fatigues.

Oh great, I bet this one knows Judo.

Frantically, I reached for the hammer in my belt. I'd just cleared it when the freak made impact. Falling backward, I twisted. We rolled, and luckily, I ended up on top. Breaking my hand free from the freak's clawing, I swung down as hard as I could. It sounded and felt like I'd just burst a watermelon like Gallagher. The struggling figure went limp. I wiped the gore off the hammer and stuck it back into my belt. I sat there for a second, looking at the freak's blood oozing from its pale translucent skin onto the deck. I wondered who he'd been, before all of this happened.

Still breathing heavily, I rose quickly and stepped back to the hatch. I released the mechanism and stepped through, slamming it shut behind me and spinning the wheel.

A sudden panicked thought coursed through my mind: *Did I just lock myself in a room full of these things?*

I spun around and raised the hammer. Nothing. I slumped to the floor on top of a big coil of rope. I was in the forward storage locker where they kept the lines used for tying up the ferry when it docked.

Max & Lisa
7:15 p.m.
SeaTac Airport

Well, storming the front entrance didn't work, and there's no way in from the roof. That leaves the basement, Max thought.

He drove around the loop like he was leaving the airport. Just as he entered the on-ramp for the interstate, he pulled over and drove down the embankment to a copse of trees. He hadn't done any stealthy groundwork since he left Fort Lewis in 1976 as an army grunt. Back then, it was just him and a bunch of other teenagers getting high and stumbling around the woods. He moved down the man-made ravine to a massive culvert. The conduit was so large that he didn't even have to bend over to traverse the fifty-foot passage. It took him a little over an hour to reach the fence surrounding the airport. Figuring that he had about two hours of daylight left, maybe an hour and a half, he might just have enough time to climb the fence.

Emerging into a jungle of twisting conveyor belts, Lisa made her way to a catwalk that followed the maze of the baggage delivery system.

Jeez, no wonder they lose so much luggage, she thought. She had to duck-walk in most places to get through the intertwining system. Twenty feet below her, she could see a couple of workers. They were wearing earmuffs, so she didn't think they would hear her, but they would see her right away if they looked up. The extent of her plan at this point was only to get away from the airport without getting caught, and then call her dad. She was sure he was figuring another way to get her out, and she was afraid he might get himself thrown into the quarantine just to find her.

Checking her phone for the fourth time since slipping out of the baggage claim area, she still didn't have a signal. She stared at the screen, hoping for the bars to magically appear as she ducked an overhead conveyor. Concentrating on her phone, she tripped over the control cable lying in her path. Unable to regain her balance, she fell headfirst off the catwalk. Knowing she wouldn't get away from a twenty-foot fall without injury, or at minimum alerting the workers, Lisa was surprised by the sudden arrest of her tumble. Momentarily confused, she looked about and realized that she'd only fallen eight feet. Her belly flop of a landing had been softened by an overstuffed duffel bag.

Thank God for duffel bags and those that stuff them, she thought, as she lay there trying to catch her breath.

After confirming her trip had gone unnoticed, she smiled to herself and continued on. Ahead, she spotted a set of stairs leading off the carnival ride she found herself on. Crawling on her belly down the conveyor belt, she made it to the stairs.

I just have to make it to the doors over there and I will be out!

"HEY! YOU! What in the hell are you doing down here, hot stuff?" a voice called, echoing in the cavernous facility.

One of the guys she'd observed earlier was standing at the bottom of the stairs looking up at her.

"You've been a very naughty girl," he stated, leering at her breasts.

She spun to head farther up the stairs and paused. Realizing that he knew this place, including the layout of the stairs and catwalks, he would most certainly catch her. Knowing she really didn't have any other choice, she turned back to him and smiled.

"Well, good looking, are you going to give me a spanking?"

His eyes lit up like he'd just won the lottery. "Oh, hell yes!"

As his foot touched the bottom stair, a shriek erupted as though from a demon that had just received its wings in hell. The noise coursed through the vast underground complex. The man's smile slipped as he was blindsided by a coworker, still wearing his hard hat.

Lisa watched in shock. To her, it looked as if the attacker's jaw literally unhinged as he bit into the man's neck. She could hear the sound of flesh ripping through screams of pain as a huge chunk of flesh was torn away, spraying blood everywhere, some even splashing on Lisa's face. The feel of the warm liquid hitting her cheeks and forehead shook her from her paralysis. Without another thought, she turned and raced down the stairs, taking two at a time. She ran as if the devil himself was at her heels, which she thought might actually be the case.

Barely slowing to plow through the doors, she found herself at the bottom of an outdoor set of concrete steps ascending toward the back of the terminal building. Pausing only for the briefest of seconds, she ran up the stairs almost faster than she'd descended. At the top was a landscaped berm that led down over an embankment. She pushed her way through the hedges and ran sideways down the hill. Arriving at the bottom, she looked to her left.

That way leads back to the runways, she thought, turning to the right and jogging toward the next line of trees.

Emerging on the other side of the trees, she came face-to-face with a chain-link fence. To the right was the front of the terminal, and the left led away from the airport. Shrinking back into the tree line to stay out of sight, she fished out her phone. She was surprised she'd managed to hold on to it after her fall and subsequent sprint... and doubly so that it was still working. She speed-dialed her dad.

*****

Max spent a half hour trying to climb the damn ten-foot chain-link fence. Finally flopping to the ground on the other side with multiple lacerations, his phone started ringing. Retrieving it, he saw that it was Lisa.

"Lisa, where are you? Are you okay?" he asked, answering.

There was no reply. She'd hung up the phone.

She hung up the phone! Why would she hang up?

Max couldn't believe she would hang up on him like that.

She has to be under some kind of duress.

He rolled over onto his hands and knees, using the fence to get to his feet. Frantic with worry, he turned. Lisa was running straight at him from fifteen feet away. She launched herself into his arms and started to cry.

"I got you, baby! I got you! It's going to be okay," Max said, holding her tight while his own tears started to form.

They held each other for minutes before releasing.

"Dad, you look like shit. Are you okay?" Lisa said, examining him.

"I may live, but that's up for debate at the moment," Max replied.

With a couple of shoves against his old ass, Max made it back over the fence. Lisa followed, scaling it quickly. She landed on her feet next to him as he sat gasping for air and inspecting his newest wounds.

"You know, sweetie, you could have shown up twenty minutes ago and saved us both a whole lot of pain and discomfort."

She laughed and helped him up. They made their way back through the culvert and managed to reach the Land Rover.

Max started the vehicle, pulled onto the interstate, and accelerated. Pulling his cell phone out, he tried Ryan again. The phone rang twice and then went to a fast busy signal. Trying again, he received a recorded message that informed him all circuits were busy. He put the phone down and listened as Lisa filled him in on the details of her ordeal. As she talked, he interrupted with disbelief to ask about the guy going after his friend.

"Dad, I am so not making this up!" she said, frustration edging into her voice.

"Okay, okay. Let's just find a hotel in the city and bunk down for the night. I'm too tired to try and get to the island tonight."

They found a Residence Inn and pulled in around 9:45. Checking in, the manager told them to go to their rooms and lock themselves in, informing them that they were the last people he would allow to get a room tonight. Max and Lisa stared at him with some confusion.

"Haven't you been watching the news?" the manager asked.

Both shook their heads.

Arriving at their room, they immediately turned on the TV and started watching the news. The reports were startling. The world seemed to be coming apart at the seams. The president had declared martial law and ordered all civilians to remain in their homes until told otherwise. The reports were coming in from every corner of the globe; the flu vaccinations were turning people into crazed killers. Quarantine centers had been set up; they failed. Communication systems were failing due to a lack of workers to manipulate the routing and rerouting of signals. All sorts of infrastructure were seeing similar conditions. At ten minutes after ten, the TV went blank.

Max couldn't sleep. Lisa said she had a headache and went to lie down. He heard the screams first, then the god-awful shrieks about ten minutes after Lisa had gone into the other room. He turned off all the lights and drew the blackout curtains. Their room was on the second floor overlooking the parking lot. Opening the drapes just enough to see outside, he watched people being chased down under the streetlights for a couple of hours. Unable to believe what he was witnessing, and not wanting to see any more, he made himself a stiff drink and sat. With drink in hand, he stared at the wall in the darkness and listened to the world crumbling outside.

He didn't remember falling asleep, but he woke with a start. Something, or someone, was banging into the walls of the building. The tremors were faint, but they were there. He looked out the window and saw hundreds of people running back and forth between the buildings. As he watched, one person ran at full speed into the side of the complex their room was in. Bam! No sooner had he felt the vibration from the impact another would repeat the procedure.

The phones didn't work, the TV didn't work, but he still hadn't tried his laptop. Plugging in his air card, he couldn't find a signal. He tried the hotel's wireless network: no luck. Max was finally able to get onto the Internet after hooking into the hotel's Ethernet. He looked at his watch; it was 2:45 a.m. Opening his e-mail, he saw a message from Ryan. He opened it, read it, and replied that they would meet at Sarah's place tomorrow. He was moving the cursor to the send button when the connection dropped.

Ryan
5:52 a.m.
Cathlamet Ferry
Puget Sound, Washington

I woke up to what felt like a car wreck. There wasn't even time to process that I'd passed out before my head banged into a steel bulkhead. My shoulder then smacked into a girder, and I reached up and grabbed it to stabilize myself as I felt the ferry shudder and buck. After a moment, the shifting and crashing stopped. I felt my head and my hand came away sticky.

I must have split my noggin.

Then, remembering the encounter I'd had with the freak in

uniform, I shuddered and felt nauseated. I leaned back against the bulkhead to take stock of my injuries. Probing, I couldn't find a wound on my head, and although I took a pretty good shot to the shoulder, I didn't think I'd broken anything. The blood must have been from the Zeke last night.

Zeke. Yeah, that's a good name for them. Not "zombies" like Romero's, but something fast and vicious.

The ferry took another jolt and I grabbed the stanchion next to me. The ferry had either run aground or into another vessel. I rose shakily. Finding my hammer, I cavalierly opened the hatch. I'd had it with this shit; I was either going to make it or I wasn't. I was not going to just sit around waiting to die of thirst in a locked room.

Stepping out, I had to shield my eyes from the glare of the brightly shining sun. I looked around the car deck. The vehicles were jammed together like a pileup on the interstate. There wasn't any sign of the freaks, *looks like my brain is stuck with freaks,* but I wasn't about to let my guard down. Holding the hammer, I cautiously made my way to the bow.

The ferry was wedged up against an abandoned-looking pier. The Humvee that I was headed to last night when I was so rudely interrupted by its occupant was sitting with its nose through the big steel chains, blocking the vehicle exit lane. I opened the door, ready to bash anything that jumped out.

The driver was in similar shape as the not-so-fat-anymore lady upstairs. The stench was worse than a dead whore in a Mexican brothel. I stepped back and looked in the cab from a greater distance. It wasn't much better, but at least I was able to keep from gagging. I walked around to the back of the Humvee and opened it up.

Halle-frickin-lujah!

I stared at the most beautiful thing I'd seen since I left West-*By-God*-Virginia: a case of M4A1 carbines, four cases of MREs, and a box of 24 grenades. These guys must have been taking supplies from the armory in Seattle to a deployed unit on Whidbey when all this came down. After more searching and gagging, I came across a box of utility vests and six bags of loaded magazines for the M4A1s. The M4s were straight-up basic carbines. There weren't any fancy scopes or stocks, just Plain Jane killing tools with standard sights. I checked the magazines to find that although the rifles were not special, the ammo was definitely high-quality 62-grain ballistic-tipped 5.56 rounds. I pulled an M4 out of the crate, cleared it, and dry-fired. These were virgin rifles, never deployed nor assigned. I was having difficulty not crying like a two-year-old on Christmas morning. I also found the driver's vest stuffed behind his seat. It had four M9 magazines in it.

Shit! He had a 9mm pistol on him, and I have to find it.

I dug around behind his seat, dry heaving the entire time.

It's not here. Damn, I guess I have to search him.

I tried to be respectful, but my eyes were watering and snot was running from my nose. My stomach was already sore from heaving so much. Then I saw the M9 down on the floor in an inch of coagulated blood and chunks of flesh.

"I'm sorry, buddy, but I need this more than you do. Thank you for your service, and God rest your soul."

Those were the first words I'd spoken aloud since this all began. My voice sounded harsh and brittle, uncaring; but honestly, I was deeply grateful to this young man who had given his life in the course of his duty.

I retrieved my backpack from the trunk of the rental car and charged my cell phone from the laptop. It was probably a moot point, but I had pictures on that phone that I didn't want to give up. There still wasn't any service, and I didn't think AT&T would be coming back anytime soon.

I crammed as many MREs into the backpack as I could after tossing the laptop and all its accessories back in the trunk. Even if there was some chance I might be able to use it again, it was just shit taking up room. Right now, I needed food, water, and ammunition. I had a one-liter water bottle in my pack, and I knew that water was number one on the list of things I had to find. I thought about going back to get the bleach, but the mere thought of facing the unknown darkness made me forget that idea as quickly as it formed.

Finding an old, rusty ladder that I could reach on the pier, I climbed up with a great amount of huffing and puffing. I was tired and sore and hurt in places I didn't even know existed, but there was no rest in sight. I had to find some transportation; I had to get to Sarah's house.

It was eleven o'clock before I found a vehicle with the keys in it. As an added bonus, it had nearly a full tank of fuel. On the downside, the previous owner had expired behind the wheel. The mess he left me was disgusting, but I dragged him out and cleaned off the seat as best as I could. I found a blanket in the back and used it to cover what I couldn't clean. Contrary to the story about Los Angeles I'd read on the Internet last night, the roads were fairly clear. I didn't have a clue as to why, but I wasn't about to complain.

The car was a Chevy Malibu with a built-in GPS navigation system. I wasn't sure if it would work, but after typing in my niece's address, it came right up with a route. As it turned out, the ferry had beached just north of Edmonds. The pier was no longer in use; there wasn't even an access road. I'd had to climb a fence, cross two railroad tracks, and climb another fence before I'd arrived at the parking lot. A sign identified the place as Haines Wharf Park.

The GPS indicated that it was only half an hour to Woodinville, where I hoped to find Max, Lisa, and Sarah's family. The trip was uneventful and enlightening. The only places with any congestion appeared to be off-ramps leading to hospitals. Once I hit the 405, I could maintain about thirty miles per hour through the mess. Slowing to miss a few abandoned crashes and several bodies cost me some time, but I pulled up to the house just after noon. The garage door was open and there was a single SUV parked in the driveway.

Looks like Max didn't get my message, I thought, pulling in. I sat in the car, hoping someone would come out of the house to greet me. After ten minutes with no sign of life, I got out of the car. The entire neighborhood seemed abandoned. I saw the curtains in the front window of the house move.

Did I just see that or am I losing it? I thought, as the front door opened and Max stuck his head out.

"Hey, little brother!"

I ran around the car and bolted for him. I was never so glad to see anyone in my entire life, and I planned to bear hug him.

"Whoa man, hold up," he said, holding up both arms, palms facing me.

I skidded to a stop. "Why? What's wrong?" I asked, confused.

Still holding up his arms, he said, "Sarah left a note. Tim and Peter died two days ago. Sarah and the other three kids left the same day and went to Meg's."

Then he hung his head. "Lisa is sick, man. She looks real bad... I don't know."

His shoulders shook as he stood sobbing. I walked up and grabbed him into that bear hug. He tried to pull away, but he was in no shape to rebuff the support I offered.

He whispered, "I don't think she's going to make it, Ryan, and I don't know if I want to."

Just then, a plane roared overhead. I ran back into the yard, waving my arms. There was no use shouting, as I knew from my time as an air crewman in the Coast Guard. The aircraft didn't turn or acknowledge that it had seen me. I turned around and walked back to the house. Max said that I shouldn't be there, that I would be exposed to the flu if I came in.

I chuckled and put my arm around his shoulder. "Max, as you always say, 'in for a dollar... in for dime.'"

Chapter 2

Regroup

RYAN, MAX, & LISA
3:00 P.M.
SARAH'S HOUSE
WOODINVILLE, WA

I listened to the raspy breathing across the room—Lisa wasn't doing well. I found a thermometer and took her temperature: 103 degrees. Max was finally sleeping; I could hear him snoring in the next room. After I'd convinced him that he couldn't get me to leave, he finally gave in and lay down while I watched Lisa.

Apparently, Sarah had realized things were going downhill fast and filled the bathtubs with water for drinking and left some food out before leaving the house. For us, or for whoever happened across the house, I guessed. I am not a doctor, but I knew I had to keep Lisa hydrated if she was going to stand any chance at all. I woke her every fifteen minutes or so and forced her to drink some water, half of which I would end up wearing.

I searched my mind for everything I'd heard about the South African Flu. I knew the mortality rate was extremely high, but I also thought I remembered hearing that most victims succumbed to death within the first 24 hours. Max said she started showing symptoms at ten o'clock the night before. All I could do at that point was wait while my mind wandered.

I need to finish shoring up the windows and doors before it gets dark... We need to go back to the ferry to get the rest of the weapons and ammunition...

I went to check on Lisa again, jolted back to reality by her coughing. She was paler than before, her eyes were sunken back in the sockets, and she was still burning up.

I have to cool her down somehow. I know we need the water to drink, but if I can't break this fever, she's going to die, and soon. The decision made, I started stripping off her clothes.

"Lisa, I have to get you undressed and get you into the bathtub."

She opened her eyes but didn't seem to focus on me. I got her down to her underwear after much contorting of limbs and embarrassed fumbling on my part. She was as light as a feather.

It is like carrying a burning piece of charcoal, I thought to myself as I made my way down the hall to the bathroom. The water wasn't cold, but it was much cooler than she was. I lay her gently in the tub, making sure to keep my hand behind her head. I took her temp again: 104!

Come on Lisa, fight this thing!

I spent the next two hours stirring water and swishing it over her hair, not sure if it was accomplishing anything.

I heard Max call out, "Ryan?"

"We're back here, in the back bathroom."

He came in wiping the sleep from his eyes, looking like hell.

"Any change?" he asked.

"Here, switch places with me and I'll take her temperature again," I said, as I moved to let him take my seat.

I slid the thermometer under her tongue while he held her still. It was an old mercury thermometer, and I forgot to shake the mercury back down. I pulled it back and shook it. The thermometer flew from my hand and shattered on the floor.

"Shit!" I yelled.

Lisa's eyes slammed open and she sat up, coughing and shaking.

"Lisa!" Max turned her head in his hands. "Lisa, can you hear me?"

She jerked a little and said, "Damn, Dad. I'm sick, not deaf!"

I laughed loudly and got down next to them. "How are you feeling?" I asked.

"Like shit, thank you. Can you get me out of this tub? I'm freezing."

I looked at Max. "It's a good sign, I think. It means the fever has broken."

Max busied himself helping Lisa up and toweling her off, but I could see what looked like hope in his eyes.

"Jeez, Dad, you're going to rub my skin off; easy, would ya!"

Max smiled then muttered, "Oh, she's definitely getting better. She sounds just like her mother when she gets her ass up in the air."

I just grinned and said, "Come on, let's get her back to the couch."

Once we had Lisa settled back on the couch, I signaled Max to follow me into the garage. We needed to secure the house. Max was so caught up with Lisa that he hadn't been thinking about it. I am the youngest in my family so I usually defer to my older siblings, but I didn't live through yesterday just to sit by and wait for him to make the call.

"Max, we only have an hour or so of light left. We need to finish boarding up the windows and doors."

He just stared at me for a minute.

"Max?"

He shook his head once and nodded.

"That sounds like a good idea," he said, finally snapping back to the present.

Max had been a carpenter his entire life. There was no one I knew who was better with a hammer and nails. In very short order, we had completed the job and set about taking an inventory of the supplies in the house and those we brought with us, in preparation for the night ahead. The light outside was fading and I'd no idea what to expect.

Would thousands of those freaks attack us as soon as it gets dark, or would they leave us alone entirely? I had no clue.

With night looming, we sat in the living room to go over our stock. Max and Lisa came to the party with nothing but their clothes and a desire to live. We had plenty of food and enough water to last us through the night, thanks to Sarah and Tim. One tub of water upstairs was full, and there was still some left in the tub downstairs—though we wouldn't be drinking that. There was no telling what came off of or out of Lisa during her bath.

I brought two of the M4 rifles and the M9 from the ferry, courtesy of the National Guard. I managed to carry two bags of 30-round magazines, totaling about 600 rounds of .556 for the M4s. I had five 15-round magazines for the M9; seventy-five rounds of 9mm.

I'd carefully packed five of the grenades in my backpack. I had no experience with them, and frankly, they scared the shit out of me. But Max's eyes lit up when he saw them.

"Shit, oh dear, little brother. Where did you get those?" were his exact words.

We had two flashlights, my tactical 300-lumen that had been in my laptop bag and the small LED on my survival knife. We found a Coleman LED lantern with an extra battery in the garage and a few candles in the kitchen pantry. We laid out everything and split the weapons between us—Max and I that is, Lisa was still out of action. I was exhausted; Max said he was fine, so he took the first watch.

"Wake me at midnight. No lights and no sound, Bro. We've got to act like a black hole here and hope we go unnoticed," I said, and trundled off to collapse in the next room.

I thought I would pass out as soon as I hit the bed, but once I was horizontal, my mind went into high gear. A panic attack struck me as I realized that this was for real. I'd been so focused on just making it through the day, my mind had saved up all its emotional baggage until I landed. I rolled over and puked my guts out; I didn't have time to stifle the urge. It just came. Waves of worry about my wife and kids caught up with me and knocked me sideways. Tears spewed from my eyes as my breath came in gasps. The room was spinning and I thought for sure I was dying. I flopped back on the mattress and grabbed onto the bedding to keep from flying across the room. My heart rate soared as the primal *fight or flight* coursed through me.

Then it stopped. Everything slowly ebbed and I felt the panic leave me. *Face the fear,* I told myself. *My wife is strong and the kids are smart. If anyone stands a chance of making it, they do.*

"J," my wife of twenty-seven years, would be with my son Mark and his wife, Patty. They had all my prepper supplies as well as their own bug-out bags. Mark had his .45 auto and my dad's old Winchester 1894. I also remembered that Ann, his maternal grandmother, had given him his Pappy's .357.

My paranoia about our country's economy collapsing turned out to be wrong, or at least avoided by this crazy scenario. After the last big crash of the stock market in '08, I stocked the house with canned goods. I also bought an AR15 and a thousand or so rounds of .223, in addition to my shotgun and 9mm pistol.

They could hunker down in town then beat feet for the camp—a 4.5-acre piece of land with a double-wide on it near Tygart Lake in West Virginia, about two and half hours north of them. We lived there for several years before I transferred to Charleston.

My daughter, Auddy, lived in South Carolina, and that was my biggest fear. She was afraid to own a gun; all she had was a damn Taser and some mace I'd bought for her. Her boyfriend was smart and tough and would do what he could, but the not knowing haunted me.

Somehow, I managed to fall asleep in spite of the rantings of my conscious mind.

I woke to Max's whispered insistence. I sat up and tried to make sense of what he was saying.

"Ryan, wake up! Something is out there, Ryan!"

I sat up and waved him quiet. Listening for a minute, I could hear the shrieks I'd come to associate with the freaks. *Yeah, that name is going to stick,* I thought before my mind flicked back to Max.

"Are they trying to get in?" I asked him, feeling around for the M9 I left lying next to me on the bed.

"No, but there seems to be a bunch of them running up and down the street."

He was standing by the window, peering out of the cracks he left specifically for that purpose. I cupped my hand over the end of my flashlight and flicked it on and off to check the batteries, then located the M9, holstered it, and got up to stand next to him. We stood there together, looking out through the crack and over the driveway to the street.

It was a rare clear moonlit night in western Washington, and I could see fairly well. Several of the freaks were jogging down the middle of the road. They stopped and lifted their faces toward the sky, as if they were sniffing the air. Every so often, one would break off from the pack and head off on its own. This was the first time I saw that type of pack mentality. Up until then, I'd only experienced them *mano-a-mano.* This was new, and new scared me. It meant they were developing traits they didn't possess last night, or perhaps I just hadn't seen it. It showed a level of intelligence, this cooperation between them, and that didn't bode well for us. Their methods had not found us yet, but it was concerning nonetheless.

"How is Lisa doing?" I asked, almost too low to be heard. "And what time is it?"

Max looked at his watch. "It's 1:30, and Lisa seems to be

35

resting much better than earlier. Without the thermometer, though, I can't tell if she still has a fever."

"Well? Does she still feel hot?"

Max shot back a hurt look. "How the hell am I supposed to tell?"

We are making too much noise. I raised my hand to try to quiet him. I had it about halfway up when I heard a loud shriek right outside the window, then another at the front of the house. That's when the banging started. It sounded like they couldn't tell the difference between the boarded windows and the exterior walls.

The booming noise grew more frequent, and Max raised his M4. I began waving frantically in the half-dark room at him. Thankfully, he saw me, lowered the rifle, and mouthed "WHAT?" back at me.

I pointed to the other room and made what I thought was the universal sign for someone sleeping, then pointed again, hoping he understood we needed to go to Lisa. He looked at me as if I'd lost my mind. *No, dumb shit, I don't want to take a nap.*

"Go to Lisa," I whispered and pointed again.

He acted like he couldn't read my mind and flipped me off as he headed to the front room. I turned the flashlight on again, keeping my hand over the light, letting just enough spill for me to see my way. When I got to the couch, Max was there feeling Lisa's forehead.

I heard panting noises coming from the door a few feet away. As quietly as I could, I crept over to it. We had only put a couple of two-by-fours across the front door in case we needed to use it as an exit. The door was steel, with a deadbolt in addition to the normal door lock. I crouched down and eased up with my back against the wall right next to it. I could still hear the panting outside and wanted to see if it was just one. *Probably just a dedicated Jehovah's Witness... right?* I turned to face the door and slowly elevated to the peephole. It reminded me of U-boat movies where the captain raises the periscope to see if the destroyers are still there.

Steeling myself for whatever I was about to see, I pressed my eye to the lens. What I saw was a freak running full speed toward the door. I almost got my face off the door before he hit. The force of the impact combined with my initial backwards motion launched me onto my ass, taking out a little table and the knick-knacks it held. The crashing wood and breaking glass figurines sounded like a car wreck. Lisa came to with a scream and Max started unloading his M4 at the door.

By the time I got to my feet, Max had burned through one magazine and was loading another.

"STOP! HOLD IT!" I blurted.

I went back to the door and peered through one of the new holes provided by Max. On the porch, a single body lay on its side. I stood up and opened the little portal that surrounded the peephole like a speakeasy password door. My nostrils were immediately assaulted by the smell that I would now forever associate with these... these... freaks!

I only had to look at the body for a second to verify that it was not getting back up, and then I looked to the street beyond. *Shit!* Fifteen to twenty of the freaks were running full tilt down the street toward the house. I turned and yelled,

"Run! Go to the utility room!"

Max grabbed Lisa's arm, yanking her to her feet just as I got to them. I grabbed her other arm. You would never have guessed that two overweight fifty-plus-year-old guys could move like we were. We dodged around the obstacles we had set up earlier in the day, making it to the kitchen just as the first of the freaks hit the door. It shook, but held. I slipped a little making the turn toward the stairway that led down to the utility room, landing on my left knee. The one the doctor said would never be right again, even after he replaced half of it with titanium.

I dropped Lisa's arm and kept shouting to them, "Go... Go... Go!"

I turned to the door and brought the M4 up. The door still held, but I didn't know how long it would. One after the other, the freaks launched their bodies at the door. They were all shrieking.

Probably calling all the freaks in Seattle to the buffet, I thought, as I waited to see if they'd get through. Each time one hit the door, I winced. They kept it up for a good while. I don't know how long I sat there kneeling with the M4 pointed at the door. I just know that my knee was killing me. I slid to the floor and belly-crawled to the stairway. I could barely make out Max at the doorway of the utility room in the basement.

I set the last trap as I heard the frame of the front door crack. I didn't know if it would continue to hold, but I wasn't sticking around to find out. I turned over onto my ass and bumped down the stairs like a two-year-old looking for a good time. When I got to the bottom, Max grabbed my hand, pulled me into the room, and slammed the door shut.

"Did they get in?" Max asked, hammering two-by-fours over each corner of the door and frame. He told me earlier that it gave more surface strength to the door than simply nailing them across the frame.

"I don't know," I replied, rubbing my knee and making a pouty face.

"Why in hell's name did you shoot the hell out of the door?" I asked in a reasonable tone, which probably came out sounding more like, *"WHAT THE HELL WERE YOU THINKING, YOU IDIOT?"*

Max didn't miss a lick. "Oh, I dunno. Maybe because I just saw my little brother go flying backward and I thought it might be a good idea to stop whatever was trying to break in and eat his ungrateful, useless ass."

"Hmm..." I replied thoughtfully. "Well, you know that every

one of those things within miles is probably headed for this house now, looking for an easy meal."

Max briefly paused his hammering and said, "I guess I should have just let them eat you then."

He finished nailing up the boards that we stored down there for this very purpose. Earlier, we had set up the utility room as our fallback position. All our weapons and ammunition, some water, and some food were down here. He'd, however, left the five grenades upstairs, set up with trip wires around the house as a surprise for our guests. Thankfully, we hadn't tripped them dragging Lisa across the living room, which could have happened easily since she wasn't in on the plan.

The house shook and dust fell on us from the ceiling. "One down," Max said, and lifted four fingers, his thumb crossing his palm. The second grenade exploded, sending another massive quake through the house. Max folded over a finger. Again, the house joggled; again Max put down a finger. I just covered my head and hoped the ceiling stayed in place.

"Jeez Max, get down," I shouted...

Max just smiled and looked up. A thump that felt like a blow to the gut rattled the room. Max bent down and covered his head, which was what I told him to do, but it did not instill a lot of confidence in my expectations. I grabbed Lisa and covered her as best I could. The walls literally bowed inward, my ears felt the compression, and the world went dark.

Max shook his head and wondered how long he'd been out. He found Ryan's tactical flashlight and turned it on to check on Ryan and Lisa. They both seemed to be unconscious, but okay otherwise—no bloody ears, noses, or eyes.

He got up and surveyed the damage. The room itself was still structurally sound. Stuff had fallen off the shelves and the drop-down ceiling tiles were lying about, making the room seem in disarray. Not bad. His booby traps had all gone off without completely destroying their HQ.

It was just like his days in the army, although he'd never actually been in combat. All they had ever done was train, sit around, and then train some more. He was glad to see that the training had stuck thirty-five years later. He looked at the time, 5:20 a.m.—still a few minutes before the sun would come up.

He got up and went to the door. He put his ear to it to see if he could hear anything moving in the basement. His hearing wasn't great before the grenades went off, and now there was a persistent high-pitched ringing, but he concentrated on trying to locate any movement outside the utility room.

After a few minutes, he decided to do some recon. He pulled the boards from the doorframe with the claw hammer as quietly as possible. He started to open the door, and then stopped. He checked his rifle and made sure there was a fresh magazine in place with a round in the chamber. He cautiously opened the door and stepped out, closing it behind him.

*****

I don't know how long I was unconscious, but as I came to, my ears were ringing and I was covered in debris. I lay there for a moment to get my wits about me. I felt someone moving under me and remembered trying to cover Lisa. I rolled to the side a little.

"Lisa, are you okay?"

She ran a hand through her hair and looked as if she was contemplating an answer. "Yeah, I'm fine. I actually feel hungry," she finally replied.

I chuckled. "Well, that's a good sign, I guess."

I moved around and threw some of the ceiling tiles off me to see if I could locate Max. The last place I'd seen him before the grenades went off was over by the door. He wasn't there. I noticed that the boards were missing from the doorframe, although the door seemed to be fine and was still shut.

I collected myself and cleared away the junk, which was mostly ceiling tiles and boxes from the shelves. Having tidied up a bit, I decided to go look for Max.

"Lisa, I need to go find out what Max is up to. Why don't you try to find the least disgusting MRE there and eat a little? Don't overdo it."

She gave me a weak smile. "Okay, and what if the monsters come eat me while you're out looking for Max?"

"Valid point, my dear." I unholstered the M9 and held it up. "Have you ever fired one of these?"

She reached up and took the weapon, popped the magazine out, racked the slide, and caught the round that was in the chamber as it flew out.

"Please... your brother had me shooting before I could spell my name."

"Okey-dokey, Annie Oakley," I said with a smile. *Damn, I wish I'd done the same with Auddy. Please God, let her be okay.*

I handed her one of the extra magazines. "We need a password to make sure we're good when we come back. What works for you?"

Lisa came back quickly with an answer. "I'll be Raven and you can be Chicken One, and Dad can be Chicken Two."

"Chicken One? I think I can come up with something better than that."

"Nope. I insist. Besides, who is ever going to guess that?"

I had to admit that she had me there. "Okay, but if someone has me at gunpoint or something, I will change it to Eagle One, okay?"

"Good thinking, Chicken One!" she giggled.

I grimaced and continued, "Right, so I will only go out and look around for a few minutes, then I will come back and check on you."

"Roger that, Chicken One!"

I am definitely changing this shit soon. If she thinks it's cute I will let it go for now, but Chicken One? Really? In all the books I'd ever read, the guys always had really cool names. Chicken One is bullshit—although it did make me laugh.

I cracked the door and peeked out. "Roger that, Raven," I said over my shoulder. "I will be right back."

Oh crap, Sarah is going to be pissed when she sees what Max did to her house.

I looked up the stairway to what used to be the first floor. A predawn hue promised another day, something that I realized was no longer to be taken for granted. I stepped over some pieces of unidentifiable debris.

The top of the stairs ended in the kitchen, or where it used to be. I could see the sky. *Hmmm... not good, not good.* As I climbed the stairs, I heard something moving around.

"Max? Is that you?" I called out. "Yeah, just me, and a bunch of zombie parts," he answered back.

I crested the stairs and turned toward the front room. The house was a total loss. There was a big hole that used to be an exterior wall. The interior walls were peppered with shrapnel and stains of what must have been the blood of the freaks.

"Zombies are undead things that you have to decapitate or shoot in the head to kill," I said, approaching him. "These things aren't dead and can be killed with a body shot." I put my hands on my hips. "And furthermore, they don't get back up after you shoot them."

"I stand corrected, little brother. And what other conclusions have your skilled observations helped you arrive at?" he said, mimicking my stance.

His sarcasm ignored, I went on. "Well, it appears they don't enjoy the sunshine, or even the overcast skies of the great state of Washington."

He interrupted again, "And the bastards can't stand a good fragging."

I looked around at the devastation his grenade traps had caused. "You realize that if Sarah ever comes back here, your ass is kaput."

"What? They were your damn grenades."

I just shook my head. "Come on, we need to get Lisa and talk about what's next on our agenda."

We collected everything that we thought would be useful and packed it into the two vehicles. Then we sat down to discuss our next move. Lisa was still nowhere near one hundred percent, but she had a vote in everything we decided.

Max and I each had our own ideas about what to do. I, for one, said that we should head up to Parker's house in Everson after returning to the ferry to collect the rest of the guns and stuff I left there. Parker was our older brother. He lived a short distance from the Canadian border and kept a bunch of stuff we could stand to have, especially his local knowledge. He and his wife, Rhonda, were mother-earth kind of folks. She was retired now, and Parker worked for the state fish and game department. He got the job because of his extensive knowledge of the peregrine falcons in the area, and all other manner of bird species. His love of falcons was second only to his love for his wife, although she debated that.

Max wanted to go to the ferry also, but then head directly for Meg's house in eastern Washington to hook up with her and Sarah and the kids. Lisa didn't really care either way, but tended to side with Max just because. There were other things to take into consideration.

I'd one or two concerns. "Max, who was still trying to make it to the reunion? Is there a chance anyone got all the way to the island? Or maybe someone who might still be stuck at the airport?"

He rubbed his temples and thought for a minute. "Well, everyone from San Diego was going to drive up. Jake and Carla were going to bring Lauren and Steve and stop in Portland to pick up Conner, and..."

I'd been holding up my hand since he got to the part about Jake and Carla. I choked up a bit and took a deep breath.

"Jake died from the flu. I don't know what Carla was planning, but I doubt they left San Diego."

Max knew how that had to have affected me, and just said, "Aw shit, sorry man."

I waved my hand in a circle indicating he should continue.

"Well," he said, "that means Barb and all of her clan probably didn't head out either." Barb was our oldest sister and her clan was composed of about twenty other nieces, cousins, and assorted family.

"I don't know," I said. "What about Maddie, wasn't she flying up from Texas?"

Max gave a quick shake of the head. "No, she and her husband were borrowing a friend's RV and driving. Jean was flying to Colorado to hook up with Lynn, and they were going to drive to Meg's before heading out to the coast."

So, that accounted for all of our immediate family, as Jean and Lynn were our other sisters. There were still more cousins and our one surviving aunt, but neither Max nor I knew their travel plans.

"What about Trish?" I didn't want to ask because Trish was his daughter from his first marriage. I knew it was a touchy subject, but I touched it anyway.

Max got a faraway look in his eyes, as if remembering a long ago time when life was just getting started.

"She's at her mom's place with Frank. They were going to come over for a day, but with what happened, they are probably going to hole up at the farm."

He grimaced, then said, "Damn place is way the hell out in the boonies, so they're good for now."

I put both hands on my knees and sighed. "I would feel better if we at least did a drive-by at Parker's before heading to

Meg's, but I will go along with whatever you guys decide."

Max looked over at Lisa. "What do you think?"

She pursed her lips. "Look, Uncle Parker can take care of himself, and he may even think to come here. I think we should leave a message for him, telling him our plans and asking him to check the island to see if anyone got there. Then we should go get the stuff from the ferry and head to Meg's."

I must have done a double take, because she just looked at me and said, "What?"

I laughed and stood. "Lisa, that is probably the most cogent, well-spoken idea that has been put forth at our little meeting; I second that, let's go!"

Max grinned. "That's my girl! Let's do it!"

Chapter 3

Family

MADDIE & HARRY
SOUTH OF RAYMONDVILLE, TEXAS
ONE WEEK BEFORE OUTBREAK

At sixty, cousin Maddie was still beautiful. She had to fight to keep ol' man time from getting the best of her, but she was active and physically fit. She would go down someday, she knew, but it would be kickin'-n-screamin'. Her strawberry blond hair had some gray to it, but she'd taken to dying that out years ago. She rode her horses, tended to her livestock, and was about as real a cowgirl as you would ever meet. She could sing like an angel and drink you under the table if she'd a mind to.

She'd lived a good part of her life as a singer in multiple country western bands after migrating to Texas in her twenties. Maddie was also a nurse anesthetist by trade and had the funds to support the lifestyle she'd become accustomed to. She had a son, Branson, from her first marriage; he was on his own, living life as a twenty-eight-year-old.

Maddie had met and married Harry a few years ago; robbing the cradle, so to speak, as he was forty-nine now, and barely able to keep up with her. That's not to say he wasn't in good shape. He weighed 175 pounds, but at 5´9˝, he was solid and strong. He had blue eyes and blond hair and the women said he was cute, in a manly way. Harry owned a towing company and specialized in towing big rigs and unusually large vehicles. He was constantly teased because his last name was Towes—no kidding, Harry Towes. He'd become quite the fighter in grade school, where the other kids teased him about his hairy toes. Even after he was much older, he'd been in a few scraps over his name. Eventually he got past it and used it to promote his business.

Harry mostly just nodded, throwing out an, "uh-huh," and a "you bet, sweetie" every once in a while, while Maddie held up the conversation.

She was a prepper. That is to say, she was sure the government was heading to hell in a hand basket, and she would be ready when it happened. She and Ryan had kept in touch over the years, both leery of the direction the country was headed. Where Ryan was somewhat prepared for the collapse of society, Maddie was *fucking A* prepared. Perhaps even a little bit anxious to try out all of her goodies. She wasn't paranoid, just prepper-anoid. She would tell you this and then laugh with such gusto that you had to laugh with her.

She'd given thought to calling off the trip when the flu started in South Africa, but Ryan had given her a hard time. He joked with her that if the shit did hit the fan while they were at the reunion, he would need her help protecting all the helpless liberals. She laughed and told him she would see.

Once she'd decided to go, they made the decision to drive because Harry didn't like to fly. It wasn't that he wouldn't, just that he didn't like to. They were due for some time off anyhow, and Harry's kids wanted him to get away from the shop for a while.

Maddie looked around at RVs and thought about buying a camper to tow behind one of their trucks. She changed her mind when a wealthy client, who was also a good friend, asked Harry if he wanted to borrow his Marathon motor coach[1]. Harry didn't explain to Maddie that they were going to Oregon, drop it off, and pick up a new one his client had ordered.

---

[1] See diagram on page 327

Maddie literally did a little dance when she saw the coach for the first time.

"DAMN Harry, this thing is a mansion on wheels!" she said, feeling the custom wood finish inside the door. "This is too nice; we can't borrow this."

Harry smiled. "Uh-huh, you bet we can, sweetie." And that was that.

She spent the next day and a half loading the considerable storage areas with all the things a prepper considered nice to have in case of TEOTWAWKI. She was looking forward to the trip north, which would take them through some of the most beautiful country in the world.

Carla
9:00 a.m.
San Diego International Airport
One Day before Outbreak

Carla Wilford sat in the Range Rover in the cell phone lot. She marveled at how excited she still got picking up Jake from his frequent business trips, even after twenty-eight years of marriage. He worked for a marketing firm that handled all of the mailers and telemarketing for one of the big three automakers. His territory had increased over the last couple of years as the company merged with another company and cut staff, increasing his workload, the number of dealerships, and trips away from home. He didn't complain, as the pay was good. He enjoyed the work, and most importantly, he still had his job.

She was also excited to be leaving for two weeks of time off with the family. Lauren and Steve, her daughter and son-in-law, were waiting at the house, ready for the long road trip to Portland, Oregon. There they would pick up Conner, the youngest Wilford, and head the rest of the way to Whidbey

Island in Washington for the reunion. Conner was just finishing his last semester of college, and after the reunion, they would all head back to Portland for his graduation ceremony.

Carla was the shortest member of the family, but she ran her clan like a congenial chief boatswain's mate. Jake was the man of the house and often equated himself to the captain of the ship. He did what the chief said and basked in the glory of being captain.

Lauren and Steve had just moved from the East Coast after finishing their university experience. Steve was in the Navy ROTC and needed to complete a yearlong internship before his commission as a chaplain came about. Lauren, following family tradition, was a registered nurse. Two of her great aunts, Jean and Meg, were both RNs, and Lauren had always thought that it was cool. After two years of actual nursing experience, however, she realized that "cool" was a matter of perception.

Carla glanced at her watch for the third time in as many minutes. The flight was two hours late as it was; Jake should be on the ground, headed for baggage claim. She thought about just heading over now, but she'd jumped the gun before and suffered the wrath of the airport police for loitering too long in the pickup area. She would wait for him to call.

Her mom and sister were also going to Washington but wouldn't leave until tomorrow, as the rest of the family had to work right up to their departure. She was glad they would be traveling separately. Their group might be twenty-plus people, and that always led to drama and delays.

Her thoughts were interrupted by the familiar "YO-HO-BLOW-THE-MAN-DOWN" ringtone. They were a nautical kind of family; at least Jake thought they were, as he clung to his old Coast Guard days. She pushed the phone button on the steering wheel.

"Hey Hon," she answered, putting the Rover in gear. "On my way."

"Okay," Jake replied, not sounding his usual chipper self.

"Are you okay?"

"Yeah, just got a bit of jet lag, I think," he replied. "We were sitting on the ground for two hours in Hawaii waiting for clearance. There was some kind of BS about the Department of Homeland Security or something. Anyhow, I will be at the curb in a couple of minutes."

"I will be here waiting," she said, as she jockeyed between two limos for a spot.

Four hours later, they were on the 805 Freeway, headed north to Interstate 15, then on to the I-5. This would take them inland a bit and was an easier route than trying to hug the coast all the way to Oregon. Carla was worried about Jake. He'd thrown up at the house before they left, although he insisted he just needed some sleep. She'd been seeing the South African Flu story on the news, but that was on the East Coast, and Jake had been in Honolulu for the last week. Oh well, even if he picked up a bug, she would pamper him back to health over the next couple of days. She just felt bad for him, being sick while on the road.

Looks like Steve and I will be doing most of the driving, she thought, as she watched Jake sleep fitfully.

Jean, Lynn, Madison, & Tyler
8:00 a.m.
Butte, Montana
One Day Before Outbreak

"She'll be coming around the mountain, she'll be coming around the mountain, she'll be coming around the mountain when she comes..." Aunt Jean finished with a flurry and everyone giggled.

"Let's do Michael Finnegan," shouted Tyler from the backseat of the Prius.

"Uuughhh!" Madison cried. "We've been singing that one for the last twenty-four hours!"

"Oma," Tyler complained to Lynn, "why do we always have to sing what Madison wants?"

They were on the way to Aunt Meg's house in Washington, and were two hours on the road after stopping for the night in Bozeman, Montana.

"Listen you two, do I have to pull this car over and give you what for?" Lynn couldn't finish the sentence with a straight face, and everyone burst into a fit of laughter.

Jean had flown to Denver from Ft. Lauderdale, Florida, where she lived, to catch a ride with Lynn and her grandkids to the reunion. Of all Ryan's brothers and sisters, these two were as thick as thieves. Jean was the second child and Lynn the fourth. Lynn also had the distinction of being the youngest girl. That being said, neither were spring chickens. Jean was sixty-six, and she and Max were the rebels of the family. She would fit most comfortably in the "tough old broad" category these days. You did not fuck with Jean. Lynn was only a step behind Jean, but had somehow inherited a bit more tact from the family gene pool—not much, but enough to be a calming force in tense situations. The two together were hell on wheels.

Lynn was a motivational speaker, a life coach, and ran a successful art camp for women. She prided herself on her fitness, both mental and physical. She'd toned down many of her business interests in favor of caring for her grandkids, whom she loved and helped raise when their father turned out to be a dud. Lynn was a "can do," type-A personality and knew that she could defeat any obstacle put before her, given enough time and resources.

Jean was a nurse; she now relied on that vocation more so than she had for most of her life. She'd worked the yachting scene in the Caribbean for a long time. That came about from an extended job in Alaska during the building of the Alaskan pipeline, a very lucrative time for her. She'd taken the money and invested in a schooner with two of her doctor friends, and they chartered cruises for the near rich in the Caribbean.

When that ended, she went on to work other big yachts as a nurse and head steward. As she got older, the yacht gigs went by the wayside, and now she did home health care when not out socializing with her friends. On the flight from Florida, she'd observed several people who looked like death. She knew what that look was, having seen it before. She dug around in her purse, found a surgical mask, and wore it for the rest of the trip. She really didn't want to be sick for the reunion.

In between singing silly songs, watching for cars with only one headlight, and seeing how many different state license plates they could collect, they listened to the radio; NPR mostly, and what they heard was not good. The CDC was now calling for everyone to get vaccinated against the South African Flu immediately. Jean and Lynn discussed it and decided to wait until they got to Meg's house to see if she'd been giving out the vaccine, and if she had any on hand.

The Barbara Bunch
8:00 a.m.
San Diego, CA
Day of Outbreak

Barb was seventy years old. She was the matriarch of her branch of the family tree. She gathered part of the family at her home in El Cajon, a community just east of San Diego. Her daughter Carla and son-in-law Jake had already left for the reunion. Barb's oldest, Hope, was helping to organize the caravan of travelers prior to their departure. Hope usually left this kind of stuff to her younger sister, Carla, who loved it.

"Okay, everybody, we leave in ten minutes," she said, knowing it would be more like thirty. "Make sure to hit the bathroom before we leave. Our first stop will be hours up the road."

She knew this also was not true but said it anyhow, almost hopefully. Hope's oldest, Diane, directed her five-year-old daughter, Lila, to pee again. Barb's oldest son, Joshua, was hustling around, helping to load the last of their luggage and pillows and whatever else they had deemed necessary for the trip.

Without Carla and her clan, the family caravan would consist of only three vehicles.

Hardly a caravan at all, Barb thought. Denise and her new husband, Larry, were late: the first of what would be many delays in their journey north. What was normally close to twenty people was now a mere handful. Joshua had just gone through his second divorce and had not brought along his newest girlfriend. He was 5′10″, good-looking, strong as an ox, and had forty-five years of bad luck with women.

In the lead car, Barb occupied the navigator's seat. She was looking at the road map; she liked having it. GPS was just not her thing. Josh was driving and Grandpa Don rode in the backseat. Hope was in the second vehicle with her husband Dale, Diane, and a most-excited Lila.

They had just about given up on Denise when Hope got a call. "Mom, this is Denise. We have another employee that called in sick. We are going to have to stay."

"Oh, are you sure, honey?" Hope knew that Denise and Larry's lunch truck was doing well and thought they deserved to get away.

"Yeah, Mom, we just can't leave without Carver running the truck. He's the only one we trust to do it, and now he has the flu."

"Well, okay then, we will miss you. Love you!" Hope was

disappointed but also proud that her daughter was taking care of business, like an adult.

"Believe me, Mom, we really wanted to go. We love you too. Have a safe trip."

As they disconnected the call, neither of them knew it would be the last time they would ever speak to each other. The two cars pulled out and headed for the freeway to begin the trip that would prove to be anything but what they expected.

Josh looked in the rearview mirror every few minutes to make sure Dale was still there. They were ten hours into their trip and the sun had set, making it hard for Josh to tell if the car trailing him was Dale. He slowed to let the car behind him catch up a little. When it did, he said, "Uh oh!"

Barb looked over at him staring in the mirror. "What's the matter?"

"I lost Dale. I thought the car behind us was him, so I don't know how long ago we lost him."

Barb turned in her seat to look back. "It couldn't have been long, or they would have called."

Josh nodded as he turned on the signal to stop on the shoulder of the interstate. "We'll just wait and let them catch up."

As soon as they stopped, Barb tried to call Hope. *"All circuits are busy, please hang up and try your call again..."* She hung up and tried again with the same result. "I can't get her cell. Do you think we should turn around and go back?"

They were all peering out of the rear window in anticipation of the missing family members pulling up behind them.

"Let's just give them a few minutes; I'm sure they are just lagging behind a little," added Grandpa Don.

The sky melded from twilight into darkness as they sat and waited. About twenty-five minutes later, a highway patrol car sped past in the opposite direction with all its lights on and the siren blaring. Josh could make out more emergency lights heading south farther up the road.

"Oh no, turn around now!" Barb shouted at Josh.

Josh waited for a break in the traffic, made an illegal U-turn, and almost got stuck in the median. Thankfully, the car survived the bumpy median and lurched onto the southbound side of the freeway. They sped south, following the Highway Patrol's lights in the distance.

They crested a hill to the scene of a massive car accident on the northbound side of the road. There were several police cars and emergency vehicles on both sides of the interstate, their harsh lights strobing off the devastation. Josh pulled over.

"Wait here!" he said, opening the door. Barb ignored his directive and got out of the vehicle, leaving Grandpa Don in the car.

They crossed to the northbound side, expecting to find someone in authority directing the scene. What they found instead caused Josh to immediately bend over and begin retching. A body with its head caved in was halfway out of the passenger side of an SUV's windshield. The driver also appeared to be dead or unconscious. The SUV was pinned to the guardrail by a semi-truck on its side, which Josh recalled passing an hour or so ago. The windshield of the semi was missing, as was the driver.

The scene was surreal, like a nightmare. The lights flashed, and the smell of diesel fuel, gasoline, and burnt rubber hung in the air. There were people calling for help, people screaming, the sound of hot motors ticking, and cars passing by in the southbound lanes. Barb made her way around the truck and SUV to look for Hope and her family. Josh recovered and followed her over the guardrail toward the other vehicles in the pileup.

The complete chaos of cars and trucks thrown together made the mangled wreckage that much harder to search. Josh grabbed his mom by the arm.

"Did you hear that?" he asked her.

Barb continued on. "We have to keep looking."

"Mom, did you hear that shrieking?"

Barb ignored him and peered into the debris. Josh stopped and turned his head, trying to locate the sound. It was then that he heard it again, but this time gunshots rang out in response. Josh started jogging toward the sound. He passed a box truck, and there he saw Dale's Lexus.

"Mom!" he called out. "I found their car!"

Josh approached the car with caution, afraid of what he would find. The entire front end of the car was ripped off, the rear smashed all the way into the backseat. He didn't even realize he was crying until his mom appeared around the overturned box truck.

"Oh no, oh no, oh no," she kept repeating, as she stumbled toward the Lexus.

"Mom, wait!" Josh stood frozen to the ground, unable to draw any nearer to the horror that waited, promising to sear itself into his brain forever.

Barb continued into the wreckage and yelled back to Josh, "Hurry! Hope is still alive!"

That broke Josh from his stupor. He raced forward to help Barb free Hope, but before he made it two steps, Barb began to scream. That's when he saw Dale standing where the front of the car used to be, his arm bent at an unusual angle.

Looks like he smashed his mouth on the steering wheel. There was blood all over his face and down the front of his shirt. He tilted his head back and let loose a shriek that made Josh's skin crawl.

A gunshot sounded from behind the Lexus, and Dale crumpled to the ground. Josh ran to him, unsure of what to do. As he got closer, he saw a highway patrolman leaning against the truck that the Lexus crashed into. He looked up at Josh, smiled, stuck the gun in his mouth, and pulled the trigger. Josh saw what looked like mud splatter against the door the patrolman had been leaning against. It took a millisecond for him to process that it wasn't mud; the patrolman slid down the truck in a heap.

He checked Dale's pulse and found none. He walked over to the cop and checked on him as well. It was obvious he was dead, but it looked like a wild animal had gutted him. Josh relieved him of his weapon, a Smith & Wesson 4006. He looked for additional magazines on the officer's belt and found two.

Josh stood and went to help Barb, who was again attempting to free Hope from the wreckage, though by all appearances, she didn't stand a chance. Blood was no longer pouring from her shoulder and neck.

How did she get such horrific trauma from a car accident?

"Mom..." Josh stepped up next to her and laid a hand on her arm.

She whirled around and pushed him. "No, no, no... she will be okay!" she screamed at him. Then she turned back to Hope and said, "You'll be okay, you'll be okay!"

Josh let his mom try to extricate Hope while he looked into the backseat. Diane was obviously gone; her once-beautiful eyes fixed upward, meeting his gaze. It was hard, but he looked over at Lila's booster seat.

"Mom, Lila's not here!"

"Help me with Hope, then we will find Lila!"

"Mom! Hope is dead!"

Barb fell forward onto the car. "Oh God, why would you let this happen?"

Josh tried to convince his mom to return to the car and wait while he searched for Lila. She refused and began calling out for her great grandchild.

"Lila! Lilaaaaa!"

Josh stuck the patrolman's gun in his belt and looked under both the car and the truck for her. Not finding any sign of her there, he had a hopeful thought—*she must still be alive or she would be right here!* He began calling for her as well, frantically searching around the other side of the wreckage.

Back at the car, Grandpa Don sat in the backseat. He'd rolled the window down to listen for any sign of his family. He suffered in silence, waiting for them to return. He heard the plaintive screams of those in pain, the shrieking of... he didn't know of what. He'd just decided to go after his wife and Josh when something zipped past in his peripheral vision. It was too quick to identify, but he smelled something horrible.

Several years before, he'd undergone a brain surgery that had affected his sense of smell; however, he was sure this smell was real, not imagined as some were. He opened the door and stood next to the car. He thought that he heard something or someone in the bushes next to the road. He moved toward the bushes.

What was that sound? It almost sounded like a dog panting, or someone who had just run a mile trying to catch their breath.

"Josh, is that you?" Whatever it was, it wasn't Josh. It let out an unbelievable shriek that sent Gramps hustling back to the car.

He made it to the car, slammed the door, and tried to roll up the window, but he'd turned the ignition off after opening it and now there was no power. The thing from the bushes ran into the side of the car, bounced off, and tried regaining its feet as Grandpa Don lurched forward over the seat to turn the key. Accomplishing this, he was reaching for the window button next to the driver's seat when he felt the thing grab him from behind. Then he felt a searing heat in his right leg.

He turned to see Lila, his great-granddaughter, leaning halfway through the window, viciously biting his leg, ripping the flesh off his calf. Then a second one came to likewise reach through the window, grabbing at him. He successfully jerked his leg away from Lila and pushed her back against the thing behind her. He was able to hold her back far enough to roll up the window. Just as it was about to close, it stopped, blocked by the toe of his shoe.

He wrenched his foot free, but the thing behind Lila managed to get its hand through the crack. Thinking it would try to pull free from the door, Gramps lowered the window a half-inch, but instead of pulling its hand out, the monster pushed it further through, almost managing to get its whole arm inside the vehicle. Grandpa Don quickly closed the window up tight against it.

His leg was a mess. The wound was bleeding freely, and it took all his effort to crawl into the driver's seat. He started the car, put it in gear, and swung out onto the southbound lane, gathering speed as he mashed the accelerator all the way to the floorboard. The thing managed to keep on its feet for about twenty yards before tripping.

Now dragging the thing alongside the car, Grandpa Don yelled, "Take that, you son-of-a-booger!"

He aimed the car toward a police car sitting on the shoulder of the road, its lights flashing. His right front fender made contact with the left rear quarter panel of the old Crown Vic.

The screeching of metal drowned out the shrieking thing right before it was sandwiched between the two vehicles. Its bones were shattered instantly by the collision; blood issued from its mouth and eyes in response to the intense pressure created by the crash. Grandpa Don swore under his breath as the car fishtailed. He tried to regain control as he bounced off the police cruiser. When he managed to stop the car, he turned in his seat to look back. There was the arm of the thing—half-in, half-out of the window.

For whatever reason, the traffic seemed to have disappeared from the interstate. Grandpa Don turned the car around and drove north in the southbound lanes, the car making unusual sounds and the steering wheel pulling hard to the right. He manhandled the car back toward where they had parked earlier and activated the high beams, looking for Lila.

He didn't care that she'd attacked him. That was his great-granddaughter out there, and he was going to help her if he could. But his head swam, and before he could find her, his vision started to tunnel into darkness. He passed out and his head came to rest on the horn.

Josh heard the car horn and stopped his search. "Mom, is that Dad?"

Barb also stopped and listened. "It sounds like our horn."

Josh walked back to her. "Come on, he must need us!"

They made their way back around the pileup to see the car facing the wrong direction, the entire right side smashed up.

"What the hell?" Josh uttered. He ran toward the car and saw his dad slumped over, head resting on the steering wheel. He ran around to the driver's side and opened the door, reached in, and gently laid him back in the seat. It was then that he saw the blood.

"Mom, come here, quick!"

Barb hustled as quickly as possible, which was a halting jog with a walking step thrown in here and there. She made it to the car and saw the arm hanging in the window. She was no wimp, but the sight of it combined with the crazy state of affairs surrounding her was just too much; she fainted and fell to the ground like a sack of spuds.

Josh, caught off guard, didn't know what to do. *Do I leave Dad to help Mom?*

He opened the back door, pulled Gramps out of the driver's seat, and laid him in the backseat. He took off his belt, put it around his dad's leg, and tightened it as much as he could. That accomplished, he went over to his mom, who had started to come around. He helped her back to the car and got her over to the passenger seat with a little pushing and shoving.

Once he had everyone situated in the car, he started forward only to realize the damage was so bad that it was close to undrivable. He looked back and saw the flashing lights of what looked like an ambulance a quarter-mile south. He fought with the wheel, got turned around, and slowly made his way in that direction. It took several minutes, but he made it. He pulled up behind the ambulance and jumped out of the car.

He noticed something was different than it was just a few minutes ago.

The quiet! The sounds of people screaming had stopped, and there was no shouting between emergency workers. *What the hell?*

He stood there for a minute trying to figure out what was going on.

"Where is everyone?" Barb asked, leaning over toward the driver's side.

"I don't know, Mom, but we have got to get Dad to a hospital. Are you well enough to help me move him to the ambulance?" He half expected her to argue with him about stealing the ambulance, but she just nodded and got out of the car.

They moved Grandpa Don into the ambulance and laid him on the floor; there weren't any stretchers. Barb got in with him. Josh closed the back doors and went around to the front of the truck, got in, and started it. The radio squelched and he grabbed the mic off the dash.

"Hello, is there anyone out there? Hello?" Nothing. He threw the truck in gear, did a three-point turn, and headed north.

Chapter 4

Heading Out

RYAN, MAX, & LISA
7:00 A.M.
HINES WHARF PARK

The trip from Woodinville to the ferry went without incident: no resistance, no survivors. The ferry was still where I'd left it, securely wedged into the pier. Max wanted to pull the fence down so we could back the vehicles up to the pier.

"Max, I think we ought to leave it up. Let's check the ferry before we do something we can't undo," I argued, finishing the energy drink I'd taken from Sarah's stash.

"Why?" was his only reply.

"Well, I thought we might be able to get the ferry running eventually... and even if we can't, it's a good place to keep as a secured area."

Max mulled that over for a few seconds and nodded. "Okay, so what's your plan for today?"

We discussed in detail how we should approach the situation, and came to an agreement. Lisa would stay with the vehicles and signal us if anyone else showed up while Max and I retrieved what we could from the decks of the ferry without going inside; once that was done, we would inspect the rest of the ship, time permitting.

"Okay. Lisa, are you good with this?" Max asked.

"It's Raven, Chicken Two. And yeah, I'm fine."

I hadn't explained our code from earlier to Max, so he wasn't in the loop.

"Chicken Two?"

Lisa laughed. "Yeah, you're Chicken Two and Uncle Ryan is Chicken One. I'm Raven."

Max's only comeback was, "So why is he Chicken One?"

I threw the empty can I was holding at him. "Come on, let's get this done."

Max and I scaled the chain-link fences, cussing and bitching the whole time. We caught our pants and shirts on the loose metal ends and tried not to impale any important body parts. Once over the fences, we made our way to the ladder.

"Man, what's up with this pier?" Max asked as I climbed down to the ferry.

"I read on the placard in the park that it was an old Coast Guard patrol boat station in World War Two. Some guy bought it and made it into a fishing pier that closed sometime in the late '60s."

"Huh, learn something new every day," Max said as he made his way down.

We went around the vehicles to where the Humvee was located and began to move the contents up to the pier. It was hard, sweaty work, but after a couple of hours, we had four cases of MREs—minus what I'd already pilfered—the remaining six M4s, and the nineteen remaining grenades. In addition to that, I'd missed the 5.56 ammo boxes under the case that held the M4s.

"How much of this ammo should we take?" I asked Max.

"All of it. You never know if we'll ever make it back here."

I blanched. "But that is like five thousand rounds, dude."

He just smiled. "Quit bitchin' and start pitchin', recruit."

"Okay, Chicken Two," was the only comeback I could think of.

It was two o'clock before we got it all loaded into the vehicles. The Malibu sat on its haunches like a cat pissing.

"Looks like we need to find better transportation," Max said, pointing at the Malibu while sitting back against the wheel of the Rover.

"Well, I don't think anyone is going to throw us in jail if we just go find a dealership and requisition a couple of trucks," Lisa offered.

"Another great idea, Lisa, we'll do that," I said. "Do you think it's too late to hit the road for Meg's?"

Max shook his head. "I think we should go find a truck and transfer everything into it and go. Once we get out of town, we should be safer. Don't you think?"

I nodded. "I would still like to explore the ferry and see if it's salvageable; but you're right, the longer we stay in a populated area, the longer we will be surrounded by thousands of these freaks."

We loaded ourselves into the vehicles. I drove the Malibu and Max drove the Rover, with Lisa riding shotgun. As I drove, I couldn't help but think about my family back in West Virginia. *Were they still alive? Did Auddy make it home from South Carolina? I need to find out! How would I ever make it all the way home? I need to get to Meg's house for now, then I can figure out what to do next.*

I came out of my reverie suddenly when I caught motion out of the corner of my eye. I slammed on the brakes and Max almost rear-ended me. A gaunt black cat ran across the road in front of us.

Great! Just what I needed, seven years of bad luck! It was the first sign of life I'd seen all day. *Well, I guess the pussycats made it through the outbreak.* I released the brake and waved to Max and Lisa to follow me.

Once we were back out on the Pacific Highway, I stopped and went back to the Rover.

"Which way?" I asked after Max rolled down his window.

"I think our chances are better if we head toward Lynnwood," Max said, looking both north and south on the highway.

"Looks like the businesses pick up that way," Lisa threw in.

I peered down the road. "Okay, south it is." I got back into the Malibu and turned right. The car bottomed out with every bump I hit. If we didn't find something soon, I was sure I'd lose the muffler.

Not more than a half-mile down the road, I saw that Max had chosen well. There was a Ford dealership just ahead, and it was a large one. I pulled up in front of the showroom and stopped. I looked around but saw no signs of life; it was eerie how quiet the world was in the absence of all normal human noise. I got out of the car as Max and Lisa exited the Rover, grabbing the M4 as I went.

"Let's have a look."

Max had his M4 and Lisa carried the M9. We moved around to the side where the main doors were located.

"Looks like someone beat us to the punch," Max observed.

The glass doors were shattered and there were what looked like muddy footprints covering the floor just inside the door.

"Something, not someone. I think we found a nest of freaks, Max," I said.

Lisa took an involuntary step backward, but Max lean forward for a better look.

"Yeah, I think that's dried blood."

He reached down and ran his finger across one of the footprints. It didn't smear, so it wasn't fresh. Max stood up and pointed to a beautiful white F350 Super Crew Platinum four-wheel drive truck in the showroom.

"That's what we want, right there."

It had the eight-foot bed and was probably twenty feet long in total.

"That thing is a monster," I said. I'd wanted one of its little brothers, the F150, for some time now.

"Do we risk looking for the keys, with those things in there?" I asked.

"Well, with the light from the big windows, it should be

safe... I think," Max said as he ducked under the door handles and stepped into the building.

I checked my M4 and made sure it was locked and loaded. I took the safety off and followed him in, Lisa close behind me. The showroom was a hundred feet long and fifty wide. The sales offices were little glassed-in cubicles running down the back wall. I began to check them for the manager's spot, hoping to find the keys. No luck. I noticed there was office space on the second floor that looked over the showroom.

"How do we get in there?" I said, pointing it out to Max and Lisa.

There was a lounge area at the other end of the room, and next to it was a hallway. Above the hallway entrance was a sign for the restrooms and another sign that said "Manager's Office, Parts Department, and Service" with a little arrow pointing down the hallway.

Max frowned and said, "That way, I would guess."

The path of bloody footprints went from the front door to the hallway and beyond.

"Great," I responded, not really meaning it.

The light from the showroom windows shone all the way to the far wall. A double door led to the service and parts department on the first floor. Another sign pointed up at a stairwell that said, "Manager's office." *Sonofabitch!*

I looked at Max and he shrugged. "If we want the truck, that's where we have to go."

The prospect of exploring the dark stairwell took me right back to that first night with the freaks. My adrenal gland started pouring its magic sauce throughout my body.

"Okay, Lisa, trade me weapons."

I put the safety on the M4 and showed her how it worked. I gave her the four mags of .556 for it, and in exchange took the four mags of 9mm from her. I checked the automatic to make sure it had a round in the chamber, and moved toward the stairwell.

"Okay, Max, I'll try to stay low. You got me covered?"

I could see by his eyes that the adrenaline had him in its grip as well. "Yeah, got you covered, Bro." We slowly moved up the steps.

I got to the first landing and pulled out the flashlight, and Max followed suit. The combined effect was to illuminate the entire stairwell up to the second floor. I put my foot on the next step and heard panting. It was hard to tell where the sound was coming from, as the linoleum floor and enclosed concrete walls formed an echo chamber. I took the next step and the panting grew in intensity.

I could now see a window at the top of the stairs to the left, looking back in the direction of the parts and service departments. I pointed at my eyes and motioned to Max that I was going to try to look to the right at the top of the stairs. He nodded that he understood and pointed his rifle at the corner. I felt the telltale sweat dribble down my side as I moved up another step.

The panting seemed to pick up even more. I knew it was probably just my imagination, but I could swear that the freak knew I was coming.

Well, no shit Sherlock, your shadow is as plain as skywriting. I crouched even lower. I could almost see around the corner when Mr. Sales Manager jumped at me with a blood-curdling shriek. I fired two shots, more a reflex than anything else. My shots struck it in the chest. I watched as if it were a slow motion replay, and I couldn't figure out why its head had exploded.

It wasn't until I rolled it off me that I realized Max had fired as well. His shots had literally blown the thing's head half off. The freak's blood had covered my shirt, which I immediately pulled off. I wiped my face off with a clean spot and threw it on top of the now-dead freak.

I looked at its skin; this was really the first time I'd

examined one closely. The skin was pale. It looked almost translucent, and I could see the veins running under its skin like dark roadmaps. Max and I hadn't said a word up until then.

"Pretty fucking scary looking, eh?" Max whispered.

"Are you guys okay?" Lisa yelled up the stairwell.

"Yeah, we're fine. Don't come up," I yelled back.

There was no need to subject her to this scene, and another person would just be in the way. I stepped back against the wall and let out a deep breath.

"You ready?"

Max nodded. I scaled the steps quickly this time, fearing I wouldn't be able to move at all if I thought about it too much. I aimed the light down the hall; it was clear. Max followed me up and we slowly went forward. The unnatural quiet enveloped us as we moved toward the first door. I could picture the hustle and bustle of a car dealership, people scurrying around trying to get deals done. The darkness carried its own malevolent presence that made the air itself feel heavy.

I had to consciously fight the urge to flee that was running through me. The first door we came to was open. I paused to listen for any sign that the room had a freak in it. I didn't hear anything, so I motioned Max to go in and to the right and I would go in and to the left. He nodded, and we went in fast and low. I kicked a small metal trashcan as soon as I came through the doorway, and sent it sailing across the floor where it crashed into a metal desk as loud as a fart in church. I shined the flashlight around the left-hand side of the room, expecting an attack at any second.

Max cleared his side of the room and said, "That was graceful."

"Yeah, not exactly textbook, was it? Do you hear anything?" I asked.

"No, and if there were any more of those things in here, they would be screaming and hissing about the noisy guys in the next room."

I flipped him off and went back into the hallway, shining my light down each way just to make sure we were still alone. The other rooms proved to be empty, and we chalked all the bloody footprints up to the sales manager's exploits.

We found the key rack in the manager's office, and on it, the keys to the F350.

"Should we just take this whole board downstairs and save the next guys a little trouble?" I asked Max.

"Nah it's too heavy. Just grab another set of keys to a 4×4 diesel; that way we only have to find one kind of fuel."

I searched the board with the light and found a tag identifying a 4×4 Super Duty crew cab F250 King Ranch model and we beat feet back downstairs.

We couldn't find the keys to the doors that they used to move the vehicles in and out of the showroom.

"Well, now what?" Lisa said.

I responded, "You think we can shoot the lock out of that door without breaking the glass?"

"I think I can," said Lisa, sizing up the shot.

We all got behind the truck, and she braced her arm on the bed. She leveled the M4 and took three deep breaths, letting the last one out slowly as her finger tightened on the trigger. The shot took her by surprise, and echoed around the room. I walked around the truck to the doors and inspected the damage.

"Perfect damn shot, Lisa. You are promoted to rifleman first class!"

I pushed on the door and it slid in its tracks back into the wall. Max released the finger locks on the other slider and moved it out of the way. I tossed him the keys.

"I'll take the other one, you can have the F350."

With that, I went out to the car and got a clean shirt.

Going to have to go to Wally World and get some more shirts, I thought to myself. I went to find the other truck. I pushed the alarm button on the key fob and tracked down the F250.

Max and Lisa were already transferring the stuff from the Rover and Malibu into the F350 when I rolled up in my new ride. The King Ranch was one step down from the Platinum, but was no slouch. It was dark blue with gold trim, all leather, fully loaded. I liked it.

"Never figured I'd get to own a brand new one of these," I said, stepping down from the cab. I owned an old '97 F350 with the 8.3 power-stroke motor, but I'd always dreamed of having a new one. "This F250 is supposed to get 20 mpg highway," I added.

Max stopped loading long enough to tell me to go cannibalize a couple of spare tires for our use. I found a jack and a lug wrench, and went to get us each an additional two spares.

I found a work truck that had the same size tires with just plain steel wheels. Not as cool as alloy, but it would work. I jacked up the truck, took off the left front tire, and lowered it down onto the ground. I would normally have found a block or something for it to sit on, but in this new world, it didn't seem important.

I finished getting all four tires off but realized I wouldn't be able to retrieve my jack from under the truck after all the wheels were off. My remedy was simple: I bashed in the window of the work truck and took the jack out of it. By the time I was done with my cannibalization, Max and Lisa had finished loading the trucks up and were ready to go.

We drove the trucks over, put the extra spare tires in, and pulled out of the dealer's lot. I signaled Max to pull alongside me.

"We need to find a hardware store and a sporting goods

store. There are a few more things we need before we take off."

Max gave a thumbs-up and I pulled back out onto the Pacific Highway.

We hadn't even gone a block when I spotted an auto parts store. I swerved into its parking lot and Max followed me. I hopped out of my truck, went up to the front window, and peered in.

Max walked up behind me. "What do you see?"

"Nothing bad," I replied.

The entire front of the building was floor-to-ceiling windows, letting light penetrate far into the store. It was dark in the back, but I didn't see the need for us to go in that far.

"Look over there." I pointed to a shelf with 5-gallon gas cans. "We need those and a few other things out of here." I went back to the truck and grabbed my M4.

"Come on, Lisa, we're going to need your help."

We went to the front door, which was still intact. I picked up a rock from the landscaping and tossed it at the door. It smashed, gloriously sending the glass cascading downward to the floor inside. Immediately, we heard a loud shriek as things crashed around in the back of the store. I looked at Max.

"Should we risk it?"

He looked into the store and blew out his air, puffing his cheeks as he did. "Yeah, we are going to need this stuff, and we're going to run into these things everywhere we go—so why wait? I'll go in first. Lisa, you grab a cart. Ryan, you cover our six."

"Copy that, Chicken Two!" Lisa said.

"After you." I bowed and motioned him through with a sweeping arm gesture.

My bravado was short-lived. As we entered the aisle holding the gas cans, a shriek bounced off the walls that I could feel all the way in my bones. Max swung toward the sound, and when he turned to look back, his eyes were as big as saucers. Lisa filled the cart with gas cans and hurried to the front of the store. I went as far as the end of the aisle to cover her and Max at the same time.

The freaks were howling and shrieking, and although I'd heard this before, it felt like the first time. Max waved at me to get my attention and pointed to the next aisle. I nodded, and he moved back to go over one aisle and stepped into the murky area of half-light leading to the parts section. I looked over to Lisa and back, and he was gone! *What the hell!*

I ran to the end of the aisle and heard Max scream.

"Shit, shit, shit!" I scrambled for my utility knife and turned on its flashlight. I held the M4 in my right hand and stepped around the corner. A freak had Max on the ground and I couldn't tell much more than that. I couldn't shoot the damn thing with it right on top of him, so I ran straight at it and ploughed into them, stabbing with the knife, trying to cut its damn head off.

I rolled off Max, losing my grip on the M4 but not the freak. I kept stabbing ferociously with my left hand, holding onto the freak's head with my right. I couldn't see anything, as the knife and the flashlight were now covered in blood.

Max began popping off rounds with his M4. The muzzle flashes were like a strobe light, freezing the image of a second freak right over him, then back a step, then another, and finally backed clear against the wall.

The freak I was fighting was incredibly strong, and my knife seemed to have no effect. I felt my body giving up. My mind screamed at me, *Don't you quit, you pussy... don't you dare quit!*

The freak pushed me against something. I could feel his fetid breath. All of a sudden, my vision faded and I saw a very bright, white light.

So this is how I go out? I Love you J, Mark, Auddy...

The light exploded, and I felt the heat of the blast as the freak flew off me. I looked up to see Lisa standing over me, a halo around her head.

This is weird.

"Uncle Ryan, are you all right? Oh shit, oh shit, I killed Uncle Ryan!"

I tried to say something, but my voice failed me. As quickly as it started, it was over. Max was helping me up, half-dragging me back to the front of the store. Once we reached the light, I finally was able to blurt out, hoarsely,

"I'm okay, I think."

Max eased me to the ground and sat down heavily next to me. Coughing, catching my breath, I tried to sit up. Lisa was still in a tizzy; her hands were going all over me.

"Lisa, I'm okay," I said, firmly.

She sat down hard and started sobbing. Max scooted over next to her on his butt and pulled her into a hug.

"Did it bite you, Max? Hell, did it bite me?"

I started feeling around my face and neck. There was a lot of blood on me, but thankfully, it wasn't mine.

"We've got to be more careful," Max said over Lisa's shoulder.

"Ya think?" she managed to get out between sobs.

She started getting it together—a deep breath, a hitch, another deep breath.

"Thanks, kiddo, you saved my ass," I managed to mumble.

"While you were saving my ass," Max added.

"Look, we are not trained special operators. We have to sit down and plan these foraging trips a little more thoroughly," I said as I rolled over onto my hands and knees to get up. I grunted and groaned as I used the shelves to get to my feet.

"I thought I shot you in the head back there," Lisa said, on the verge of getting worked up again.

"Look, you didn't. You shot the freak. If you hadn't, I would have been toast!"

She just nodded, turned her head, and puked all over the shelf next to her. Max rubbed her back and held her hair.

She held up her hand. "I think I'm okay now."

We collected everything else that we thought we might need: more flashlights, two full shopping bags of batteries, and a hand-crank pump as well as a battery-powered pump. We also got two batteries for the trucks and a bunch of tubing we could use with the small pumps that we found to siphon fuel.

Once we loaded the trucks with our bounty, I could see the exhaustion written across Max's and Lisa's faces. I'm sure mine looked as bad, if not worse.

"Look guys, I am voting we find someplace secure and hunker down for the night. I'm zapped."

Max smiled and pointed at something over our heads. I looked up and saw the billboard: "Adventure Sports: Guns and More" with a big arrow pointing to the right. "Just one block and make a left on Scriber Lake Road."

"That should work!" I said as we saddled up and started the trucks. We headed toward the other side of the parking lot, and right there in front of me was a Starbucks.

I swerved over and stopped. I hopped out and ran up to the window. The well-lit shop was all I needed to see. I went back to the truck, grabbed my M4, turned the safety off, and pelted the front of the store with about twenty rounds. Max got out of his ride and asked me what in the hell I was doing.

"Coffee," was all I said.

I walked up to the counter and grabbed as much ground coffee as I could carry, a bunch of cups, and some filters too. I came out of the store with a shit-eating grin on my face.

"I don't care if I have to boil it in a boot, I am going to have some coffee!"

We got back into the trucks and peeled out of the parking lot onto 200th street. The first intersection we came to was Scriber Lake Road. A Courtyard Hotel was on the corner. Just past it was a small two-level building, built back into the hillside, the lower portion facing the street and the top floor accessible by a driveway past the parking lot.

Immediately disappointed by its size and lack of burglar bars over the windows, I thought to myself, *this won't work. How can a gun shop not have security bars?* I pulled right up to the front doors and parked.

There were several cars in the parking lot, and I knew we would have to clear the building.

I asked Max exactly what I was thinking: "Is it really worth it?"

He walked up to the doors and pulled on them. The left door swung open; he almost fell down, not expecting it to be unlocked. He quickly shut it and put his hand on the glass.

"This is one-inch Lexan," he said.

"What's Lexan?" Lisa asked, sparing me the trouble.

"Bullet-resistant polycarbonate plastic, just as good as bars on the windows," he answered.

The fact that the place was unlocked was curious. Most gun shops left their doors locked, even during business hours, and used an electronic lock to buzz people in once they eyeballed them with a camera. Whatever the reason, we had access, but I was still leery of going in after the debacle at the auto parts store.

"Man, I just don't know if we should risk it," I said.

Max seemed to ponder it for a minute. "I think it's something we have to do. It's secure, and look at all the shit in there."

I didn't like it, but I acquiesced. "Okay, but we have to come up with a better strategy than we used in the auto parts store."

We took a walk around the building to make sure there were no obvious breaches that might indicate a freak nest. The bottom floor, basically a basement dug into the hillside with one side facing the street, looked secure. The top floor was office space that was locked up tight and didn't appear to have been broken into. We discussed in detail how we would go in, what we would do, and how we would retreat if necessary.

I felt better, even though in reality we were still three civilians who weren't trained for this kind of action.

It is what it is... God, I hate that cliché, I thought as we stacked up next to the front door.

Max was again the first one in, carrying his M4 up and ready. Lisa kept her hand on his shoulder, the M9 pointing out to the right and down, ready to bring it to bear. I followed right behind Lisa with my M4 up and pointed to the left. Max had duct-taped the flashlight to the end of his M4, although the room we entered had plenty of light.

As soon as we stepped over the threshold, I knew there was something dead close by. It lacked the smell that I'd come to associate with the freaks; it just smelled like ordinary, everyday death. Lisa gagged but didn't throw up. I felt the tang in my mouth that usually preceded a full-on ralph attack, but managed to keep it down.

Max led us right up to the glass display counter at the back of the room. He leaned forward and shined his light back and forth, surveying the situation.

"Oh shit!" he said with a disgusted tone, and made for the end of the counter. We stuck together as if an invisible rope connected us. Lisa's hand never left his back, and I found myself bumping into her whenever they stopped.

"This room is clear," Max said, lowering his rifle.

I went behind the counter and saw what Max had already discovered. It looked like a double murder, with a suicide to boot. An older woman sat slumped over, her brains all over the mirrored wall next to her. A smaller form, which looked like a girl, lay prostrate on the floor with a similar head wound. Next to the older woman sat a man staring directly at me, the entire top of his head missing, a Taurus Judge lay beside him.

"That pistol, it can load both .45 rounds and .410 shells. As far as I can figure, he shot both of them with .45 rounds, then sat down and did himself with a .410."

Max nodded. "Yeah, he didn't want to risk flinching and ending up a vegetable."

Lisa had gone to the other end of the counter and was holding up a ledger.

"He left a note," she announced, and went on to read it out loud. "Whoever finds this, we decided as a family that we did not want to live in a world that was ruled by zombies. Take whatever you want, 12-29-16-12; Mel, Trina, and Beth."

"That's pretty fucked up," said Max, lowering his head.

"Let's move some supplies in for the night and get some extra protection against those doors," I said, not wanting to dwell on the three lying there.

"Don't you think we ought to at least move them out of here?" Lisa asked.

"Yeah... Max and I will put them in that dumpster out front," I answered unenthusiastically.

We wrapped them up in a tarp we found in the back room. I just opened the door, went in, and looked around, shining my light on all the stored equipment. I never once thought about the possibility that freaks could be in there. Luckily, they weren't.

Max vetoed putting them in the dumpster; instead, we loaded them into the back of his truck. We then went for a ride and placed them in a vacant lot about six blocks away.

Driving back, my mind wandered as it was wont to do while I wasn't busy figuring out how to stay alive.

J, I miss you, I will find my way there no matter how long it takes. I'm sorry I wasn't there for you. I wish I could hit the rewind button, go back, and fix this. Survive baby, just survive...

"Hey, shithead, stop dwelling on it," Max said, looking over at me.

"What?" I said.

"You're beating yourself up over shit you cannot change. I can see it pulling you down."

"Thanks, Sigmund."

I turned back to the window.

"Hey, pull in here!"

Max did as I asked and pulled into the gas station.

"Look, let's not mess with the fuel today. Let's just get back and get shit squared away at the gun shop," he said to my back as I walked away from the truck.

"I'm not worried about the fuel," I said over my shoulder as I bent down, picked up a trashcan, and threw it through the window of the gas station.

I climbed through and grabbed a carton of Marlboro Lights and a six-pack of lighters. I got back into the truck and said, "Go."

He didn't say another word. I'd quit smoking a few years before and started using an e-cigarette, which had stopped working about an hour into this ordeal. I ripped into the carton, smacked the top of a pack on the heel of my hand a couple of times, then opened it and lit a cigarette. The smoke curled around my face as I took a drag, sucking it down into my nicotine-starved lungs.

As I exhaled, he just said, "Aw, shit."

He reached over and grabbed a pack. After a few minutes of us sitting there quietly smoking, we both just started laughing. Lisa shook her head.

"What the hell, give me one. Doesn't matter anyway, right?" she said.

As soon as we got back to the gun shop, we got busy setting up for nightfall. We draped tarps over the windows and pushed a heavy gun safe over to the doors, laying it down sideways to get it off the casters. It looked like it would be enough, but we got a second one and did the same.

"There, that's not going anywhere," Max said.

"I hope not. Still, let's set up our stuff in the back where there are no windows." When hiding from things that go bump in the night, I am a firm believer in two zones of protection.

We moved into the storage room and tried to make it as comfortable as possible. We still had some daylight left, so we set out to enhance our weapon load. Max gravitated to the shotguns, and I wanted to find a 1911 .45. I found what I was looking for right away—two sets of matched Sig Sauer 1911 C3s, a smaller version of the 1911. Each had a 4.2-inch barrel, rosewood grips and polished steel frame with a seven-shot magazine.

"Hey Lisa, come over here and check these out."

She made her way over and I held one out for her to see.

"Wow, I like the feel of that," she said, moving it around, checking the balance.

"Yeah, it's a .45, with a lot more punch than the M9 we have now. Now, let's find some comfortable holsters."

It didn't take long to find two sets of holsters that would work. With two guns each, the math was easy. "Seven rounds, plus one in the pipe, will give us sixteen rounds each," I explained. The same number of rounds as the M9, but with much better knockdown power.

"Sold!" she responded with a grin.

We found two extra magazines for them, in addition to the one that was in the case. The C3s had tritium sights for low-light situations, and all around, I thought it was a better handgun than the M9.

"We'll hit the range in the morning and get you familiar with them," I said as she continued to admire her new friends.

Max came over carrying two tactical shotguns.

"Wilson Combat? Never heard of them before," I said as he handed one to me.

"They take the Remington 870 and add a few bells and whistles, like the 120-lumen light with quick-on button."

Max pointed out each feature to me as he listed them aloud.

"Eighteen-inch barrel with a modified choke, Trak-Lock ghost-ring rear sight, and ramp front with tritium insert."

He flipped it over and continued, "The follower is neon green, makes it easy to see in the dark."

"What's a follower?" Lisa asked.

"It shows you where to stick the rounds when reloading. It takes six 2 ¾ shells or four 3-inch magnums. There's a clip here to carry six extra rounds."

"Nice find," I said.

"Yeah, there's a lot more here that we can use, but it's getting dark. You guys wanna eat and call it a night?" Max asked.

We were all beat, and it sounded like a good plan to me. We took our new weapons and ammo back to the storage room and fixed some MREs. There was a short couch long enough for Lisa to stretch out on and a couple of old lounge chairs. We flipped for who had watch. Max didn't get his finger up fast enough, so he had first shift.

"Wake me in four hours, Bro." I crashed onto the La-Z-Boy and quickly fell asleep.

Chapter 5

Go Back or Go On?

CARLA'S GROUP
9:00 P.M.
BAKERSFIELD, CA
ONE DAY BEFORE OUTBREAK

Carla sat next to Jake's cot in the hastily created triage tent of Mercy Southwest Hospital. Their travel north interrupted, as Jake's flu was worse than he'd let on. He started the day with a headache and nausea, but the further they drove, the sicker he became. At Lauren's insistence, Carla had finally relented and made the call to go to the hospital, and they veered off Interstate 5 toward Bakersfield at five o'clock.

When they turned off the Rosedale Highway onto Old River road, the two lanes of northbound traffic in front of the hospital were closed and tents were erected on them. It took four hours to get Jake situated and examined by a nurse, who spent just a few minutes with him and wrote a number in red on the back of his hand.

She turned to Carla and asked, "Have you been vaccinated?"

Carla shook her head no.

"Roll up your sleeve." Carla blanched and asked why.

The nurse said matter-of-factly, "It's too late for me to inoculate him, but I have the vaccine and you should take it."

With tears running down her face, Carla took off the shirt she was wearing over her spaghetti-strap camisole, but as the nurse came at her to administer the vaccination, Carla had a premonition.

"No! I changed my mind. I don't want it."

The nurse wasn't in the mood; having too much to do, she dismissed Carla with a, "Whatever, lady."

Lauren and Steve had gone to find a hotel, but they had already gotten the vaccination at the Naval Base in San Diego, *or had they?*

Jake stirred and opened his eyes. His dry lips cracked as he smiled at Carla. "Hey beautiful," he croaked. "What's a guy gotta do to get a drink in this joint?"

Carla held a cup of water with a straw up to his mouth so he could get a sip. He coughed up what little water she got into him. Carla kept wiping him down with a cool washcloth and he slipped back into unconsciousness a few minutes later. They were giving him fluids via IV, but his body was burning them off as quickly as they were going in.

The doctor finally visited a couple of hours later and asked Carla if Jake had been awake at all. When she said yes, that he'd been awake for a few minutes, the doctor said that was a good sign and left.

Two hours later, Jake's breathing became labored and then just stopped. Carla screamed for the nurse, but no one came. She tried to do CPR and gave up only when the nurse finally showed up and pulled her away. Carla was devastated; she folded to the pavement and lay there weeping. The nurse helped her onto a chair and stayed with her until she was finally able to get somewhat under control.

She called Lauren and told her that her dad had passed. Lauren started with the questions that couldn't be answered before giving up and handing the phone to her husband while trying not to give into the shock. Steve got on the phone.

"I'm so sorry. Carla..." he started, but the Navy chaplain knew there were no words that would ease the pain she was feeling.

"Jake loved you, Lauren, and Conner, so much. He's no longer in pain," he continued, trying to find the right words. At a loss, he simply admitted, "There is nothing I can say that will help you hurt less; just know that we are here for you."

Carla asked Steve to bring Lauren back to the hospital and hung up. When the nurse told Carla they would have to take the body away, she asked with an angry edge to her voice, "Can't you even wait until my daughter gets here to say her goodbyes?"

"I'm sorry, but we have to take precautions with deaths from the South African Flu. We don't have the space to quarantine you, or we would do that as well. Has he been in contact with anyone else in the last twenty-four hours?"

Carla laughed mirthlessly. "Are you kidding me? He has been in contact with literally hundreds of people in the last twenty-four hours!"

The nurse tried to keep her cool. "Ma'am, I am just trying to help here. I should be at home with my family! His body will be cremated and his ashes will be sent to you once this has all settled down."

Carla knew her anger was misplaced. She walked away, over to Jake's cot. She got down on her knees next to him, ran her fingers through his hair, and then put her hand on his bearded cheek.

"I love you, Jacob Floyd Wilford. I will always love you. I will be with you again; save me a seat." She kissed him gently on the forehead, stood, and walked out of the tent, not wanting to look back, knowing that it wouldn't change anything.

Carla called and arranged to meet up with Lauren and Steve. Lauren had made it through the denial stage and onto anger, and like Carla, directed her wrath at the hospital. "What the hell, they aren't going to release Dad? What the hell!" she repeated.

She regained control on the twenty-minute drive back to the hospital. When she saw her mom, however, they both broke down again into a sobbing hug that lasted several minutes. Steve just stood back, giving them the space and time to deal with the suddenness of Jake's death and the hole he left in their hearts.

They got back to the hotel and talked about getting some food, but no one was hungry. They flipped on the TV for some kind of a distraction. The news was following the South African Flu.

"Do you want me to turn this off?" Steve asked.

"No!" they both said at once.

"We need to see what's going on, and we need to talk about what we're going to do," Carla added.

The 24-hour news network's background banner declared *BREAKING NEWS*. That could mean anything these days, the term so overused as to be completely irrelevant. The ticker at the bottom of the screen, however, made the banner actually seem relevant, as it scrolled a running tally of the dead in Europe and South Africa. The total deaths in South Africa were over 200,000, and even the UK had risen to over 85,000. The ticker continued even though the station was running a commercial for erectile dysfunction.

Back from the commercial break, the anchor began speaking after the *BREAKING NEWS* graphic spun up behind him:

"More disturbing news just in from our correspondent Jim Covett, covering the Pentagon in Washington, D.C. Jim?" The camera cut to the remote unit outside the Pentagon.

"Thanks, Chuck. High-ranking officials here are denying the rumors that U.S. military personnel are reporting in sick by the thousands across the country and around the world. There are also unconfirmed reports that many have died and that we have lost contact with several key bases in remote locations such as Diego Garcia. One official, who spoke to us on conditions of anonymity, said that six different overseas bases had gone dark this evening, and that efforts were underway to reestablish contact. Other reports from Stuttgart

Army Air Base in Germany claim that some of the personnel have attacked their own troops. These reports have been officially discounted due to the extreme nature of the attacks and reports of cannibalism. The Joint Chiefs are furious that anyone would slander our troops with such unbelievable claims..."

Steve turned the channel to another news program and the reports were more of the same. A woman reporter standing outside of a large hospital was speaking.

"We are receiving reports from all over the country of hospitals being overwhelmed, like this one behind me here in Los Angeles, by the number of cases of South African Flu, and those seeking the vaccination against it. They are now requesting that only those who have not already contracted the flu come to the hospital for vaccinations. All those showing symptoms of the flu should remain at home, drink plenty of fluids, and get as much rest as they can. They are admitting there is nothing they can do for—"

All of a sudden, the report cut off and a graphic filled the screen reporting that a technical problem had occurred and that the station would come back on shortly. Steve changed the channel, only to see the same screen. Every channel he tried carried the same thing.

"That's strange," he said, and looked over at Carla, who was busy trying to make a call.

"I can't seem to get a call out. I keep getting an 'all circuits are busy' message." She then sent a text and got a *send failure* message.

"The system must be overwhelmed by traffic," Steve offered.

"Well, we need to discuss what to do now," Carla replied, throwing her cell phone on the bed. "If we go home, we will have to make arrangements for Conner to stay somewhere until graduation."

Lauren shook her head. "Mom, do you really think he's

going to want to wait around up there for two weeks for graduation with all that has happened?"

"No, you're probably right. We can just send him money for a plane ticket."

Carla seemed lost in thought. Steve stood up and put his hands on his hips. "Look, I know that with what's happened, you want to get home, but we're about twelve hours from Portland. I suggest we load up the Land Rover and head in that direction. I don't think any of us are going to get any sleep tonight, and I think we need to get to Conner."

Carla thought for a moment and then nodded slowly. "Regardless of what happens, I don't want to tell Conner over the phone like I did with Lauren. I should have waited, but I was kind of in shock."

"It's okay, Mom." Lauren put her arm around Carla and gave her a gentle squeeze.

They loaded up the Rover and got back on the road. Steve volunteered to drive. He was amped up from drinking coffee all night. Carla and Lauren rode together in the backseat, holding hands and talking quietly about Jake. Every so often, one of them would break down into tears and the other would provide comfort. This went on until both of them fell asleep, worn out by the constant grind of grief.

It was 3:00 a.m., and Steve was feeling really weird. The white lines on the road dimmed, then suddenly got brighter. The oncoming headlights seemed painfully bright. He would flash his high beams, only to have the other vehicle flash theirs back to indicate they were not already on. His head hurt, and he would be cold one minute and hot the next.

"Hey Lauren, you awake?" he asked.

Lauren stirred from a half-sleep when she heard her name. "What's up, babe?"

"I have got to stop and get gas and something to drink. I'm feeling weird." Steve felt stupid; he was just tired and needed a break.

"That's fine, honey, just use the debit card," Lauren said, not really processing what he said. She turned to her other side and drifted off again.

Steve saw a sign for a gas station at the next exit and pulled off the freeway. As he pulled up to the gas pump, Lauren woke up again and asked where they were.

"Just north of Stockton," Steve snapped at her. He slammed the door and went to pump the gas.

Carla awoke at the slam of the door. "What's that all about?" she asked.

"I don't know; I just asked where we were and he got all huffy."

Lauren was sitting up, looking back at Steve. He was fumbling with the gas cap, then he turned around and staggered toward the storefront of the station.

"What is he doing? I told him to use the debit card." Lauren got out and yelled at him, "Honey, just use the debit card!"

He didn't turn around or even acknowledge her. Lauren went around the Rover, swiped her debit card, and started pumping the gas, fuming at Steve's behavior.

Carla cracked her door and said, "Don't sweat it, sweetie. He's tired and we've all been through the mill tonight."

"That's no excuse for being a total ass, Mom," Lauren said. She finished pumping the gas and got back in the car, taking the driver's seat.

"Come on, Lauren, don't react like this; you'll just make it worse."

"I don't care, Mom. He has no right to be mad at me, dammit!"

They sat there for five minutes, then ten. Lauren was working up a good head of steam; she was really going to lay into him when he got back to the car.

"What the hell is he doing in there?" she snapped, banging on the steering wheel.

"Calm down, honey. Let's drive over there and pick him up

at the front of the store."

Lauren started the Rover and chirped the tires, swerving around the pumps, and pulled up in front of the store. She put the Rover in park and looked through the store's windows, trying to see Steve. There he was, leaning over the cashier's counter, covered in... blood?

Lauren screamed and started to get out of the Rover. Carla had seen the same thing from the backseat and grabbed Lauren by the arm. "Wait!" was all she said.

They both looked on as Steve pulled the attendant over the counter to the floor and continued the vicious attack. He was tearing at the man's throat with his teeth, pulling mouthfuls of flesh and sinew. Blood was spurting a foot in the air from the man's neck as Steve raised his head and let out a shriek that they could hear clearly.

Lauren began sobbing and screaming, "What is he doing, what is he doing?"

"Move over!" Carla commanded Lauren. She leaned over from the backseat and pulled her daughter over the console into the passenger seat. Carla squeezed into the driver's seat, threw the shifter into reverse, and slammed her foot down on the accelerator. The Rover's V8 responded, tearing at the asphalt with both rear wheels smoking. Carla swung the nose of the Rover around and shifted into drive, not even waiting for it to stop. The Rover bucked and the gears crunched into place. She sped toward the exit, narrowly missing first the pumps, then the sign pole. When the Rover was back straight on the road after slewing around two corners, Carla slammed on the brakes and put it in park. She opened the door and puked what little contents her stomach held onto the side of the road.

She shut the door. "Lauren, give me your phone."

"Mom, what in God's name is going on?" she said, shaking, crying, and handing Carla her phone all at the same time.

"I don't know, but whatever it is, we need to call the police."

She dialed 911 and an operator answered on the second ring. "San Joaquin County 911, what is your emergency?"

"We just witnessed a fight between two men at the Mini-Mart gas station off Interstate 5. There was blood everywhere," Carla told the operator.

"Are you still at the scene?"

"No, ma'am."

"Do you know either of the people fighting?"

Carla hung up the phone. She set the phone down and started praying aloud. "Lord, I don't know what's going on, I am scared." The phone interrupted her prayer. She picked it up and saw that the 911 operator was calling back. She shut the phone off completely.

"How do I get the battery out of this thing?" she asked Lauren.

"You have to unscrew the case with a screw driver," Lauren said.

Carla didn't have a screwdriver. In frustration, she opened the door and threw the phone out. She then slumped forward, her head resting on the steering wheel.

"Mom, we have to go back. We have to find out what happened. Steve would never do that! Why would Steve do that?" Lauren knew she was in shock, but it didn't matter; she still thought she was being reasonable.

"No, Lauren, we cannot go back. Do you remember the report on TV that said our soldiers were attacking each other?"

"Yeah, Mom, I remember. I also remember that they said those rumors were unsubstantiated."

Carla looked across at her daughter. "Well, I think we just substantiated them, don't you?"

Carla pulled the Rover back onto the road, turned up the freeway onramp, and merged onto I-5 north. "What are you doing, Mom?" Lauren asked.

"I'm going to go get my son, that's what I'm doing," Carla responded.

"So, do you really think this flu virus is causing people to go insane like Steve did?" Lauren said like she didn't believe any of it.

"No, I think it's the vaccine." The words came out of Carla's mouth without passing through her normally highly sensitive thought process.

"Oh my god, Mom, did you get a vaccination?"

"No, I was about to, but for some reason I didn't. When did you get yours?"

"I didn't. I was off the day Steve went, remember? Then one thing or another kept me from rescheduling it. I never did get it done," she said, with a look of realization cresting her face.

"Open the glove box," Carla said. Lauren opened it to find her dad's .45-caliber pistol and a box of ammunition. "Get it out and load it. We may need it before the night is done."

Lauren shook her head, "Mom, I think you are wrong. I think Steve just snapped."

"Lauren, you know Steven better than I do. Do you really think that?"

Lauren sank in her seat; she took the pistol out and saw that it was already loaded. She closed the glove box. "I don't know what I think, Mom, I really don't know."

They drove north for another eight hours on I-5, both of them in shock and with no more conversation than was necessary. At one point, Lauren demanded that her mother turn around and go back, but Carla refused, saying that getting to Conner was the only thing that mattered.

They arrived in Portland at ten o'clock the next morning. Conner answered the door in his boxers, his eyes squinting behind his hand, held up to block the bright morning sun.

"Hey guys, I didn't think you'd be here until tonight. Where's Dad?"

Conner didn't believe them when they told him what happened. He just sat on the couch, shaking his head.

"If this is some kind of joke, it isn't funny!"

Carla put her hand on his knee. "I wish it were a bad joke, son, but it's the truth, and the sooner we deal with it, the better."

"Deal with it? You want me to deal with it?" He stood up and threw the coffee cup he was holding. It smashed into pieces as it exploded against the wall. Conner began to cry as he stared at the coffee dripping down the wall.

"Mom, why didn't you do something? You always do something."

"Conner, there was nothing I could do... there just wasn't." Carla began to weep also.

He went to her and they embraced. Carla stroked his hair. "It will be okay," she said.

She closed her eyes and asked Conner the question she was terrified to know the answer to. "Honey, did you get the vaccine?"

"No, I slept in the day I was scheduled to. So, I won't be turning into a cannibal like Steve?"

"We think that's what caused it, but we're not sure."

After cleaning up the mess, they sat down and turned on the TV. Most of the stations were playing their normal broadcast schedule of taped shows. There was an unfamiliar anchor on the first news channel they found. He explained he was filling in for the regular anchor, who was away on assignment. The anchor then spoke with a panel of government experts about the South African Flu.

"Jessica, is it true that the vaccine developed by the CDC and the World Health Organization has been recalled?"

"Yes, Walter, the vaccine that we thought was effective against this flu has been recalled. The recall came because it is believed that, though it was originally effective, the virus has mutated and now the vaccine needs to be changed to combat this mutation. No one should take the old vaccine; it just is not working any longer."

"Jessica, there are rumors flying around the Internet that the vaccine is causing people to become violent; is this true?"

"Well, Walter, while a very few people have reacted that way to the vaccine, we believe it is a very small percentage of those inoculated, and that the vaccine was effective in containing the virus in its original form. However, no one should get the vaccine at this point. It is not worth the small risk of the side effects."

"So Jessica, the government has now changed what they are telling people to do. They are telling people to stay home if you or a loved one are showing symptoms of the flu."

"Yes, Walter, until the new vaccine can be developed, we are recommending that everyone go into lockdown mode in order to stop the spread of the flu. We are setting up new facilities around the country, but they won't be ready for people until tomorrow at the earliest. Only essential public works and infrastructure workers should be going anywhere. Everyone else should shelter in place, drink plenty of liquids, and rest. We will be distributing food and water starting tomorrow. The worst thing you can do at this point is go out into public places. Stay calm and stay at home. Your government is confident that we can fix the vaccine and provide safe water and food for everyone; everyone just needs to be patient."

"What a crock!" Lauren said. "Look at them trying to calm the masses with this crap! Change the channel, Conner."

Conner did as Lauren requested. Every news channel they went to had the same anchor and panel.

"I think you're right, Lauren. I think we are being lied to," Carla said. "I think Lauren and I need to try and sleep for a while. I need to make some calls first, though."

Carla tried to call her mother. The phone rang once, then went to a message saying that the caller was not available at this time. She tried her uncle, Ryan, with the same result. Everyone she tried either didn't answer or the circuits were reported busy. She tried using Conner's phone and got the same thing. Giving up on the phones, she used Conner's laptop to get onto her Facebook account, where she was able to leave a post telling people that Jake had died from the flu and that she was sorry she couldn't reach any of them by phone.

The house, occupied by four other tenants besides Conner, belonged to a friend of the family who had reluctantly agreed to rent it out to the five college boys, with a hefty security deposit. All the others had already left to go home for the summer except for Sam, the only other senior of the five. Sam was at his job. It was his next-to-last day before he quit delivering pizza.

Both Sam and Conner were outdoorsy types. They would often spend time hiking in the mountains or kayaking in the ocean. Sam had been raised by his uncle and was well off, financially. He'd received a settlement from the accident that killed his parents. He still liked to work, though. He said it wasn't right that some people just sat around wasting air because they could. He could have easily afforded his own place, but he and Conner had been friends since grade school, and he liked hanging out with the guys. Sam paid a little extra on the rent to keep his Jeep and assorted toys in the garage. Truthfully, he spent most of his time in the house and only occasionally slept in his own room, the loft over the garage. More often than not, he would end up sleeping on the couch in the living room.

"When is Sam due home?" Carla asked Conner.

"He worked the day shift today because so many people called off that they actually have him making pizzas." He made a face as if he would never eat a pizza that Sam made. "He should be home by five."

"Does his uncle still plan on being here for the graduation ceremony?"

Conner nodded. "Yeah, he's supposed to be here next week."

Carla thought about this for a minute. "I don't want to leave Sam here alone, and I do plan on leaving before next week. We need to get back to San Diego."

"Okay, but Sam can take care of himself fine, Mom." Conner stopped, not wanting to say what he was going to say.

"What?" Carla said looking at him.

"Nothing." He paused for a good ten seconds, but Carla stared him down.

"It's just that Sam's been buying survival stuff all year, and I didn't want to get him busted because I know you will rat him out to his uncle."

"Why would that bother Tom? Oh, I see, he's been buying guns, hasn't he?"

"Mom, you can't tell Tom. You know what a left-winger he is. It's bad enough that he has control over Sam's money until he turns twenty-five. If he finds out that Sam has been spending money on guns, he'll go ape shit."

"First of all, watch your mouth. Secondly, Tom is Sam's legal guardian, and he has done all right with that for twelve years, hasn't he?"

"Yes ma'am, but Sam is not a little kid and Tom still treats him like he's fifteen... sorry I swore."

Carla shook her head and smiled; he was his father's son. That thought brought the grief boiling up inside her. She had to turn away to collect herself. Conner, thinking he blew it again by making his mom cry, felt like an ass.

"No, Mom, I really am sorry, I won't do it again."

Carla wiped her eyes. "Make sure you don't. You know what your father would say."

They said in unison, "Your mother brought you into this world, and I can take you out!" They laughed with tears in their eyes.

"I love you, Mom."

"I love you too, Son."

Chapter 6

A New Ride

MADDIE & HARRY
8:00 A.M.
MARATHON COACH HEADQUARTERS
COBURG, OR
DAY OF OUTBREAK

Maddie sat in the comfortable custom-made leather chair across from Harry as they pulled into the Marathon Coach headquarters. Harry was worried that he'd made a critical error in judgment; Maddie loved the coach and talked about how they needed to look into buying one. What worried him even more was that he'd begun to daydream about owning one, too.

They spent the previous night at an RV park just off Highway 58 in Oakridge, Oregon. Harry finally told Maddie that they would be dropping off the coach at the Marathon headquarters. When she asked what they were going to do for transportation from there, he simply said, "There's a ride waiting on us."

The ride waiting on them was Don's brand new custom Prevost coach. Marathon's reputation was that if you could dream it, they could build it, and they had done just that. Don McClure wanted a coach that he could take anywhere and have no fear of being stuck or brought to heel by anyone. He designed the coach to survive the worst humanity could dish out and keep him living in style and comfort.

Harry parked the coach in front of the offices, where the president of the company was waiting to greet them. Normally, the site manager would have been there, but he was out with the flu.

"Good morning, I'm Warren," he said as he shook Harry's hand. "You must be Harry. Don told me to expect you today. I'm sorry Don couldn't be here for the delivery, but he said we should fully brief you on all the systems onboard the coach so that you can bring him up to speed when you get home." Harry introduced Maddie and they spent a few minutes making small talk.

Maddie caught on right away and gave Harry the eye for letting her think that they would be giving up the coach for a lesser mode of transportation. Harry ignored the eye, so she added a quick elbow as well. Harry winced and smiled as Warren escorted them into the building.

"Would you folks like something to drink, or would you like to get right to it?"

Harry looked at Maddie, deferring the decision to her. "Let go see it!" she said, with a big smile.

Warren laughed, "Yeah, we get that a lot here. I used to drag people to breakfast and give them a tour, when all they really wanted was to see their new coach. Okay then, if you will follow me, I will introduce you to our VP of Design and Engineering; he will spend the day with you to make sure you're comfortable with all the features of the coach."

They made their way through the offices to an attached giant hanger-like building that housed the manufacturing department. Warren knocked on the edge of an open doorway to an office that overlooked the entire production area.

"Hello, anybody home?" Warren called out as he entered.

A beautiful brunette stood and walked across the room toward them. Her smile and demeanor, meant to put even the most nervous client at ease, worked exactly as intended.

"Hello, I am Sourires. You can call me Sophie," she said, hand outstretched.

After the introductions, Warren asked, "Is Robert here? I

spoke with him yesterday about doing the delivery for Mr. McClure's coach because David is out sick."

She frowned. "I'm sorry, sir, but I just found out that Robert is out as well."

"Oh my," Warren said. "That is unfortunate."

He turned to Harry. "I am really sorry about this, but this flu going around is about to cripple us here. Over half our work force has called in sick this week; we just had a doctor out here on Tuesday to give the remaining employees the vaccination."

After a few unproductive phone calls, Warren looked at Sophie with his eyebrows raised. Sophie quickly volunteered to assist with the delivery, and Warren promised to come find them at lunchtime to give them a break for a few minutes. He apologized again before heading back to the front offices.

"Wow, this flu is really starting to cause problems, isn't it?" Maddie offered.

Sophie blew an errant bang of hair back with a long breath. "You have no idea. We are never behind around here, but it's really starting to take its toll on us. I am just glad they finished Mr. McClure's coach before you arrived."

Sophie led them back out to the floor of the production area. "I have never done a delivery before, so please bear with me."

Maddie tried to put her at ease. "We're just the hired help," she said, with a chuckle and a smile.

They went out a door to a large parking lot. Sophie took them about a hundred feet away from the building, then turned them around. A large roll-up door began to open and the outside speakers started playing *Flight of the Valkyries*.

The custom H3-45 Triple Slide coach appeared like a bull entering the ring. Maddie let out a little gasp and was immediately embarrassed. Harry's jaw loosened and he heard himself making a rather unmanly noise. Sophie was watching them, not the coach, and was grinning from ear to ear.

"I could get to like this part of the job," she said. "Watching your faces, well, it's very gratifying."

Sophie rattled off a few stats on the coach. "The coach is 45 feet long and eight and a half feet wide. Some of the features are: a gourmet kitchen, a large walk-in shower with two rainfall showerheads above and eight body spa total-immersion showerheads down the sides, three queen beds, two pullouts in the salon and one in the rear bedroom. Two single bunks across from the bathroom. There are three slide outs, two in the main cabin and one in the rear bedroom. The paint is not one of our usual colors, either. Don requested a camouflaged paint scheme, but changed his mind after viewing our computer mock-ups of this one."

Harry nodded, noting how the paint seemed to absorb the colors of the surrounding landscape as the coach moved through the parking lot.

"It's beautiful!" Maddie exclaimed.

"Wow," was all Harry could offer. The coach pulled up and stopped in front of them.

Thomas, the company engineer who drove the coach out, began briefing the group at the rear bay. "This is the power plant for the coach. Don opted for the Detroit S-60 over the Volvo engine. The S-60 turbo produces 515 horsepower and 1950 foot-pounds of torque. There are three alternators—two for the house batteries, which are also charged by four 100-watt solar panels on the roof, and the third alternator for the 24-volt batteries, which are also trickle-charged via solar. As you can see, there is redundancy for each system to ensure you don't ever find yourself without power."

He closed the rear bay doors and moved to the right side of the coach. "This next bay is custom for this coach. You open it using the Crestron remote or manual release; I will further explain the remote later. As you can see, this bay is just aft of the rear axles and is fairly narrow, but extends up behind the rear of the cabin. It houses two Kawasaki KX250 motorcycles."

He pushed a hidden button in the wheel well, the bay door

opened, and a rail holding the bike automatically extended. He unfolded the end of the rail, which acted as a ramp, unfolded the handlebars of one motorcycle, and rolled it down to the ground. "As you can see, we had to slightly modify the handlebars to fold down and lock; they are actually stronger than the originals." He reversed the process and explained that the other motorcycle could be accessed the same way on the other side.

He paused at the wheel well and rested his hand on one of the tires. "These tires are the first run-flat tires we have ever installed on one of our coaches. In addition to these, the bullet-resistant windows and Kevlar window blinds make this coach as close to a tank as anything I've ever worked on.

"This next bay houses the 20 kW diesel generator, mounted on air cushions for vibration-free operation and this pull-out shelf for ease of maintenance. The bay has soundproofing such that you can barely hear it running when you shut the bay door. It also has a 110 compressor that powers the A/C."

He closed that bay and moved forward to the next one. "This one is for storage, and as you can see, is open all the way across to the other side. Along the back of this compartment are the circuit breakers for a lot of the equipment as well as a manual generator panel. The generator is also operated by the Crestron remote."

Sophie's cell phone rang. She excused herself and stepped away from the group. Maddie thought she heard her say something like, "Are you kidding me!" in a hushed hand-cupping-the-phone kind of way. She hung up the phone and came back over as Thomas was explaining the water system bay to them.

"I'm so sorry, but I have to head back over to the office. I'll be back as soon as I can. Thomas, can you continue with Harry and Maddie?"

Thomas shrugged and said, "No problem." With that, she

turned and practically ran back to the building.

Harry looked at Maddie with raised eyebrows as if to ask what that was all about; it was Maddie's turn to shrug.

"As I was saying," Thomas continued as he crouched down next to the coach, "this panel controls the water manifold. You can see that both hot and cold systems have multiple lines. This allows you to shut them off individually in case of a leak in any one line and maintain water access across the rest of the system. There is a 500-gallon clean-water tank that can be serviced from here."

He pointed to a connection on the panel. "This one is for clean water, and once connected, it will monitor the tank. When the tank is full, the valve will close. That means you can hook it up and go do something else while it fills. This button will lower a door below the coach that will give you access to three different things."

He pushed the button and a door dropped from below the coach. "If you push this switch labeled 'Shore Connection,' it will release the electrical hookup for external power for the coach." He pushed the button and out popped the electrical cord. "It will extend twenty feet—just keep holding the button for the desired length. Then just push the top of the switch to retrieve the cord until it retracts all the way in."

He was about to tell them about the waste disposal when he got a call and excused himself to answer it. He listened for a minute as Maddie watched the color drain from his face. "Sophie! Sophie, are you still there!"

He listened for a few more seconds and then let his arm drop to his side. "Uh, that was Sophie, and, um, she said something about people in the factory going crazy and that we should get the hell out of here, then she screamed and dropped the phone. I could hear what sounded like a scuffle, and then it went dead."

Maddie stuck her hand in her back pocket and came out

with an LCP .380. She looked at Harry and asked, "Do we leave, or do we look?"

Harry took a deep breath and sighed. "I guess we look. Let's go back to the other coach out front and get some more firepower just in case there really is something going on."

Thomas drove them around to the front of the building and parked next to the old coach. Just then, the floor-to-ceiling windows of a second floor conference room exploded and a chair landed on top of a car parked below, activating its alarm. Next came Sophie. She flew out of the space, locked in an embrace with another woman. As they fell, the two women appeared to be struggling. They landed behind the car with the blaring alarm, out of their direct line of sight.

"Holy shit!" Thomas yelled, leaning back and away from the scene.

Harry threw the door open, and he and Maddie ran to help Sophie. They rounded the damaged car to find Sophie lying on her stomach next to the other woman. Sophie was covered in blood and was trying to get up, but the fact that her right arm was missing below the elbow was slowing her progress. She looked up at Maddie and said, "I'm really sorry for this inconvenience," then fell over on her side, eyes open and fixed.

The other woman was obviously dead, but upon further inspection, Harry found her skin was a translucent with blotches here and there. As he watched, her skin turned red and blistered, like a sunburn developing instantaneously over all exposed areas. He turned toward Maddie, who was checking on Sophie.

"She gone?"

Maddie nodded and looked over at him. "What about her?"

"Yeah, come check this out. She was all pale-looking, then right before my eyes she turned red with a postmortem sunburn."

Thomas disabled the car alarm so they could hear

themselves think. "What the hell is going on, guys? I'm working seven days a week, twelve to sixteen hour shifts, to meet our deadlines. Last week they announced that we needed to be here to get our vaccinations against the South African Flu."

Harry interrupted him. "So, you got the vaccination?"

"No, we had an issue with the motorcycle lift on Mr. McClure's coach, so I stayed on the floor and didn't get it. I sent everyone else, though. I actually had my foreman sign my name on the list so I wouldn't get in trouble."

"Well, all we know is that when we left Texas, they were saying the virus had spread to Europe from South Africa and that the CDC had developed a vaccine that was mass-produced in labs all over the globe. We weren't too concerned about it, as we were not going to be hitting any major cities and figured we would just get it when we got home." Maddie looked over at Harry, who was quietly rubbing his chin in thought.

"Look, this coach is supposed to have all the latest communication gear on it, right?" He directed the question at Thomas.

Thomas nodded his head, frowning. "Yeah, but that was the electronic engineer's specialty. I know where it all is, but I'm not the designer. Their shop spent the better part of six months installing and configuring all that. They were supposed to bring you up to speed on that this afternoon."

Maddie pointed at him. "You stay here and start trying to figure all that out. Harry and I will go see what's going on inside."

With that, Harry and Maddie went to the old coach and opened the storage bay. Thomas went to the hidden file cabinet in the desk right behind the driver's station and found the DVD labeled *Communication*.

Maddie selected her favorite 5.56 caliber AR15 with Eotech close-combat hologram site, and her Taurus Judge. She strapped on the Taurus holster and checked to make sure that all the ammunition loops held .410 shells. "I'm good to go."

Harry grabbed a Mossberg 930 SPX 12-gauge and his old reliable Smith & Wesson M&P 9mm that held 17+1 and 4 extra magazines. He also grabbed a bandolier of 55 2.75 double-aught buckshot and strapped it tightly to his chest. He took a Remington 870 pump shotgun to Thomas.

"Hey, you know how to work one of these?"

Thomas looked up from the computer. "Sure, point the end with the hole toward the bad guys and shoot." Harry showed him how to load it and where to find the safety, and left him with a box of shells.

Back in Texas, Maddie and Harry had converted an old barn on their property into a shoot house. They could set it up with multiple different floor plans and they practiced clearing rooms together. They did it for fun, and never thought they would ever actually get to put this skill set into practice. Maddie pestered Harry to go play S.W.A.T. with her and he usually gave in with a promise of a reward later.

"You know how hot it makes me, Harry," was usually all she had to say.

They lined up outside the door to the offices. Maddie held the door handle and Harry staged to the left. He counted down: three, two, one... Maddie swung the door open and Harry quickly moved through it and to the right. Maddie followed closely and cleared the left. Harry called out "Clear" and moved to the next doorway. The front reception area was deserted, and the only sound they heard was the hum of the A/C.

Harry pointed at the door to the hallway they had gone through earlier that day with Warren. Since the door opened inward, this was a bit more challenging.

"Okay, remember: I clear right, you clear left, and we hold in the hall. Anything hinky and we blow back into this room, got it?" Maddie nodded once and gave him a thumbs-up.

He counted down again and pushed the door open, following it through as it moved into the hallway. Concentrating on her job, Maddie started forward and began to look to the left. She made it almost through the doorway when Harry slammed into her, knocking her back into the foyer. She heard a loud shriek and the sound of Harry's 18.5-inch barrel exploding at the same time.

Maddie was staring at the ceiling of the reception area for an instant before rolling to her left to come up on one knee. She pointed at the hall and saw Harry crouched there, looking back at her, his shotgun pointing up.

"Sorry about that sweetie, kind of ran into someone."

She waved off the apology, moved back over to him, and saw what was left of the buxom blond receptionist. She was now minus her buxom, as it was currently spread all over the wall behind her. Maddie had worked in emergency rooms all her life and the sight did not affect her much, but the smell was horrendous.

"God, why does it smell so bad? She smells like she's been dead for a month."

Harry shrugged while checking up and down the hall. "Don't know, baby. Which way?"

They heard another shriek and the sound of a person screaming in abject terror or pain; they weren't sure which.

"I guess we go toward the screams, eh?" Harry said.

Maddie moved to go.

"Wait—me first, Mad."

"Okay, macho man, be my guest."

Harry peeked around the corner and hustled down the hallway to the first office. Maddie slid down the wall and came up behind him. They both heard heavy panting from the interior office.

"I'm going to cross to the other side of the door," Harry whispered back to her. She gave a quick nod. Harry crouched and started to lunge across the doorway, but was sideswiped immediately by a fat little guy in a suit.

Maddie couldn't shoot without hitting Harry, so she screamed instead.

"Harry!"

The little fat man didn't pay her any mind and appeared to be close to biting off Harry's ear. She flipped her AR around, grabbed it like a baseball bat, and swung like she wanted to hit the wall on the other side of its head. The shock of the impact went up her arms as the butt of the AR sank into its temple and blood splattered across Harry's face. She lost her grip on the rifle and fell forward on top of both of them. Without even knowing why, she wrapped her right arm around its neck and rolled to the left, pulling it with her off Harry.

Harry held his 9mm to its head and pulled the trigger. Maddie watched in fascination as the bullet neatly entered the thing's head, just inches above her. She would swear later that she could see the shock wave ripple across its scalp as the bullet passed through and erupted out the other side. The bullet's exit was anything but neat; the fragments of bone and brains, mixed with bright red blood, burst like a volcano, spewing its contents like lava all over the wall to her right.

Maddie struggled to get out from under the damn squealer and the gore still dripping from its head. Harry stood with his hands on his knees, breathing in ragged gasps.

"That kind of took me by surprise," he croaked.

"Yeah, me too." She located her AR. Its extendable stock was broken. "Wow, didn't know I was that strong."

Harry, still trying to catch his breath, just shook his head. "Thanks."

Maddie loosened the sling on the AR and put it over her back. She drew the Judge from its holster and held it with both hands.

Harry looked at her and asked, "Why are we doing this? I think it's pretty obvious that there is nothing but these things in here."

"There may be someone that needs our help," she said, thinking how utterly stupid it sounded as it came out of her mouth.

"Yeah, we might need help ourselves if this keeps up." Harry bent down and picked up his shotgun. "Keep going, or go back?"

"Live to fight another day?" Maddie proposed, and Harry agreed.

"Sounds like the smartest thing I've heard all day."

Chapter 7

Meg's House

Meg looked over at Andy sleeping next to her in the king-size bed. Sadie and Beth had already gotten up and were out rummaging around in the kitchen, fixing themselves cereal. Andy had been up half the night crying inconsolably over his father's death. He missed his brother Peter terribly, but he couldn't accept that he no longer had a dad. "Why Grammie? Why?" he'd wailed plaintively. Meg had no good answer for him, nor for Sadie and Beth.

They didn't want to hear that God wanted Tim and Peter to come live with him in heaven. Beth said God was mean and she hated him. Sadie, ever faithful, still could not understand why Jesus took her dad and brother away. Sarah had relied heavily on Tim to share the parenting duties of the four, now three, children and was trying her best to keep it together.

Meg went out to the living room to find Sarah watching the news.

"They are saying the vaccine has been recalled and they're ordering everyone to stop taking it," Sarah said as Meg sat down.

"What? I've given it to hundreds of people over the last two weeks." Meg leaned forward to listen for a reason why it was recalled.

"Did you take the vaccine, Mom?" Sarah asked.

"No. I'm allergic to one of the proteins listed in the

ingredients, so I didn't."

"Well, the kids and I went to get it at our clinic last week, but they were out and told us to come back. We never made it. Then, when Tim and Peter got sick, I was mad that they ran out and called and read them the riot act." Sarah looked at nothing with the thousand-yard stare once reserved for those with PTSD.

"Honey, there is obviously some reason for the recall, so it was a blessing in disguise," Meg tried to comfort her.

"I don't know, Mom. What if it could have saved them?"

"There is no way they would be stopping the program if it was working. You couldn't have done anything different, nothing that would have changed where we are now." They went quiet and watched the news.

Reports from London of serious rioting as the fatality rate of the flu reaches eighty-two percent. Stores are being looted for antiviral medications, reportedly ineffective against this strain of flu. Additional reports, unsubstantiated at this time, claim that people have turned violent and are attacking those around them for no apparent reason; some have described these attacks as horrific to the point of cannibalism.

Meg stood up. "I have to get to the office to find out if we have any more information on what's going on."

"Mom, you need to stay here; it's not safe out there. Lynn, Jean, and the kids will be here soon. Why don't you wait until they get here?"

"Sarah, you don't understand, I have patients that I'm responsible for."

Sarah stood, crossed the room, and grabbed her mother by the shoulders. "Mom, you have responsibilities here. I cannot lose anyone else to this thing, don't you get it? This is not just another flu, this is killing people everywhere!"

Meg saw the look on her daughter's face and knew she was right, but she still had to check in at work. "Look, I have to go in, even if it's just long enough to shut the place down and send everyone home. I will stop and stock up on supplies while I'm in town."

She went to change clothes and run a brush through her hair.

Meg's place was ten miles from Oroville, Washington, a small town on the Canadian border east of the Cascade Mountains. It was considered high desert and had supplied the United States with most of their apples. Now the apple orchards were being systematically torn out because they couldn't compete with South American produce. The rural farms that once fed the nation were dying... and the population with them. Most of those who lived here were the last generation of farmers. Their sons and daughters moved away to the big cities, where they could earn a decent wage.

Meg provided health care to them as a traveling nurse; she'd been the director of the home health care service for Okanagan County until the company changed hands. The new director had no clue how to operate the business, and most everyone brought their concerns to Meg. She basically ran the clinic, and the new director accommodated her because it was convenient. Meg had another couple of years until she could retire, at which time she planned to move to the coast to be near her daughter and grandkids.

All that apparently had changed now. A line formed outside the clinic for those who had not already succumbed to the flu. They looked like they were waiting for a miracle to stay their disease and make them whole again. Meg greeted them as she walked into the clinic from the parking lot. She knew most of them by name.

She stopped at the front door and turned. Her voice carried well and she spoke clearly.

"The vaccine has been recalled. I don't know why. I only know that we have been instructed not to inoculate anyone else."

The crowd murmured at this, but they trusted her and listened.

"Go home and stay away from anyone showing signs of the flu. If you are already sick, we will set up an infirmary at the high school gym. Please go there now, or head home. There is nothing more we can do, other than pray and care for the sick in hopes that this will pass."

She'd planned to return home immediately but couldn't just leave these people to their fate. She went in and directed the workers and volunteers concerning the setup of the infirmary.

She called home, and Sarah answered on the first ring.

"Sarah, I know you don't want to hear this, but I have a responsibility to this community. I have to stay in town and set up an infirmary for those that are too sick to care for themselves. I'll be at the high school gym until everything is set up, and then I'll head home for dinner."

"Mom, you can't save the world, come home now!" Sarah pleaded.

Meg replied thoughtfully, "I know I can't, honey. I am just trying to make these people more comfortable until this thing runs its course. I'll be home soon. Get the turkey soup from the freezer downstairs and heat it for dinner. I'll see you soon."

Sarah hung up the phone only to have it ring again before she could take two steps across the room. "Hello?"

"Hey, this is Lynn. We're just about there. We're going to stop in Oroville to pick up groceries. Can you think of anything we might need?"

"Aunt Lynn, have you been listening to the news?"

"Yeah, it's sounding worse. We figured we'd stock up on some supplies to try and have enough on hand to last it out. It may be a couple of weeks until things settle down. It doesn't look like we're going to make it to the reunion."

Lynn sounded matter-of-fact about it—just another bump in

the road of life. This bolstered Sarah's spirit a little, and she told Lynn about Meg's plan. She also told Lynn to buy all the canned goods they could and come on out.

"Okay, sounds like a plan. We will see you in a bit."

Lynn hung up and told Jean what was going on. Jean immediately called Meg.

"Hey Meg, Jean here. I am coming over to help you get this infirmary set up. Lynn is going to hit the store and then head up to the house."

Meg sounded rushed, but thankful. "Thanks, Jean. I could use the help, I have a bunch of volunteers here but need another nurse to get this working."

"What's a big sister for?" Jean replied.

They got directions to the school and headed that way. Madison and Tyler were disappointed at the delay but understood the change in plans was unavoidable. Madison, fourteen going on twenty-eight, explained to Tyler, twelve going on... well, twelve, that life wasn't always fair. It hadn't even dawned on Lynn to ask why Sarah wasn't out on the coast.

Meg contacted the Red Cross representative, who happened to be a deacon at her church.

"Maggie, we need all the beds you have in storage and as many people as you can muster."

The emergency response team for the county had twenty hospital beds in storage at the high school and access to the regional emergency pharmacy for IVs and antibiotics. While Meg got the ball rolling on the infirmary setup, she also called a couple of people to bring food and water to the shelter. Normally, it would have been a few quick calls to key people who would rally the troops to get things done; however, she was having no luck reaching them. No one was answering their phones.

Meg arrived to find the beds already being moved into the

gymnasium. Lynn, the kids, and Jean were waiting on her in the parking lot. They all exchanged quick hugs and got down to business.

"Lynn, I need you to get some supplies and head to the house. Sarah is having a hard time coping without Tim." She saw the confused look on Lynn's face. "Oh, didn't Sarah tell you?"

"What?"

"Tim and Peter both died from the flu; that's why they're here." Jean frowned and Lynn put an arm around Meg, giving her another hug. Meg took a deep breath and exhaled slowly. "We can't dwell on that right now, we'll have time to grieve later."

"Anyhow, Sarah and the kids are there, and I would feel better knowing you were too," Meg said, as she signed off on the medical supplies a staffer dropped off.

Jean got right into gear and started arranging for people to take information from those who had already showed up for help. Lynn and the kids got back into the car and left for the grocery store on the way to Meg's house. It was just twelve-thirty and the sun shone brightly on the eastern Washington town.

Meg was in the gymnasium and had just briefed a young volunteer on how to fill out the forms listing a person's critical info when he suddenly became ill. His name was Cam, he was sixteen, and he went to the same high school where they were setting up the infirmary. Cam was an Eagle Scout and had come to help get the shelter ready; he was always on hand for community outreach and did whatever was asked of him. Meg knew him well; he'd been in her Sunday school class back when he was in the second grade and was always around during church functions. Meg admitted to Cam that the bustle of activity at the school made her comfortable; she felt she was doing something to combat the chaos that the flu was wreaking on her home. When he turned toward Meg, she saw that his face was ashen and he was sweating profusely.

"Cam, are you all right?" she asked, leading him to a chair and sitting him down. He stared blankly at her and began to shake. Meg yelled for Jean and they laid him down right there and began to take his vitals.

"Look at his skin," Jean remarked, as she worked at getting his pulse. He was not only getting paler by the moment, but his skin was taking on a translucent quality before their eyes.

"His pulse is skyrocketing," Jean reported.

His eyes snapped open and he looked at Meg, who was trying to take his blood pressure. He grabbed her arm and rose off the floor toward her; she drew back trying to gain control of his arms, only to find her hand in his mouth. He bit down, severing her pinky and ring fingers in one quick motion. She screamed in horror as he chewed on her now detached fingers.

Seeing this all take place, Jean let go of him then grabbed him by the hair and bashed his head against the floor. Meg scooted away, holding her mangled hand and shaking her head, unable to comprehend what had just taken place. Jean continued to beat his head against the floor and Meg screamed at her to stop. Across the gym, another person attacked a Red Cross worker, shrieking like a banshee. Jean dropped the boy's limp body and scurried over to Meg, who was up against the wall trying to stop the bleeding.

She gathered Meg up and pulled her toward the door. "We have to get this cleaned up," Meg said, going into shock.

"Come with me now!" Jean yelled at her just as a third person shrieked, pounced on top of a patient recently placed in one of the beds, and began biting at his face. Jean fell backward into the double doors, pulling Meg with her as they stumbled out into the lobby. The left door started to close. The right one remained open, and Cam got up and came charging after them. He reached the lobby only to throw his arms over his face, shriek, and turn back for the gymnasium once the light from the windows touched his skin. Jean managed to get Meg on her feet, and together they ran out of the building into the parking lot.

Lynn didn't want to freak her grandkids out, so she played down the emerging crisis as they drove to the grocery store.

"Aunt Jean and Aunt Meg are going to help these people get better."

Madison looked at her and said, "Oma, the news said the sick people were all dying."

"No, they said that some of them were dying."

"Yeah, like eighty percent of them!" was Madison's reply.

"Well, it's what Aunt Jean and Meg do, guys. They help sick people."

"Oma, I'm scared," Tyler complained.

Madison added, "If those people have the South African Flu, they could give it to Aunt Jean and Aunt Meg!"

Lynn tried to think of a reasoned rebuttal as they pulled into the grocery store parking lot.

"They know what they're doing," was the only thing she could come up with. "I want you two to stay in the car. I am going in and will be back in fifteen minutes, tops. Stay in the car and keep the doors locked."

They started to argue, but when she fixed them with a grandmotherly stare, they both nodded and quit fussing.

Lynn entered the store and grabbed a cart. She headed down the closest aisle, throwing in anything nonperishable. Her main goal was speed and getting as much food as she could. The store wasn't that busy, which puzzled her. She came head-to-head with another woman who was frantically filling her cart with frozen dinners. She thought about telling her frozen food wasn't the best option at this point but kept the comment to herself. She made the turn onto the canned food aisle to find it well stocked. Again, she was surprised; if this were Denver, the first sign of a good snowstorm would have cleared the shelves. She wasn't highly selective, but took a minute to try to get a variety of canned goods.

Someone in the back of the store interrupted the quiet.

"Hey, hey, hey!" It was a man's voice. It initially sounded mildly perturbed and quickly escalated to a panicked objection. That was followed by the crash of someone locked in a full-on wrestling match, knocking over displays and banging into shelves. She then heard what sounded like a wounded mountain lion shrieking a loud wail of either pain or agitation.

Her fight-or-flight instinct triggered. She wheeled her cart toward the front of the store. She just cleared the aisle and was almost to the checkout when she saw and heard the woman in the freezer section scream. The bagboy had her on the ground and was tearing into her arm with his teeth. He flung blood in a wide arc as he wrenched a piece of flesh from her bicep, working his way toward her neck, shaking his head like a pit bull.

Lynn's bowels turned to water and she broke into a full-fledged run, pushing the cart straight past the cashier, who stood frozen in horror. The boy looked up from his feeding frenzy and shrieked at another shopper standing a few feet away. The shopper was a middle-aged man who dropped the fish sticks he was holding and started to run. The bagboy leaped up from the floor and onto the man's back, biting down on his shoulder.

"Get off! Get off!" he screamed as he ran, beating at the boy with his free hand.

As they passed the stunned cashier and entered the front of the store where the sun shone through the windows, the bagboy let him go and backpedaled quickly, looking like he couldn't get away fast enough.

The cashier broke for the front doors and almost caught up to Lynn.

"I'm done, I'm outta here!" He pulled off the store apron, wadding it up as he ran to his car.

The shopper who had been bitten fell, got up, and staggered to his vehicle. Lynn crashed the cart into the rear quarter panel of the Prius and was shaking so badly she couldn't push the release button for the hatch. Madison unlocked the door and started to get out to help.

"Get back in there!" Lynn screamed at her. She finally activated the hatch and threw all the groceries in as fast as she could, looking over her shoulder at the front doors of the store.

Jean pressed the cool washcloth to Meg's forehead. Meg was unconscious, lying on the couch back home. When Jean got her home, Sarah had helped half-carry, half-drag Meg into the living room. Jean had cleaned and sutured the wounds and was monitoring her closely. Lynn and the kids arrived right behind them.

Lynn prepared soup and peanut butter and jelly sandwiches, listening while Jean explained what happened. Jean told her story as she stood in the doorway connecting the kitchen and living room so she could keep an eye on Meg. The kids were occupied in the back room, watching a DVD.

"I wouldn't believe you if I hadn't been through the same thing at the grocery store," Lynn said after Jean finished.

Sarah just sat there, not saying anything. The stress of the last few days had worn her down. She was afraid, she was a widow, and she didn't know if she could take much more. Jean saw the stare and correctly assessed that Sarah was at the breaking point.

"Sarah, don't feel like this is all on you. We will get through it as a family."

Sarah's shoulders slumped, and she quietly began to cry. "I just don't know how I am going to do it," she mumbled. "With Tim gone, and Peter... how am I supposed to raise these kids without Tim, especially now?"

Lynn crossed the room and hugged her. "Like Jean said, we will do it together."

Sarah nodded and wiped her eyes with her sleeve. "How is Mom?"

Jean looked back into the living room at Meg. "She should be okay; she didn't lose much blood and as long as we can keep the wounds from getting infected..." What she didn't say was she wasn't sure if the bite had passed the infection on to Meg. "We will just have to wait and see..." she let the sentence hang there like a cartoon thought bubble.

Lynn finished cleaning up the kitchen after everyone ate their fill of soup and sandwiches. Jean kept a close eye on Meg, who was still unconscious. Sarah lay on Meg's bed while the kids continued to watch movies in the back bedroom. Lynn walked into the living room, drying her hands on a dishtowel.

"Should she be waking up?"

Jean glanced at Meg and frowned. "Everyone is different. Her vitals are good and she doesn't seem to be in distress, but I don't like the fever."

Meg's temperature had been over a hundred all afternoon. "I think letting her rest is more important than anything else right now."

Jean checked the IV she'd started and was thankful that Meg's supply of such medical equipment was so complete. "I've got her on a saline drip with an antibiotic that should fight off any infection for now."

"What about the boy who attacked her?" Lynn asked. "What are the chances that he passed something to Meg when he bit her?"

"That's the million dollar question, isn't it?" Jean replied.

Meg looked down on the scene. Lynn and Jean stood over her body laid out on the couch. She could hear the discussion plainly, as if she were participating in it. Her first thought was that she must be dead and would be drifting off to heaven any moment now. Many of her patients had described this type of out-of-body experience to Meg in her years of nursing, but she always credited the stories as a phenomenon of the brain trying to fill in the gaps. It always happened when someone had been in a life-threatening circumstance. Now, it seemed as normal as brushing her teeth.

While dwelling on the significance of this, she realized she was no longer hovering over the living room. Now the world was totally black—no, not totally, now pictures began to flash by quickly: the gymnasium, the grocery store, a dark hall in a house she didn't recognize. Was she dreaming? The pictures didn't feel like they were something she'd witnessed, but something that was being shown to her by someone else. She felt something else, too... fear! It was not her fear. It belonged to someone else; someone was showing her their fear. Not just one person, but many; the pictures flashed by faster and faster until her mind cried out, *STOP!*

She opened her eyes and Jean and Lynn were standing over her.

"How are you feeling?" Jean asked.

Chapter 8

A Day Full of Surprises

RYAN'S GROUP
7:00 A.M.
LYNNWOOD, WA
ADVENTURE SPORTS

I awoke to the smell of coffee. The night had passed with no visits from the freaks. I had the midnight-to-four watch and heard plenty of shrieking. Either we had hidden well, or they had easier prey at hand. I wasn't going to complain.

I pushed the recliner down and had to kick the leg rest several times to get it to stay. Max had removed the tarps from the front windows to let in some light. I could see Lisa standing behind the counter through the storage room doorway.

"I smell coffee," I said, as I wandered out of the back room.

"'Bout time you got up, sleeping beauty," Max replied.

"Hey, Uncle Ryan, come look at this note again. I'll get you some coffee," Lisa said, putting the ledger down on the counter for me.

"First tell me how you made coffee without electricity."

I picked up the ledger and reread the note Mel left. She handed me a Styrofoam cup full of hot steaming coffee.

"What, no cream?"

She punched me, and I spilled a little of the precious liquid. "Hey now, you give me coffee only to burn me with it?" I sipped the coffee and noticed a few grounds on my tongue. I thought better than to mention it. "Oh my god, that's good!"

Lisa smiled. "I used a smelting kit to make it." I spit the coffee out and looked at her. "You mean the one that they use to melt down lead?"

119

She laughed, "No, this was a 'new in box' set, silly."

I held up the ledger. "So, what am I reading this for again?"

She pointed to the end of the note where Mel had signed. "What do you think these numbers are?" Right there in his note, Mel had put *12-29-16-12* in front of his name.

"Hmmm, you know, I went right by those yesterday, thinking they were a date; but that doesn't make any sense, does it?"

Max ambled over after overhearing our discussion. "Let me see."

I flipped the ledger around so he could have a look. "I missed that too. Now that I'm looking at it, it looks like a combination."

I raised my eyebrows. "Okay, to what, though?"

We all looked at each other. Lisa was the first to speak. "Could it be to one of those gun safes we used to block the doors last night?"

Max shook his head. "I don't think so, why leave the combination to an empty gun safe?"

I went over to the gun safes. Max and Lisa had pulled them away from the doors, but they were still lying on their sides. I looked in the plastic bag attached to the top of one of them. "Nope, the combinations for these are here, with instructions on how to reset them."

Max scratched his beard of three days. "Why wouldn't he write down more information? He gives us the combination to a hidden safe, but doesn't tell us where it is."

We all scanned the room again, looking for something obvious that we might have missed. Nothing stood out. I put my hands on my hips and gave them both a flummoxed look.

"Well, let's search the place carefully and see if we can turn up anything."

We split the entire store into thirds and began searching in earnest. The floor in the front room was tile and there was no floor safe, neither there or behind the counter. We moved everything hanging on the walls and knocked on the sheetrock to no avail. After a full hour of searching, we came up empty.

"What the hell?" Max said.

"Well, we have the storage room and the shooting range," I offered.

Max shrugged and said, "Okay, Lisa and I will look in the storage room. You take the range."

The range could barely qualify as a range. Three shooting lanes, maxed out at 25 meters. Nonetheless, I took one of the large flashlights we had procured from the auto parts store and began looking around. I couldn't find anything. I went back to find Max and Lisa going through the storage room with similar results.

"Maybe he was just fucking with us," Lisa commented.

"I don't know," I said as I stood back and looked over the layout of the store again. "Something is not kosher here. Look, if we go into the storage room and pace off the distance from the door to the wall..." I demonstrated. "I come up with about twenty-four feet."

I walked over to the door to the range, entered again, and paced off the distance between the door and the interior wall. "If I go in here and do the same thing," I said from inside the darkened range, "I come up with about the same, twenty-four feet."

Max tilted his head, doing the math. "I come up with forty-eight feet; that would leave about ten feet of missing space. That's an awful lot of dead space. Maybe a secret room?"

Lisa chimed in, "Yeah, but we searched the damn rooms and didn't find a door. How would you get in there?"

With my thumb, I pointed over my shoulder to the mirror we were all standing directly in front of. "How about through the looking glass, Alice?"

Max and Lisa were on the other side of the counter and I was standing behind it. I turned and looked closer at the mirror. It was made up of three four-foot-wide sections. I pushed on the one to my left, nothing; I pushed on the middle one, nothing again. I pushed on the right one, and it didn't move much, but I thought I could feel more give than with the other two.

"There's some movement here," I said.

Max rushed around the end of the counter and we tried pushing on it again. It moved, but not more than a quarter inch. We looked all around the edges and couldn't find any kind of latch.

"What about in the ceiling?" Lisa pointed at the drop ceiling above us. I looked around and there under the counter was a small wooden stool. I pulled it out and stepped up. The extra twelve inches was just enough, and I lifted the ceiling tile up. Off to the right and just above the edge of the section was a plastic knob. I turned it to the right; Max was still pushing on the mirror.

"I felt it click!" He released the pressure and the mirror popped out. I replaced the tile and got off the stool.

On the other side of the mirror was a steel door with a combination wheel and a handle inset into it. Max moved to my right so we could open the mirror further and I tried the combination. Left two full cycles then stopped on 12, right to 29, left to 16, then back right to 12. I pulled down on the handle and the door released inward.

I turned on the flashlight and moved into the room. Max and Lisa were right behind me, both with flashlights. My first thought was, *why in the world would they have killed themselves with this kind of resource at hand?*

Max summed it up succinctly: "Shit." It made me think of an article I read about being prepared for the end of the world as we know it. The mental fortitude and the will to live were two things that many preppers fail to take into consideration when planning for the fall of civilization. There were literally thousands of dollars' worth of preparation in here, yet they did absolutely nothing to protect Mel and his family from succumbing to the realization that the world would never be the same again.

The room itself was not large—probably seven hundred square feet. It felt smaller due to all the stuff that was crammed in it. Some light filtered in through the one-way mirror and a Lexan window next to the door looking out into the store. Next to the door was a weapons rack that held some serious firepower.

A beautiful TP AR 7.62 NATO rifle stole my heart right from the start. TrackingPoint was a relatively new company that built different weapons platforms integrated with a micro-processing riflescope that could make anyone into an expert shooter, even at long range. The scope could lock onto a target and the target could be marked by pressing a small button next to the trigger guard; the shooter would be alerted when they lined up correctly. This technology worked even if the target was moving at up to ten miles per hour. I knew exactly what I was looking at, as I'd seen a demonstration of this particular weapons system on the Internet. The scope even came with its own Bluetooth connection so that the shooter could see exactly what they were aiming at on their tablet or smartphone. Below it were two TP AR 5.56 NATO rifles that used the same technology. These made our M4s seem like muzzle-loading antiques.

The weapons rack sat above a large Craftsman toolbox. I opened the top drawer to find a full complement of suppressors laid out in foam cutouts, each labeled by bore size. There were two 7.62 and four 5.56. The 5.56 would fit our M4s, and 7.62 would fit the TP AR 7.62.

The next drawer down held four pistols already equipped with suppressors: two Sig Sauer Mosquitos .22LR and two Sig P226 9mm, with two extra magazines for each.

There was more ammunition here than we could possibly load into the two trucks and still have room for food and water. We also found military-grade communication gear, complete with mobile radios that were supposed to be good for up to 25 miles. The whole setup would fit into a backpack, and it even had a Goal Zero Sherpa 100 charger with a 20-watt solar panel.

Beyond the weapons rack were two sets of bunk beds, a desk, and a kitchenette. The entire left side of the room was stacked with gourmet freeze-dried food in five-gallon containers. *That will come in handy.* Toward the back of the space was another door. I opened it and found a full-service bathroom. To the rear of the bathroom was another door—this place was full of surprises. Behind this door was a generator and what looked like a large water tank.

I walked back to the front where Lisa was inspecting the freeze-dried foodstuffs and Max was checking out the rifles.

"This is a pretty sweet setup, Max. If we weren't so gung-ho to hit the road, I would say we should just make this our home."

He looked at me and nodded. "We should definitely make sure this is all secured when we leave, to try and keep it for a fallback position."

Lisa was sitting cross-legged and going through a pail of food. "Uncle Ryan, look at all this food! Can I make us a big batch of it before we leave?"

I smiled. "Sure, I'd like that; how about you, Max?"

Max agreed. "Sounds good to me. She can do that while we load a bunch of this stuff into the trucks. These rifles are amazing; I've been reading the manual on 'em and they are some sci-fi shit."

I picked up the 7.62 version and turned it in my hands. "I've seen them demoed, and they're easy to use, too. Just put the reticle over your target, hit the tag button, then wait for the reticle to turn green, and squeeze the trigger. I saw a twelve-year-old girl hit targets at 250, 500, and 1,000 yards with one—very impressive. That solar battery charger for the radios will come in handy; these scopes do eat up the batteries."

After a filling batch of chicken à la king, we put the tarps back up on the front window and secured the store. We found the keys to the front door in the secret room. It was eleven o'clock before we finally pulled out of the parking lot, heading toward Interstate 90 east.

I did a radio check. "Chicken One to Raven, you copy?"

"This is Raven, I copy."

We were trying out the throat mikes, held in place with a nylon choker. It wasn't real comfortable, but I guessed we would grow used to it. The earpiece felt like a finger stuck in my ear, but at least we could communicate. "Chicken Two, follow me to the fueling point we discussed earlier, copy?"

"Copy."

We pulled into the gas station where we had procured the cigarettes the night before and stopped next to the fuel tank access point off to the side of the storefront. Max mounted an electric pump to a board and used the 12-volt plug that fit into the power access point in the truck. We used to call it the cigarette lighter, but that was no longer politically correct. One thing we'd found in the secret room was a bolt cutter. Max used it now to snap the lock on the diesel fuel cover. We lowered the tubing down into the tank, still unsure if there was any fuel left in it. The output tubing was exactly the right size to fit the nozzle receptacle on the truck's fuel tank.

"Well, that worked out well, didn't it?" I said as Max powered up the pump.

"Yeah, now let's hope this works."

The pump hummed while we watched the tube coming out of the ground, hoping for the best, fearing the worst. After what seemed like an eternity, Lisa let out a half-whispered "Yes!" as she saw the diesel fuel coming up the tube. Our system worked, but it was slow; it took nearly twenty minutes to fuel both trucks, even though the tanks were three-quarters full to start with.

"We're going to have to work on speeding that up if we can," I said, as we started packing up the pump.

Max agreed. "Yeah, that took too long... Lisa, go get us a shitload of cigarettes, kiddo."

Lisa ran off to get the smokes and Max turned toward me. "Ryan, without making it obvious, look across the street at the second floor of the building on the corner and tell me what you see."

I walked over to my truck and grabbed an open pack of cigarettes off the dash, popped one out, and while I cupped my hands around the lighter, I casually glanced at the building. I walked back over to Max.

"Looks like someone is checking us out."

Lisa walked up with her arms loaded down with multiple cartons of smokes. "This work?"

Max nodded and said, "Thanks, put them in the backseat and stay in there once you're in."

She gave him a puzzled look. "What's up?"

I reached over and took a carton of Marlboro Lights from her, and as I leaned in, I smiled and said, "Just do what he said, 'k?"

She shook her head and muttered something but did as she was told. Max and I still had our M4s because we hadn't had a chance to check out the new 5.56s. I stood with my back toward the street, turned away from the building, hoping whoever was watching us would relax if they thought we were heading away from them.

"I'm going to go back to my truck and get in, which will probably get their attention. If you see a gun or anything, I would appreciate a heads up."

Max opened his door and moved behind it as I turned away

and walked over to my truck. I opened the door and heard Max yell: "Duck!" I dove into the cab, banging my head on the console. I heard a pop, and then the whack of the bullet hitting the metal of the truck. Max began shooting three-round bursts at the culprit across the street. Lying on my side, I started the truck, sat up, shifted into drive, and jammed on the accelerator. The tires screeched like one of the freaks as I flew out of the gas station.

I sped up and pulled into a parking lot with a fence and trees around it about three hundred yards down the road. I slid to a halt and bailed out of the truck, opened the back door, and grabbed the 7.62 Tracking-point rifle. I ran to the end of the fence and deployed the bipod on the front of the rifle. I lay down and began scanning for the shooter. I zeroed in on where I'd last seen movement in the windows of the building. I didn't have a good angle on the building, but the magnification on the scope helped me spot the rifle barrel sticking out of a window. I moved the reticle about two feet back from the end of the barrel and hit the tag button. Once the tag was made, the reticle turned red for an instant; when I was on target it turned green. I gently applied pressure to the trigger as I exhaled, and the rifle bucked in my hands. The recoil was greater than the M4, but not bad.

My ears rang from the shot, but I could hear Max like he was standing on top of me. "You got whoever it was."

I didn't know how that made me feel right then, other than I was glad they could no longer harm my brother or niece.

"Get out of there now," I shouted at him.

"We're moving," came the reply.

I heard the truck coming before I saw it, my eye still on the scope, looking for any signs of movement from the building.

"Just keep driving, I'll be right on your ass," I said as I got to my feet and stowed the bipod. I hustled back to my truck, threw the rifle in the backseat, and tore out of the parking lot, looking in my rearview to see if anyone was following.

"I don't see anyone following. How far ahead are you?" I asked as I switched from looking behind to trying to see Max and Lisa ahead.

"We are just coming up on one hundred and ninety-sixth."

"Okay, head for Interstate 5 and I will be right behind you. Wait for me on the freeway unless I tell you otherwise." I still didn't see any pursuit, but I wasn't about to quit looking for it. A couple of minutes later, I turned right onto one-ninety-sixth and made for the freeway.

I pulled around Max and stopped. I got out of the truck and leaned against the side. I felt shaky and a little light-headed. I'd never experienced this much adrenaline in my entire life and I had to fight the urge to puke. I was tired of giving up my nutrition to the roadside every time I got my belly full.

Lisa ran up to me and gave me a hug. "You okay?" I nodded.

Max walked up. "I thought you ran off on us back there for a minute."

"I had to get some separation from the area to try out our new toy."

He lit a cigarette and said, "Yeah, I thought that was a little louder the M4. Hell of shot from that angle."

I reached out and took his smoke. "To be honest, I wasn't going for a kill shot. I just wanted to get them to quit shooting at you."

Max stuck his finger in the bullet hole on my doorpost and whistled, then lit himself another cigarette.

"Well, it worked out that way just the same. You okay to drive or do you want Lisa to for a while?"

"You know, that's a damn good idea, Max. Lisa, you okay with that?"

"Hell yeah!"

We got back on the road heading for I-90 east. We had discussed the trip to Meg's house several times. The route we ended up agreeing on was the major interstate over the Cascade Mountains, the logic being that there would be more chance for us to find fuel. I pointed out that, with our twenty-five gallons of extra fuel per truck, we had enough to make it all the way there. I thought the truth was that Max didn't trust the rural route. It really didn't matter in the long run, as I felt that we would make it regardless of which road we took. So I sat in the passenger seat and drank beer to calm my nerves. We found the beer in the sales manager's mini-fridge at the Ford dealership. The first two were cold, but by the time I grabbed the third it was warm, so I dumped it out the window.

"What the hell are you doing?" Lisa yelled at me.

"I'm pouring out this warm beer, why?"

"That's alcohol abuse! This is the damn apocalypse; don't be pouring out our beer!" I'd never seen her that animated and laughed, "Okay, I won't ever do it again, promise."

We took Interstate 5 north to the 405 to go south toward I-90. Lisa proved to be a good driver, as she was confident enough to go fast when she could but also responsible enough not to overdo it. We threaded our way through the wrecks and bodies scattered along the road. Anytime we talked, the voice-activated mics on our throats would transmit the conversation to Max, who was following closely behind.

"So, how many people do you think survived this, Uncle Ryan?" Lisa asked as she picked up speed on a relatively open section of road.

"Well, from the lack of folks we have run across, I would say less than I thought originally. I'd hoped there were more like us, you know, out on the freeways, trying to find family, or just leaving the city. But from the looks of it, that isn't the case. We do have some info. The death rate from the flu was really high and there were very few who were immune to it or the vaccine that produced the freaks. I figure that with the combination of those factors, we are part of a very small group of survivors."

Lisa persisted, "Like what, twenty-five percent?"

I shook my head. "I think that is a little high, more like ten to fifteen percent."

She slowed the vehicle as we came to a large bunch of abandoned cars. I scanned the vehicles with the binoculars we salvaged from Adventure Sports.

"I'm seeing several bodies but no movement. Just keep to the left."

We were coming up on exit 15, State Route 900. Based on the number of vehicles, I figured we must be close to a hospital. A road sign soon confirmed that indeed there was a hospital ahead. Lisa skirted the massive parking lot of vehicles.

"So, that's still, like, thirty million unaffected people left, right?" She was still trying to make sense of a senseless situation.

"Yeah, I guess; and that's all it is—a guess. Another thing to consider, Lisa, is that since it began, how many of those thirty million have been killed by the freaks, and how many have been killed by each other? How many have done what the gun store owner and his family did?"

She shuddered, visibly shaken by the thought. "How many people do you think turned into freaks?"

Max cut into the conversation over the radio. "Lisa, there is no way to know, and all this talk is just freaking you out, so just let it go for now."

"No, Dad, I think we need to be realistic here, try and figure out what we are facing. How many freaks are out there? I'd say that is pretty relevant to our survival."

Max was silent on his end for an entire minute. Then he clicked back on. "Without any specific numbers, or an actual count of how many got the vaccination, we are just blowing smoke. My guess would be in the neighborhood of two hundred million."

That effectively ended the conversation.

We had been driving for about a half an hour; after that, I must have dozed off. I woke with a start as Lisa slammed on the brakes. We were in the mountains and had come around a corner; there was a red Acura parked facing west in the eastbound lane. It was jacked up and a guy was changing the tire. I hit the release on my seatbelt and was out of the door with my rifle up and pointed at him before I even thought about it. He looked scared, not threatening, and slowly raised his hands.

By the time Max made it to the party, I'd already found out the guy's name was Andrew. He was a student from Seattle trying to get to Spokane.

"Why are you headed toward Seattle if you're trying to get to Spokane?" I asked.

"The pass is blocked by several accidents, and I was backtracking to find another way."

This sounded semi-logical, and since he wasn't armed, I figured it wouldn't hurt to hear him out. Max poked his head around the end of my truck with his M4 leading the way.

"Easy, Max, he isn't armed, and says he's just trying to find a way over the Cascades, says the pass is blocked ahead; sounds like he just saved us a wasted trip." Max grunted, but didn't lower his weapon.

"You hungry, Andrew?" I asked.

He nodded as if I'd read his mind. "Yeah, some food would be great!"

Max had finally lowered his M4 around the time Andrew had broken into his second MRE.

"How bad was the pile up? Could we use the trucks to clear it?"

Andrew shook his head. "If it was only one, maybe, but there was one on this side going east that had ten cars and a semi involved. I found a place to cross over to the westbound lanes but ran into another one further east. That one was just as bad and there were lots of bodies at both. I don't think it would be worth it. I turned around to go back to Route 2, which crosses over further north. There is a road down about ten miles in North Bend that connects to it."

I looked at my group, then at Andrew. "Would you be opposed to us tagging along?"

"Hell no! I mean, that would be great. I don't even have a gun, so any friend with one would be greatly appreciated. You are friendly, aren't you?" he asked with raised eyebrows.

"About as friendly as you'll likely find these days," I chuckled.

"Good. My dog, Sam, would really miss me."

We helped Andrew finish changing his tire, which was a full-size spare, thank God. Then we turned the trucks around and headed back toward North Bend. I led the caravan, Andrew took up the middle, and Max and Lisa brought up the rear. In just a few miles, we came up on North Bend. I would have missed it, but Andrew flashed his lights at me and motioned for me to get off on the ramp. Driving backward on a highway, the signs aren't easy to read.

"Hey, Chicken Two, I'm going to stop and talk to Andrew for a minute."

"That's fine, and stop calling me that!"

"Communication security, brother, communication security." It wouldn't really matter but I liked that it rankled him.

"Roger, Chicken One; I suggest we come up with better handles, then." I pulled my truck to the side of the road while laughing to myself.

"What's so funny?" Andrew asked when I got back to his car. I must have still been grinning at Max's comment.

"Oh nothing, just something Max said. So, you know this road?"

"Well, not this particular one. I have been across Route 203 several times and this is 202, which should hit 203 just up the road a piece."

"Isn't Treehouse Point around here somewhere?" I asked.

"Yeah, it's about ten miles from here."

There was a program on TV that I loved, back before all this happened, about these guys who built custom tree houses—and when I say tree houses, I don't mean the little backyard affairs you're used to.

"Be a good place to stop for the night, but we have a lot of daylight left."

Andrew nodded. "Yeah, there are plenty of places we can stop across Route 2, if we need too."

"Okay, why don't you lead then?" I banged on his roof twice and returned to my truck.

Andrew pulled around me and started down the road. I hopped back in the truck and followed.

"What was all that about?" Max asked.

"He knows the route better than we do, so I figured he should lead."

Max came back immediately, "You think we can trust him?"

"Max, quit being so paranoid. Yes, I think we can trust him."

We drove along Highway 202 north to the junction of 2 and headed east. The coastal valley narrowed as we drove into the foothills, through Monroeville and Sultan. The lush marshes with red cedars and bigtooth aspen thinned out; lodgepole pines and Douglas firs took their place as we climbed higher. The Cascades reared their magnificent peaks ahead, mostly covered in snow, even this late in the year. The foothills gave way to mountains. The shift was dramatic to say the least. The trees thickened and crowded the road until they blocked any view beyond. Then, just as suddenly, the trees opened up and mountains surrounded us, huge rock walls carved into the mountainside by men to create the winding road. Sheer rock jutted up on our right, while the other side dropped away to the valley far below. Waterfalls shot off the mountainside, pouring the frigid snow melt into the streams and eventually the ocean.

We reached the crest at Stevens Pass and wound our way down the eastern side. Eventually arriving at the junction of Route 2 and Route 97, I flashed my lights at Andrew. He pulled over and we all got out to stretch our legs and say goodbye to our new friend.

"Well, Andrew, it was a pleasure, but this is where we split up," I said.

"I hope you find your family okay," he said, and reached out to shake my hand.

"Just a minute, Andrew... Max, Lisa, can I talk to you guys for a minute?" We walked to the back of my truck; Max was already shaking his head.

"I know what you're thinking and the answer is no!"

"Why not? We have more of everything than we need, and this kid is unarmed with no supplies to speak of."

Max put his hands on his hips. He took in a deep breath, and let it out. "You are one softhearted and softheaded SOB, you know that? All right, but take it easy; we don't have *that* much."

I smiled and Lisa added her two cents. "It's the right thing to do, Dad."

I retrieved one of the M4s from the case and several full mags. "Lisa, grab some of those MREs and some water."

We went back to Andrew's car where he was leaning against the hood. "Andrew, we talked and we want you to take this." I held out the M4.

He reached out and took it. "I would be stupid to say no to this offer, so I won't." He threw a bear hug on me. "Thanks, Ryan, Max, Lisa, you guys probably just saved my life."

He released his grip and Lisa gave him the MREs and water. She received the same bear hug in return. He let her go and turned toward Max. Max quickly held out his hand. "Don't you go hugging on me, kid!" he said, unable to hide a smile. Andrew shook his hand enthusiastically.

"You know how to use that thing?" Max said, pointing at the M4.

"Yes sir, I do, and thanks again."

"Don't thank me, thank my softheaded brother over there, and ah, be careful, kid."

Andrew got in his car after giving Lisa and me another quick hug and pulled out on 97 South.

"I hope he finds his family," Lisa said with wet eyes.

"Come on you two do-gooders, before you find someone else to give our shit to," Max said gruffly as he headed for his truck. I could have sworn I saw him wipe his eyes, maybe not. It was funny, we had only met this kid earlier today, but somehow, just the thought of him out there by himself made me feel like I lost someone. Probably the fact that my son was out there somewhere, I hoped, trying to survive without me. Four hours later, we pulled up to my sister's house where we found a lot more hugs.

Chapter 9

No Way Home

Carla woke up with a bit of a headache. She looked at her watch—6:23? She was confused, not sure if it was evening or dawn. She got up and stumbled a little. Steadying herself by putting a hand on the wall, she made her way to the kitchen. There was no sign of Conner or Lauren. Light spilled in through the window blinds.

Wow, I must have slept through the night, she thought.

She made her way to Conner's room and quietly opened his door a crack; his bed was a mess, but he wasn't in it. She went by the laundry room on her way to the living room and saw the washer pushed up against the door. Her heart rate increased as fear seeped into her mind. She turned the corner into the living room and found Conner slumped in a chair that was pushed up against the couch with several other pieces of furniture, all in front of the door. She shook his shoulder and he scrambled to his feet, grabbing a rifle, which until then Carla hadn't noticed.

The look on his face was one of terror and shame. "Oh my god, I fell asleep!"

Carla, confused, asked, "Why are you sleeping here, what happened?"

He just kept repeating himself. "I fell asleep, oh my god, I fell asleep! Where is Lauren?"

That got Carla moving. She headed back to the hallway to look for Lauren.

"Lauren!" she yelled. "Lauren!"

Then she heard Lauren's response from the laundry room. "Yeah, I'm in here," she said weakly.

Carla ran down the hall and skidded to a stop. "Are you okay?"

Lauren was sitting on the floor with a pistol in her lap. "Yeah, I'm okay, I feel horrible though."

Carla helped her up and they went back into the living room, where Conner was hurriedly pulling furniture from the barricade.

"Conner! Stop and talk to me!" Carla barked at him.

He looked at her as if it were the first time he'd ever seen her. "Mom?"

Conner folded in on himself, fell to the floor, and curled into a fetal position. "I killed my friend, I killed Sam; I killed my friend."

It was clear that he was in shock and that it was escalating into a dangerous mental breakdown. Carla went into the kitchen, grabbed a pitcher of water from the refrigerator, and threw it on him. She didn't know if it was the right thing to do, but she had to try to break the pattern he was in. She got down next to him and embraced him.

"It's okay, it's okay," she repeated, over and over, holding him tight. Slowly, he started to calm down. He came out of the fetal position and clung to his mother, crying and mumbling.

After twenty minutes of this, Conner seemed to be breathing normally again and had passed out. Carla dried him off, and Lauren put a pillow under his head and covered him with a blanket.

Carla took two extra-strength ibuprofen and made some coffee. She decided to let Conner sleep while she and Lauren talked about what happened.

"So, what happened after I went down last night?"

Lauren sat staring into her cup of coffee. "I went to lie down as well, but I woke up to the sound of Conner yelling. I got up and went to see what was going on. It was dark and Conner was out back by the garage. When I got there, he wasn't yelling anymore; he was standing over someone with a baseball bat. I called out to him and he screamed at me to get back in the house. The way he said it scared the crap out of me, and I came back in. I was looking out the window, trying to see what was going on, but I only caught bits and pieces. I heard a loud shrieking sound, something like the mountain lions we used to hear when Dad took us on backpacking trips, ya 'know?"

Carla nodded and motioned for Lauren to continue. "I saw Conner go into the garage and I heard more of those screams. It seemed like hours but I'm sure it wasn't but a few minutes. Conner came back out carrying some stuff. He came back to the house and was acting weird. He shoved this pistol into my hands and told me to guard the back door and to shoot anyone who came in. Then he tore the hoses off the washer and we pushed it in front of the door. He told me to stay there and I heard him out in the living room moving furniture around. I kept asking him what was going on, but he just turned off all the lights and told me to be quiet. We heard more of them out there through the night, but they didn't try my door, and eventually I fell asleep."

Carla put two and two together as she listened to Lauren. Conner said that he'd killed Sam. Sam must have turned into one of those things and attacked Conner last night. She hoped that the thing with Steve was an isolated instance, but between what they heard on the news, and what they experienced themselves, it appeared that this was happening everywhere.

Carla asked Lauren to write down everything she could think of about the virus, the vaccine, and the people who had turned. Then Carla sat down and also wrote out her thoughts on a pad of paper. It always helped her to write things down. She listed who, what, when, where, and why. This tried-and-true investigative process allowed her to see the big picture. She listed all her immediate family members under the "who" column. Then she listed what she knew about them, when she'd last heard from them, and where they were at that time. The why was obvious.

They had been writing for about an hour when Conner stirred. He didn't seem to be as agitated as he was earlier, but he was clearly troubled.

"Hey, Conner, you okay?" Carla asked.

He sat up and rubbed his face. "Only if everything that I remember was just a terrible nightmare. It wasn't, was it?"

Carla shook her head sadly. "Come on and sit with us. I'll make some breakfast and we can talk about it."

While Carla made scrambled eggs, toast, and a fresh pot of coffee, Lauren told Conner what she'd told their mother while he slept. They ate their eggs and drank their coffee without much conversation after that. Lauren cleaned up the dishes and wiped the table off, and they both looked at Conner.

"So, can you fill in the blanks of what Lauren told me?" Conner began to recount the previous day's events.

"It all started shortly after it got dark. I was worried that Sam wasn't home yet, but I figured they had asked him to work over. I was playing *Call of Duty* when I thought I heard something out by the garage. Thinking it might be Sam, I hurried out the back to tell him you were here. When I got out there, there was no one around. I can't explain why, but I got a really bad feeling, so I went in the house and grabbed my softball bat. I went back outside and yelled for Sam, thinking he was in the garage. He didn't answer, but I heard a shrieking sound from out front. It sounded like a wounded animal, but I knew it wasn't.

The back porch light was on and I could see down the driveway a few feet, but not really well. Then I heard what sounded like bare feet slapping the pavement, and Sam came running up the driveway. He was covered in blood, and I thought he'd been in a car accident or something and I started toward him. That's when he attacked me. I was lucky; I managed to fend him off with the bat. I was closer to the garage than the house so I went in there. Sam must have left the door up when he left this morning and I was thinking about the weapons he had in there. The motion light in the garage lit up and I saw several more people running up the driveway. I ran to the back of the garage and hit the door button and it started to close. It almost made it, but one of them set off the safety thingy and it started opening again. I hit the button again and ran for the back door. I made it out and heard the garage door close, but then I saw Sam standing there. He screamed at me, making that awful sound, and ran right at me. I didn't have any choice, Mom." He started weeping again. "I had to do it, or he would have bitten me. I swear, Mom, I didn't want to, but I killed him."

Carla had moved around the table and was rubbing his shoulders. "Conner, you had no choice. We saw the same thing happen to Steve, and it was horrible. I don't think there is anything else you could have done, really."

Conner nodded. "I guess that must have been when Lauren saw me and came out. I was pretty pissed off at that point and yelled at her to go back inside. I knew there were a couple of them still in the garage and I went in there and bashed the crap out of them. It was stupid, but I blamed them for Sam and I just went nuts. I grabbed this rifle and a pistol and headed back for the house. We barricaded the doors, turned out the lights, and waited. I heard them on and off all night; guess I fell asleep at some point. Lucky we didn't end up like Sam."

"I don't think that's the way it works," Carla said.

They all sat at the table, their notes spread out in front of them. "I spent a couple of hours trying to make sense of this. God knows it doesn't make any, but I think we can make some decisions based on what I have here. The one thing that sticks out to me is that these are not zombies, even though they are cannibalistic. They are just really sick people. Another thing is, they don't come out during the day. Lauren and I only saw them at night on our way here, and then last night they didn't show up until after dark. Based on what we have seen, I would say there is a good chance that they are nocturnal. The other thing that's bothering me is that the news we have suggests that the vaccine is what caused these people to change. We don't know that for a fact, but we haven't had the vaccine and none of us have changed. Either way, we need to monitor the way we are feeling and let each other know if something is going on with us physically. This morning I woke with a headache and was dizzy, but since then I've felt fine. How about you guys? Anything physical going on with you? Headache, stomachache, diarrhea?"

They both said they were fine. "It doesn't mean we aren't changing, so we have to be careful regardless. If any of us do change, the others will have to be willing to... you know."

Conner stood. "I will not do to you what I did to Sam. I can't."

Lauren nodded her head in agreement. "Me either, Mom."

Carla knew she would be unable to put down either of her kids and realized they felt the same. "Okay, but if it does happen, we have to at least be willing to leave the one that changes, agreed?" They both nodded.

"After looking at all our options, I think we should head back home today. We'll take all the supplies and weapons that Sam has here. We need to set up a rig to siphon gas. Conner, can you find that for me?"

"Sure, Mom," Conner answered, "but I think we also need to take two vehicles, in case one breaks down."

"That's a good idea; we'll look for one when we leave here. Anything else I haven't thought of?" Neither Lauren nor

Conner could think of anything, so they went to work getting everything packed into the Rover.

They left the house at noon. Carla thought she'd steeled herself for what she would see upon leaving Conner's house, but the utter desolation made it hard to breathe. The streets were empty: no people, no animals, nothing but abandoned vehicles and loose papers floating across the road like ghosts. Their first priority was to find a suitable second vehicle. Conner suggested a 4×4 truck, but so far, they hadn't seen one that fit the bill.

Mount Hood stood off to their left as they got onto the interstate heading south. "I have seen that every day for the last four years. It looks exactly the same as before, but now it makes me feel small," Conner said, gazing at the beautiful snow-covered peak.

Conner looked just like Carla's grandfather Brant, who in turn bore a resemblance to Clark Gable. Conner was 6'4" with broad shoulders, dark hair, brown eyes, and a well-groomed moustache. He'd been studying for work in Christian ministry, and like the rest of the Wilfords, he was devoted to serving God by serving those around him.

"How could this fit into God's plan?" he asked no one in particular. "Why would God allow this to happen?"

Carla spoke up without any hesitation. "I don't know, but I have a feeling that this has more to do with decisions made by men than divine intervention."

"Huh." For all his education, it was the only thing he could say at the time. Two days ago, he could have spent hours discussing the theological reasons for the fall of civilization. It was no longer a hypothetical thesis up for debate, but a cold hard reality.

It was slow going. There was no traffic, but there were wrecked vehicles every so often, abandoned—or worse, with bodies strewn about them. They came across several vehicles they could have taken, but they made one excuse after another to forgo splitting up.

As they came over a rise, they saw something they didn't expect. There was a car in the distance, heading north toward them.

"What should we do?" Conner said as he double-checked the AR15 that he'd taken from Sam's cache.

Carla had no illusions as to how dangerous other survivors could be, but there were no other vehicles in sight and the car was moving, not waiting in ambush. She flicked her lights a few times at the oncoming car and slowed.

"Be ready to shoot, but keep the rifle out of sight unless they do something stupid," she said.

"I am going to try and talk to them, but I will hit the gas at the first sign of trouble. You two be ready to duck, got it?"

"Yes ma'am," they replied in unison.

Carla rolled her window down and came to a stop a hundred yards before the other vehicle reached them. She raised a hand out the window in a way that made it obvious that she wanted to talk. They could now see two people in the approaching car—a man and a woman. They stopped down the road a little way; they looked like they were arguing. Finally, they slowly moved closer and the man rolled down his window.

"We don't want any trouble," Carla called out.

"Neither do we." It was an older gentleman with what must have been his daughter or much younger wife. "There is no reason to head that direction," the man said, giving Carla a hard look, trying to evaluate the situation.

"Why?" Carla half-yelled back.

"California has sealed its borders. We just came from there and there's no way around it. We even tried the back roads; everything is blocked or blown up. You can keep going, but *we* couldn't find a way through."

Carla waved and shouted, "Thanks for the info!" The man

smiled, waved, and then drove away, rolling up his window.

"So, now what do we do?" Lauren asked from the backseat.

Conner chimed in, "I say we go for it. If this route is blocked, we can head for the coast."

Carla hadn't started moving yet. She sat there with her head on her hands, leaning forward against the steering wheel.

"It's already five o'clock. By the time we get down there and look around, it will be too late to start on a different route. Let's look for someplace secure to spend the night and think about our next move." She stepped on the accelerator and started looking for the next exit, which turned out to be a little town by the name of Halsey. It didn't look like much, which suited Carla fine.

"Okay, guys, look for a small building with as few windows as possible." It took about twenty minutes to find what they were looking for: a small auto repair shop about two miles from the interstate. It was a cinder block building with a rollup door and small windows set high off the ground. They stopped in front and looked around for any signs of life.

"Looks like nobody is home," quipped Conner.

"I hope not," Carla said.

They got out and walked around the entire building. All the doors were closed and the windows unbroken. "Okay, let's see if we can get in—and pay attention, there could be one of those things inside," Carla warned.

They found the rollup door locked; there was a hasp on the main entrance door with a sturdy padlock. It took Conner several tries, but he eventually broke the lock with a large rock. They cautiously entered the dimly lit office. It smelled of grease and tobacco, and it was obvious that no one bothered to do much janitorial work; but it had a couch, a desk, a few chairs, and a couple of vending machines. The repair bay was empty, and once they found the locking mechanism, they drove the Rover in and parked it on the lift.

As twilight fell, they settled in and secured the building.

Conner stacked boxes of lead acid batteries outside in front of the main entrance door, then came in through the rollup door and locked it from inside. The space was small, but they felt safe and sat down to a meal of cold canned ravioli. Conner said a short prayer over the meal and asked God to watch over their family wherever they might be on this night.

They took turns staying awake, and the night passed without incident. In the morning, Conner went outside to pee and found footprints around the exterior of the building but wasn't sure if they were from last night or not. He'd heard the things shrieking in the distance, but not close to the building. He finished his business and went back in, where he didn't say anything about the footprints. He didn't want to freak out his sister.

They broke into the vending machines and had Pop-Tarts and Danish for breakfast with warm sodas. It was Carla who finally raised the question that none of them wanted to address.

"If we can't get into California, we will have to head north, to Seattle or Whidbey Island, and see if we can locate any of the others who may have made it to the reunion before this all started."

Conner still wanted to try to make it back to San Diego. "Mom, we can't just take the word of some stranger we happened across on the road. We need to try and get home."

Lauren agreed. "Mom, I want to go home."

Carla sighed. "Okay, so what if we get to the border and can't find a way across?"

Conner smiled. "Then we will head north; what do we have to lose?"

Carla reluctantly agreed and they broke camp, which consisted of looting the rest of the goodies from the vending machine and all of the sodas.

They headed back to the interstate and stopped at a gas station they had seen the night before. Conner got busy siphoning gas from an abandoned pickup truck while Carla and Lauren went to check out the station's convenience store.

With Jake's .45 in hand, Carla peered through the glass door and saw that the store looked like any other she'd ever seen. She tried the door and it swung open. The stench hit them like a wave: both of them began gagging.

Lauren held her hand over her mouth. "Oh man, I'm going to spew!"

Carla let the door close. "Obviously, there is something ripe in there. Let's go get something to wrap around our faces."

"I'm not going in there, you're crazy!"

Carla was already walking to the Rover and said over her shoulder, "Quit being a drama queen; we need supplies from in there, and I'll need your help."

They both found T-shirts and tied them around their faces. "Okay, kemosabe, let's go rescue that rotting corpse," Lauren said.

Carla laughed and headed toward the store. Carla entered first and shined a flashlight down the aisle by the door.

"Stay right with me, okay?"

"Okay," Lauren said, breathing through her mouth. She was still having issues with the smell and was focusing on not throwing up.

Carla moved across the front of the store, shining the light down each aisle. She leaned over the front counter and shined the light behind it.

"Nothing here, grab some bags." Lauren got the bags and started filling one with beef jerky.

"Don't forget to take all the batteries you can find."

Lauren finished stuffing every piece of beef jerky she could find into the bag and then started on a new bag with the batteries. Carla concentrated on making sure nothing snuck up on them. "Okay, Mom, I'm going to set this outside, I'll be right back."

Lauren stepped out the door and Carla moved down the first aisle toward the cooler. The odor changed subtly; it still smelled like death, but now she detected a hint of sourness. Maybe it was just her imagination. She stopped and listened— still nothing. She opened the cooler door, reached in, and started unloading bottles of water, stacking them on the floor. She heard Lauren come back in and looked back up the aisle toward the front of the store.

There were bottles around her feet and she held the mini-flashlight in her mouth, the pistol in her right hand.

She talked around the flashlight, "Hey, grab some more—"

Carla was suddenly pulled from her feet; something clenched her left arm inside the cooler. Her head slammed into the cooler door. She pushed against the frame with her right hand, losing her grip on the pistol.

"Lauren, help!" she screamed, and one of those things shrieked back at her from inside the cooler.

The only thing between her and the sicko's mouth was the bottle rack. The thing pulled her into the cooler up to her shoulder, as far as it could. Lauren screamed for Conner and ran down the aisle toward her mom. Carla tried to gain some traction, but her head slammed into the doorframe repeatedly. Her vision narrowed and she felt herself slipping into the foggy tunnel of unconsciousness. She thought she heard an explosion just prior to everything going dark.

Conner splashed water on Carla's face, slapping her gently until she came around.

"What happened?"

"Lauren blew a hole in that guy who was trying to squeeze you through the shelves."

Lauren had grabbed the .45 off the floor and went to the side door of the cooler, opened it, and unloaded all six rounds of hollow-point ammo into the thing. Luckily, it was the only one in there. Carla would see some bruises and she had a cut on her temple, but she was okay.

"Where is she?"

Conner chuckled. "Outside puking her guts out."

They collected all the supplies they could carry and pulled out with a full tank of gas and with Lauren somewhat nauseated. They made it as far as Grants Pass before running into a problem.

"Why the hell would they do that?" Conner marveled, staring at the scene in front of them. The bridge that once crossed over the Rouge River was destroyed.

"It had to be either the governor of Oregon or California, trying to stop the spread of the virus," Carla said. "Let's backtrack and try some other crossings; they couldn't have destroyed them all."

Five hours later, after driving every back road and even one train track, they gave up.

"We can head west and try the coast," Conner suggested.

"Look, Conner, I want to get home as much as you do, but from what we have seen, I think it would be a waste of time," Carla argued.

Lauren joined the discussion. "What about heading east, then south?"

Carla was tired and just wanted to get out of the car for a while. "We can try, but we are talking at least a week to get home at this rate."

Conner was visibly upset. "So, what? We're just going to give up?"

Carla rubbed her temples. "No, but what do you expect to find if we do make it back home?"

The question hung in the air like a fart. No one would claim it, or comment on it. Carla finally broke the silence.

"Let's find some maps and a place to crash for tonight and figure out what to do." She turned the Rover around and they started their search for a suitable place to spend the night.

Chapter 10

Alone Again

Barb was tired. She kept an eye on her husband of fifty years and was amazed at how quickly the wound on his leg was changing. She didn't know how long ago they had left the scene of the accident. It couldn't have been more than a few hours ago. In that time, Grampa Don's leg had turned from a bloody mess into a hotly infected combination of corruption and decay. The smell turned her stomach, but she used the alcohol she found and tried to clean it.

She lay her hand on his forehead and whispered, "I think we are at the end of this part of our journey, honey. We've done our best and I know that we will just be a burden to everyone from here on out."

She lay down next to him and thought about her family. Her oldest, Hope, was gone. She'd no idea where Carla was. Josh, her oldest boy, was trying valiantly to save his dad; and Tobie, her youngest, was in Virginia with his own family. The many grandchildren passed through her thoughts as she said a prayer.

"Please watch over them, Lord. I know I have failed them often in life but I always loved them without condition. I don't know why this plague has befallen us, but I trust in you. Keep them safe, and if that isn't possible, please don't let them suffer. I'm ready to come home, Lord."

A feeling of peace settled on her as she reached down and

held Don's hand. She noticed he wasn't breathing any longer, but that was okay, he wasn't suffering—an answer to her prayer. She drifted off into a peaceful sleep and dreamed of heaven.

Josh had a sudden urge to pull over and check on his mom and dad. He couldn't find a hospital and was becoming concerned that his dad's wounds would turn him into one of the crazy ones. He pulled to the side of the road and got out. He noticed immediately that the light in the rear of the ambulance was out. Maybe he shouldn't disturb them; they had been through a lot. His fear overcame his desire to just get back in and drive.

He approached the doors, and as soon as his hand touched the handle, he knew. He bent his head and took a deep breath. The door swung open, almost of its own volition. He turned the overhead light on and knelt beside them. His mom had a peaceful smile on her face; he put his fingers on her neck and found no pulse. His dad was obviously gone, already gray and cold. There was no sign that he was turning into one of those things like Dale. Apparently, suffering a bite was fatal but not transformative.

He leaned back against the interior and felt like giving in to the moment. This was just like the last ten years of his life. He was alone again, and then he heard something. His mom's voice, as plain as if she were alive. *Get off your duff and move. Quit feeling sorry for yourself. You aren't Job; go find Uncle Ryan in Washington.* It startled him so badly that he literally jumped and then double-checked her pulse.

That was just way too freaky, he thought, as he closed the back doors of the ambulance.

Chapter 11

Another Day

MADDIE, HARRY, AND THOMAS
11:36 P.M.
HARRISBURG, OR
WILDWOOD ESTATES

They sat in the comfortable main salon area of the coach. Thomas was showing them some highlights of the onboard communications systems. The group was parked at Thomas's home, ten or so miles out from the Marathon factory.

"These images are real-time satellite photos of Sydney, Australia, taken by the Skylark system. A private company recently launched their thirty-third satellite into orbit. The company's brain trust owns a Marathon coach, is on the board, and provides this service at a greatly reduced fee to their fellow Marathon family members. The satellites are much smaller than those that belong to telecommunication giants or governments. They are about the size of a mini-fridge and cost about 350 thousand dollars a pop—not a billion dollars, like Uncle Sam's. They don't do anything but take high-resolution photographs. Their main clients are corporations and those interested in day-to-day changes in large areas of the globe. With improvements in their software, they can take more chances with maneuvering the satellites without risking huge losses. In other words, if they lose a satellite, it is not the end of the world."

Maddie interrupted him. "So what good is it to us? I don't need to know what's going on in Sydney."

Thomas waved his hands back and forth. "No, no, the

reason we are looking at Sydney is because it is daytime there right now, not because we are restricted in what we can see. I wanted you to be able see more than the lights of the cities in the U.S., or should I say the lack of lights."

He made a few taps on the tablet he was holding and the picture changed to a view of Florida. The only reason Maddie knew it was Florida was because it was printed right at the bottom of the screen: *Miami, Florida.*

"Two days ago, you would have seen a clear demarcation between the coast and the sea. Today, as you can see, a large percentage of the lights in Miami are no longer burning." Thomas let that sink in for a moment.

"What you are saying is that there are already large power outages," Maddie answered. It wasn't a question.

Thomas typed away at the tablet and the picture changed again. This time, the screen split to show two pictures.

"Here is a side-by-side comparison. The one on the left is from two nights ago, the right is about three hours old."

"Oh my God!" Maddie exclaimed. The difference was stark.

"Normally we wouldn't be able to get actual real-time pictures because there is a queue for requested overflights assigned by your company code. I signed in with Larry's code, the communications director at Marathon and a board member of Skylark. I just happen to know the admin password for Marathon's network—please don't ask how. The satellite dishes on the coach track multiple satellites and autocorrect as we drive. Your friend Mr. McClure spared no expense on this beauty," Thomas said, patting the armrest of the chair he sat in.

"When I said multiple satellites, I meant hundreds. There are at least six hundred purely commercial satellites in orbit, not to mention those that are government-owned and privately operated. While we don't have access to spy satellites, we do have access to many that are government-owned."

Harry interrupted this time. "You said you didn't know much about this stuff. Sounds like you know it pretty damn well."

Thomas smiled. "My knowledge is skin deep. If Larry were with us, he could log into the Pentagon's network."

"What else can you get on that dad-blame thing?" Maddie said in her thickest country drawl.

Thomas smiled again. "More than we can discuss in one sitting, that's for sure."

Harry rubbed his chin, as he was wont to do. "So, Thomas, we haven't officially asked you this, but how would you like to sign on with us permanently?"

Thomas mimicked Harry's chin rubbing. "Well, I don't have any family around here, and if you wouldn't be opposed to it, I would love to join your merry little band."

Maddie clapped her hands and got up. "Well, stand up, Thomas. We're a hugging family." Thomas blushed, stood, and accepted his hug.

They were all tired from the long day full of stress and said their goodnights. Thomas headed to his house from the driveway; he stopped to listen to the sounds of the night. The canopy of stars was always a sight out here away from the city, but somehow they seemed even brighter tonight. He stood there for a few minutes, smoking his last cigarette before bed, wondering when the zombies would show up this far out in the boonies. He stubbed out his smoke and went inside.

A black figure bounded across the room and slammed into his chest, attacking his face. Thomas laughed as the chocolate lab licked and chewed on his ears.

"Stop it, stop it," he chuckled, which did nothing to halt the attack. He bent his lanky six-foot frame down and hugged his best friend, Rico, by the neck. He stood the Remington in the corner next to the door.

"Hey buddy, looks like we're going on an adventure." He

went into the kitchen and checked on Rico's food and water. He wandered into the bathroom and relieved his bladder; he looked at his reflection in the mirror as he washed his hands. The gray hairs were more noticeable than they had been just a year ago. He spoke to the image looking back at him.

"You're never going to snag another one like Trina with that mug." His wife, Trina, had died of cancer the year before.

"Especially now that the zombies are out and about," he continued to himself while brushing his teeth. Rico followed him into the bathroom and stood staring at his friend, who looked and sounded funny, talking with his toothbrush stuck in his mouth. Thomas spit in the sink. "Let's get some shuteye, Rico; tomorrow's gonna be another day."

Thomas woke to the sound of Rico's low warning growl. Rico was as friendly as any dog Thomas had ever owned, but he was also one of the best watchdogs ever. He didn't bark when he sensed danger. He would alert Thomas, then stand ready to attack whatever the threat was without making another sound.

Thomas lay there listening. He didn't hear anything, but Rico was good at his job and Thomas trusted him. He looked over at his alarm clock to find that the power had gone out. He quietly got out of bed and padded into the living room, Rico following close behind. He retrieved the shotgun and went to the front window. Rico stood as still as a statue, his ears and tail up, nostrils working overtime.

"What do you smell, ol' buddy?" Thomas whispered. "One of those zombie things out there?"

Maddie woke up. She'd been dreaming of her cousin Barb. In the dream, they were standing in the kitchen of the old homestead on Whidbey Island, chatting while Barb made something in the oven. Barb walked over to the window, looked out, and said,

"It's time to wake up, there's something outside." Maddie looked at her watch and saw that it was 3:18.

She nudged Harry, sleeping next to her, and whispered, "Harry, wake up, I think there's something out there."

Harry woke up and realized he was in an unfamiliar place. A second later, he heard Maddie whispering to him.

"Okay, I'll go check it out."

He got out of bed, went to the main cabin area, and put on his boots. Maddie came out of the back room fully dressed, carrying her rifle.

"How'd you do that?" Harry said, pointing at her clothes. She looked at Harry standing there in his boxers, boots, and holding his shotgun, and burst out laughing.

"What," he said, "you've never seen my security outfit?"

Maddie shook her head and picked up the tablet that Thomas had used last night to show them the satellite photos.

"I wish Thomas had shown us how to use the security cameras instead of the satellite stuff."

"Come on, we'll do it the old fashioned way. Probably just a coyote or something," Harry said as he went to the door.

Thomas had a flashlight but didn't turn it on; he knew his land like the back of his hand. He crept around the pine trees in front of the house, making his way to the driveway. He'd just cleared the pines...

Maddie and Harry had just climbed down from the coach and were hunched down and listening. Harry heard something off to his right. He turned on the flashlight attached to the shotgun with a flick of his finger and spotted a naked figure hiding in the trees. He started to squeeze the trigger, but Maddie knocked the barrel away a millisecond before it went off. A loud scream and a stream of cuss words followed the boom of the shotgun. Maddie was running toward the trees, shouting "Dammit, Harry, you just shot Thomas!"

Harry felt like a complete ass. Thomas was sitting on the couch with a robe on while Maddie examined a couple of scratches from the near miss on his arm.

"You're lucky Maddie deflected my shot. I am so sorry, man!" Harry said.

Thomas shook his head. "Should have put on some pants before I went out to investigate. I can't sleep with clothes on."

Maddie chuckled. "You're probably going to have to learn how; can't have you two out traipsing around naked, shooting at each other."

They all laughed while Rico tilted his head and growled. Thomas was the first to notice. Although the coach was insulated well, he heard a faint shrieking sound and knew exactly what it was. Before he could say anything, there was a loud bang and the coach shook. Rico was at the door, scratching to get out, his hackles at attention. There was another loud bang. This time, as the coach shook again, the shrieking was hard to miss. Thomas grabbed the remote and turned on the TV. He pushed a couple of buttons and the TV showed the infrared feed from outside on a tiled screen.

"That would have come in handy about a half hour ago," Maddie said

The screen showed a 360-degree view of the area around the coach. What they saw was a group of twenty-plus attacking. There didn't seem to be any coordinated effort to suggest high intelligence. They just kept coming.

"Rico, come, sit." He did as his master bade him, but he did not look happy about it. He was shaking and whining, with a growl thrown in for good measure.

"He woke me up about a half hour ago. I guess you sensed something after all, buddy." He bent and scratched him on the neck. "Good boy!"

Maddie stood looking at the things bashing into the sides of the coach. "Can they get in?"

Thomas laughed. "No, there is no way in hell they can get in, unless we open the door."

Harry spoke up, "I suggest that we don't do that, then."

They all exchanged looks. "I don't like that we're stuck in here without being able to do anything about them ravaging the coach," Maddie said.

Thomas pulled a binder from the desk drawer. "Here is the hard copy manual for everything this coach has installed. Let me show you a couple of features that might help our current situation."

"Well, unless you have a 30mm Gatling gun or flame throwers around the exterior, I don't know how. Do we have either of those?" Maddie asked hopefully.

Thomas shook his head as he leafed through the manual. "No, nothing like that, sorry—but we do have some options." He got on the computer at the desk and started clicking on the desktop. "I could do this with the Crestron remote or the tablet, but I prefer working on the computer."

A diagram of the coach was now on the screen, and Thomas held the cursor over a specific spot on the exterior and right-clicked. The drop-down menu came up on the screen, from which he selected "outside lighting." When he clicked the left mouse button, the area around the coach lit up like a football stadium. The cameras automatically changed from infrared to HD, and the group saw the attackers blasted by light. It kept them at bay for a minute, until they discovered that the light did not hurt; then they redoubled their attack.

"Well, that doesn't seem to affect them," Maddie offered.

Thomas then right-clicked another part of the diagram and left-clicked a lightning bolt symbol.

"What does that do?" Harry asked.

The words were barely off his lips when one of the creatures ran toward the coach, hit the side, and was blown back about five feet. It looked stunned.

"I wasn't sure how that would work," said Thomas. "It's called the zapper. It delivers 50,000 volts and is adjustable from ten milliamps to 50 milliamps. I had it set to the max. It won't kill a normal person, and apparently it won't kill one of these."

The thing had gotten back on its feet and attempted another run at the coach, with the same results. This time, though, it did not come back for more. They watched as various others tried their luck, only to get shocked. After about five minutes of this, Thomas sighed and turned it off.

"Why did you turn it off?" Maddie protested.

"Because we don't want to drain our battery bank completely, and it isn't going to kill these things. I may be able to reengineer the system to actually be lethal, but we couldn't do that at the plant for obvious legal reasons. Harry, could you please start the coach? It will help recharge the system. There is one other thing we can try," Thomas said.

"What?"

Thomas pointed toward the roof. "We can get up there and shoot the bastards."

Between the bunk beds and the restroom was a hatch that led to the roof. "You won't have much room up there, and be careful not to damage the solar panels, satellite dishes, or any other important-looking stuff up there," Thomas told Harry as he climbed up the ladder.

He'd changed into a set of black Army ACUs, since he didn't think his boxers were sufficient clothing for the occasion. A nylon rope was tied around his waist to make sure he wouldn't fall off—or if he did, so they could reel him back in. Maddie was pissed because she wanted to be the one to go topside, but Harry told her there was no way in hell he was going to let her have all the fun.

He successfully made it onto the roof, and Maddie handed up one of the AR15s with holographic sights that she'd selected from her collection to bring on the trip. He also wore a utility vest with several thirty-round magazines shoved into various pockets made for that purpose.

"Wish me luck!" he said, and disappeared.

Harry had a radio with an earbud and throat mic on. "Can you hear me, Sugarbooger?" he transmitted.

"Yes, I can hear you, and cut the crap. This is serious," Maddie replied. She and Thomas watched on the monitor as Harry carefully made his way toward the front of the coach.

The creatures continued their attack, shrieking and running at the coach. The zapper had deterred them, but once it had been turned off, they quickly resumed the battering. Once Harry was in place, he watched, trying to discern a pattern. He finally gave up and just picked one. He steadied his aim and gently squeezed the trigger until he felt the rifle buck against his shoulder. The bullet ran straight and true, hitting the thing center mass. It was quite anticlimactic; there was no massive trauma apparent, and the thing just fell to the ground and did not move.

Rather disappointed, Harry called over the radio, "Huh that was anticlimactic. Do you think it's dead?"

"Give it a minute," Maddie answered. They all waited, expecting the thing to get back up and renew its attack. After a couple of minutes, Harry just started shooting. He'd pick a target, aim, and fire. The others just kept going on as before, as though they didn't even notice. It wasn't until he'd killed about half of them that one of the creatures standing back from the light let out a shriek that sounded slightly different than the others. The creatures ran off into the darkness and Harry safetied his weapon.

"Do you think they're gone, or just regrouping?" he asked over the radio.

Maddie doused the lights, turned on the infrared again, and searched the area for any heat signatures.

"Looks like they have vamoosed, El Guapo."

Harry stowed his gear and poured himself a whiskey. He smacked his lips with satisfaction after taking a sip. Maddie and Thomas had recorded the entire episode; they all watched it and reviewed what they could learn from it.

"They are definitely not zombies in the traditional sense of the word," Maddie said.

Thomas and Harry both agreed. Harry took another sip of his drink.

"I thought for sure they would just get back up after the body shot. I've read too many zombie books, I guess."

"Yeah," Maddie said. "This brings up a whole different discussion."

"What's that?" Thomas asked.

"Is it right for us to just indiscriminately kill them? I mean, what if they can be cured?"

Harry shook his head, not believing what he was hearing. "You're kidding, right? Of all people, I never thought I would hear that from you."

"Why? Just because I am prepared to defend myself doesn't mean I don't value life."

Thomas held up his hands. "No need for us to decide the morality of killing zom– these *things*, right now. Let's see if we can catch a couple more hours of shut-eye before we start our day."

Thomas and Rico spent the rest of the night in the coach. Thomas slept on one of the comfortable crew bunks and Rico on the other. They woke to the sounds of Harry making breakfast.

"How do you like your eggs, Thomas?"

"However the cook makes them!" he called out as he went into the bathroom. "Man, this bathroom is sweet!" he said.

"Yeah, kind of like staying at Trump Plaza, isn't it?" Harry half-shouted.

Maddie opened the sliding door that separated the main cabin from the bedroom.

"Y'all are some noisy motherfuckers." She was not a morning person.

"Oh, calm down and come drink some of this coffee," Harry said as he stirred the scrambled eggs. He'd added some sausage, some cheese, and a couple of cloves of garlic to the eggs. It smelled wonderful.

They talked while they ate. "Thomas, do you think we could add a catwalk up top? To make it safer to do what I did last night?" Harry asked.

"Well, we could head back down to Coburg and find a welding shop; I don't want to tackle killing all my old friends back at the plant, even if they are turned."

"Do you know of any small shops that would have everything we'd need?" Maddie asked.

"Yeah, I know of a couple that might be workable."

"Okay, let's get whatever you need from the house and head out. That all right with you, Harry?"

Harry drank the last of his coffee and stood. "Yeah, I'll clean up the breakfast mess. What are we going to do with those?" He pointed outside at the bodies.

"I have a backhoe; if you guys will help, we can bury them in the pasture," Thomas said.

They spent about an hour burying the bodies. The smell of the things seemed to permeate their clothes, even their hair.

"Jeez, have you ever smelled anything so rank? We should have held off on breakfast." Thomas wiped his mouth with the back of his leather glove after losing his eggs.

"I agree," Harry said.

Maddie, the only one of the three not to have puked, looked at them and grinned.

"Ya pussies!" she exclaimed, then laughed. They both flipped her the bird at the same time, which just made her laugh harder, especially since she'd called dibs on the first shower.

It was still early in the day when they set out to find a suitable welding shop. Thomas was listening to ham radio feeds via satellite as they drove, trying to get more information on the state of the rest of the world. He also set one of the dishes to scan for signals in hopes of finding a live feed that was still broadcasting. He'd programmed the location of his best hope for finding what they needed into the GPS, and Harry followed the waypoints to their destination.

The shop they were heading to was just off I-5. It serviced a large truck stop as well as the public. Thomas had done business with Jerry, the owner, over the years, and hoped to find him alive and well.

Harry pulled up to the front gate and blew the coach's horn. After several minutes of waiting with no results, Thomas and Maddie disembarked and approached the gate. They found it locked up tight with a large chain and a heavy-duty padlock.

"You want me to get the bolt cutters?" Maddie asked.

Thomas produced a lock-pick kit from his bag. "Let me give it a go first. It's a behemoth; I'm not sure the bolt cutters would even work." Several minutes later, Thomas opened the lock with a "Ta-da!" Maddie laughed, and they rolled the gate open and waved Harry in.

Thomas found everything he needed to make the modifications and asked Harry for help taking some measurements. Maddie watched more of the videos on the coach's display while she cleaned the AR15 Harry had used last night.

An hour later, Harry held a piece of metal in place for Thomas to weld. He told Harry to look away while he welded to avoid damaging his vision. Harry averted his eyes toward the back of the coach and noticed two small boxes. The top on one of them slowly opened. Seconds later, a small, unmanned aerial vehicle (UAV) appeared. It looked like a white X with a helicopter rotor at the end of each arm and a camera hanging down on a gimbal below it. It came up to Thomas and Harry and hovered over them. Then he heard Maddie over the radio.

"I see you, Sugarbooger."

"What the hell?" was all Harry could say.

"We have three of these things, two like this and one airplane," Maddie said. "I don't even have to fly it. I just click on the map and it goes to that coordinate and waits for its next command. Isn't that cool?"

Harry laughed, "Yeah, sweetie, that's cool. Don't break it."

"I won't. I am going to take it out a ways and then use the RTB."

"Okay," Harry said, "I'll bite—what's RTB?"

He knew what it meant, but he didn't want to disappoint her. "It means return-to-base, silly."

Harry laughed, "Oh really, huh, learn something new every day." The UAV zipped off and Harry went back to helping Thomas.

Maddie clicked on I-5, which was only a quarter mile away, and the UAV flew straight there and went into a hover. She clicked on the "scan" button and it began to turn slowly in a circle. When it pointed south, Maddie thought she saw something moving. She frantically looked for a stop button, but couldn't find one, so she clicked the cursor on the map a little further south. The UAV spun around and started heading toward the target, and in the distance, she could just make out a vehicle heading their way on the interstate.

Chapter 12

Dumb Luck

They had tried several roads leading off the interstate toward the east. Each time, a downed bridge, dead end, or some other barrier prevented them from making their way east to find a way south. The beautiful mountain conifers like the grand firs and Jeffrey pines had given way to high valley oaks, cottonwood, and alder as they wound their way along the Willamette River. Conner held out hope that State Route 228 would be open. Routes 58, 222, and 126 all proved what the old man told them yesterday.

"It's only about forty miles to Route 228, Mom," he said.

"Okay, whatever, would you hand me a water, please?" Carla didn't think California was in their future, but Conner was dead set on getting back there sooner rather than later. She accepted the water from Lauren and took a long pull on the bottle. It was good, even if it was warm.

"Hey, did you see that?" Conner barked, and Carla swerved, almost crashing into an abandoned vehicle.

"Conner!" she said in her best peeved-mother voice. "You trying to get us killed?"

"Sorry, Mom, but I thought I saw something flying over the road up there."

Carla immediately went on red alert. "Where?"

Conner pointed straight up the interstate. "Up there."

"Do you still see it?"

Conner squinted and held up his hand to block the sun.

"No, it was just there for a second. It could be my imagination, or even a bird."

"Both of you get your guns ready. Keep the safeties on, but make sure they are loaded and ready to go," Carla said, scanning the road ahead for any possible ambush. They drove for another ten minutes without seeing any sign of a confrontation.

They were almost to the place where Conner had spotted what he thought was a plane. Carla stopped the car and they all got out. They searched the skies in all directions, but came up empty.

"Must have been a bird," Conner said.

They took advantage of the stop. Each of them took turns relieving themselves while the other two stood guard.

"Well, let's get back on the road," Carla said, no longer sure of what they were doing. They had just started getting back in the Rover when they heard what sounded like a horn honking.

"Did you hear that?" Conner asked.

"Yes," said both Lauren and Carla. They searched the area again, looking in every direction.

"There!" Conner said.

"Where?" Carla turned to look in the direction he was pointing. About a mile north of them was an overpass, and on it was someone waving a white flag back and forth.

"What do we do?" Lauren asked.

Carla thought for a moment. "Okay, here is what we are going to do."

Carla drove the Rover slowly up the interstate. She slowed down even more to weave around a couple of wrecked vehicles as she approached the overpass. She stopped about one hundred yards from whomever it was standing up there. He didn't appear to be holding a weapon, but it would be the perfect place for an ambush. Carla was shaking and sweating as she exited the vehicle.

"Who are you?" she yelled at the man.

"My name is Harry Towes! I am from Texas. Who are you?" he yelled back.

Carla's first thought was, *Harry Toes? He has to be telling the truth; no one would make that up.*

"Who are you with?" she yelled back, not wanting to give out too much info and trying to feel the situation out.

He rolled up his flag and put it away. She saw that he was standing next to a large dirt bike. He cupped his hands over his mouth again and yelled.

"Can I come down there, so we don't have to keep shouting?"

She thought for a moment. She'd dropped Lauren and Conner out the back of the Rover as they drove past the wrecked vehicles and was sure that they could shoot well enough to hit this guy if he did anything funny.

"Okay, but walk down and keep your hands where I can see them!"

He raised his hands and walked to the end of the overpass, stepped over the guardrail, and carefully made his way down the slope. When he was on level ground, he raised his hands again and walked down the middle of the northbound lanes. He made it to about fifteen feet away when she said, "That's close enough."

"Pleasure to make your acquaintance. Harry Towes at your service, ma'am. Where y'all headed?"

"Just passing through, how about you?" Carla answered his question with a question.

Harry smiled. "Well, me and the missus were headed to Whidbey Island when all this crazy stuff started happening." Harry figured a lone woman was no threat, and he didn't see any sign of more people coming up the road. Besides, Maddie had them both under her watchful eye, looking through the scope of a .308 sniper rifle.

Carla was suddenly at a loss for words. These people were headed to Whidbey Island? What were the odds that she'd find someone else heading to the exact same place? *Am I wearing anything that may have given away my destination? We didn't write "Whidbey Island or Bust!" on the side of the Rover.*

How in the hell? She found herself thinking that several times a day lately.

"Mister Towes, if that is really your name, how do you know where I am going? I will tell you that, right now, you have two rifles pointed at you; one signal from me and you'll be dead."

Harry's smile vanished. "Look, little lady, you are making it hard to be friendly here. I don't know where you are going because you, as of yet, have not told me! Furthermore, I will be frank with you and tell you that you also are in the crosshairs of a rifle. In the hands of an expert, I might add."

They stood there in the proverbial Mexican standoff. Neither one of them knew what to do next.

"Harry, hand her the radio, would you? I want to talk to her." He wasn't wearing the earpiece or throat mic, so Maddie's voice seemed to emanate from Harry's butt. Carla's eyes widened. Harry held his hands up in front of him and turned slowly so that Carla could see what he was reaching for. He carefully unclipped the radio from his belt and handed it to her.

"Hello?" Maddie said over the radio.

Carla pushed the talk button and said, "Hello."

Then Maddie started talking a mile a minute. "Listen, honey, we aren't going to do you any harm. We are just surviving out here like you appear to be, is that right?"

Carla held the button down again. "That's all we are doing, yes."

"Well, let me tell you, we have to come to some kind of an agreement about what to do; we all can't just sit around here

167

waiting for it to get dark, now can we?"

Just the way Maddie said it made Carla relax. "No, I don't suppose that would be a good idea."

Maddie came back on. "Are you hungry? We've got all kinds of good food, and depending on how many hundreds of snipers you got hiding out there, we can probably feed y'all." She said it with a chuckle, and Carla finally made her decision.

"Okay, we would love to have dinner with you. Can we put the guns down now and meet?" Carla released the talk button as she saw a figure rise up from the side of the road not more than a hundred feet away, wearing some kind of bush on her back. Carla turned around and gave the all-clear signal to Conner and Lauren. They cautiously poked their heads out from behind the wreck. Maddie shed her ghillie suit, unzipping it and peeling it off as Harry helped her out of it.

She then walked over and said, "I'm Maddie Towes. Glad to meet y'all."

She was holding out her hand. Carla just stood there looking shocked.

"What's the matter? You okay?" Maddie looked concerned.

"Your name is M-M-Maddie?" Carla stuttered.

"Yes, and you are?"

"Your name is Maddie, and you're from Texas?"

Maddie was starting to wonder if this woman wasn't a few bricks short. "Yes."

Carla, still looking shocked, said, "Are you related to anyone named Brant?"

Now it was Maddie's turn to look shocked. "No fucking way!" Maddie squealed. "What's your name, darling?"

"My name is Carla Wilford. My grandmother's name was Muriel Brant."

Maddie just started laughing, and continued to laugh. By this time, Lauren and Conner had walked up, wondering what was going on with this crazy lady.

"You're my damn cousins!" She was still howling with laughter as she looked at Harry. "They're my damn cousins!" Now everyone was laughing. "No way! No fucking way," she kept repeating in between her raucous bouts of laughter.

Carla cringed at the vulgar language but was relieved they had found family and that she now had someone with whom to share the burden of leadership.

Chapter 13

Bad Luck

I stood on the porch drinking a cup of freshly brewed coffee. For whatever reason, the power still worked in this part of the country, and that made our lives much easier. I sipped the coffee and thought about my family back in West Virginia. I sent up a little prayer and frowned. I was not a practicing anything, but I was raised in a Christian home and knew God personally. We weren't always on good terms, but that wasn't his fault.

"So, what are you going to do?" Max had a bad habit of sneaking up behind me.

"I don't know," I said. "Once we get everything squared away here, I'll probably head east."

Max lit a smoke and took a big drag. "Ya know, Meg still won't let me smoke in the house. End of the fucking world and I still have to go outside to smoke."

He laughed. I chuckled in return, "Probably still a good idea for the kids anyhow."

"Yeah, whatever." Max smiled and flicked the ash from the end of his cigarette. "Dad smoked like a freight train around us growing up and it didn't affect us too badly," he continued.

I laughed aloud. "Yeah, let's see, out of seven kids, how many of us have smoked at one time or another?"

Max pretended to count on his fingers... "Six, and I'm not

sure Barb didn't sneak one in there at some point."

I smiled at him and took the pack of smokes from his front shirt pocket. "I don't blame Dad for my bad habits, but I do think that we should encourage the youngsters to abstain." I lit my cigarette and took another drink of coffee.

"Yeah, it would be a bitch to keep all these people in smokes," Max said sarcastically.

Meg stepped out on the porch and leaned on the railing. She seemed to have recovered well from the attack and looked no worse for wear, other than being a couple of digits short. She reached over and borrowed my cigarette, took a quick hit, then handed it back. Max shook his head and went back inside after depositing his butt in the ashcan.

"What's his problem?" she asked.

"Nothing," I said. "How are we set for supplies?"

"With what you guys brought and what I have here, we should be good for a month or so, if we're careful. The creek is a little low, but it looks like a storm is brewing in the mountains, and that usually brings the level up some."

Max and I worked on the barbed-wire fence all day and rigged a section across the opening out in front of the house.

"It should keep out any stragglers, but I doubt it would stop a determined assault," Max said.

"Yeah, I think we should take the trucks, go find some chain-link fence down in town, and fortify this place," I said.

Max put his hands on his hips and surveyed the surrounding countryside.

"Once we get that done, I think Lisa and I are going to head back over to see if anyone else made it to Whidbey."

I nodded. "I think this area will be more secure than the coast, mostly because of the population density. You may want to stay here."

"Ryan, I know you feel like you have to go back to West

Virginia, but what do you think the chances are that you can make it? And there is no guarantee that they'll be there."

When he saw the look in my eyes, he held up his hands. "Bro, I'm just saying, it would be a suicide mission."

I took a deep breath and let it out slowly. I knew he was just concerned for my safety, but it also pissed me off.

"Look, I have to; it isn't a question, period."

"Okay, okay, don't get pissed. I'm just trying to keep you alive, is all." We collected our tools and headed back down to the house.

Meg's garden was not going to win any awards at the fair, but the fresh vegetables were delicious and won a blue ribbon from everyone at the table, even the kids.

"Man, that squash was good!" I said, as I finished the last bite.

"I'm partial to the green beans," Jean said, and burped. The kids giggled and she said excuse me.

Lynn and Jean had agreed to be the designated cooks but pointed out that Max and I would be the designated dishwashers.

"I think you should put the kids to work on that. It will give them a purpose—besides, we are security," I pointed out politely.

"Just like when we were growing up, you guys skated out of every chore given to you." Rather than start an unwinnable argument, I slid out of my chair and motioned to Max that it was time for a smoke.

It was only four o'clock and nowhere near sundown, but the gathering storm clouds had blocked the sun for most of the afternoon, creating an early twilight. Lynn and Jean were cleaning up the kitchen. Sarah and the kids were watching *Frozen* for the fifth time in as many days.

Jean yelled out the door, "These dishes will be waiting for you boys!"

I shook my head and realized there was no point in fighting it. Max, Meg, Lisa, and I were on the porch going over plans to further fortify the property. As we talked, the wind picked up noticeably. I held down the butcher paper we were using to sketch out our plans in crayon and looked up at the ridgeline to the east, where I caught flashes of lightning.

"Let's take this inside, you guys; it's getting a bit breezy out here." We retreated to the kitchen and continued our planning session there.

When the rain came, it was as if someone were spraying the windows with a fire hose.

"Holy moley! We better make plans for an ark instead of a fence," Lisa said.

She no sooner said that than the power went out. Everyone groaned simultaneously. We heard the kids scream, and then the patter of feet as they ran down the hall.

"It's just a storm guys. It's okay, we'll be fine," Meg assured them.

As Meg had predicted, the storm passed and we awoke to a beautiful clear sky the next morning. Max and I took my truck and went to town to see if we could find some chain-link fence and a generator. We needed one now that the power had failed. On the short drive to town, we saw absolutely no one. We searched around the small town to no avail.

"There is a Home Depot and a Lowe's down in Omak," Max said. Omak was quite a bit bigger than Oroville, but it was forty minutes away.

"You think we should risk it?" I asked.

Max didn't say anything, he just shrugged, so I added, "I tell you what, let's go back to Meg's and we'll make the trip to Omak tomorrow. I would rather have the whole day, and besides, we told them we'd be back in a couple of hours."

"Sounds good to me," Max said.

We swung by the grocery store and looked it over. "We

should get some meat; it's going to go bad shortly and I could use a big fat steak tonight," Max said, getting out of the truck. I followed, not sure it was a good idea but liking the sound of meat.

"Why do you think the power stayed on here longer than over on the coast?" I asked.

"Obviously the lines come from Spokane or a plant on this side of the Cascades that hadn't failed yet," Max said.

We loaded up and checked our weapons. We both chose tactical shotguns; they were unbeatable in close combat. We each slung a bandolier of shotgun shells over our shoulders and headed to the store. I double-checked my 1911, locked and cocked with one in the pipe. Max had taken to wearing the nickel-plated Judge that he picked up from Mel at Adventure Sports; it was now his daily carry sidearm.

We approached the store with care. Lynn had told us her story, and we expected to find some freaks inside.

"Okay, remember to keep your head on a swivel while we're in here," Max said.

"Got it." We were wearing the radios, and turned on voice-activation mode. Max adjusted his throat mic.

"Radio check."

"Copy," I said, as we headed in.

The store was dark except for the very front where the sunlight shone on the checkout counter. We moved to the counter and stopped. Max flicked on his shotgun's flashlight and I followed suit.

"Do you know where the meat department is?" he whispered over the radio.

"Yeah, I've been in here many times. Follow me and watch our backs."

I grabbed a shopping basket and stayed low while we moved to the end of the aisle. When we stopped at the end cap, I heard the telltale panting. I motioned to Max, held up one finger, and pointed around the corner. He nodded. I stepped around the corner and shined the light down the aisle: nothing. Max grabbed my shoulder and pulled me down. I heard and felt the shotgun go off over my head as I ducked. I looked up just in time to see the freak knocked backward off the top of the shelf and into the next aisle. I'd little time to recover, however, because the sound of bare feet slapping the tile floor sounded to my right. I turned to see a freak in mid-flight as it dove at me from five feet away.

I pointed the shotgun in its general direction and pulled the trigger three times. The semi-auto shotgun responded by sending twenty-four double-aught pellets to meet it. It looked like Wile E. Coyote as it hovered in midair before dropping straight to the ground, splashing in a puddle of its own blood.

I heard Max's voice in my ear, "Clear?"

I responded, looking quickly in both directions: "Clear."

We quickly walked to the back of the store, both our flashlight beams dancing around the room, looking for any more freaks.

"Well, so much for the steaks," I said, pointing to the meat counter.

The freaks had completely devoured all the meat. It looked like the Tasmanian Devil had been through.

"Fuck me dead," Max said.

That pretty much summed up my thoughts, too. "Let's get the hell out of here."

On the way back to the front of the store, we passed the wine rack. I somehow had managed to hold onto the hand basket and filled it with six bottles of red.

"Not an entirely wasted trip," Max quipped.

We drove out of town without having seen a living normal person.

"You think everybody's either dead or changed?" I asked.

"Hard to say, little brother; there have to be a few survivors."

"You'd think they would've made themselves known to us," I said.

"Yeah, two guys looting the grocery store with tactical shotguns, who wouldn't?"

"Good point."

We got back to Meg's and found everyone waiting anxiously in the driveway... well, not everyone. They all talked at once as we got out of the truck.

"Hold on!" I held up my hands. "Meg, what is going on?"

"Jean is missing. She and Lynn were picking berries and Lynn came back to get another container. When she got back to where they were picking, Jean was gone."

"Where is Lynn?"

"She refused to wait for you. She took off and went looking for her."

"Shit!" Max said.

"Okay, everyone but Meg, back in the house. Lock the doors and don't let anyone in. If someone tries to get in, Lisa, shoot them. Come on, Meg, show us where they were picking berries." I grabbed my TP5.56 with the TrackingPoint sight and we headed off across the pasture.

We worked our way down the creek looking for the berry patch where Meg had sent Lynn and Jean. When we were close, we started checking the ground for any sign of tracks.

"What are we looking for?" Meg asked.

"Footprints or any kind of disturbance that will give us an idea of which way they went."

There were several sets of footprints in the sandy soil, but with our lack of experience in tracking, we couldn't make any sense of them.

"I wish I'd paid more attention to all the hunting shows I've watched where they explained this stuff," I mumbled.

We covered the path leading down from Meg's house and we couldn't see any way out of the area except up and over a steep hillside that lead to a mesa.

"What's up that way?" I pointed toward the hillside.

"There are a couple of ranches, but they are two miles away at least," Meg said.

We crossed the creek and started searching. "Hey, look at this!" Max said.

He found the hoofprints of several horses along the base of the hillside. There was no sign of a struggle—but then again, we probably wouldn't have known the difference.

"Okay, I think we should go back to the house, take my truck, and go check out these ranches Meg mentioned."

We left Lisa with Sarah and the kids; Meg came with us. We headed down the main road for about a mile. Meg pointed out a dirt road that made a hard turn back toward the bluff. I turned in.

"Keep it slow, Ryan," Max said. "We don't want to advertise our approach with a big dust plume."

I slowed the truck and looked back to make sure I wasn't kicking up the dust too badly. I stopped the truck just short of the crest of the hill. We got out and walked up until we could see across the mesa. We scanned the area with the binoculars, looking for any movement. I thought I saw something and retraced back across the path I'd just scanned. In the Coast Guard, they taught us not to concentrate on one spot when searching an area, but to let your eyes pan. You are much more likely to see something with your peripheral vision than directly where you are looking. I saw it again. It was Lynn; she was headed away from us, but I recognized the funky yellow felt hat Meg had inherited from our Uncle Herb.

"Come on!" I said as I raced back to the truck. "I see Lynn!"

We kept our speed down but caught up with her in short order. She turned when she heard the truck and looked like she was trying to find somewhere to run to. I rolled down my window and waved my arm up and down, not knowing if that would get her to stop or cause her more distress, but she stopped and waited for us to pull up.

"Well, I'm glad I didn't shoot at you," she said as I climbed out.

"Yeah, me too. You want a ride?"

She got in the backseat with Max. "I followed the tracks and they seem to be heading toward the mountains over there," she said, pointing due east.

Max handed her a canteen and she took a drink, thanked him, and then took another.

"How far away is the first ranch, Meg?" I asked.

"Probably another mile and a half. The ranch sits in the valley just on the other side of the mesa," she answered.

"Can they see us approaching?"

"No, not until we start down the other side."

We stopped well short of the edge of the mesa, not wanting to silhouette ourselves against the ridgeline. The mesa consisted of high desert brush and baby's breath. Yeah, the same kind that comes in flower bouquets. Some stories held that a con artist sold the people in the area on the idea that they could farm it and make a fortune. Unfortunately, the invasive and aggressive plant now covered the desert landscape. We hacked our way through the brush to a spot where we could look down on the ranch unseen.

The ranch looked well taken care of. I could see vegetables growing in a large garden, and hay fields surrounding the property. Three horses were picketed in front of the house, still wearing their saddles, grazing on the front lawn. I handed my binoculars to Lynn.

"Looks like we found them; now what the hell do we do?"

We decided against storming the place in a frontal attack, figuring we couldn't risk Jean getting caught in the crossfire or perhaps getting killed by her captors. The next best plan was to get close and watch for an opportunity to exploit. After much debate, we settled on Meg remaining on the Mesa to act as an overwatch while Max, Lynn, and I got as close as possible to see if we could somehow cause a distraction that would leave Jean free to escape. It wasn't much of a plan, but we weren't leaving without our sister.

I crept up the ditch line in front of the house. I'd switched out the TrackingPoint for my M4 with one of Mel's suppressors attached. The ditch had a foot of water in it and the grass around it was knee high. As long as I moved slowly, I could keep out of sight. Max came up from the west side and made it to the barn next to the house. Lynn crawled through the hay field, coming in from the east.

I'd just made it about halfway down the ditch directly across from the horses when I heard someone coming out of the house. Meg came over the radio. "I have a boy coming out of the house with a dog."

I peeked through the grass and saw a Weimaraner bounding across the yard. It started barking and I was afraid I was going to have to shoot it. That would lead to an all-out firefight with whoever just exited the house.

I sighted in, but heard someone yell, "Damn it, Yogi, if you spook them horses again, I will beat the shit outta you!" This was followed by the dog yelping as it ran off toward the back of the house. He must have thrown something at the dog, because he was still coming down the front steps. He appeared to be sixteen or maybe younger and had a sour expression on his face, like he was mad, but also scared. He was talking to himself as he made his way to the horses.

"Do this, do that, I'm gonna fuck that old man up one of these days." He approached the horses and his demeanor changed.

"Easy girl, I won't let that scrawny dog mess with you." He patted the horse on the neck and scratched between its ears.

I spoke in a normal voice. He was close enough that I was sure he would hear me.

"I have a rifle pointed directly at you and if you so much as fart I will drop you where you stand." His eyes widened, but he didn't react other than to look around for me.

"I said don't move."

"No you didn't, you said don't fart."

I had to give that to him. "Okay, if you ever want to fart again, then don't move."

He stood still with his arm still around the horse's neck.

"Max, are you in position at the barn?" I asked over the radio.

"Yep," he replied.

"Okay, I am sending someone your way. Take him into your care when he gets there."

Max came back quickly, "Roger that"

"Okay, I want you to collect the horses and take them to the barn without making any move to alert those in the house. Remember, you have a rifle pointed at you, and if you screw this up, you will be dead." I moved up the bank of the ditch to where he could see my rifle barrel sticking out of the grass.

"Okay mister, don't go killing me, I ain't done nothing." I actually grimaced at his use of a double negative, but I decided not to shoot him for it. He collected the pickets and led the horses to the barn.

"I have him," Max radioed.

"Okay, ask him about Jean, and what's going on in there."

"Copy," was all Max said.

I waited for what seemed like hours; finally, Max came back on the radio.

"Okay, he said his little sister went crazy yesterday and that they locked her in the basement. They knew of Meg; they thought she was a doctor. They went over with a horse to bring her over when they ran into Jean and thought that she was Meg. Jean declined their request, but told them that as soon as we got back she would have us drive her over to the ranch. The kid says that's when it went south, says his dad drew down on her and forced her to go along."

"Is she hurt?" I asked.

"He says no, but that after she explained what she thought was happening to his sister, his dad smacked Jean and told her she better come up with something to fix his kid. That's when his dad sent him to take care of the horses."

"Okay, I am going to try and get his attention and see if we can't avoid bloodshed here, okay?"

"Okay, I will make my way with the kid toward the back and make sure he doesn't send someone out to flank you," Max replied.

"Lynn, Meg, did you get all of that?" I asked.

"Lynn here, I got it and I am where I can see the front and the east sides of the house. I will keep you covered from here."

"Copy, Meg?"

"Yes, I heard too. I can only see the front and I have the rifle you left with me, but it's been years since I've shot anything."

"I understand. Just keep watch and let us know if you see something we don't," I said.

"Okay. Over," Meg said.

I yelled toward the house, "In the house—we have your son. Come out, bring my sister, and we will trade!" I waited for several seconds, then repeated myself.

The door inched open. "You better get the fuck outta here or I am going to kill her!" he yelled back at me.

"Listen, mister, nothing has happened here that we can't forget about. Just let my sister go and we will let your boy go and leave."

"No! She's gonna fix my girl, she has to fix my girl!"

I didn't want to tell him that there was no hope for his daughter and that Jean couldn't help her. That might just push him over the edge.

"Look, I have some medicine she will need to fix your kid;

she can't do it without the medicine." Of course, I had nothing, but it was the only thing I could come up with that might get us in there.

"Max, are you getting all this?" I whispered over the radio.

"Yeah, I got the kid tied up in the back of the barn. Get the dad out front and I will get Jean out the back," Max said.

"Look, can we just put down the guns and I will bring you the medicine?" I shouted at the door.

"You put down your gun, and come up on the porch!" he shouted.

"I will, if you put your hands out of the door where I can see them."

He opened the door wider and stood there with his arms at his sides. I put down my rifle and moved toward him. "Okay, just take it easy," I said as I slowly approached.

"Let me see that medicine."

I held up my canteen. "We keep some on hand for people we run into that have been exposed," I lied.

I made it halfway across the porch when he reached behind his back and drew his pistol. I couldn't tell what kind it was; I just saw what looked like a cannon pointed at me. Flame spouted from the end of it and my world slowed to a crawl. I felt a searing fire in my side as I dove to the right, hoping to clear the porch railing. I landed short and the rail collapsed under my weight. I looked up while trying to pull my .45 and saw him turn toward me, pistol raised, to finish what he'd started.

A thought crossed my mind.

Hmmm, I must be going to make it through this, my life is not flashing before my eyes. I cleared the holster just in time to see the look of a crazy man in his mad-dog expression. He turned sharply to his right as if he'd suddenly decided to change direction. The report of the 7.62 reached me a second later as the second round tore through his neck. It was strange, watching the layers of flesh peel back as the bullet ran through him, creating a torrent of blood that splashed outward like a Japanese fan. Time resumed its normal pace as he crumpled to the ground. I heard another shot from inside the house as darkness crept around the edges of my vision.

I awoke in bed. The curtain on the window fluttered inward as a breeze wafted across my brow. I tried to sit up but felt a hot poker jab me in the side and take my breath.

"Just lie back and try to relax," Jean said. "And thank you for coming after me." I turned my head toward her voice and she gave me a smile.

"Reminds me of the time you cut your foot on the beer bottle playing in the drainage ditch, except you didn't scream as much this time."

"I don't think it was because I didn't want to," I said in return.

"How long have I been out?" I laid my head back down.

"Three days. I gave you enough pain-killers to keep you unconscious. We cut them off this morning because we have to leave."

"What? Leave? What are you talking about?"

"The thunderstorms the other day started fires south of us, and by the looks of it, we have about ten hours before they get here," Max said from across the room.

I raised my head again and looked at him. "What happened after I got shot?"

Max frowned. "I came in the back door as soon as I heard the first shot. I thought it was you shooting him, not the other way around. When I came in the back door, the mother was going for a shotgun. I had to end her."

"What about the little girl, and the son?"

"There was nothing we could do for the girl, she was a freak; and as for the boy, well, we are still debating that."

"Meg is the one you need to thank; she took out the son-of-a-bitch that shot you."

"How's she doing? I'm sure it was hard on her."

"Believe it or not, her biggest worry was that she wasn't able to figure out the TrackingPoint fast enough to keep you from getting shot! She said she had him in her sights, but followed your instructions on how to mark the target then wait for the reticle to turn green." Max chuckled.

"I'm glad my instructions and her studious attention to them is so amusing to you! So, how bad is my situation?" I directed the question to Jean.

"You're going to live, but it's going to be a while before you're on your feet. The bullet went through your side and missed your vital organs, but unlike on TV, you aren't just going to jump up and start running around."

"How are we going to leave if I can't jump up and run around?" I asked no one in particular.

"Max and Lisa went out and found a truck cap for the back of your 4×4, and we put a bed in the back. It won't be real comfortable for you, but we have good drugs," Jean said.

"Let's hold off on the drugs until I see how I feel; I don't want to be out of it if we run into trouble," I said.

Jean rolled her eyes. "You just had a trauma that would have landed you in ICU for a week, then in rehab for a month. The entry wound was clean but the exit was a mess. We had to put twenty-three internal sutures and forty-six external. Don't be a hero!"

I held my ground. "Only if I can't handle it, I'll let you know."

Jean got up in a huff. "Men! God put you on earth just to piss me off with your idiocy."

"I thought you didn't believe in God," I shot back as she strode from the room.

"Not a good idea to piss off the person responsible for your medical care, bro," Max chuckled.

"Whatever," I said.

They had spent the last three days planning for our return to the coast. We couldn't head back the way we came, as it was engulfed in flames. Being out of the picture, I'd no say in the plan, but Max filled me in and said that he acted as my proxy when it came time to vote.

"Wonderful," I said.

The plan was to head into Canada and use their roads. We had done so many times in the past, because that was where our brother Parker lived. We would head northwest on the Crowsnest Highway, then hit the Trans-Canada Highway west of the border crossing just north of Everson. Everson, Washington, a small rural town of twenty-five hundred, was just south of the Canadian border, and was where Parker called home. Normally, the drive would take four to five hours, but we had no idea if we could make it in one day or not.

About an hour after I awoke, they were loading me into the bed of the F250. I was already reconsidering the drugs Jean had offered, but bit my tongue, not wanting to give her the satisfaction. We gave the kid from the ranch a second chance and were taking him with us. His name was Chris and he rode in front with Lisa, who was driving my truck. Jean rode with me, surrounded by supplies stacked to the ceiling of the truck capper. Meg drove her Subaru Outback filled with Sarah's gang, and Max brought up the rear with Lynn, Madison, and Tyler.

It was hot in the back of the truck, even with the rear window of the cab open to allow the air conditioning to flow into the capper. After about an hour of bouncing around, I begged Jean for the drugs. She didn't gloat too much as she injected something into my IV. All I remember was her saying, "Goodnight!"

Chapter 14

Parker

PARKER
6:48 A.M.
PUGET SOUND, WA
FIVE DAYS AFTER OUTBREAK

Parker couldn't tell if the taste of salt was from the spray of the ocean or the tears running down his face. They mixed in his graying beard as the wind blew across the bow of the boat. He stood six feet tall and he was slim without being skinny. His brown eyes continued to mist as he steered the Zodiac through the waves. His mission today was twofold: lay the love of his life to rest, and check if any of the family had made it to Whidbey.

He met his wife, Rhonda, through his sister Jean in New York back in the seventies. Their spirits connected immediately, even though it would be several years before they acknowledged the inevitability of spending the rest of their lives together. She was several years older than Parker, but they were perfectly matched. Their love for the natural order of things kept bringing them together until they finally acquiesced.

Now, he was alone again. Being alone didn't bother him—it was being without *her*. He was a loner. Rhonda always knew that and gave him the space he needed to spend days, even weeks at a time chasing his birds. He was a falconer. She was strong-minded and enjoyed being with him, but she didn't have to be right next to him. She let him fly away, knowing that he would be there when she needed him. He was her falcon, released from his tether. He would soar off to hunt, only to return with a bounty to lay at her feet.

The boat settled as he pulled back the throttle of the fifty-horse Honda four-stroke outboard. The dogs, Poncha and Lefty, were subdued as well; they knew the form wrapped in the blankets was their pack leader's mate. She was also their mother and they smelled death mixed with her familiar scent. They grieved as well. Poncha was a Scottish deerhound. Her name, modified to fit her gender, was taken from her predecessor, Poncho. Lefty was a mutt, and together they formed Parker's pack.

Parker had weighed down Rhonda's body with two large rocks from their garden wall. The rocks were handpicked and named as they built the rock wall together. It was silly, but she'd been like that with certain things. He shook his head and said goodbye as he rolled her off the boat and watched her disappear below the waves. Neither of them were religious; in both their opinions, once you were dead, you were dead.

They both thought they had escaped the virus that had taken the world by storm. They remained secluded in their home once the news broke of the highly contagious flu. But then, three days ago, Rhonda fell ill. He tried to get her to go to the hospital, but she refused. She'd been a nurse for forty-five years and told him there was no cure other than to stay hydrated and rest.

He'd narrowly escaped death twice himself. The screamers, which only came out at night, found the screeching sound of his falcons' calls irresistible. A small pack of screamers had come the night before Rhonda took ill; they snuck around the house all night, never finding a way in, then disappeared an hour before dawn.

The next night, one of them made it into the backyard. It came through the doggie door he'd built into the wall next to the porch for Poncha and Lefty. He was asleep in a chair in the living room when the thing attacked. The dogs woke him, barking and growling as it slid through the thick plastic flap. He had a .44 magnum pistol that he kept for his trips into bear country and got off a hasty shot as the thing came at him. He was glad that it was a reaction shot and not one that he had time to consider; the thing had once been the neighbor's ten-year-old daughter, and he was sure he wouldn't have shot her if he'd realized it at the time.

His second encounter came the next morning. He went into town to see if the pharmacy had any antiviral drugs that might help Rhonda. He was not being overly cautious, as he knew the screamers only came out at night. He walked right into the darkened store, turned on his flashlight, and headed for the pharmacy in the back.

He was halfway through the store when he heard the shrieking just a few feet from where he stood. Being unprepared almost cost him his life. Wilson, whom Parker had known for 15 years, appeared in his lab coat, covered in blood. Instead of his usual friendly greeting, Wilson came at Parker with bad intent. Parker backpedaled, keeping the big six-cell Maglite out in front of him. Wilson plowed into him, knocking him backward toward the front of the store. Parker looked over his shoulder as he fell and saw he was still fifteen feet from the door. He held Wilson at bay with the long flashlight, kicking his old friend in the balls as hard as he could. It had no effect at all. The only thing that saved Parker was that, in Wilson's effort to rip into Parker's throat, the two were propelled down the aisle toward the front door. The second they entered the square of sunlight coming through the glass door, Wilson recoiled.

He had to get to the antiviral drugs he hoped Wilson kept in the back. Parker knew Rhonda was dying. He retrieved the pistol from the truck and went back in.

"Hey Wilson, I'm back! What do ya say old friend, can you

spare a few drugs for old time's sake?"

He heard panting coming from the darkness like Poncha after a hard run. Holding the flashlight in his left hand and pointing the .44 down the aisle with his right, Parker inched his way into the darkness. He wasn't a gun enthusiast; in fact, he hadn't shot the .44 mag more than three or four times before killing the screamer the other night. His hand shook a little as the adrenaline coursed through his veins, the panting growing louder and faster the further he crept.

In all his outdoor adventures, he'd learned how to regulate the effects of the adrenaline rush. He focused on breathing slowly through his nose and reminded himself that he was capable and well prepared. Wilson came from his right. Parker didn't see him coming until the last second. He whirled and the boom of the .44 echoed off the walls as the bullet tore through Wilson's eye socket. Blood and little chunks of skull and gray matter flew everywhere. The bright beam of the flashlight amplified the vivid red color of the blood as it fanned out behind Wilson as he fell. The quiet returned as Parker stood there, his ears ringing, looking at the pitiful remains.

He continued toward the back of the store. The smell of something dead reached out to him from the hallway beside the pharmacy. He pointed the flashlight down the hall that led to the offices, but decided he didn't want to know what was producing that smell. He opened the door to the pharmacy, and after a thorough search, found some Theraflu. It was the only antiviral he could find, and he hurried back home.

Poncha and Lefty didn't meet him at the door upon his return. That was unusual. He went up the stairs, excited to bring the medicine to Rhonda, but knew as soon as he stepped into the bedroom that she was gone. Both Poncha and Lefty were lying on the bed guarding the lifeless body of his love. He fell to the floor and cried out. Poncha came to him, whining, and licked at his face as he lay there sobbing.

That had been two days ago. Yesterday, he made the two-hour trip to Woodinville to check on his niece Sarah. He found the house in ruins with a note nailed to the garage door.

Parker, wanted to leave this note in hopes that you would eventually come by. Max and Lisa met me here the day after all this shit came down. The freaks attacked us that night but we are okay. We're heading out to Meg's place. We hope this finds you and Rhonda well. We plan to stay at Meg's until this settles down. We hope to come back to check on you and see if anyone else made it to the island for the reunion. Could you check out Whidbey and find out if Cousin Molly is at the farm in Coupville, and if anyone is at the rentals? Sarah and the kids left a note, which is under this one. They left for Meg's sometime before we arrived. Much love, Ryan

Parker read Sarah's note and felt another pang of loss. Tim had been a great husband and father, and then there was eight-year-old Peter. He and sixty-two-year-old Parker had become good buddies since Sarah and Tim had adopted him. He would miss them both. He got back into his truck and drove straight home.

Today, he was intent on finding out whether any of the family had made it to the houses they had rented for the reunion. There were three different houses to check, as well as the farm in Coupville. Two of the houses were located in Penn Cove, which was about three-quarters of the way up the eastern shore from Whidbey Island's southern tip. He carefully checked the tides in his book before leaving Bellingham; he would have to navigate Deception Pass in order to reach the other side of Whidbey.

Deception Pass got its name in 1792 when explorers Vancouver and Whidbey had initially missed the pass and thought that the island was actually a peninsula. Toward the end of their exploration, however, Vancouver sent Whidbey on one last expedition to map the inlets along the northwestern shore. Whidbey found the pass and successfully made his way through to the eastern side of the island. Vancouver, pleased with Whidbey's circumnavigation, named the island in his honor.

The reason it was necessary to know the precise tidal schedule was because Deception Pass was dangerous to navigate unless the tides were static. It narrowed to less than a thousand feet wide where the bridge crossed from the mainland, and there were many submerged rocks that could ruin your day and your boat. If the tides were going either in or out, the pass would be violently pushing or pulling billions of gallons of water through its tiny passage and could actually create class-3 rapids and huge standing waves. He normally would have launched the boat from one of the many places east of Whidbey, but with the current state of affairs, he felt safer on the water than he did traveling the roads. It had also allowed him to say goodbye to Rhonda in a way that somewhat soothed the ache in his heart.

He'd timed it correctly and approached the pass when it was relatively safe to navigate. The fourteen-foot Zodiac with its fifty-horsepower engine was nimble, and Parker's experience made the passage uneventful. He drove under the bridge and he and the dogs motored south to Penn Cove.

He docked at the Port of Coupville, which was little more than a pier and a smattering of businesses. It was still early in the day, and the hike to the farm was only about a mile. He figured on going there first to see if Molly and her husband Henry were okay. Molly and Henry ran the last producing commercial farm on Whidbey Island. Most of the island had become a bedroom community for Seattle, but they still eked out an honest living tilling the soil. The 200-plus acre farm, started in the early 1900s by Henry's grandfather, grew mostly squash. Parker's stomach growled as he thought about Molly's squash soup.

He and the dogs made their way up Main Street. The small town of Coupville was deserted. It was amazing to Parker how quickly the world had gone from its hustle and bustle to dead quiet—during the day.

He arrived at the farmhouse with high hopes. He tried the front door first, knocking and loudly calling out. There was no response. The rest of the house looked secure: no broken windows, no signs of life or death.

Parker wandered around the house to the garage. He opened the garage door and found Henry's 1967 GTO 442 parked in its place of honor. Parker knew where Henry kept the key. He retrieved it from its hiding place in the garage and sat down behind the wheel. He turned the key and the Pontiac roared to life without any hesitation. He covered the backseat with a blanket out of respect for Henry, then tried to get Poncha and Lefty to hop in. Lefty jumped right in, but Poncha was leery of the rumbling beast. Parker finally shut it off.

"Come on Poncha, or I'm leaving you here!"

She tilted her head then jumped in. He fired it back up and the beefy engine kicked out a belch of throaty thunder, causing Poncha to pace nervously in the backseat. He pulled out of the garage and onto the pavement. He couldn't resist the urge and spun the tires as he turned onto the main road.

"Yeeeehaaaa!" It had been years since he'd been in a car with this kind of horsepower. He went through the gears, doing a hundred miles an hour before backing off.

"Woo-wee Poncha, this is fun, eh?" Oddly enough, Poncha didn't agree, and buried her head under the blanket.

He wasn't out for a joyride. He headed for the house that Max had rented on the north shore of Penn Cove. When he got there, it appeared abandoned. No cars were parked in the driveway, and he peeked in every window.

"Nobody home here, guys," Parker said to the dogs. "Let's go check out the other house."

The other house on Penn Cove was all the way back through

Coupville and close to the eastern point that demarked the entrance to the cove. He'd been there once before to check it out for Jean.

He found the place by looking for the natural stone walls that bordered the driveway. It was lined with evergreens, their branches creating a tunnel leading toward the water. The driveway turned to the right and into a clearing. The house faced the cove; it was bigger than he remembered. His pulse quickened when he saw there were several vehicles parked around the circular drive.

The next thing he noticed were several people with rifles pointed at him. He braked suddenly, and Poncha and Lefty slid off the backseat onto the floor. Parker heard a familiar voice yelling.

"Don't shoot my car! Don't shoot my car!" Henry popped up from behind a Lexus, waving his arms frantically and running toward him.

Parker smiled until he saw the sawed off shotgun appear next to his head.

"It's me—Parker Brant. Don't shoot, I'm related!" Once he said it aloud, it sounded ridiculous. He looked up the barrel at his Cousin Merle.

He was surprised at the number of people that had made it there. Once the initial confrontation subsided and Henry agreed not to hang Parker for bringing out his GTO, they all retreated to the great room in the house. Parker counted twenty people, and most of them were family somehow. Those who didn't live on the island had arrived the weekend before the outbreak. The group originally was scattered around the three rentals and the farm. They all pitched in and fortified this house because of its size and location. A large cistern on the hill provided the house with a gravity-fed water system, meaning the toilets would function as long as the sewers remained clear. Sheets of three-quarter-inch plywood covered the windows and all but one door. The great room, once a cheery and bright gathering place, became a cave, dimly lit with candles and LED camping lights. The lovely view of Penn Cove was now replaced by a bleak darkness, both of the heart and the sun.

Parker spent some time answering questions about what he'd seen as he made his way to the island. They all talked about the people that had turned into rabid animals, and the attacks they had fended off since it all began. Molly and Kathleen, Merle's wife, cooked a lunch of fresh vegetables, squash soup, and bread. Parker ate for the first time since the day before. Henry showed him around the place and pointed out the tree house where they stood watch. It was about fifteen feet off the ground, attached to several large pine trees. A ladder made of two-by-fours reached all the way to a hole in the bottom of the structure, the top eight feet covered with plywood.

"How do you get up there with that plywood on the ladder?" Parker asked.

"I fixed that up. There are hinges on the plywood like shutters, and a lock. You unlock it on the way up and then, once inside, you close it and relock it from the top," Henry said. "Come on, I'll show ya."

The tree house was ten feet by ten feet with windows running around each side at seated eye level. There was a cot, a kerosene heater, two chairs, and a footlocker. Henry flipped open the top on the footlocker and retrieved one of two rifles from it. It was an M1 Garand. Originally used in the Second World War, it was a staple of the military for many years.

"Springfield thirty-aught-six," Henry said. "No fancy sights on it or nothing, but it's my favorite."

Parker looked into the footlocker. There was also an AR15 with a red-dot scope in it, as well as enough ammo to supply a platoon.

"You can use the sissy gun in there if you want, but me, I like my rifle like I like my women," Henry said.

"Okay, Henry, I'll bite. How do you like your women?"

"Reliable," he said with a smile.

Henry went on to explain to Parker that the house had solar panels and a bank of batteries, which he'd disconnected from the house. They used the system mainly for perimeter lights, which triggered with motion detectors.

"We wired a bunch of them up around the property, in the trees, and around the house," Henry said, pointing them out. "When the vectors show up, we sit up here and pick them off. The only blind spot is the far side of the house, which is guarded by somebody in the attic."

Parker nodded. "Why do you call them vectors?"

Henry shrugged. "It's what doctors call anyone who's been infected with rabies. I know that isn't one hundred percent accurate, but it was the best we could figure when it all started."

"Huh, Ryan called them freaks in the note I found at Sarah's in Woodinville. I guess one name is as good as another," Parker replied.

Parker had already decided to spend the night on the island. He'd missed the turn of the tide, and he wasn't planning on being out and about when darkness fell. Henry asked if he would take the overnight watch with him in the tree house. Parker agreed, and they settled in around eight o'clock, just as the sun was setting. It wouldn't be fully dark until close to nine, but in this case, better safe than sorry.

Henry lay down on the cot and Parker took the first watch. A Navy sound-powered phone sat in the corner connected to the house. It was old tech, but it worked. Henry's instructions to Parker were simple. If the vectors showed up, call the house and warn whoever was on watch there, and wake them up, too.

Parker spent many hours staking out owl nests in his life prior to the outbreak, so he was used to staying awake for long periods. He sat facing the woods toward town. Henry had told him that they didn't show up every night, and when they did, it was usually only a small group.

Whidbey Island's population fluctuated from between sixty and seventy thousand; this being the height of tourist season, it would be closer to seventy. While Coupeville was the county seat, its population was only eighteen hundred, give or take.

Parker sat there doing the math in his head.

The South African Flu's morbidity rate was high, and the average age of people in the area was fifty-something. Older folks tended to be more likely to have received the vaccination, as they visited the doctor more often than young people did. He figured that if half the population died of the flu, and three out of four that survived had gotten the vaccination, then... still a shitload of vectors!

He wondered how so many of his family had survived both the flu and the vaccination. Immunity or resistance to both must be hereditary, something to do with genetics.

A light popped on in the trees, pulling him from his thoughts. He searched the area for whatever had triggered the motion detector. It wouldn't do to wake Henry up only to find that a raccoon was poking around. Before he could locate the source, several more of the perimeter lights came on. He reached over and shook Henry.

"Henry, we've got company."

"How many do you see?" he asked quietly as he sat up on the cot, rubbing his face.

Parker was about to tell him none, but as he formed that thought, several of them ran into the clearing.

"Small group, probably six or seven, yeah, seven," Parker whispered. "Over in the clearing to the south."

Henry focused on the lit area. "Let's see what they do. If we start shooting, it will draw any others close by. They may just keep moving."

Henry called the house. "We have a group of seven to the

south; don't start shooting unless we do."

The small pack of vectors were all lifting their noses to the air, trying to get a scent. One let out a shriek that sent the others scurrying. Parker heard another shriek off in the distance to the east.

"Sounds like we may get more regardless; those things communicate with all that damn shrieking," Henry said. He moved to the window, swung it up, and hooked it.

"Do you think you can take out the one making all the racket?" he asked Parker.

"I don't know, Henry, I'm not much of one for killing unless we have to," Parker answered.

"There is something you need to realize, Parker: It's us or them. We are going to have to kill, and keep killing, until either these things are all gone, or we are."

Parker had killed things when necessary throughout his life. He fed himself and Rhonda with the kills his falcons made. He killed birds to feed to his falcons, and now he faced having to kill people to survive. He killed Wilson, and the little girl next door, and it made him feel like shit, but there was no arguing that these things were trying to kill them.

"Okay, I'll do it." He picked up the AR15 and braced it against the windowsill. He located the vector that was obviously the leader. He breathed slowly, remembering the lessons his dad taught him all those years ago with the twenty-two. He lined up the dot on the center of his target and began to ease pressure onto the trigger.

The trigger pushed the sear up, releasing the firing pin that ignited the primer in the .223 round. The primer's ignition set off an explosion in the 25 grains of gunpowder. This, in turn, expanded the shell casing, sealing off the barrel, forcing the 62-grain jacketed hollow-point bullet to begin its journey. The twisted grooves inside the barrel began to spin the projectile as it exited the rifle. Traveling at 3,050 feet per second, the bullet tore into the chest cavity and created a path of destruction through the vector's heart. This all happened before it heard the report of the rifle.

As the vector crumpled to the ground, Parker heard Henry begin to fire on the others. Parker located another vector as it turned and looked in their direction. Through the lens of his scope, Parker saw no recognition in the thing's face that it was about to die. He watched his shot hit it above the right eye; its head snapped back and it fell in a heap. Unlike any movie he'd ever seen, each vector that he shot simply dropped to the ground. None of them flew through the air or did a back flip, they simply dropped.

After what seemed like both an eternity and an instant, the gunfire ceased.

"Be ready, the second group will be here any minute," Henry said.

Parker could barely hear him over the ringing in his ears. "What the hell, don't they realize that the noise means death?" Parker shouted back.

Henry looked at him quizzically, and then remembered that it was Parker's first battle with a pack of vectors.

"No, I guess they haven't put two and two together where that is concerned." Parker just shook his head and looked out over the scene of death he'd helped bring.

"What if they find a cure for this? We are killing these people, your neighbors, possibly even relatives, without a second thought," Parker complained.

"You obviously haven't seen someone who has been torn to pieces by one of these things yet, have you?" Henry asked, all the while keeping an eye out for more of them. He continued, "They have no mind, Parker, just an unstoppable desire to feed. If someone comes up with a cure I will be alive to feel regret that I had to kill so many, but I'm not going to let them eat me, or you for that matter."

They waited and watched. After several minutes, Henry spoke.

"Well, maybe they are learning. That ain't good."

The rest of the night passed without incident. In the morning, they climbed down from the tree house, and with the help of the group, cleaned up the mess. After they took the bodies to the farm and burned them, Henry and Merle dropped Parker and the dogs at the pier.

"I'll be back soon," Parker said as he leaned against the door. He ducked his head and looked across the truck at Merle and gave him a nod.

Henry smiled at him.

"You take care out there, Parker. Remember what we talked about up in the tree house. Those things won't feel bad about killing you." With that, Henry fired up the truck and headed back up the road.

Chapter 15

Whidbey Bound

They sat around the table having just finished a wonderful meal. Harry and Maddie made a canned ham with macaroni salad and candied yams. Conner ate the last piece and was in the process of communicating his undying love for his newly found cousins.

"I haven't eaten anything that good, ever," he said, as he rubbed his full belly.

"Well, I hope you liked the macaroni salad; I made enough to feed an army," Maddie said.

"Liked it? I loved it! But I couldn't eat another bite; I'm stuffed." He leaned his head back against the plush headrest of his seat in front of the desk next to the dining table. The chair could turn toward the table and lock, or turn toward the desk. The coach was all about efficient use of space.

Once everything was cleaned up and put away, Thomas gave the newcomers a tour.

"The couch on the left, as you enter, is a queen-size pull-out bed that will only deploy when the slide is out. The sink and storage cabinets begin the galley area, below is the dishwasher drawer. Next to the sink is the two-burner stove, with the speed oven and microwave above it."

He got up from the table and motioned for everyone to follow. They moved to the center of the salon and watched as he manipulated the Crestron remote, which could run every feature on the coach. The table they had been sitting at slowly descended into the floor, the slide-out retracted into the coach, and the bench seat they had been sitting on came toward them.

"With the slide-out and the table retracted, the seating area can be converted into another sleeping area. Across from the galley is more storage space and a subzero refrigerator with a two-drawer freezer." He didn't point out the secret gun locker next to the fridge, because he wasn't sure Maddie wanted them to know about it.

"Go ahead and show them the weapons bay, Thomas," Maddie prompted.

The front of the fridge had the same high-quality walnut veneer as all the cabinets, and next to it was what looked like a six-inch wall, again with the same wood trim.

"If you push here," Thomas pointed to the bottom kick plate as he pushed against it with his toe, "you will activate the lock that holds this floor-to-ceiling storage area." He pulled it out.

"Nice," Conner said under his breath.

The storage bay held two tactical shotguns and two AR15s, as well as two nine-millimeter MP5s.

"These are all from my personal collection; they did not come included with the coach, and I will train you on their use as we travel. Don't get in here without asking, unless the situation is grave. The ammunition is stored in these drawers, and as you can see, we have a lot, but we will never have enough," Maddie said, closing the drawers under the freezer.

"Continue, Thomas," Maddie said, giving the floor back to the engineer.

"Okay, these two bunks can be converted into a wardrobe closet, but with there being six of us, I won't even bother to show you that feature. If you look on the ceiling above the bunk, you will see a docking station for your phone, as well as a tablet that you can use to view all of the same things that you can on any of the onboard TVs or the computer. Across the hall from the bunks is the restroom."

The shower, toilet, and small sink, beautifully crafted, pulled a "sweet" from Carla. They moved through the air pocket doors into the master suite/office.

"This room was completely customized from our normal floor plan. Normally, this area is a luxurious bedroom or a high-end office, not both. On this wall is a motorized queen-sized Murphy bed, which when in the up position as it is now, has a table attached that unfolds as you see here. The chairs are stored in this cabinet," Thomas said, pointing to another closet.

"On the opposite wall is a set of drawers that also has a 50-inch flat screen TV that can be raised and lowered. With the bed down and the TV in its stored position, you have two sets of windows. There is normally another restroom in the back, but we used that space for personal storage and the motorcycles." Thomas finished the tour and told them that he would continue to teach them about all the features as it became necessary.

Maddie and Carla talked while Lauren took a nap and the boys worked on the catwalk.

"So, what are you planning on doing?" Carla asked.

"We talked about heading back to Texas, but with all the family heading to Whidbey, we thought we would go and find out if anyone made it," Maddie said.

Carla looked down at her hands, trying to fight back the tears.

"We lost my husband to the flu, and my son-in-law to the vaccine, and well, I don't know what to do. Go home to San Diego, go with you to Whidbey? I am so confused."

Maddie reached out and took Carla's hand.

"Listen, honey, you don't have to decide right this minute. Do you know where any of your other family is?"

"No, I'm not sure; when this all started, I couldn't reach any of them. Mom and Dad, my sister Hope and her family, and my brother Josh were supposed to leave the day after we did. I have no idea if they actually did," Carla said.

"Well," Maddie looked pensive, "I only know that the big cities are going to be teeming with these things, plus it can't be coincidence that we found each other. I had a dream the other night. Your mom and I were in the kitchen of the old homestead in Langley just chatting, and then she looked out the window and told me to wake up, that something was outside. We got up, and an hour later, the creeps showed up. I don't know if it was just because I planned on seeing her at the reunion that she was in my dream, or if she was reaching out to me. Either way, it convinced me to head to Whidbey."

"Let me talk to Thomas and ask him to give us a satellite shot of San Diego," Maddie said. "Maybe we can we get an idea of what's going on down there."

Carla wanted to be able to give Conner a good reason not to head directly home.

"I would appreciate that," she said.

Carla fell asleep on the couch in the salon and woke up several hours later. It was dark and no one else seemed to be up except for Thomas, who sat at the computer watching the camera feeds.

She lay there thinking.

What should I do, Jacob? I need your help, give me something. She drifted back to sleep. Her dreams filled with horrible scenes from what looked like her home. An ethereal feeling encompassed her. A strange, hollow, echoing feeling; she was standing in her living room and Jake was standing next to her.

Don't go back, baby; there was a bright flash of light. The air was sucked from her lungs and the heat felt like every description of hell she'd ever imagined. She awoke with a gasp, knowing that the only thing to do was to head away from home. She wasn't sure if Jacob had really come to her in a dream or if it was just her subconscious, but the dream seemed very real. She had to convince Conner that going home was not an option. She went back to sleep without the horrors of the dreams, just the knowledge that they must not go back.

The next morning, she woke with a purpose. She looked around to find Conner, who wasn't in the coach. She finally found him sitting on the top of an old '57 Chevy, a rusted-out hulk of a once-powerful muscle car. She groaned as she climbed up the bumper to the rear deck and then onto the roof. She sat down beside Conner, who looked like he was in deep meditation as the sun poked its head up over the mountains. She rested her hand on his shoulder.

"Conner?"

He didn't move; his voice sounded resigned.

"I know, Mom, I know, we can't go home... I saw Dad in a dream last night; he said we could never go back. God, I miss him. I know it sounds stupid, but the dream seemed so real. Do you think I'm losing it?"

Carla held him close and pressed her lips to his ear.

"No, you're not losing it." She didn't tell him of her own dream; she didn't know why, it just didn't seem like she should. "Your dad lives inside us, he still loves you, he will always love you, Conner."

"Hey y'all, want some breakfast?" Maddie called from the door of the coach.

Carla hooked her arm around Conner's neck.

"What do you say, boy? You want some breakfast?"

"Yeah, Mom, let's get some breakfast."

They climbed down from the Chevy and made their way back to the coach. As they entered, Harry gave them both a smile.

"How do you like your eggs? Scrambled or scrambled? We're down to the powdered stuff now."

After breakfast and some discussion, they decided they would all travel in the coach. They could always pick up another vehicle down the road if they needed it. Leaving the Rover was hard—it was a part of the family, and it had been Jacob's.

They rolled out at around eight in the morning, topping off the diesel from one of the many abandoned eighteen-wheelers at the truck stop.

Carla was worried about Lauren.

"We're going to be okay, honey."

Lauren looked up.

"Nothing is ever going to be okay."

Chapter 16

Rebound

Josh stood next to the two graves. He'd no tears left to shed and was glad for the cool breeze that blew in from the ocean. He pounded a makeshift cross at the head of each grave and said a prayer over his mom and dad. The gravesite was on a bluff overlooking the surf. He figured his mother would approve. She'd always loved the ocean. He decided on coming to the coast for two reasons: First, it was where he wanted to bury his parents, and second, Highway 101 avoided some of the bigger cities. After finding his parents had passed, he continued to drive north, aimlessly at first. He had a run-in with a group of crazies in a town where he stopped to look for help. They had surrounded the ambulance and almost succeeded in tipping it over. He headed west from there, not knowing where he was, but knowing he would eventually run into the coast. His idea was to drive up the coast, avoiding large populations, and eventually try to find a boat large enough to get him to Whidbey Island.

The ambulance had provided him with some very handy items. There were tools used for extracting victims from vehicles that gave him some hope of survival. He found bolt cutters, a crowbar, a folding shovel, high tensile rope, and much more. He chose a wrecking bar from the inventory to use as a weapon. He only had a limited number of bullets for the pistol he borrowed from the CHP. The wrecking bar was 30 inches long and weighed at least ten pounds; it would definitely do some damage. There was also a good bit of drugs onboard. He didn't know what many of them were for, but there was a medical book that he figured would clue him in.

His first priority now was to find some food. The ambulance had water, both drinking water and sterile water for medical use, but no food. He set off to scavenge something.

The road stretched out in front of him with nothing but trees in sight. The two-lane highway was empty of any traffic and Josh wondered if he made a bad decision. Where he lived, you couldn't drive more than five minutes without seeing a Ralph's, a Vons, or a Kroger supermarket.

The highway expanded to four lanes outside of Coos Bay, and a few businesses appeared. Trucking companies, tire companies, and a sawmill, but nothing that might provide him with food. A tawdry-looking strip club on the right offered a full buffet. *Dine while they Dance,* the sign proclaimed. That would rank right up there with prime rib at the bowling alley; besides, he wanted non-perishable foodstuffs. He kept his eye peeled for any signs of life as well as groceries. He couldn't believe how deserted the place seemed.

He passed a burned-out 7/11 and a Subway, still no sign of anything good. As he crossed a bridge over a sliver of the bay, he finally saw something: a large, white building. He didn't recognize the name on the side, but thought it was worth checking out. He pulled off the highway, which had transformed itself into the main street of Coos Bay, and into the parking lot. The main sign proclaimed *FOOD-BAKERY-DELI!*

"This is more like it," he said aloud. He stopped the ambulance right in front of the main entrance and got out. His salivary glands started pumping and his stomach growled just at the thought of food. He retrieved his wrecking bar and flashlight from the ambulance and walked up to the doors. As he approached, the smell became a mixture of rancid meat and ammonia.

God, what is that? he wondered.

The doorframe was still standing but the glass was completely broken out, and there was garbage all over the place.

"Hmmm, looks like I'm not the first customer," he said, as he flashed the light into the store.

Something ran through his flashlight beam, but he couldn't follow it.

"Hey, is somebody in there?" he yelled.

Then he heard it: the shrieking, the same shriek that Dale had made. He took an involuntary step backward. He put down the wrecking bar and pulled the pistol from his belt. He checked to make sure the magazine was loaded and that there was a bullet in the chamber. He ducked under the crossbar on the doorframe and shined the light around slowly. He didn't see anything, so he moved a little further in and repeated the process.

"Come on, mister boogeyman," he shouted, trying to instill a little bravado in his voice. It would have been more effective if he hadn't warbled like a cockatoo on the last couple of words.

He was too hungry to pass on this store; he was craving Oreos, but would settle for anything at this point. He took another step and a shriek sounded right in front of him. He shined his light up just in time to see not one, but several rabid-looking people charging straight at him. He turned and fled for the door—he made it in three long strides and dove back out under the crossbar, landing flat on his face, skinning up his left hand and chin in the bargain.

He rolled onto his back, expecting the attack to continue, expecting to see the horde of pale, terrifying, plague-infested monsters ready to pounce, but they had stopped. He could hear them panting, trying to catch their breath—no, wait, that was him. His heart beat so hard he could feel it in the top of his head.

God, what are these things? He got to his feet and remained bent over, trying to catch his wind. There was no way in hell he was going back in there. He would have to keep looking. He took the time to clean and bandage his hand and chin, applying antibacterial salve liberally to the wounds—there was no telling what kind of crap was on the ground here.

He got back into the ambulance and drove around the building, looking for a miracle. It presented itself in the form of another store: a Safeway.

He laughed. "I even have my preferred customer card for Safeway." He winced at the pain in his chin and rebuked himself for the new habit of talking to himself.

"Got to quit talking to myself. Somebody might think I'm crazy." This only made him laugh again.

He held his hand up to block the glare and looked into the Safeway. It was nowhere near as big as the other store and it had skylights throughout. Much better, at least he would be able to see what was coming at him. The doors were still intact, until he swung the wrecking bar into them. The shattered glass cascaded down, nearly causing him another trip to the back of the ambulance for more bandages. He danced out of the way just in time to avoid cutting himself to ribbons.

He stopped and listened at the door. He whistled loudly, then waited for the shrieking... nothing.

"Okay, let's take this slow, Josh." He stepped inside, the glass cracking under his feet. He didn't look down; he was scanning the store, his head whipping around like he was at Wimbledon. There was a very bad smell, but it wasn't the same sour smell as in the last place. It reminded him of the smell in his garage when a rat or mouse had been lying in there dead for a while... only about a hundred times worse.

He had to get some food or he wouldn't last much longer.

He kept moving forward, the gun in one hand and the wrecking bar in the other. He got a shopping cart and started looking for the canned goods. He found the store to be well stocked. It was hard to believe there hadn't been a run on the place, or any looting.

This thing came on suddenly and with a vengeance, he reminded himself.

He became more comfortable as he shopped. The absence of shrieking and the plentiful light helped him relax. He even shoved the pistol into his belt and put the wrecking bar in the cart. He filled up the cart and took it out to the ambulance, unloaded it, and returned for another load. He bent over to pick up the last can of chili.

"Hey!" someone said. He screamed and jumped straight into the air; his response was met with an equally loud scream. He fumbled for the pistol the whole time, thinking the next thing he would hear was the sound of a shotgun blast tearing him in half.

"Hey, hey, don't shoot, don't shoot, okay?" a female voice said. He finally located the source of the voice. It was a beautiful woman, holding her hands out toward him in a way to indicate that she wanted him to stop.

"God lady, you scared the shit outta me! Literally, a little I think, anyhow."

She was 5′7″, short blonde hair with beautiful blue eyes; in a word, she was flawless. Red flags popped into Josh's brain like a fireworks finale. He quickly checked all around the immediate area. He pushed his cart toward the front of the store.

"Hey, where are you going? Hey, hold on." She chased him down the aisle.

Josh continued to scan every corner of the building, expecting the beefy boyfriend with the gang of thugs to show up at any minute.

"Leave me alone, lady. I don't want any trouble," he said as he wheeled his treasure of canned food away.

She looked around mimicking Josh's wild search.

"Look, I need help. I don't want any trouble either."

Josh stopped; he pointed the pistol at her chest.

"Where are the others?" Josh asked.

She started to lie but caught herself.

"I'm alo– look, we need your help."

Josh smiled.

"Wherever you are, you better stay right there!" he yelled, "or I will shoot her."

Her eyes widened.

"Oldest trick in the book, lady; send the pretty girl to distract the mark, then jump him while he's stunned by her beauty." He kept looking around, sure he was about to be attacked.

"Listen to me!" she stomped her foot. "I am not alone, but the only other person here is my daughter. Stacy, come out!" she called.

Fearing it was the signal to attack, Josh took two strides and had her in a headlock.

"Anybody moves and I blow her brains out!" he screamed.

She flailed about trying to break his hold, but he was too strong. They stood like that for a full minute, both of them breathing hard, hearts pounding.

"Look, just leave. Go. Don't hurt me."

Josh eased his muscles a fraction, she slammed her foot down on his arch and bit his arm at the same moment. His immediate reaction was to release her, but as she stepped away, he grabbed for her again. He felt the blow to the back of his head but it didn't register.

How did she hit me, she's in front of me, he thought as he fell to the ground. The dust bunnies under the edge of the shelves came into focus as his world slowly faded to black.

When he came around, he was lying in the same place, but tied up, both hands and feet, and his face was in a pool of his own drool. He pulled his face away from the floor only to have piercing shock waves roll through his head. He felt his stomach roll and its contents spewed out of his nose and mouth.

"Ewwww, gross," he heard a high-pitched voice offer.

"Mom, he's awake and he puked all over the place," he heard the voice call out. She was relaying the scene to someone on the other side of the store.

"Just stay away from him, Stace, I'll be right there," the woman's voice called back.

"Oh, don't worry, I'm not getting anywhere near him. Yuck!"

After he quit gagging, he was able to see the girl sitting on a milk crate ten feet down the aisle from where he lay. Her blond hair was in a ponytail and her freckly nose scrunched up in disgust. She looked to be about ten years old. He tried to roll over onto his back, but his bound hands made it impossible. He ended up lying on his side with his ear in puke. Luckily, since it had been so long since he'd eaten, it was nothing more than bile and water.

"Well, mister, I thought maybe you could help us, but given the fact that an eleven-year-old girl knocked you senseless, I don't know what good you are." The woman squatted next to her daughter, holding Josh's pistol in her hand.

"Jeez, lady, I thought it was a setup, figured your gang was gonna jump me. I guess they did, huh?"

This drew a giggle from the girl. "Whopped you right upside the head with a rolling pin," she said with a laugh.

"Stacy, stop!" her mom scolded.

"So now what?" Josh asked.

"So now you and I are going to talk for a while. Depending on how I feel after that, we might just leave you lying here for the ghouls to eat, or maybe we'll let you live, that's what."

"Can you at least sit me up, and let me have a drink of water?"

"You going to behave?"

"Yes, I'll behave," he mumbled.

"What?" she said.

"I said I'll behave, ma'am," Josh said clearly.

"Name's Olivia, and if you want to lie there in your puke for a while longer, just keep calling me ma'am."

Josh started to say something but began gagging again.

"Oh, for crap's sake. Stacy, help me get him sitting up before he pukes again."

They got Josh sitting up and gave him some water. "There, now what's your name?" Olivia asked.

"My name is Josh, I'm from San Diego."

"Well, Josh from San Diego, tell me your story."

Josh figured he didn't have much to lose, so he told her about his trip so far and how he'd just buried his parents.

"Man, that sucks," Stacy said when he finished.

"Yeah, listen, I'm sorry for the way I acted here, but you can understand me being freaked out, can't you?" Josh stared at his feet, not wanting to look them in the eye.

"Okay, Josh, I am going to have Stacy untie you, but I'm keeping your gun for now."

Olivia prompted Stacy to untie Josh. Once freed, Josh pulled off his shirt and used it to wipe his face clean.

"Got some in your hair there you missed," Stacy pointed.

Josh smiled and poured some water over his head, wincing at the sting.

"Damn, girl, you pack a mean swing," he said as he felt the spot where Stacy had knocked him on the head.

"Softball," she said as an explanation.

"Ah," Josh said. "Do you think I could eat something? I'm starving."

Stacy pulled a can of franks and beans from the cart he'd filled, popped the top, and handed it to him. Josh tilted the can and gobbled down the room-temperature concoction. Seeing how quickly he finished it off, she did the same with a can of peaches. He made quick work of the peaches, and said "thanks."

"Got any Oreos and milk?" he asked.

Olivia ignored his request. "Josh, there's a locker room in the back if you want to clean up. I think there might even be some clothes you could wear."

"Are you saying I stink?" Josh asked with a smile.

"I didn't, but you do," she replied.

They followed him to the back of the store and pointed out the locker room.

"You trust me to go in there alone?" Josh said.

"I have your gun and I have been through everything in there, so yes. And there's only one door."

Josh shook his head and went in.

"Hey, it's dark in here."

Olivia handed him an LED lantern. He spent about three minutes in the cold shower and dried off with paper towels. Stacy had left a brush and some Secret deodorant on the sink, so he used both. He found some clothes that fit and even a pair of Timberland boots in one of the lockers.

He came out.

"Tada!" he said, holding out his arms.

Stacy laughed and Olivia lowered the pistol she'd been pointing at him.

"Well, you clean up pretty good. So, what are your plans?"

"Well, that kind of depends on you," Josh said.

She removed the mag from the pistol, racked the slide, and ejected the round in the chamber.

"Here." She handed him the pistol, but stuck the magazine in her back pocket. "I'll give you your bullets when you leave."

He didn't mention he had three other magazines, and shoved the pistol into his waistband at the small of his back. He spent the next hour going through the store, stocking up on everything he could think of. Stacy and "Liv," as she preferred to be called, helped him load it all up.

"I'm heading to Whidbey Island to meet up with some family; you're both welcome to come. It may be safer than staying on the mainland," Josh offered. He didn't want to appear forward, but he also could imagine them all hanging together. It would beat being alone.

Liv tilted her head to the side and looked him straight in the eyes.

"What strings are attached?"

He knew exactly what she meant.

"Look Liv, you are a beautiful woman, and even though we had a rough introduction, I really like you. There are absolutely no strings attached. I will never push myself on you, and there's that safety in numbers thing, ya know?" Josh was actually blushing and had to restrain the urge to kick at the ground in an "aw shucks" kind of way.

Olivia had her hands shoved in her back pockets with her hip cocked to the side, making her look pretty damn sexy.

"Let me and Stacy talk about it. Stacy, come inside with me." Liv tipped her head toward the store.

Stacy followed her mom into the store.

"So, what do you think, Stace? Do you think we can trust him? Should we go or stay?"

Stacy could tell her mom kind of liked Josh, but didn't let on that she knew.

"I think we are going to want to find other good people before long, and I don't know if staying here would accomplish that... I think Josh is okay. What do you think?"

"Well, he doesn't make a good first impression, but he does have a cute butt." Liv smiled.

"Ewwww, Mom, that's gross!" Stacy swatted her on the shoulder.

They came back out of the store and approached Josh, who

was just finishing packing up the ambulance.

"There is no way we're going to make it all the way to the peninsula tonight. Why don't we stay here tonight and get an early start in the morning?" Liv said.

"You're coming with me? Uh... cool, um, I mean great! Where are we going to stay tonight? I broke the doors out, remember?"

"We can stay in the locker room. It's secure. Lock up the ambulance and come in. Stacy and I will cook you dinner."

Chapter 17

Recalled

MEG'S GROUP, LYNN'S GROUP, & RYAN'S GROUP
4:30 P.M.
HOPE, BRITISH COLUMBIA, CANADA

Meg was having a hard time concentrating on the road. Max and Lisa had been talking on the radio. Max said they were making good time and should make it to Parker's well before sundown. It was raining, and she tried to focus on Lisa's taillights ahead.

All day, Meg had been getting flashes, the same kind of pictures in her head that had plagued her after her ordeal at the gym. At first, they only happened while she slept, and she wrote it off as the stress of the situation they were in; but for the last few days, they had started coming to her while she was awake. She wouldn't lose consciousness or zone out. It was more like random thoughts passed in and out of her mind throughout the day. She hadn't mentioned it to anyone because she thought it was just her mind's way of coping.

There was also a weird feeling that had begun to accompany the pictures, the kind of feeling you get when you're standing in the middle of a large crowd. It got worse whenever they passed through a town, and as they approached Hope, B.C., it was becoming very distracting.

"Mom, look out!" Sarah screamed.

Meg slammed on the brakes and the car slid sideways toward the edge of the road. Lisa had slowed for a curve, and this time, Meg had zoned out. The car skipped over the wet road, the brakes doing little to slow its momentum. They were heading for the guardrail at a speed Meg knew would send them plummeting to their deaths in the river below. As the car skidded toward the rail, Meg saw Max's massive truck zooming toward them out of the corner of her eye.

Great, we're all going to crash into the river, she thought.

The next thing she knew, Max's truck had blocked the car's path to disaster, and the two vehicles crashed together. The sounds of metal collapsing, windows breaking, and kids screaming combined to give the moment a surreal soundtrack that would forever remain embedded with all involved in the crash. Max's truck had stopped them mere feet from the guardrail.

"Is anyone hurt?" Meg asked, frantically looking at the kids. All three of them sat staring at Meg, eyes as big as saucers. Then they all burst into tears. Sarah tried to quiet them as Meg did a cursory examination, twisting around in her seat. Max pulled open the back passenger door only to see the exploded airbags hanging down from above the doorframe.

"Is everyone okay?" he asked, pulling at the now-deflated bags. He finally got past the airbags and saw that everyone was fine.

"Whew, that was fun, eh guys?" he said, trying to ease the intense vibe in the car.

They all looked at him like he was crazy, but it did distract the kids from the situation enough to stop their crying. The worst injuries were a cut to Sarah's forehead from flying glass and a jammed knee for Meg from the crushed panel on her side of the car. Max's truck had a few dents in the side and a bent Nerf bar, but the car was a total loss. Lisa didn't even know there was a problem, and only stopped and turned around after Max had radioed her.

The crash and the ensuing activities of emptying the car of supplies and reassigning passengers took a couple of hours. It was evident that they wouldn't make it to Parker's before dark.

Awake, but still half-loopy from the drugs, I heard the harrowing story of the crash from the kids in the backseat.

"I thought we were going to explode, Uncle Ryan!" Andy said in conclusion.

"That only happens in the movies," Beth informed him.

Max had taken the lead and was looking for a secure place for us to spend the night in the town of Hope. He settled for an auto repair shop at the western edge of town with two separate concrete buildings, each housing a single car bay. After Lisa and Max cleared the buildings, we moved in.

With Jean under one arm and Meg under the other, I made it out of the truck. I almost passed out from the pain when I came off the tailgate. The eight-inch drop made my side explode like the car in the movie Beth had referenced earlier. After swearing a blue streak, which got me severely reprimanded by Meg, I sucked it up and didn't even cry like a little girl. They placed my mattress against the back wall facing the entrance. I convinced them to lean the top up against some boxes so that I could recline, instead of lying flat on my back. They parked Max's truck in the other building and then everyone took shelter with me. The kids would bed down in the truck and the adults would have to make do. The waiting room had a single glass door that Max and Lisa stacked 50-pound bags of rock salt in front of, outside and in, two rows wide, all the way to the top of the door. There was no couch in the shop, but Lynn found a couple of old chaise lounge beach chairs on the flat roof that could improvise as cots. Max claimed a bench seat that the mechanics must have removed from an old station wagon; he could lie on it with his upper body comfortable and his feet resting on the ground.

The kids were restless, feeling cooped up. Sarah cleared away a spot on the concrete floor and drew a hopscotch pad. Jean joined in with them and the sight of her playing hopscotch had all of us in stitches—me literally. The release was palpable, and everyone was in a much better mood. The night didn't seem as foreboding somehow. The MREs were passed out and everyone sat around chatting and enjoying their meals.

Meg came over and sat next to me on the mattress.

"Jean is pretty tired; I told her I would watch you while she sleeps."

I laughed, "I'm fine, but you can sack out on my bed." I was feeling better; I wasn't making that part up. "Besides, I slept all day. I'll wake you if I need something." She lay down. It was a little tight with both of us on the mattress, but it was doable. I put my arm around her and told her thanks for taking care of me.

She chuckled. "Watch it, little brother." I laughed and patted her on the shoulder.

"How are you doing? I mean, you're recovering too," I said.

She was quiet for a moment.

"I'm okay. I've been having some really vivid dreams, and it's messing with my brain some, but physically I'm great.

"Well, relax and try to get some rest," I said.

Meg went quiet again and I thought she'd drifted off but before long, I realized her eyes were open and she was shaking.

"Meg, are you all right?" I looked at her. Her eyes were wide open.

"Run!" she screamed. "Everyone run!"

She rolled off the mattress and grabbed me by the arm.

"We have to get out of here now, Ryan, right now!"

By this time, Max and Lisa had run into the service area from the waiting room. Lynn and Jean were sitting up on the chaise lounges, everyone staring at Meg. Chris, who had been asleep on a pallet next to the rollup door, was the only one not looking at Meg. He turned toward the crack between the door and frame.

"They're out there!" he said without raising his voice.

In that moment, there was perfect silence. It only lasted a

fraction of a second, but it was the quiet before the storm. All at once, a chorus of shrieks sounded outside. I struggled through the pain and got to my feet. I had the .308 next to me and a bag full of magazines.

"Max, the roof!" Lisa and Max ran to the stairway.

"Meg, help me into the waiting room!" I yelled. She just stood there mumbling.

"Jean, help me to the waiting room!" Jean reacted and ran to my side. Lynn came along, each getting under my arms. They half-dragged me as I felt the fire in my side reignite. It felt like the devil himself was tearing me apart.

"Lynn, Chris, get Meg into the truck, be ready to go. Lock the doors and be ready!"

The kids were fully awake and crying. Sarah tried her best to calm them but was losing the battle. I saw Chris run by me toward the stairway with one of the shotguns.

"Chris, get back here!" I yelled, but he wasn't listening and he disappeared up the stairway. Jean got me to the waiting area.

"Go get in the truck; if they get in here you're going to have to drive through them and out of here. Get all the kids into the cab, leave the tailgate down, and be ready to go, do you understand?"

"Yes," was all she said as she headed to the truck. Backing in when we arrived turned out to have been a smart move. I only hoped we would live through this so that we could congratulate ourselves on how smart we were.

Max looked down from the roof at a sea of freaks, every one of them trying to breach their sanctuary. The rage inside him gave him the urge to flip the selector switch to full auto and start spraying them with bullets, but he realized immediately that would be a mistake. He left the selector on semi-auto and brought the rifle up to his shoulder, peered through the ACOG scope, and began to shoot methodically, one target at a time. Lisa, standing next to him, burned through a magazine on full auto. When she reloaded, she noticed that her dad was shooting one shot at a time. She didn't know why, but figured he knew something that she didn't. She switched to semi-auto and began following his lead. She had one of the M4s with the close-combat EOTech holographic sights. She lined up a freak and shot it through the chest. The round entered exactly where she aimed and the freak dropped out of sight under the mass of bodies clamoring to get at her family. Chris had somehow gotten his hands on a shotgun and was standing at the back of the building, shooting down on the freaks.

I heard the gunfire from the roof continue unabated. The building shook from the assault of the freaks. I felt my side and realized that my wound was bleeding. I stood in the doorway between the garage and the waiting room, hoping that the door would hold. I hadn't been wearing my throat mic since my injury, but I still carried my radio with me at all times. So did everyone else. We had long since dispensed with code names, and our radio transmissions were usually without any regard for military protocol.

"Max, can you hear me?" We would be screwed if he didn't have his earbud in; he would never hear me over all that gunfire. He and Lisa wore their throat mics and earbuds pretty much 24/7, so my worry was for naught.

"Max here, how can I be of service?" he replied.

"How many freaks are out there?" There was no reply for several seconds. "Max, you copy my last?" I said into the radio.

"Roger that, too many to count," came the reply.

"Jean, are you listening?" I asked.

"Yes, I'm on, over," she replied.

"There's an ammo bag with duct tape around it in the back of the truck. Can you bring it to me?"

"Yes, Lynn is going to look for it."

I saw Lynn get out of the truck and disappear around the back. It must have taken her a minute to find it, but she hurried back toward me carrying the bag.

"Wait," I told her, and retrieved two of the remaining grenades from the bag, sticking one in each of my front pockets.

"Take the rest of these to Max and Lisa, and then get back to the truck!"

She didn't even reply, she just turned and ran for the stairs. People could say whatever they wanted about my family, but we were good under pressure. A couple minutes later, she reappeared at the front of the truck and gave me a thumbs up.

"Jean, be ready to haul ass if you hear me screaming," I said into the radio.

"Yes sir," she replied.

Max's ears rang like the bells of Notre Dame, but he smiled when he heard Ryan send Jean the message about the bag. Sure enough, a few minutes later, Lynn tapped him on the shoulder, handed him the bag, and ran back down stairs.

"Lisa, get over here."

She stopped shooting freaks and looked over at him. He waved her over. There were still hundreds, if not a thousand of the freaks crowded around the building.

"Listen, there is no way we are going to take out all of these things, there are just too many of them. Take Chris and go downstairs and get Ryan into the back of the truck," he yelled above the shrieking and constant ringing in his ears.

"What are you going to do, Dad?" Lisa eyed him suspiciously.

"I'm going to blow these bastards up and clear a path out of here!"

"No way, Dad, I'm not leaving you!"

"Don't worry, I plan on throwing about half of these, then I'll beat feet down stairs and we'll ride out of here in style. Now go!"

She didn't argue. She turned, ran over, and grabbed Chris.

"Come on!" They headed downstairs.

"Ryan, this is Max. I'm going to use the grenades to try and clear a path. Lisa and Chris are coming to help you into the truck. There are too many of them, bro, we've got to jam!"

I heard him and understood his plan, but like Lisa, I didn't trust him.

"Don't try and be a damn hero, Max. We aren't leaving without you!" I shouted into the radio.

"Why does everybody think I have a death wish? I'm Chicken Two, for Pete's sake. Jean, I want you to wait until I jump in the back of the truck, then drive straight through the garage door and hang a left; head for the freeway and don't stop for anything!"

"This is Jean, I got it!" Just then, Lisa and Chris came and hustled me to the back of the truck. I sat down on the tailgate; they got in and pulled me in with them.

Max pulled the pin on the first grenade and lobbed it into the freaks in front of the door. He knew he should duck, but he had to see what impact it would have on the crowd. The explosion almost knocked him down, and it had a devastating effect on the freaks. Max thought he was hit with shrapnel but realized it was pieces of the freaks flung at him from the blast. After that, things really got messy. He started pitching the grenades as fast as he could pull the pins. He didn't wait to see the results. He threw the tenth one and ran for the stairs.

I heard the first explosion and then a pause. Then, the explosions kept coming, one after another. The next thing I was aware of was Max diving headfirst into the bed of the truck, screaming at the top of his lungs, "Go, go, go!"

Jean didn't hesitate; she plowed through the garage door and straight into the mayhem. I almost passed out from the pain but held on to my consciousness long enough to see the carnage left in our wake. A few of the freaks lucky enough to survive Max's bombardment fell prey to Jean, barreling forward with total disregard for the truck's fenders. As we drove through the pack of freaks, Max pulled the pin on one of the remaining grenades, shoved it into the bag, and threw the whole thing out of the truck. The resulting explosions lifted the rear tires off the ground; when it came back down, I didn't see one freak left standing. The truck swerved back and forth, throwing us around in the bed like rag dolls. I heard Lisa scream Chris's name, and then I did pass out.

An unusually big bump woke me by throwing me a couple of feet in the air before depositing me back onto the hard metal of the truck bed. *Whoooof,* went the air in my lungs. A lot of football in my youth helped my brain recognize the feeling of having the wind knocked out of me. There was nothing to do but be patient and take short breaths until it returned. The added bonus of having a gunshot wound in my side was a new twist, one that I would have gladly foregone.

Around the time I started to get my wind back and the pain in my side had dwindled to a mere *Oh my god I'm gonna die* type pain, the truck slid to a stop. It was very dark and it was a minute before anyone found a flashlight. I saw someone coming down the side of the truck wearing a headband light; by the height, I reckoned it was Jean. I'd no idea how long I'd been unconscious, but my impression was that it had not been long.

"Is everyone all right back here?" Jean asked.

"We lost Chris out the back after the last explosion," Lisa said. There was no emotion in her voice and it was clear that we were not going to go back to find him—he was just lost.

"Ryan, how's the side?" Jean shined her light on me.

I squinted at her. "I'll live, I'm afraid. How's everyone up front?"

"Crowded, but other than that, and being traumatized, we're all okay."

"Where are we?" Max asked.

"We're about ten miles from town. I saw this barn and thought we should regroup, but wanted to ask you guys what you thought," Jean explained.

"Yeah, that sounds like a good idea." Max slid down from the truck bed to the tailgate and got out. He found his flashlight then went off to examine the barn.

Before Jean could leave, I asked her, "How's Meg?"

"She's pretty shook, keeps saying that she brought them to us, that and she thinks she's turning into one of them."

"That's bullshit," I said.

"That's what I've been telling her, but she blames herself. She wanted me to stop and let her out so she wouldn't eat any of us. That totally freaked out the kids. So, yeah, it's a little tense right now."

Max came back over to the truck. "Okay, pull it inside, Jean; it looks like a good place to hole up for a while."

I got out of the truck by rolling over on my stomach and pushing myself off the tailgate. I'm not sure if I was getting any better or if I was just finally getting used to the pain. Someone had turned on a couple of LED camping lights and I found a hay bale to sit on. I leaned back against the wall of the barn and tried to look at my boo-boo. My shirt was fixed to my skin with half-dried blood, so I decided to just leave it alone. Meg found me and sat down.

"You're going to have to kill me, Ryan," she whispered.

"Would you stop with that shit, Meg," I said. "I am not going to kill you; you haven't shown any signs that you're turning into one of those damn things. Look at your skin."

She held out her arms, and even in the dim light, it was plain that they looked normal: no graying, no blotches, nothing.

"I'm telling you, I've been communicating with them; they're in my frickin' head!"

Her voice steadily rose as she talked. That was about as close to swearing, other then maybe a dammit here and there, as I'd ever heard from her. I took her hand.

"You may want to cool it and slow down a minute. You have the kids half-convinced Grammy is going to eat them. Look, let's get everyone settled, and then we can talk about this more. Now go tell the kids you're sorry for scaring them, and tell them you're all right."

"You mean lie," she said, as she got up and left me sitting there.

Lisa came by a few minutes later.

"Hey," she said.

I could tell she was down in the dumps.

"Hey, kiddo." I gave her a hug with my good side. "What's up?"

"I'm tired of this shit, Uncle Ryan. It's never going to be normal again, and I'm worried I won't be able to keep my shit together."

Her eyes watered up. This was the first chink I'd seen in her armor. She'd had a rough life after Max and her mom split, and it hardened her against showing her feelings much. She ended up married to a good guy, but her examples of how to be married had, let's say, not been stellar. She'd only mentioned Jack a couple of times since we had met up and I didn't want to pry, so I'd left it alone.

Now, she seemed like she wanted to talk, so I asked.

"How were you and Jack doing when you came up here?"

A tear slipped out of the corner of her eye.

"Oh, okay, I guess. We butt heads quite a bit. I miss the shit out of him right now." She smiled. "You think he's all right?"

227

What do you say to that? When eighty to ninety percent of the world is dying, dead, or turned, it's hard to put a good spin on it.

"Look kiddo, I'm not going to blow smoke up your ass and tell you I'm sure he's fine, but look, were doing fine, right? So there is a chance he's okay. I'm in the same boat. My family is in West Virginia, and I don't have a clue if they're alive or not. Tell you what, after we get all these people settled in on the island, you can come with me if you want. I'm going to go find out, one way or another. Besides, how am I going to survive without Raven on my six?"

She laughed and gave me another hug. "Thanks, Uncle Ryan, you're the best."

Chapter 18

Repair

MADDIE, HARRY, THOMAS, & CARLA'S GROUP
2:00 P.M.
OLYMPIA, WA
INTERSTATE 5

Harry was taking a turn at the wheel while Thomas worked at the computer station. For some reason, he couldn't get the radios to work. Finally, he declared, "We're going to have to stop for me to be able to get these radios working. It has to be a connection problem and I can't remedy that while we're driving."

They had made incredible time since leaving Coburg and Harry didn't want to stop, but the radios were a priority.

"Okay, I'll look for a good spot for a stop," Harry said. Maddie and Conner began gearing up. They decided that any stop from now on would be under armed guard. The closer they got to any major metropolitan area, the more likely it was that they would run into other survivors.

"We're coming up on an overpass that looks like a good place," Harry called out to the rest of the group over his shoulder.

"Sounds good," Maddie replied.

Harry maneuvered the coach to the exit ramp.

"Trosper Road, Tumwater, Washington. Fifteen minute stop, folks, smoke 'em if ya got 'em."

Harry played the part of the bus driver well, and this reference made Thomas happy. He hadn't had a smoke for the last five hours. Harry stopped the coach in the middle of the bridge over I-5 and everyone got out to stretch their legs. Conner walked down the road to the western end of the overpass and Maddie took up station on the east end.

"Nothing moving over here," Conner called in over the walkie.

"Same over here, over," Maddie said.

Lauren and Carla took up watch on the top of the coach on the catwalk Thomas had constructed.

"We have a pretty good view from up here and I don't see anything either," reported Carla.

Thomas and Harry, feeling well protected, got busy working on the UHF/VHF radios and the satellite linking equipment. Thomas climbed in one of the back bays that held the equipment, and Harry was his step-and-fetch-it guy.

"I need a nine-sixteenths box wrench," Thomas said from inside the bay.

"Coming up," Harry said as he located the proper tool.

"Oh, and some needle-nose pliers, also."

"Yes, sir." Harry found both and passed them to Thomas.

Lauren grabbed Carla by the arm and pointed to the north.

"Guys, we have company. Red pickup truck coming south on I-5 about a mile and a half out," Carla said over the radio. "I'm heading down to the monitoring station to pull them up on the cameras."

Carla headed for the access point and Lauren followed.

"No, I need you to stay up here. Cover Conner and Maddie if they need help."

Lauren had an MP5 submachine gun, which was not a good weapon for long distances.

"Here, trade me the AR. I can't hit anything with this."

They traded weapons and Carla took a moment to make sure Lauren remembered how to operate the AR15. She might not be experienced, but at least she could throw some lead at the bad guys if needed.

"Don't shoot your brother," Carla said as she disappeared down into the coach.

Lauren had withdrawn into herself recently. Carla had noticed but didn't have time to deal with it right this minute.

"Maybe I should just shoot myself and end this," Lauren said to no one. She looked back up the road through the binoculars and saw that the red truck was closing the distance.

Harry picked up the AR15 that he'd claimed from Maddie's weapons cache and charged it.

"What do you see, Carla?"

"Okay, I have them! Two males in the cab and two males in the bed of the truck, all of them are armed."

"Patch me through to the PA system, Carla; Conner, Maddie, come back to the coach. If we have to, we'll button up and haul ass," Harry said.

"Roger," Conner replied instantly.

"I'm going to take up a spot down here, where I can have a good angle for a sniper shot," Maddie transmitted.

"Maddie, damn it, just do what I ask this one time!" Harry said, the frustration in his voice evident.

"Yes, dear," was Maddie's only reply.

"Okay, Carla, put me on the PA."

When the truck got about a hundred yards from the overpass, Harry held up his hand, motioning for them to stop. The driver slowed and stopped about seventy-five yards away.

The passenger opened the door and stood on the step of the truck, where he proceeded to lean against the top of the door.

"Howdy," he yelled. "Where you folks headed?"

Harry pushed the transmit button on the handheld and feedback screeched from the coach speakers. He quickly released the mic button and walked out from in front of the coach to a position where he hoped he wouldn't cause any more feedback. He pushed the button.

"We are headed north," he said. There was a slight squeal of feedback, but nothing unbearable.

The man was observant and could see they had the bay open.

"Are you broken down? Do you need some help? We have a base camp just up the road; if you need somewhere to hole up for the night. It's safe and secure."

Harry did not intend to take them up on the offer, but he needed to stall so Conner and Maddie had time to make it back to the coach.

"I tell you what, let me confer with my group and see what they say."

Then, without waiting for an answer, he said, "Everybody meet me at the coach."

Hoping everyone in his group would take the hint and get inside the coach, he held up a finger as if to say, wait a minute, and walked over to meet Thomas as he was walking toward the front of the coach after shutting the bay doors.

Carla quickly shut off the PA and came across the radio.

"They're backing up to get on the ramp, looks like they're headed this way."

"Okay, everyone in the coach now!" Harry said into the radio.

He and Thomas ran to the door, where they met Maddie coming toward them from the east. Lauren scrambled down the ladder into the coach.

Harry looked up.

"Conner, hurry the hell up!" There was no sign of him.

They all piled in the coach and Harry fired it up. Carla yelled at Harry,

"We are not leaving Conner!"

Harry yelled back, "I'm not leaving him, I'm going to find him."

The coach lurched forward to the west.

"Anyone see him?" Harry yelled.

Carla, still on the camera, searched the area with the camera set to wide angle.

"No, oh shit, Conner, where are you?"

Maddie called Conner over the radio.

"Conner, this is Maddie, where are you?" The radio was silent for a minute, and then she thought she heard something.

"Everybody quiet!" Harry stopped the coach and they all listened.

"This is Conner, they have me."

"Thomas, get the UAV up!" Maddie wasted no time. She grabbed the tablet and her hands flew over the surface. The picture from the drone would show on the TV in the salon.

"Maddie, you don't need the drone, they're coming up the road," Harry said. Sure enough, the pickup stopped a hundred feet from the coach.

The leader got out and pulled Conner after him.

"Harry, on the roof. I'm going out to see what they want," Maddie said.

Carla was about to protest, but realized that Maddie was probably a better choice to deal with these bastards in this situation. She took one of the MP5s and followed Harry onto the roof. Lauren sat staring at the TV, watching the pictures provided by the external cameras on the coach.

Maddie exited the coach and stood next to an abandoned Jeep. She carried her AR15 pointed safely at the ground. Conner stood next to a smiling man with a full beard, who appeared to be in his forties.

"Hey there, lady, no need for the firearms, we're friendly," he said, his hand on Conner's shoulder.

"What do you want?" Maddie said without a hint of a smile.

"Well, for starters, we like that RV you're driving," he laughed. The two men in the back of the truck leaning over the cab thought that this was hilarious.

The man started to speak again, but never finished opening his mouth because a bullet hole appeared over his right eye. Maddie dove behind the abandoned Jeep and looked to see who had fired the shot. Conner fell to the ground and rolled under the truck as the idiots in the back fumbled to get a shot off.

Lauren had gotten out of the coach and snuck around the other side, and was calmly walking toward the pickup, shooting at the driver. He ducked down and hit the accelerator, rocketing the truck backward away from the coach.

This left Conner exposed, but both the men in the back of the truck were more concerned with the fire from Lauren, and now Harry, who had begun to shoot from the catwalk.

Maddie brought her rifle up, but the truck was a half block away and turning onto a side street. She ran to Conner, who by this time had made it to his knees. She quickly cut the zip ties that bound his hands, and they both ran for the coach.

They climbed aboard to find Thomas in the driver's seat, Carla at the computer station, and Harry coming down the ladder.

"Where is Lauren?" Carla asked, looking frantically at Maddie.

"Right here, Mom," Lauren replied as she climbed the steps up to the coach. No one said another word as Thomas closed the door and backed the coach away from the scene toward the northbound onramp. The bearded man lay where he fell, obviously dead. Whoever these guys were, they were definitely going to have to come up with a better plan to rob people.

They headed north on Interstate 5, which merged into U.S. 101 just before entering Olympia. Carla was checking on Conner, going over him with a fine-toothed comb.

"Mom, I'm fine," he complained.

"Just hold still and let me clean up the scrape on your arm," Carla said. Lauren had curled up on the couch and hadn't said much.

Maddie sat down next to Lauren.

"You okay? That was an amazing shot out there, what made you do it?"

"Well, to answer your first question, I'm okay. To answer your second question, those men were going to kill us and take what we had, so I decided to act," Lauren said matter-of-factly.

"Well, you probably saved us. Honestly, I didn't know what to do," Maddie admitted.

"Yeah, I could have gotten us all killed, too," Lauren said with a faraway look in her eyes.

"But you didn't, and I am glad you did what you did," Maddie said.

"Maddie, I killed a man, a living human being. Not one of those crazy zombies, but a..." Lauren began, but tears began flow and she collapsed into Maddie's arms. Maddie stroked her hair and held her.

"And it's a damn good thing that you did. They were going to do the same to us, or worse."

Lauren cried until she fell asleep, Maddie holding her the entire time. Maddie didn't get up when Lauren fell asleep; she continued to sit with her, looking out the window.

Chapter 19

Three For the...

Liv shook Josh by the shoulder. She'd been on watch since two o'clock and caught herself nodding off.

"Hey, wake up, Josh, hey." It took a couple more shakes, but Josh opened his eyes and smiled.

"Is this heaven?" he asked sleepily.

She shook her head. "That's a pretty lame line, Josh."

"Hey, give me a break. I just woke up," he said. "Did we have any visitors?"

"No, it's been quiet, and I'm starting to doze off. I figured it wouldn't hurt to get an early start."

He rubbed his face and ran his hands through his hair. "What time is it?"

"About six. It should be starting to get light out, enough that the ghouls will have gone into hiding, anyway," she said.

They ate Pop Tarts for breakfast and made some peanut butter and jelly sandwiches for the road. Stacy walked around in an early morning daze eating handfuls of Lucky Charms straight from the box.

"Stacy, stash those in your pack and wash up. We're going to be leaving in ten; make sure you pee."

"Gosh, Mom, could you be any more embarrassing?" Stacy shot daggers at her.

Liv shrugged. "Sorry, I'll try to be more sensitive; now go get ready please."

Josh pretended not to have heard the exchange and finished rolling up his sleeping bag that Liv had given him last night.

"That's the first I've slept since this all began," he said.

"You were snoring like a freight train. I was afraid you were going to bring the ghouls down on us there for a while," she said, only half kidding.

"Why do you call them ghouls?" Josh asked.

"I don't know, what do you call them?" she said.

"Huh, I don't know, haven't talked about it with anyone until now. I think of them as people—crazy people, but people."

Liv was shocked by that.

"Are you frickin' kidding me? These things are definitely not people anymore. Have you had any direct contact with one yet?"

"Yeah—I told you about Dale, my brother-in-law. Also, a couple of nights ago, I ran into a bunch of them that tried to tip over my ride, but I just drove off. Then, before Stacy beaned me over the head, I ran into a group of them in the Fred Meyer's store. They looked horrible and they chased me, but like I said, they were just people acting crazy, maybe rabid."

She looked at him and shook her head for the fourth time that morning.

"Josh, these things eat people. They don't want to chat or ask how your day was. They're only interested in one thing: eating! Like zombies, but they aren't zombies, they're still alive..." her voice faded and her eyes glazed over as if in reminiscence.

Her whole body quaked in a spasm of fear, then she finished.

"They can't go into the sunlight. It burns them like the old vampire stories, but it doesn't burn them up; they just get all red and blistered and then they die. They are definitely not people anymore."

"Okay, okay, I get it," he said, not sure if he really got it or not. He knew they were bad news, but he would have to take her word for the rest.

"Let's just get out of here."

They found two different diesel trucks in the parking lot; they filled the ambulance and a couple of gas cans and were ready to roll.

As they drove through town, Josh felt the need to explain his route.

"I think we should keep along the coast on 101." They were all in the cab of the ambulance; no one wanted to ride in the back. Stacy, fidgeting, sat between Josh and Liv.

"If you're gonna stay close to the coast, why don't we just take Uncle Phil's boat?" she said, flipping through a first aid manual she found in the back of the ambulance. Josh looked over at Liv with his eyebrows raised. Liv was staring at Stacy with an astonished look on her face.

"It never even occurred to me," Liv said. "My brother Phil has a fishing boat docked in Charleston, just down the road."

"Have you seen him since this all started?" Josh asked. Her eyes moistened and she quickly averted her attention to something out the passenger window.

"Mom locked him in our garage," Stacy said as if she were talking about the weather. Josh looked over at Liv, who shook her head. Josh took the hint and didn't pursue the issue.

He switched subjects. "How big is Uncle Phil's boat?"

"Oh, it's big—ginormous!" Stacy said.

"It's not that big, Stacy," her mom corrected her. "I think it's twenty feet or so."

"It would take us longer to get there, but it's not a bad idea. Is it seaworthy?" Josh asked.

"I don't know a thing about boats," Liv replied.

"Well, what do you think? Should we check it out, or just keep driving? I planned on stealing a boat once we got up north, but if we have access to one down here..." he said with a shrug.

"Make a left at the next intersection," was all that Liv said.

"Hey, we don't have to, it's just an idea." Josh could see that Liv was not thrilled.

"It's just that I'm not a boat person. Phil tried to get me to go with him all the time, but I always found an excuse not to."

"I went with him a bunch of times," Stacy said. "It was a blast!"

Josh laughed. "I guess that means you'll be the first mate then," he said, poking her with an elbow. Josh was still skeptical about hitting the water, but if it meant not having to deal with the crazy people, he could get into that.

After following Liv's directions for twenty minutes, they finally arrived at the Charleston Marina. She pointed at a building on the far side of the lot.

"He has a locker over there. We'll have to break in; I don't have a key."

Josh drove around the lot a couple of times, looking for any sign of survivors. He gave up and drove to the building that Liv pointed out. The building was a long, concrete block affair with roll-up doors that had numbers stenciled on them.

"Each of the slips has their own storage area," she said, stating the obvious.

"What number are we looking for?" Josh asked.

"Twenty-four," Stacy chimed in. "It's right down there." She pointed to the end of the building. Josh rolled the truck around the end of the building and up next to number twenty-four.

Josh got out and examined the locking mechanism on the door. It was held in place with a heavy chain and three padlocks connected to each other to complete the loop. He'd seen this setup before on farm gates that more than one person or company needed access to. Uncle Phil must have had a couple of partners or friends who had access to the boat, only one padlock needed to be unlocked to remove the chain. Josh went back, got the bolt cutters out of the ambulance, and made quick work of one of the padlocks. Stacy and Liv joined him to open the locker. It was full of all kinds of fishing gear: poles, crab pots, nets—you name it, it was there. The keys to the boat hung on a nail with a float attached. A handwritten sign above the keys said, "Always leave the boat clean and the gas tank full."

It sounded as if one or more of the partners had neglected one task or another before and needed reminding. Josh took the keys off the nail. He still had no idea if the boat was suitable for what they had in mind, and he wanted to look at it before they started moving any gear.

"Where's the boat, Stacy—I mean, first mate?"

"It's over here," she said, and scampered off toward the docks. Josh and Liv followed along, Liv still looking rather perturbed at the prospect of going to sea. Josh had lived near the coast all his life, and while he'd never owned his own boat, he'd been on many and was confident he could safely operate one as long as it was in good repair.

They came to the marina entrance and a locked gate. Josh looked at the keys, determined that it must be one of the four on the key chain, and began to try them. The second key he tried fit the lock, and they went through the gate.

"Which one is it?" he said, looking down the row of boats, hoping it was one of the nicer ones.

"It's the blue one over there," Stacy pointed.

Josh smiled. "Definitely not a POS."

"What's a POS?" Stacy asked.

"Piece of sh–" before he could finish, Liv smacked him on the arm.

"Josh!"

"Shit?" Stacy asked. "Mom, it's not like I've never heard you say 'shit' before."

It was a beautiful Duckworth 26 offshore welded aluminum boat. It had a fully enclosed cabin and couldn't have been more than a couple of years old. They walked down the dock to slip twenty-four, and when Josh saw the two Yamaha F150XA four-stroke outboard motors hanging on the back, he knew instantly that this boat would do nicely. He lifted Stacy over the gunnels and hopped on himself, then held a hand out for Liv.

"I'll wait here until we have everything ready to go," she said.

Josh could see the fear in her eyes.

"Liv, this is one hell of a boat. It's made for the ocean; it has an eight-foot beam, the V-hull with those two motors—it's completely safe."

"You sound just like Phil. He would rattle off all that technical stuff and tell me what a pussy I am for being afraid. That is an awfully big damn ocean for such a small boat!" Liv half-shouted at him.

Josh realized he'd made an error in judgment. He should have approached it from a different angle.

"Liv, how many of those ghouls do you think we'll run into out there in that big ocean?" he asked.

She pouted and gave him the stink-eye, but relented. She took his hand and let him help her onto the boat. He unlocked the cabin door and went in. Phil and his partners had spared no expense. The cockpit boasted a Funuro NavNet 3D UHD Radar with 10.4-inch color display, a GPS navigation system, and VHF marine radios.

"What did your brother do for a living?" Josh knew that this rig and this equipment was well out of range for most weekend anglers.

"He was a drug dealer," Liv said without a moment's hesitation. She laughed at Josh as he fumbled for something to say. "He was the northwest regional director of sales for a large pharmaceutical company in Portland."

Josh laughed, "That would explain it."

Josh spent all morning going over the manuals for the boat's operation. He knew it was no substitute for experience, but he wanted at least to read up on the basics. The GPS was fairly simple, but it still took him about an hour to program it. It allowed him to set waypoints, which allowed him to avoid potential trouble spots he could see on the navigation charts. The boat's 175-gallon tank was full, and according to the manual, they should be able to cruise at 28 mph while burning about twelve gallons an hour. He figured that was about three miles per gallon, but he planned to double-check his figures during the trip. In any case, they would look for fueling opportunities along the route. He brought the siphoning equipment with them that he'd used for the ambulance. The radar was a little more complex, and it took him a while to figure out how to change from weather radar to standard mode.

The passage out of Coos Bay went without a hitch. They passed the outer buoy 173 nautical miles south of the Columbia River, their first waypoint, at 3:01 p.m.

The seas were calm, two-foot swells with a northwest wind blowing at a moderate ten miles per hour. Josh showed Stacy how to steer the boat and follow the line on the GPS. She was elated that Josh trusted her to drive; she paid close attention to what she was doing.

Josh had laid their course far enough offshore to avoid accidentally running into anything, but close enough that they could return to land quickly in an emergency. He sat on the bench seat behind Stacy and surreptitiously watched to make sure she remained on course. They had packed the cabin space under the bow with all kinds of supplies, but there was still enough room for someone to lie down. Liv said she was tired, and crawled into the space to catch a nap. Josh checked the radar, switching between weather mode and standard. The weather looked fine and they weren't in danger of running into anything.

"Stace, do you think you can handle this if I take a nap, too?"

"Yep, no problema, señor.'"

"Okay, if you have even the slightest inkling that there is a problem, you wake me up, okay?"

"Yes sir, Captain," she saluted.

"And even if there is no problem, wake me up at six o'clock, okay?"

"Would you go lie down already?" Stacy said, waving him off like it was no big deal.

Josh crawled into the cabin next to Liv, shutting the hatch behind him.

"Ah, you mind if I join you?"

Liv smiled. "I was hoping you'd take the hint."

She snuggled up against him when he lay down. Josh immediately felt the stirrings of desire and bent his head toward Liv's smile. He kissed her gently and brushed her bangs out of her eyes.

"Still no strings," he said.

"Hey, you never asked if there were any strings attached from my end." Liv chuckled, pulled him close, and kissed him deeply.

They made out like a couple of teenagers in the backseat of dad's car for a while, but stopped short of disrobing.

"I think I'd better go check on Stacy," Josh said, knowing that if he didn't, he would be too far gone to stop.

"I think you'd better lie back and think about baseball or something before you do," Liv laughed.

"Um, ah, yeah, you have a point." After a few minutes of chatting and talking about the trip ahead, Josh's stature had somewhat returned to normal.

"I think that's as good as it gets, for now." He smiled and shimmied his way toward the exit.

"That didn't take long," Stacy snickered.

"What? I couldn't fall asleep," Josh said, blushing bright red at her smiling side-glances.

"We didn't do anything, Stace!"

She laughed, "It's okay, Captain, I'm just teasing you."

"What are you, eleven going on thirty? And quit calling me Captain," he said, trying to change the subject. "How are we doing, are we still on course?"

"Gosh, you were only gone a couple of minutes."

"Stacy, stop it, okay?" Josh begged.

She laughed again, "Right on course, Skipper." Josh just shook his head and checked the radar again.

The seas had picked up with the wind. Josh reduced their speed a little to make it more comfortable. Liv had gotten up around five o'clock and she and Stacy played Rummy for an hour. They all enjoyed the beautiful sunset and ate ramen noodles for dinner. The boat had a small—*very* small—galley. Not more than a couple of propane burners with a small sink, and the only counter space was the table directly behind the passenger seat across from the pilot's chair. The passenger seat could swivel around to face either forward or backward toward the table. After dinner, Liv wanted Stacy to lie down for a nap, and joined her until Stacy drifted off. She came back into the main cabin looking a little pale.

"You feeling okay?" Josh asked.

"I am a little nauseated, now that you mention it," Liv replied. "I took those Dramamine you gave me before we left."

"Why don't you take some more? You should be good; that was eight hours ago at least, right?" She didn't answer Josh, but stood up and ran for the cabin door. She managed to make it to the rail before throwing up her noodles, but just barely.

Liv was sick all night long. Josh had her drinking diet cokes. That helped, but she kept getting sick. Stacy slept through the night, missing the never-ending moaning that had Josh about to commit Liv to the deep. Liv finally fell asleep around 4 a.m., lying on the floor of the main cabin with her head under the table.

As the sky in the east turned pale gray, announcing the coming sunrise, Josh turned at the Columbia River Buoy. They still had plenty of fuel, as they had been traveling much slower than he'd originally planned, but he was sure that they could make it the rest of the way if they topped off the tank here. It had taken them fourteen hours to make it this far, which meant they were only making about twelve or thirteen miles an hour.

Liv stirred as he pulled into the fueling dock of a little place called Ilwaco Harbor, at the mouth of the Columbia River. The wind was pushing the boat against the dock, so he'd no trouble leaving the helm to tie it off.

He went back in.

"Liv," he said quietly. She moaned. "Liv, wake up. We're in Washington."

Her left eyelid cracked open a fraction.

"Oh god, I don't think I can do that again," she mumbled. "I feel like crap and my mouth tastes like someone died in it."

She whimpered as he helped her sit up. She held her hand out.

"Oh god, I'm gonna puke."

Josh had expected this and pulled out the five-gallon bucket he'd retrieved from the dock for this exact purpose.

"Go ahead, get it out of your system."

She vomited up nothing but diet coke, then dry heaved for a minute or two.

"Oh God, just fucking shoot me!"

She started crying. Josh got down on the floor and held her, trying not to puke himself. With snot and vomit on her face, she looked at him and wailed like a—well, like a woman who had been puking all night. The commotion woke Stacy and she came barreling out of the bow berthing area, looking totally freaked out.

"Mom, what's the matter?"

Josh held up his hand.

"She's going to be fine, Stace, she's just been a little seasick."

With that, Liv bent forward and dry heaved a few more times.

"A little?" she managed to say between heaves, then continued crying.

"Stacy, come sit with your mom while I go check this place out," Josh said. "I may be gone for a while, so I'm leaving the pistol with you guys." He grabbed his wrecking bar and headed out.

"Be careful, Josh," Stacy said.

They had plenty of food and water, but Josh sorely wanted more firepower. He was also looking for something else: some pot. He remembered a fishing trip when he was really seasick and one of his friends offered him a hit off his joint. Josh didn't smoke the stuff, but he was desperate and willing to try anything. The one toke was magic. A few minutes later, the seasickness was gone. He knew they had recently legalized marijuana in Washington, so he felt his chances of finding some were good.

He climbed the ramp leading from the fuel dock to the parking lot. There were a few cars and trucks parked around. He walked over and began peering in the windows. If he didn't find anything, he was facing a long hike to the other side of the harbor, where the shops and hotels were located. He didn't find anything of interest in the first couple of vehicles, except a couple of bodies. One looked like it had been attacked by one of the crazies, but he couldn't see any physical damage to the other—maybe a flu victim. He wasn't going to break into a car with a body unless he saw something he couldn't live without.

He saw a pickup truck with an NRA sticker in the window.

That's promising, he thought.

He walked around the truck, checking under each wheel well, hoping to get lucky and find a key keeper. No such luck. He used his universal key to bash in the passenger window. The wrecking bar was quickly proving to be his favorite tool. He reached in, unlocked the doors, and began searching the vehicle. He found nothing under or behind the seats. He opened the glove box only to find nothing of value. He flipped up the lid on the center console without much hope; it was too shallow to hold a gun. Sure enough, there was no gun there.

Must have taken his gun with him, Josh mused. Then he saw the set of keys under some loose papers. He pulled them out and clicked on the lock button, *bah da bing!* Now he didn't have to walk. He hopped in the driver's seat and stuck the key in the ignition. It started up without a problem. He put it in drive and headed for the other side of the harbor.

As he drove, he passed a storage area with a bunch of boat trailers. It gave him an idea. What if they pulled the boat out of the water and towed it to Port Townsend? It would save time, and besides, getting Liv to go back on the water was going to be a tough sell. He could just steal a boat when they got there, but he really liked this boat and was becoming familiar with its operation. He would have to think about it.

He passed several restaurants, hotels, and salmon charter places, but no pawnshops, gun stores, or marijuana dispensaries. His hopes waning, he almost missed the Pacific County Sheriff's SUV parked at the Harbor Lights Inn & Lounge. The doors of the Ford Expedition were open on both the driver and passenger side. Josh stopped and got out of the pickup. He approached the sheriff's vehicle cautiously. There was no sign of the deputies. The keys were in the ignition, and it appeared they had abandoned the vehicle and left it running. The shotgun was missing from the rack and there were no weapons in the back, either. A sign on the wall said "Lounge," with an arrow pointing toward the back of the building, which faced the harbor.

He went down the breezeway, and as he came around the building, the stench hit him like a cold fish to the face. A cloud of blowflies ascended from two bodies and swarmed around his face. Josh backed up, spitting and cussing at the same time. He pulled his T-shirt up over his mouth and nose to keep from inhaling the flies. Neither of the bodies was a deputy, but both had been shot with a shotgun and looked like they had a really bad sunburn. What was it Liv said? The ghouls didn't burn up, they just turned red and died. This proved that theory, he supposed.

He opened the screen door to the bar. As he turned, he pulled down his T-shirt, thinking the worst was behind him— but the death and devastation was everywhere. Strewn around the entrance were a dozen or more corpses. They stank so bad that Josh couldn't hold back; he blew chunks all over them. Even as he threw up, he thought, *Now I have to dig through this pile to find the cops and their shotgun.* There wasn't enough left of them to really make out whether they were women, men, cops, or crazies. It was just a jumble of maggot-infested chewed-up bodies, some of which seemed to stare at him accusingly.

"Oh God, I don't know if I can do this," he said aloud. He stood there for a full minute just looking.

He sighed. "Job's not going to do itself."

He looked around the bar. The only light was from the door and a couple of windows up high on the wall, but it he hoped was enough to keep any more of them from attacking. He tiptoed through the mess and got a pool cue from a rack on the wall. He used it to poke around the bodies, trying to refrain from touching them. He thought he found one of the deputies wearing what looked like a gun belt. He would have to roll the body over to make sure, and he couldn't do that with the cue. He thought about just leaving, but he needed the guns. He reached down, grasped the boney shoulder with one hand and the pelvic bone with the other, and rolled it over. Sure enough, there was a semi-auto pistol on the floor. He picked it up and set it on a chair near the door.

He went back to the body, unbuckled the gun belt, and tried to pull it free. Instead of pulling free, the belt caught ahold of something and the lower half of the body turned as he pulled. The upper half did not follow it and lay there facing him. He began dry heaving and couldn't stop. He staggered back, pulling the body along with him. He tripped over another body and fell into the pile, all the while gagging so hard it hurt his ass cheeks.

He rolled over onto his hands and knees. Now covered from head to toe in maggot-infested flesh goo, he scrambled to his feet and screamed at the top of his lungs.

"Fuck you, fucking fuckers!"

He got back down on his hands and knees and tore through the remains of what had once been people. He flung body parts and bits of flesh and bone against the walls and ceiling, screaming profanities at them for being dead. He found the shotgun about halfway through the pile and sat there and cried. He rocked back and forth, sobbing, holding the shotgun and gun belt close to his chest. He eventually calmed down enough to retreat from the bar, retrieving his pistol on the way out. The flies greeted him as soon as the screen door banged shut, but they didn't faze him. He just stepped over the bodies and kept walking. Back at the truck, he threw the shotgun and pistol in the cab and went back over to the deputy's SUV. He opened the hatchback, dug through the boxes in the cargo area, and found a case of shotgun shells. He strode back to the pickup and threw them on the seat, got in, and started it up. All he could think of was getting back to the boat and washing the shit off him.

Liv, still feeling the effects of no sleep, and still constantly throwing up, had lain down in the forward cabin after Josh left. She left Stacy in charge of watching out for any strangers, with orders to wake her if she saw anyone.

Stacy had gotten bored about an hour after Josh left, and fell asleep sitting at the table. She woke with a start after hearing tires squeal and a car door slam. She looked up to see a man coming down the boat ramp, covered in blood, carrying a shotgun with a crazed look in his eyes. She grabbed the gun, opened the door, pointed it in his general direction, and pulled the trigger. She got off three rounds before the gun hit her in the face with its recoil.

Josh realized his mistake as soon as he heard the first bullet whiz by him. He dropped the shotgun and dove headfirst into the water. He surfaced and heard Stacy crying.

"Stacy! Stacy, are you all right? It's Josh, Stacy. I'm sorry I scared you," he called out from behind the dock.

He waited for a response, and when he didn't get one, he pulled himself up onto the dock and got to his feet. As he stood, Liv plowed through the cabin door, screaming.

"Stace! Stace, oh Stace, what happened, are you okay?"

He ran to the boat and found Liv on the deck, holding her shirt to Stacy's face.

"What the hell happened, Josh?"

"I came back covered in blood from a bunch of dead people and she must not have recognized me," he said, still partially covered in dried blood and goo. He started to climb in the boat.

"Josh, don't! Go wash all that shit off, she's bleeding and I don't want any of that to get on her," Liv yelled at him.

He turned, feeling about an inch tall, and went over to a hose connected there at the dock. He squeezed the handle, and a little dribble of water spurted out and then quit. He turned and jumped back into the frigid water.

Liv held Stacy tightly and kept pressure on her cut nose.

"I'm sorry, Mom, that was really stupid. I could have killed Josh."

"Sweetie, don't. I shouldn't have left you alone, and Josh should have made sure you knew it was him coming. It wasn't your fault. I guess we need to both learn how to handle a gun now, huh?"

Liv lifted the shirt off Stacy's nose and saw that the cut wasn't too deep. A butterfly bandage would probably do the trick.

"You're going to have a couple of black eyes and a cool little scar, but I think you'll live."

Josh called out from the water, "You guys okay?"

"Yeah, we're fine."

He made the girls promise to close their eyes before he climbed back onto the dock, buck-naked. He got dressed in the only other set of clothes he had. Liv made lunch and Josh told them about his plan. Stacy didn't care either way, but Liv was thrilled that they weren't going back out on the boat.

"We'll still have to put the boat in the water to get to Whidbey, but it will be a very short trip compared to what it would be from here," Josh assured her.

"Do you have something that will tow this boat?" Liv asked.

"Yeah, I saw several trucks that will work while I was out this morning. We just have to find one with keys. The truck I drove around this morning is too small. We'll all go find one together after I clean these guns and make sure they function."

Later in the day, they went out and found a big crew cab dually Silverado with its driver conveniently lying there with the keys. They collected one of the boat trailers Josh had spied earlier that looked big enough to work with their boat. By the time they got all that done, it was too late to leave, so they got back on the boat, motored out away from the dock a little, and anchored there until morning. They heard the shrieks of the ghouls off and on all night, but slept well enough knowing they were out of their reach. Once morning came, they loaded the boat onto the trailer and hit the road for Port Townsend, Washington.

Chapter 20

Back to the U.S.

Ryan's Group, Lynn's Group, & Meg's Group
10:00 A.M.
Somewhere Between Hope, B.C. and Everson, WA

We'd lost over half our supplies when we fled the auto repair shop in Hope, B.C. Luckily, we'd had the foresight to cache all our ammunition in my truck before parking Max's ride in the other building. Traveling with twelve people in the F250 was cramped but possible, since five of them were kids. Max had taken over the driving and Lisa rode shotgun, with Sadie and Beth in the middle. Lynn, Jean, and the other kids sat in the backseat, and Meg rode in the bed with me. I'd asked Jean to switch with Meg so we could talk.

Meg changed my bandages and said the exit wound was a bit messy but okay, and that the entry wound looked good. We'd been traveling for about an hour when I asked her about her visions.

"I'm sure I brought them to the shop," she said.

"Okay, I understand you think that. Can you tell me why?" I asked.

Meg continued, "I didn't realize at first I was projecting pictures to them, but when I did, that's when I told you we had to get out."

"Okay, please bear with me here," I said. "You think the freaks communicate telepathically, and they send pictures to each other rather than speaking?"

"Yes and no. There are some that are smarter than the others. They seem to not have lost all of their brains to whatever it is that's making them so crazy. Some of them are adept at sending and receiving pictures and others are not even aware that they are, but they do." She got frustrated and threw her hands up in the air. "I'm not making any sense!"

"It's okay. It's pretty hard to make sense of something like this. So, some of the freaks are smarter and they can control the others by telepathically sending them instructions, in the form of pictures, on where to go and what to do? They're like the pack leaders. And the pack members don't know how they know; they just know they're supposed to do it."

Meg nodded. "Yes, and I can see the pictures and feel when the freaks are close by, but I can tell when one of the leaders is sending pictures because they make more sense. If I see pictures of a place, it doesn't mean much, but if I see a picture of a place and have the urge to go there, I know it came from a pack leader. Some of the pictures prompt action with a feeling as well as the pictures. That's when I know a pack leader is sending it. Last night, when I figured out it was a form of communication—that the pictures of the auto repair shop were being sent to me—I realized I'd given up our location to the freaks. When they were all outside, it was like there were thousands of pictures in my head, and I could feel their hunger. It freaked me out a little... okay, a *lot*. Later, when we were at the barn and I started seeing pictures, I realized I could shut it out if I concentrate hard enough."

I'd been nodding at her the whole time she talked. I wanted her to get it all out. I wanted her to know that it was okay, that we weren't going to disown her, that she wasn't a freak.

I reached out and took her now-deformed hand.

"I think it's because of your injury. You must have gotten a small dose of whatever it is that makes them turn. I don't think it's enough of it to turn you, just enough to give you these traits in common," I said. "Just promise me you'll let me know when you get the feeling that they're close. Let's use it to our advantage."

"As long as you promise to kill me if I do turn," she said, staring me in the eye.

"I don't think you will, but I will watch you. If you start going postal, I will protect the others. That's a promise."

We'd been so engrossed in our conversation that we didn't realize we were in Everson. Max pulled the truck up to Parker's house and stopped.

I was still stiff and in pain, but I was already more mobile than the day before.

I checked the front door. It was unlocked, and I went into the mudroom. On the door into the living room was a note.

"Went fishing," it said, with Whidbey in parentheses. I tried the handle and it, too, was unlocked.

"He never was one for being wordy," Max said from behind me.

"Have everyone wait outside while you and Lisa help me clear the house," I said.

It was a two-story house. We cleared the first floor together, then Max and Lisa went upstairs and checked it. After a thorough examination of the house, we brought everyone inside. The adults gathered around the table.

"We need to discuss whether we wait here to see if Parker comes back, or if we just keep going on to Whidbey," I said.

"We don't know when he left the note; it's not dated," Jean said.

Max threw in his two cents. "Well, Rhonda doesn't go fishing with him, but the fact that she isn't here, and neither are the dogs, I'd say they planned on being gone for more than just the day."

"It's still early. I think we can make it to the island and check things out..." Lynn was saying when Lefty burst into the room through the doggie door, scaring the shit out of all of us.

Max bent down and gave him a scratch on the head after regaining his composure.

"Parker must be back."

Max headed back out the front door, where I could hear him and Parker exchanging greetings.

Poncha came bounding into the room and started making the rounds, with a big lick and wagging behind, saying hello to all the kids. Parker followed on her heels and said hello to everyone. He shared hugs with all and everybody was excited to see him. His eyes clouded over when he came to the table where I sat, and I could tell something was amiss.

"Rhonda?" I said. He shook his head and didn't say anything. Meg overheard the exchange, came over, and gave him another hug. He was the most reserved of our siblings and didn't show his emotions much. Meg knew he wouldn't want anyone to make a scene and quietly made it known to all the adults that Rhonda hadn't made it.

We talked about what we had been through. He told us about Whidbey. We told him what had happened at Meg's and in Canada on the way back.

Parker addressed the group. "I think our best bet is the island, if we can destroy the bridge and cut it off from the mainland. Then we can slowly whittle away at the vectors."

"The what?" I asked.

"Vectors; it's what Henry calls them. He said it's a term used for people infected with rabies," he answered.

"We call them freaks," I stated.

"Yeah, I saw that in your note at Sarah's. I just started calling them vectors, because I was with Henry's group and that's what they call them. They seem to die from anything that would kill a normal person. I only came back here to get my falcons. They're both imprinted on humans and I can't just turn them loose. I'm not sure how I'm going to keep them, but I have to try."

"We have plenty of daylight left. If we're going to Whidbey, then we should go today," I said.

I looked around the table at the group.

"Everybody who votes to go, raise your hand." It was unanimous.

We loaded up all of Parker's gear into his two trucks. He had a Toyota Tacoma and a larger Tundra crew cab. He drove the Tacoma, which was set up for his birds. We pulled away from the house with Parker in the lead. Jean drove my truck, and Max and Lisa brought up the rear in the Tundra, towing Parker's Zodiac.

Chapter 21

Close to Home

MADDIE, HARRY, THOMAS, & CARLA'S GROUP
10:38 A.M.
INTERSTATE 405 LOOP
SOUTHEAST OF SEATTLE

Their progress north slowed considerably as they drew closer to Seattle. They had seen massive fires just north of McChord Air Force Base. It appeared that several housing tracts were ablaze along the west side of the interstate.

Did someone start the fires to get rid of the people who turned? Maddie wondered. The smoke made for poor visibility on the road, although someone had moved vehicles out of the way, clearing a path to drive through. Thomas kept his speed at twenty miles per hour, just to be safe. Carla was at the computer station, monitoring the road ahead with the cameras and keeping Thomas up-to-date on anything she saw.

They began to see graffiti on the overpasses they drove under. Warnings were written in letters three feet tall. "Don't be out after dark!" one said. "The Shriekers can smell you!" another proclaimed. The last two said "Wood smoke can cover your scent" and "Be Quiet=Stay Alive!" Maddie sat at the front of the bus and read them aloud as they passed.

Maddie said. "It looks like there must be some survivors nearby that have banded together. Good to know for future reference."

Harry came up next to her. "Some good advice they're passing on, there. They may be the friendly sort, but I suggest we keep rolling. It could be a ploy to get us to let our guard down."

"I agree," Thomas said from the driver's seat. "Maddie, do you still want to stop at your brother's house?"

"Damn straight, I do," she came back instantly.

"Maddie, you know the chance that anyone is there is small, don't you?" Harry laid his hand on her shoulder.

"You mean the chance that anyone there is still alive is small. And, yes, I realize that," she snapped, pulling away from Harry's touch.

"Easy, Maddie, I just don't want you to get your hopes up, sweetie." Harry knew her brother, Clay, had Parkinson's disease and that it hindered his mobility. Clay had made tons of money working the crab fishery in Alaska in his youth. He still held his captains license and remained a standby harbor pilot for the Puget Sound area, but over the last several years, his ailment had been getting worse.

"The exit is only a few more miles ahead. I'm going to gear up," she said, standing. She brushed past Harry on her way to the back.

"I miss my wife," Thomas said.

Harry smacked him on the back of the head and followed Maddie to smooth things out. Thomas laughed and yelled at Harry's back,

"I'm serious, these moments are special."

Conner had been cleaning the weapons in the back room. When Maddie showed up, looking pissed, he put down the AR15 that he'd just finished.

"Gear up; we're going to clear a house in about fifteen minutes," she said, grabbing a tactical vest and swinging it around her.

Conner stood and moved to get his gear. Harry entered and Conner could feel the tension between the two.

"I'm going to go get some... um, water; I'll be right back," he said, and bolted from the room.

"Look, I'm sorry. I wasn't trying to get you to not go; I'm

just afraid for you," Harry said as he approached her.

Maddie looked up at him, tears in her eyes.

"I know. I'm afraid for me too." They embraced, and with Maddie, that meant things were good. Harry opened the closet and grabbed his gear as well.

Maddie directed Thomas to the house in Kent. It only took ten minutes once they were off the interstate. They drove down the long driveway and turned toward the house. There was smoke coming from the backyard.

"Something's burning in the back," Thomas pointed out.

"Okay, Carla stays here and monitors the area with the cameras. Lauren, can you get up top and stand watch?"

"Sure," Lauren said, and made her way to the hatch.

"Harry, Conner, you're with me. Thomas, turn this thing around and be ready to roll if we need to," Maddie spat, ordering the team like a sergeant.

Maddie, Harry, and Conner got off the coach and made their way to the fence. Maddie pulled the lanyard and unlocked the gate. They went through fast. Harry broke to the left, Conner to the right, and Maddie went straight into the yard.

Clay was sitting in a chair next to his wife, Doreen, who was flipping burgers on the grill. Their daughter, Jennifer, was lying on a nearby chaise lounge. Music was blaring from a boom box sitting on the picnic table.

"Clay!" Maddie shouted. He looked up and a big smile creased his face.

Doreen reached over and turned down the volume on the music, put her hand on her hip, and said, "Did you bring the beer?"

"Are you guys nuts?" Maddie asked rhetorically. "The fucking end of the world and you're out here barbecuing?"

"Seemed like the thing to do," Clay responded. "Are you going to come give your brother a hug, or not?" Maddie called the rest of her crew and told them to come on, and then went and gave her brother a hug.

They spent the next couple of hours catching up. Clay's Parkinson's required special medications that needed to remain refrigerated. They had a set of generators to back up the power and keep his meds cool. They explained that they had enough propane to keep the reefers running about six months, but that also meant they couldn't leave the property for any great length of time. Doreen and Jen had boarded up the house and they were doing just fine.

"Have you been attacked by the Shriekers?" Maddie asked.

"Shriekers?" Clay raised his eyebrows.

"Yeah, we don't really have a name for them, but I saw that on an overpass on the way here, and it's better than 'zombies,'" she said.

"Well then, yes, every night," he answered. "They come by and bang on the walls and scream and holler at us, and we just sit tight until the morning. Been working okay ever since this shit started."

"None of you got the flu?"

He pointed at Doreen. "She did, thought we were going to lose her there for a bit, but she's just too rotten to die." He laughed and Doreen smacked him with the spatula. Doreen did look like she'd lost a bunch of weight and her eyes appeared sunken, but her spirits seemed fine.

Maddie told them of their plan to go to Whidbey and locate the rest of the clan, if any of them had made it.

"Sounds good, but you know the ferries aren't running, right?" Clay said.

"Yeah, we figured that. We planned on going north and using the bridge."

"Well, I said the ferries aren't running. I didn't say we couldn't get them running," Clay said with a twinkle in his eye. "It's been a while, but I figure I could still drive one of those bad lads. Kind of miss being at sea, ya know."

Maddie shook her head. "Do we have enough people to make it work?" she asked. "And are you up to it?"

Doreen didn't look pleased, but Jen jumped in. "Dad told me about the reunion, and when all this happened, he said we could steal a ferry and go rescue them, but there was no way we could do it with just us."

"There are six of us, plus the three of you—is that enough?" Maddie asked again.

"Well, I could be dead by tomorrow, but I can still get around, albeit slowly, and with the rest of you following my orders, I think we could manage one of the smaller ferries."

Thomas interrupted, "I'm an engineer, and I know my way around diesels, so I could run the engine room with the help of Conner, and maybe Harry."

Maddie looked at Harry. "What do you think?"

Harry scratched his chin and looked at all of them.

"Two questions: First, can you keep Clay's meds viable? And second, would he be opposed to being carted around in a wheelchair? We have to be able to move quickly."

Maddie scowled. She knew that however bad Clay had become, he refused to use a wheelchair and fought to keep walking.

Clay smiled. "I think under the present circumstances, I could let you guys push me around a bit, and I think my meds will be fine in a cooler with some ice. We will just have to play that by ear."

Maddie added, "We have a refrigerator on the coach."

"The next question is, can we fit the coach on a smaller ferry?" Maddie said.

"Coach? What coach?" Clay asked. With the music playing, they hadn't heard the coach pull into the driveway. Maddie made a mental note to speak to Clay about security later.

"Come on, I'll show you," Maddie said.

Clay stood and took a couple of steps, then stopped, feeling the strain of his Parkinson's. It affects the nervous system, slowing or stopping the movements that we take for granted, like taking a step. It could be a few seconds before he could move, or a few minutes. Doreen knew the signs of his lockups. She'd been with him since the beginning.

"Clay, this is ridiculous, you're in no shape to go running off to pilot a ferry."

He smiled again. "You're right, hon, but if you go get that damn wheelchair, I can at least be the brains of the operation." Doreen shook her head and went into the house.

A few minutes later, she returned with the wheelchair. Jennifer helped her dad into the chair and pushed him around to the front of the house.

As soon as they cleared the fence and the coach came into view, Clay's eyes went wide.

"Holy shit! Where did you steal this thing, Maddie?"

Maddie laughed. "We didn't. We were picking it up for one of Harry's clients when all this came down."

Thomas gave Clay the whole tour and explained each of the systems to him. Clay's body was giving up on him, but his mind was still as sharp as it had ever been. He soaked up the info like a sponge. He asked questions at every turn, and two hours later, he was thoroughly impressed.

"This thing is amazing. Thomas, how in the hell does this paint job work?"

"Well, the paint itself is electrically conductive. The onboard computer uses cameras to observe the surrounding environment and basically changes the color of the coach to mimic it."

"Hmmm... what would happen if the computer failed?" Clay asked.

"The coach would look like a shiny battleship; the paint is a dark gray in its static state," Thomas replied. "We stumbled across it when we were doing research on the electrically charged defense system I told you about. Some British guy invented it."

It was too late in the day to put their plan into action, so they decided to spend the day working on the coach. Thomas went to work on radios with Harry's assistance. Maddie, Carla, and Clay spent their time watching instruction videos and reading up on the coach's systems. Doreen and Jen packed and got ready to leave in the morning. Lauren and Conner pulled security, and sat on top of the coach keeping an eye out.

Carla was a quick study and easily picked up on the coach's systems controls with Thomas's help. When they'd lost the coach's radios, they'd also lost the satellite feed, so although they were up to speed on how it functioned, they still had no idea what was happening out there in the world.

Harry stuck his head in the door and asked them to turn on the radios and scan for traffic. There was no radio traffic, but they did happen across an encrypted satellite transmission. Maddie and Harry went down and told Thomas that he'd successfully repaired the system, and told him about the transmission they had intercepted.

"Most likely military," Thomas said.

"Well, I suppose that's a good thing... or is it?" Harry scrunched his forehead and scratched his chin, thinking out loud.

"We are going to resend the request to the Skylark satellite to take some pictures of San Diego," Maddie added.

"You don't need to," Thomas responded. "It will already be on scene and following the request I sent out earlier. You just need to contact it and download the pictures."

"Oh, okay," she said, and turned to go back and tell Carla.

As Maddie came up the stairs, she found Carla staring at the computer in tears.

"Hey, you okay?"

Carla shook her head and got up from the chair. She motioned for Maddie to sit, and pointed at the screen.

"I was able to connect to the satellite identifier that was listed in the notes Thomas left. As soon as I did, it downloaded that," she said, pointing. "There is nothing left of San Diego; any of my family that were there are dead."

"What do you mean?" Maddie asked as she sat down and looked at the screen. "Oh my God," she said as it became apparent what Carla meant.

The satellite picture of the San Diego area was one of complete destruction. Somehow, the city had been nuked. Whether it was a terrorist, a foreign government, or perhaps their own government, it didn't matter. It was evident that San Diego was no more.

Maddie got up and hugged Carla, who had stopped crying and was just standing there, staring, in shock.

Carla was asleep on the couch. Maddie had given her a couple of Valium and told her to rest. They had talked and decided not to tell Conner and Lauren about San Diego right away. They were afraid that it might push Lauren over the edge.

Thomas continued to work on the coach. He made a modification to the zapper system that he hoped would result in a fatal shock for anyone or anything that touched the coach while it was activated. He'd connected the coach's electrical hookup to the house. With the generators running, it would allow them to turn on the zapper without having to run the engine.

It was decided that four of them would sleep in the coach to rotate standing guard, and everyone else would stay in the house. The night passed and Thomas was almost disappointed that none of the zombies came around to test out his modification.

During his watch, Thomas called up the Skylark satellite that he'd positioned over Washington and downloaded as many photos of the area as he could, at several different magnifications.

The next morning, they had a meeting with everyone to discuss what they were going to do and how they would do it. Clay was excited to see the satellite photos and was certain that there was a ferry docked at Mukilteo they could use.

They loaded up the coach and got an early start. The trip from the south side of Seattle to the ferry terminal took three hours. They had to exit the interstate twice to find a way around accidents that had blocked off the road completely. They arrived at around ten o'clock and parked on the ramp leading to the ferry.

They all went together to board the ferry and see if they could get it launched.

"That's weird," Clay said as they approached. "This is the *Tokitae*[2]."

"What's so weird about that?" Maddie asked.

"It's not supposed to be here, that's what," he said, a bit perplexed. "It's a brand new ferry that was supposed to replace the *Cathlamet*, but I could swear I just read that its delivery was delayed. Oh well, guess we shouldn't bitch. It's supposed to take less crew than the older models, and look, there's not a single car on it."

"We'll need to clear the entire boat to make sure there's no..." Harry paused, "what are we calling them now, Maddie?"

"Shriekers," she replied. "You know, like the sound they make"

"Like I was saying, we have to make sure there are no Shriekers on board."

Maddie agreed, "Most of the interior is lit by the windows, so that should cut down on the time we'll have to spend searching it. Let's split up. Carla, you and Lauren come with me, and we'll start at the top. Boys, you get below decks and any interior spaces on the main deck, okay?"

---

[2] See diagram on page 328

Clay protested, "What are we supposed to do?"

"Just sit here and enjoy the morning. We will clear the wheelhouses first, then come get you," Maddie said.

Maddie led the way and walked onto the *Tokitae*. They checked their radios to make sure they were working and split up once they were aboard.

Carla followed Lauren, who was right behind Maddie. They opened the door to the first stairway they came to.

"Okay, everybody got a light?" Maddie asked.

Lauren turned on the flashlight attached to the end of the Mossberg 500 shotgun that Clay had lent her. Carla put on the headlight that she carried, and Maddie flipped the switch on her AR15's tactical light.

"Here we go."

Thomas, Conner, and Harry cleared the main deck spaces without finding a single living soul. They ran across several bodies of crewmen that appeared to have turned and then died from exposure.

"Why didn't they just go inside?" Conner wondered out loud as he checked out the red, blistered skin on the body.

"Look, these doors all have actual handles; you can't just push on them to open them." Harry twisted the handle on the stairway door leading down to the engine room.

He swung it open to show Conner, and a Shrieker was on him. It came out so fast, he'd no time to bring up his weapon.

A simple mistake is going to kill me, he thought as the Shrieker closed its hands around his neck. He felt the burn of something hitting his shoulder as he fell backward.

Conner had no choice. He swung the machete as hard as he could, knowing that he didn't have enough clearance. He nicked Harry on the shoulder before burying the blade of the machete into the creature's ear. It sliced from below the cheekbone into the side of its head and got stuck about three-quarters of the way through. Instead of pulling on it, Conner stepped toward them and kept pressure on the blade. The blood poured over the blade and splattered back onto his hands, but he kept pushing. The Shrieker went sideways and lost its grip on Harry.

Conner screamed as he pushed the damn thing to the ground and drove the blade into its head.

Thomas was already at Harry's side, examining his wounded shoulder. Conner spun and looked down the stairs. There was another one, but sensing the light, it had retreated down the stairs and was panting in a darkened passageway.

"What the hell, Harry?" Conner said, his hands on his knees, breathing heavily and shaking his head.

"Sorry kid; you didn't have to cut me for it though," Harry replied, lying on the ground, bleeding from his shoulder. Thomas had his pack off and pulled out a handful of clean rags. He applied direct pressure to the wound and began taping it down.

"Hey, that's duct tape," Harry complained.

"No, that's *medical-grade* duct tape. Now shut up while I finish."

"How deep did I get him?" Conner asked, concerned.

"Aw, it's just a flesh wound." Thomas winked at him. "He's just a big pussy."

"Hey now, I'm not that big!" Harry shot back.

Maddie crept slowly up the stairs. Once she saw another door ahead, she quickened her pace.

"Ready?" she asked.

"Just go already," Lauren said.

"Ready," Carla replied.

Maddie opened the next door. To her right was the second car deck, the door standing open. To her left, a door that said "Crew Only."

"Let's keep going up." She reached across the space and opened the door leading to the next set of stairs. The light from the exterior windows on the passenger deck filtered down to them.

"Okay, I think we're good, but stay alert."

Maddie scaled the stairs quickly, and Lauren and Carla stuck to her like glue. They made a complete circuit around the passenger deck and found no one.

"All right, let's go up the stairs to the sundeck." They went back to the stairs and went up the next flight. Unlike most of the ferries Maddie had been on before, the interior stairs continued up to the wheelhouse.

"Well, this is different," she said after she tried the door. It was locked. They went to the right and exited onto the sundeck. They made their way to the exterior stairs that led up to the wheelhouse. A green chain-link fence barred their way. Maddie traded weapons with Lauren.

"Stand back," she said, and aimed at the lock. It only took her three shots to blow it open.

Her radio crackled.

"Hey, what the hell is going on up there?" It was Clay from the pier.

"Nothing, just unlocking the gate," Maddie replied. Immediately the radio came back on.

"Hey, this is Thomas. We ran into a Shrieker down here and Conner killed it, but Harry took a scratch in the process."

"From the Shrieker?" Maddie asked fearfully.

"No, no, from Conner; you may have to stitch him up, but he's going to be okay," Thomas assured her. "We are going down into the belly of the beast now, so we will probably lose radio contact. Don't worry, we're fine."

"Okay, be careful. I need Harry for stress relief," Maddie said. That got nothing in reply.

Maddie, Carla, and Lauren cleared the bridge and found no more of the creatures.

"Wow, look at this. I hope Clay can figure all this out," Carla said, looking at the high-tech equipment in the wheelhouse.

"If anyone can, he can. He has a lot of experience as a captain," Maddie said.

Thomas led the group down the next flight of stairs, since Harry was a bit handicapped. They came to the foot of the stairs, and as Conner had warned him, there was a Shrieker just down the passageway. Thomas dispatched it with a single shotgun blast to the head.

"Twelve-gauge persuasion," he said as he stepped over the body. They came to the engineering operation station, a room filled with monitors and controls for the engines and generators. It looked like the Starship Enterprise to Harry.

It took them nearly an hour to search the remainder of the engineering deck, but they found no more surprises.

"Where is the rest of the crew?" Harry wondered.

"I don't know, but there have to be more of them onboard somewhere," Thomas said.

"Well, let's go back up and tell them what we found, and help finish the search up there," Harry added.

They all met up back on the car deck. Doreen and Jen had wheeled Clay onto the boat.

"We searched all the passenger areas including the bathrooms," Maddie said.

"Harry, I need to take you back to the coach to look at that shoulder. Can the rest of you get Clay up to the bridge?"

It was slow going, but they dragged Clay backwards in his wheelchair up the stairs. He kept telling them he could walk, but Doreen just shushed him and motioned for Conner to keep going. When they got to the wheelhouse, Thomas and Clay got down to business. They started by trying to figure out how to operate the 362-foot ship.

"Before we do anything else, you're going to have to get the electrical generators up and running," Clay told Thomas. "They will be down in the engine room."

"Okay, I'll take Conner with me and see if we can't get that done," Thomas said. He got Conner's attention and they headed back down the stairs.

Back in the coach, Maddie finished sewing up Harry's shoulder.

"Hey, easy baby,"

"Oh shut it, you big baby,"

"Hey, that hurts sweetie."

"I'm sorry, just a few more."

It took fourteen stitches to close the wound to Maddie's satisfaction. She doused it with iodine just to give him one more reason to bitch.

"Now, we're going to give you antibiotics for the next few days to make sure it doesn't get infected, but you should live." She bandaged him up, gave him some Tylenol, and made a sling for him. They stepped out of the coach and the smell of the ocean greeted them.

"Ya know, Harry, I didn't realize how much I missed home until we made this trip. The thought has been nagging at me this whole time, but with everything that's gone on, it's had to take a backseat in my brain. I think I've been homesick for a long time."

Harry put his good arm around her and sidled up for a kiss.

"Let's go see if we can't help them get this boat running."

They headed back toward the wheelhouse, still being cautious, knowing the entire boat had not been cleared. When they came to the door with the "Crew Only" sign on it, Harry stopped and put his ear against it. He listened for a minute.

"I think we found the rest of the crew."

They continued up to the bridge to tell the others their suspicions. As they stepped onto the bridge, the lights came on. The main control console lit up, and different systems started beeping as they came online. Clay was holding a telephone handset.

"You got it, Thomas!" he said.

Everyone broke into applause.

Thomas had successfully started the electrical system's

generators. He, Clay, and Conner were now working on how to fire up both of the two main diesel engines that would propel them. This ferry, like most in the Washington state ferry system, was different than most other ships in that it had two bows. The pilothouse, or wheelhouse, was duplicated over both ends of the ferry so that the crew did not have to turn the ferry around during the passage between the mainland and its destination.

After another hour of fiddling around, they got both main engines started. Clay gathered everyone and explained what had to happen next.

"Okay gang, here's what I need. Thomas and Conner, I need you to operate the loading platform. Everyone else except for Harry will need to be working the lines. I will apply thrust and push the ferry into the dock. Thomas and Conner will release the lines on the pier. Once that is done, they'll adjust the loading ramp and Harry will drive the coach onboard. The ramp is run by hydraulics and will come down, but with no power onshore, it won't go back up. So, Thomas, you have to make sure you don't let it down too far. When Thomas and Conner have pulled the lines off the pier, I need everyone else to pull them onto the boat. Any questions?"

"Where do we put the lines once we have them on the boat, Dad?" Jen asked.

"Don't worry about that right now. Just pull them up onto the car deck. Any more questions?" Clay asked, excitement in his eyes.

"Okay," he continued. "Maddie, Thomas, I want you to each give me a yell over the radio when you're ready. Harry, check with Thomas before you move the coach. Let's go!"

Everyone scurried into their positions, Doreen staying with Clay to help him if he needed her.

The lines attaching the ferry to the docks were stretched tight. Thomas and Conner made it to the first one and called up to Clay.

"We're ready for power."

Clay gently engaged the propeller on what was currently the stern, and pushed the ferry up against the pilings on the pier. The lines went slack, and Thomas and Conner struggled to pull the five-inch-thick line off the cleat and drop it into the water. They ran to the other side of the pier and did the same. The only thing holding the ferry in place now was the forward pressure from the giant prop churning at the water, pushing the *Tokitae* against the pilings.

Harry sat in the driver's seat of the coach, watching and listening to the progress of the team. He was nervous; he could just see the boat slipping away as he drove off the ramp into Puget Sound. He drummed his fingers on the steering wheel as Thomas and Conner made their way to the ramp controls.

Conner stood on the big metal ramp, looking at the ferry three feet below. He ran back up to where Thomas was waiting and told him how far he would have to drop it. They agreed on a couple of simple hand signals, and Conner went back out, stood on the edge of the ramp, and gave Thomas a thumbs up. He pushed down on the lever, lowering the ramp—and Conner—the entire three feet. There was a horrendous bang as it landed on the deck of the ferry. Thomas had pushed the wrong lever and all the hydraulic pressure had been dumped out of the ramp. Conner was jolted when the ramp made contact with the deck of the ferry, and he did a forward roll onto the boat. He came to his feet and looked back at Thomas, who shrugged his shoulders as if to say "my bad."

"Roll that sucker on there, Harry," Thomas called over the radio. Harry had heard and felt the ramp crashing onto the ferry's bow, and was now doubly concerned about the safety of this operation.

"You sure you didn't break something?" he asked Thomas over the radio.

"We won't know until we try to leave. I suggest that you get a move on," Thomas responded.

Conner was waving to Harry to drive onto the ferry, so Harry put the coach in gear and started forward.

The tide must be out, Harry thought as he moved toward the ramp. *It looks like the ferry is way down there.* He gathered his nerve and accelerated down the ramp and onto the ferry. The coach scraped the front bumper on the deck and bounced violently when the wheels hit. He knew this wasn't right, but had no choice at that point. He jammed on the accelerator and shot across the deck of the ferry. He felt the ass end of the coach drop and was sure he was going into the drink.

He looked in the side mirror, saw that he was safely aboard the ferry, and slammed on the brakes. The rest of the team was still dragging the lines onto the boat when he came onboard and scattered out of the way, fearing he might run them over. He opened the door and stepped down the stairs. As he stepped out, Thomas was just making it to the end of the ramp. He saw the ramp in two pieces. Thomas had dropped the front half to the ramp, but the rest of the ramp remained in its up position. No wonder he'd bounced; his heart was still racing when Thomas approached.

"Eh, sorry about that, Harry."

Harry just shook his head as Maddie grabbed him in a full-on bear hug.

"Whew, that was interesting," was all she could offer.

"Nice job, fellas," Clay's voice came over the radio, tinged with sarcasm. He'd stopped the prop that was pushing them into the pier and had applied power to the prop on the opposite end, and the ferry began to move out to sea.

"Uh, I could use some help up here, guys. I need to get to the other pilot house." Clay didn't sound worried. "Thomas, I need you below to check on the engines and do a walk around. If you see any major red lights blinking, I would appreciate it if you'd let me know."

They moved offshore and dropped anchor. Thomas shut down the engines once they were sure the anchor was secure. He and Conner worked with Clay, going over the startup procedures several times to be ready to get underway in a hurry. They left the electrical generators running and spent the rest of the day clearing the boat of Shriekers.

Thomas and Clay remained at their posts, just to be safe, and Harry kept Thomas company. Doreen and Jennifer were not well versed in either weapons or clearing, so they stayed with Clay. The rest started at the top and went through every nook and cranny of the ferry, looking for stowaways.

They stood outside the door to the crew quarters, feeling confident they could handle anything on the other side. Maddie, Carla, Conner, and Lauren all had their weapons ready, and the lights of the ferry were on. Maddie threw the door open and stepped inside, just looking for something to kill. Lauren broke to the right as she entered and swept the room for a target. Conner stepped in, looking for a fight. The room was empty. A passageway led to the right and they fanned out immediately to cover it. Conner looked under each bunk and in each closet.

"Clear," he called out.

There wasn't enough room for all four of them in the passageway, and Maddie and Lauren were the first to make the turn. Down the hall were three doors. One was closed and two stood open. Lauren took the door to the right, which turned out to be a bathroom and showers. Maddie took the door to the left, which was another passageway. Maddie immediately let everyone know she had additional rooms to clear.

"Two doors—one left, one right."

Conner followed Maddie, and Carla followed Lauren. Lauren stepped into the room and kicked in the toilet stall door in front of her. It bounced off a Shrieker, which fell to the floor and grabbed her by the ankle. She didn't hesitate; she pointed the shotgun at the arm and blew it in half. Carla stood behind her and swung the AR15 she was carrying back and forth over the room. Lauren pushed the stall door open carefully, and point-blank stuck the shotgun in the Shrieker's ear. She pulled the trigger; brains and blood splattered across the tile.

Lauren pulled back, swung to the next stall, and kicked it in. Nothing.

"Clear," she called, and began backing out of the space. As she turned to follow Carla to the next area, she felt the teeth of a Shrieker latch onto the back of her neck. She fell to the floor under its weight. Two loud reports came from the passageway. Maddie and Conner had engaged more Shriekers across the hall. Carla moved toward the melee across the hall, and Lauren screamed as the creature ripped a ribbon of flesh from her body. She rolled to the left and her ribs smashed against the doorframe. The Shrieker wasn't slowed; it continued to rip at her.

Carla heard Lauren's scream after she took a step toward Maddie and Conner's side of the fight. She turned to see her daughter drenched in blood, a Shrieker gorging on her face. Carla began to shoot. She stuck the barrel of the AR15 into the its face and loosed the entire magazine, one round at a time, the whole time screaming at the top of her lungs.

Maddie and Conner had their hands full, as the lounge area they were clearing had five Shriekers scrambling to get at them. Carla didn't reload the AR, she just started beating on what was left of the Shrieker with the rifle, not even bothering to turn it around. *Thunk, thunk, thunk*, the barrel connected the obliterated head of the Shrieker. She stepped forward and kicked it with all her strength. It flew off of Lauren, who lay there unmoving.

Carla collapsed onto Lauren, pulling her into the passageway.

"No! No! No!" she continued to chant as she tried to save her girl.

Maddie and Conner finished clearing the other room and then came running. Conner stood over her, yelling Lauren's name. Maddie leaned back against the bulkhead and slid down to the deck, staring at the mess that used to be Lauren.

Chapter 22

Whidbey

RYAN'S GROUP, LYNN'S GROUP, MEG'S GROUP, & PARKER
11:00 A.M.
SOMEWHERE IN NORTHERN WASHINGTON

Our caravan meandered south through dairy farms, with
Mount Baker looking down at our travels. The trip was only
eighty more miles, and I was looking forward to finally
reaching the island. I hoped I would be able to recover from
my gunshot wound and rest up for a while before I began my
next adventure.

I heard Parker come over the radio. "I have a guy
hitchhiking up ahead," he said, sounding like he really didn't
believe what he was seeing.

The country surrounding us was flat and open, so I wasn't
worried about an ambush. Who the hell would be walking
down a country road by themselves in the middle of the
apocalypse?

"What do you think? Is he crazy or just stupid?" I replied.

That got a chuckle out of Max. "He's probably just another
Andrew, trying to get home."

"He has a shotgun, but he's putting it on the ground and
waving for us to stop," Parker added.

"Your call, Parker," I said, not sure what we should do. I
figured we would eventually run across other survivors, but my
first encounter had not been pleasant and it made me leery.

"He looks harmless enough. Let's see what his story is." I
could feel the truck begin to slow and pull off the road. Parker
pulled up short of where the stranger stood, and both Jean and

Max went on past him and stopped.

He stood there with his hands raised, waiting for us to initiate contact. He looked young, probably in his early twenties, straight dark hair, skinny, with a guitar strapped to his pack. Meg pushed the rear hatch of the topper open as Max walked by our truck.

"Be careful," I admonished him. He gave me a quick nod and continued toward the hitchhiker.

"Hey dudes!" I heard the young troubadour say.

"Hey," Max replied. "What's your story?"

"Just traveling the road spreading love to the masses," he said, holding his hands out wide and looking around like there was a crowd of music lovers waiting to be serenaded.

"We, my band and I, were playing a gig in Victoria and, well, all this happened. I'm just trying to get back to Bellingham."

"Where's your band?" Max asked.

"Well, I've got a song about that, but let's just say they weren't fleet of foot, if you know what I mean."

"So, they're dead?" Parker spoke for the first time in the conversation.

"Yeah man, they're history." He dropped his head for a second and stared at the ground. He looked back up.

"Can you guys give me a ride?"

Parker looked like he was going to say no, but then he always looked like he was going to say no.

"Yeah, sure, come on. Throw your shit in the back of my truck." With that, he turned and started walking back to his truck. Max turned, looked my way, and shrugged, then made for the Tundra.

"Hey, my name is Derek if you were wondering," he said as he bent and picked up his shotgun.

Max turned and pointed at the weapon. "Where did you get that?"

"Um..." he looked at the shotgun in his hands. "I found it

next to a dead guy, back up the road. I don't have any bullets for it, though."

"They call them shells, or slugs, for that type of weapon, Derek." Max held out his hand and Derek passed it to him. It was an old side-by-side double barrel with the barrels sawn off. Max cracked the breach and two empty shells ejected.

"Did you even check to see if it was loaded?" Max shook his head.

"Ahh... I didn't know how to," he stammered.

Max handed it back to him. "Makes for a nice club, I guess," he said as he walked away.

Derek stumbled, almost dropping it, and started trotting after him.

"Well, can you show me how to shoot the damn thing?"

"Maybe later," Max said. "You better hurry or Parker's going to leave without you." He pointed to Parker.

Derek put his pack and shotgun in the back of Parker's truck. Taking his guitar with him, he got in. We pulled back onto Goshen Road, then turned west on Mt. Baker Highway shortly thereafter.

When we got to Bellingham, Parker came on the radio.

"I'm going to make a short detour to drop off our new friend. You guys just head south on 5 and I'll catch up."

I immediately answered, "We'll follow you. I don't want to split up."

"Yeah, okay," he replied. If you didn't know him, you would have thought he was being an asshole. It was just the way he was, very economical with his words.

Several minutes later, we pulled up to the smoking ruins of what was once a house. We sat there for a minute, and then Parker called on the radio.

"Max, meet me at Jean's truck; we need to talk."

Parker got out of the Tacoma and made his way to the F250. They all came around the back. Jean, Lynn, Lisa, Max, and

Parker gathered around so I didn't have to get out.

"The kid doesn't have anyone left, apparently," Parker stated. "Do we keep him on, or kick him out?"

Everyone started looking at each other, trying to gauge each other's reaction. Max spoke first.

"All he will be good for is comic relief. He didn't even know how to load that scattergun he was carrying."

"Dad, not everyone had guns growing up." Lisa frowned at Max. "I'm sure he could learn."

The women all nodded; they were clearly leaning toward letting him stay with us. Lynn was frustrated.

"Look, I know it's another mouth to feed, but what are we becoming? Are we going to remain a band of paranoid survivors, or are we going to try and rebuild some kind of life?"

Parker cracked a rare smile. "I guess I could stand the company." He turned and headed back to his truck.

"Well, I guess that's decided," I said, and everyone turned to leave.

Back on the road, we made our way toward the island. We stayed on Interstate 5 until we got to Burlington, where we turned west again on Memorial Highway. It wasn't long before we made the turn for Deception Pass. Highway 20 ran all the way to the island, but it went from a four-lane highway down to a two-lane country road that twisted around like a snake. When we got to Pass Lake, I knew we were getting close.

Parker came on the radio.

"We've got a roadblock ahead."

A small island sits in Deception Pass. Pass Island is no more than a rock with trees on it, but nonetheless, it necessitated two separate bridges instead of one single span. The first span was about as long as a football field, and we came to a stop on what would be the goal line on the mainland side.

With Max's help, I got out of the F250, and together we made our way to Parker, who was looking through his binoculars at the scene ahead.

"What do we have?" I asked as we got closer.

"Looks like it was a National Guard roadblock," Parker said. "I don't think anyone is still alive, though."

He handed me the binoculars and I surveyed the carnage on Pass Island. Three Humvees blocked the end of the span we sat on. Bodies littered the ground on both sides of the roadblock.

"I can't even count the number of bodies," I said, handing the binoculars to Max.

Max looked for a minute, then handed them back to Parker.

"We need to do a little recon. I'll get Lisa and we'll scout it out."

"I'll go with you," I said, and started to go get my gear.

"No offense, Ryan, but you'd be more a hindrance than a help. Wait here and we'll let you know what's going on," Max said, and went back to get Lisa.

"What do you think?" I asked Parker.

"I think we could use one of those Humvees, and I imagine there are some more weapons we could scavenge if someone hasn't beaten us to it."

I put my earbud in and plugged it into my radio. Max and Lisa were still wearing theirs, along with the throat mic chokers.

I retrieved the TP AR 7.62 rifle, went back, and took up an overwatch position at the hood of Parker's Tacoma. Parker climbed on top of the truck with the binoculars.

"Okay, be careful, and leave your radios on voice-activate," I told Max and Lisa.

They stayed on the roadside of the sidewalk fence and zigzagged their way toward the Humvees.

Max came on the radio a couple of minutes later, sounding winded.

"Looks like these are all freaks. They all have the sunburn thing going on," he said as he reached the first bodies.

"I don't see anything moving ahead of you," I reported as I

watched through my scope. "Parker, you see anything?"

"No."

They had no concealment as they approached the Humvees. I scanned back and forth, worried that some gung ho private would appear and start shooting at them.

They made it safely to the roadblock, and I watched Lisa cover Max as he angled the corner of the Humvee on the left. He stood there for a moment with his M4 up and in the ready position, then turned and waved us up.

When I arrived, I found Lisa bent over, puking.

"I'll never get used to the smell," she said.

It did smell horrible, but being outside, the smell didn't stick to you like it did indoors. Maybe I was becoming immune to it. The bodies of the guardsmen were decimated. There was little smell coming from them; they had been picked clean. The freaks, however, were remarkably intact.

They must not like eating their own, I thought to myself. There was a group of freaks on the mainland side, and a larger group of them on the island side.

"The soldiers must have been surprised by the group from the island," I said. They came here to protect the people on the island and got ambushed by them instead. We collected five more M4s and some ammunition.

Max stood at the railing of the bridge, looking down at the water.

"Hey man, you okay?" I asked.

"Yeah, I'd been toying with the idea of just blockading the bridge instead blowing it up as you suggested, but seeing this has changed my mind." He looked disgusted. I offered him a smoke and we both took a minute to stare at the water and enjoy the nicotine buzz.

"Low tide," I remarked.

"Yeah, Parker took me through at low tide in his Zodiac a couple of years ago when I called him a pussy for not wanting to." He laughed. "Turns out he had a bigger pair than I gave him credit for. I wish I'd never called that into doubt. I nearly peed myself that day."

I laughed at the story. The water below was a churning mass of standing waves, ten feet tall in places, with currents and eddies swirling in multiple directions.

"There is no way you would get me in a boat on that!" I said, as I flicked my cigarette off the bridge and watched it spiral down.

Two of the three Humvees started. The other, apparently, had been running when they were attacked, and the battery was dead. The fuel tank was most likely empty.

The adults teamed up and moved the bodies onto the sidewalk, where Max and Parker worked together throwing them over the side. It was exhausting work and I wasn't able to help, but I made the rounds, making sure everyone had water. The kids were all playing king of the hill on the turnout area of Pass Island. It looked like the girls were all ganging up on poor Andy. He'd run up the hill only to fall prey to one or two of the girls, who held onto the high ground. Max told Andy to get used to it, that women would be doing that to him for the rest of his life. He tilted his head to the side and gave Max a queer look. It was clear that he thought Max meant girls would literally be throwing him off a hill for the rest of his life, which confused him.

Our newest member, Derek, pitched in and sang old spirituals as he dragged bodies over to Lynn and Jean, who would summarily dump them over the rail that separated the road from the sidewalk.

"Nobody knows the trouble I've seen..." I had to admit, he did have a good voice; it kept everyone's spirits up.

Two hours later, the bodies had all been given the heave-ho-here-ya-go, and everyone was bushed. Lisa and Derek were elected to drive the two working Humvees, and we headed off for Coupeville.

When we arrived, Parker started honking his horn before he even turned onto the driveway. The whole gang was there to greet us as we pulled up to the house.

Henry and Molly were the leaders of the compound. When I say compound, well, it was shaping up to be one. They had adopted another house that sat in the same clearing as the original retreat. Parker saw they had been busy since he left early that morning. The ground floor windows of the new residence had all been boarded up.

"We're going to start building a wall around the houses tomorrow," Henry said.

Molly had been making the rounds of all us newly arrived, and was full of glee.

"We hoped you'd found a few more of the clan on your return, but we never expected this many," she said to Parker. "Six of the seven Brants, we're only missing Barb now, and who knows, she may still show up."

Max was reunited with his daughter Trish. She and her mother had shown up shortly before we arrived. They regaled Max with the story of how Frank had convinced a group of marauders that he was the only one at the farm. The marauders killed him, but they escaped and made their way to the island in a small rowboat, powered by a five horsepower Evinrude. Lynn's husband and daughter were also there, but I didn't get the story as to how they had made it from Colorado.

I sat on the back deck, looking out over Penn Cove. I was grateful for finally reaching our destination, but knew I would soon have to begin my journey to the east.

Two days... I'll give myself two days to recoup... My thoughts were interrupted by the sound of a ferry's whistle.

They still refer to a ferry's horn as a whistle, but it sounded more like the blast of a foghorn. The boom echoed off the trees. I stood and walked to the edge of the deck to look toward the mouth of the cove.

Everyone came running at the sound. I couldn't imagine a ferry coming into Penn Cove, but sure as shit, there it was, a damn ferry headed toward us. Parker walked up next to me and handed me his binoculars.

"Looks like Cousin Maddie standing on the bow."

I took the binoculars and looked for myself. "What the hell, it is Maddie."

It took a while for the pandemonium to die down, during which time I passed the word around that it was Cousin Maddie on the ferry. It took another hour for the ferry to anchor up and for them to launch a zodiac for the trip to shore. I watched the whole process through Parker's binoculars. I could see several other people on the ferry but wasn't able to figure out who they were. When they finally made it to shore, I saw four people get out. They made their way up the hill from the beach, and when they got about halfway up, I recognized Carla. She was the last person I expected to see, and she looked completely wiped out. Conner was helping her up the hill. I would recognize Conner anywhere; he was the spitting image of my father. Even he seemed subdued.

Maddie made a beeline for me and was about to grab me in a bear hug when Meg stepped in and hijacked it.

"He's got a gunshot wound in his side, but I could stand a hug."

I threw up my good arm and welcomed her in with a half-hug. I finally got to meet Harry and was in the process of shaking his hand when Carla came up on the deck. She broke down and started sobbing when she saw me. I moved away from Maddie and Harry and took her into my arms. I thought she was grieving Jacob, and that wound was worse than the one in my side. I began to tear up while telling her it was going to be okay.

"No," she said, "we lost Lauren. She was right; it's never going to be okay."

It took several minutes for me to get the story of how they lost Lauren to the freaks, which she referred to as Shriekers.

"So, do you know anything about your mom and whether they left San Diego?" I asked. Not the question I should have asked right then.

"I don't know, but San Diego is gone, wiped out," she said, visibly shaking now.

I left it at that.

"Why don't you get some rest?" I waved Molly over. "Hey, can you show Carla where to find a place to rest for a while?"

Conner, Carla, and Molly went in the house, and I looked for Maddie. I found her, Parker, Max, and Jean sitting in the great room.

"Ah, I'm glad you are all in one place, saves me having to track you down. I wanted to ask what you all think about moving everyone out to the ferry."

Maddie smiled. "We were just talking about that."

It was already late afternoon, and we couldn't spend too much time debating the finer points of the plan. We decided to move everyone to the ferry and worry about the supply situation tomorrow. We would leave just a few people onshore for the night to guard the supplies.

We gathered the entire group, which now numbered over fifty, and reached a consensus that the ferry was the most logical place to stay. No one had proof, but none of us had ever seen a freak in the water. Someone made the point that we needed to agree on a name for the people who had turned. No one could agree, so we tabled that discussion for another time.

Parker and Max took Parker's boat down to the launch ramp in Coupeville, got it into the water, and we began taking people out to the ferry.

Max and Lisa volunteered to stay onshore in the tree house, and Cousin Merle and his brother-in-law Lou would stay in the house with the supplies.

It was late. Max was having trouble staying awake. He thought about waking up Lisa, who was fast asleep on the cot, but the lights around the perimeter began to pop on and staying awake became a moot point.

"Lisa, wake up!"

The freaks poured through the tree line, hundreds from all directions. Max got on the sound-powered phone and called Merle.

"Massive horde is coming at you!" he screamed, and then began to shoot.

The attack lasted for two hours. Max and Lisa fired close to fifteen hundred rounds of 5.56. The brass covered the floor of the tree house. The house had been overrun, and it didn't look good for Merle and Lou. No one answered the phone when Max tried to contact them.

At dawn, Parker and I returned to shore to survey the damage. I found Max in the house. The bodies of the freaks were everywhere. I stepped over them on my way in.

"Hey, you okay?"

Max looked like he was ready to call it quits.

"Yeah, I'm okay. Can't find Merle and Lou, though."

We searched the house and dug through the mess of freaks. After twenty minutes of searching, we found Lou upstairs. He looked like Davy Crockett at the Alamo. Dead freaks were piled up around him. Upon further examination, it appeared he'd opted to end it before being eaten alive. There was a single gunshot wound to his temple.

I bent down to get a closer look, and that was when Merle came out of his hiding spot. The room had gabled ceilings that came down to about four feet off the floor. The space in the eaves was closed off, except for the hidden section Merle had snuck into. "Hey guys," Merle said as he crawled out, "just escaped at the last minute before the barricade gave way and freaks poured into the room."

It was decided to completely abandon the compound and

relocate everything to the ferry. It took all day, but we managed to salvage enough supplies to keep the group going for a week or so. We still had the farm, which would keep the group busy and fed quite well.

I called a meeting late that afternoon. We managed to get the barbecue grills out to the ferry, and we had a memorial for Lou and everyone else we had lost up to that point. There was a lot of singing and crying, but we made it through.

It was amazing how good the hotdogs we found in the deep freeze on the ferry tasted. The walk-in freezer had stayed cold enough that nothing was ruined, and it was fully stocked with ferry food. Nothing like steak, but there were hundreds of pounds of hotdogs and hamburgers.

After the memorial, a dozen of us met to discuss the future.

"We need to establish a council that represents the group when it comes to making decisions. We can't continue to vote on every little thing," Jean said, starting the ball rolling.

"I won't be staying," I said.

Several different people were talking at once, but when I said that, a quiet came over the group. Max was the first to speak.

"Well, I tried my best to talk him out of it, but Ryan is determined to go east to try and find his family. Lisa and I have talked about it, and we will be going with him."

This was news to me, and although I told Lisa she could come with me, I'd decided to go it on my own. It was my idea and I didn't want to get anyone else involved.

Maddie spoke up next.

"We aren't staying either. Harry and I have to find our kids back in Texas, and we owe it to Mr. McClure, the owner of the coach out there, to at least find out if he's still alive."

"I'll stay long enough to help get things organized here, but we need to hit the road soon," I said.

Parker stood and motioned to Henry.

"Henry and I talked, and we need to clear the island of

vectors, or freaks, or whatever you want to call them. It will take a long time and a lot of work, but we think if we blow the bridge, we can eventually reclaim the island. I think we can do that, but I would appreciate your help getting started, and by that I mean help destroying the bridge."

Everyone agreed to work on a plan to destroy the bridge in four days. That would give me a little more time to recover from my gunshot wound, and the group enough time to come up with a feasible way to take out the bridge.

Maddie and I sat on the sun deck of the *Tokitae*, enjoying a warm day. We talked about all the shit we had recently been through, and about combining our strength. I realized it would be stupid to turn down Max and Lisa's offer to go with me, and Maddie convinced me that we should all go together in the coach. It would take me out of my way, but it increased my chances of making it to West Virginia at all.

We were making plans when Thomas came up the stairs and made his way across the deck to us.

"Hey guys. Maddie, we need to talk," he said.

"Sure thing, darlin'. What's up?"

"I love you guys, and you have become like my family, but I think Rico and I are going to stay with the folks here. They need my help, and to be honest, I'm not cut out for the road."

Thomas spoke like it was a hard decision that he'd spent a lot of time considering.

"I understand completely. We'll be screwed if the coach breaks down, but they do need you here to keep the ferry running, too," Maddie said. She was never one to candy-coat a situation.

"Harry is no slouch when it comes to fixing diesels, Maddie, and if you have issues with anything else, you can always call me on the sat phone," Thomas said.

"Yeah, as long as it isn't the sat phone that's broken," she said with a smile.

"Maddie, don't make me feel like shit here," Thomas pleaded.

"I'm sorry, Thomas. I'll really miss having you around, is all," she said, letting him off the hook. "Now go get that bottle of Fireball you've been hiding in the coach and we'll celebrate."

"Deal," he said, and went to fetch the whiskey.

Chapter 23

The Long Run

RYAN
7:24 A.M.
TOKITAE FERRY
PENN COVE, WA

I woke up with a slight hangover. Last night was the first alcohol I'd consumed since all this began other than a couple of beers. It was hard to believe that it had only been a little over two weeks ago that I was on another ferry headed for a few days of fun at our family reunion. It seemed like a lifetime ago that I left West Virginia.

I stood up and my head spun for a second; I had to grab for the table. We had taken up residence in the passenger cabin and were sleeping on the long bench seats. I made my way to the bathroom, washed my face, and brushed my teeth. The toothbrush gagged me a bit and I almost lost it before getting control.

I looked in the mirror and hardly recognized myself. The face that looked back at me was thinner, harder. I stood up and pulled up my shirt. Damn! I hadn't realized it, but my well-crafted paunch had diminished considerably. Getting chased by hordes of freaks and eating only when we got the chance had turned out to be quite the diet and exercise program. I would have to find some new clothes soon, or at least a smaller belt.

I examined my wound and found that it was actually scabbing over. It felt tight, but on a pain scale of 1-10, it was no longer a 13—more like a five or six. I used someone's deodorant that had been left beside the sink. Good old-fashioned spray. It was kind of funky smelling, but it beat my funky smell. I would have to get a bath today. I didn't plan on doing much of anything else.

I made my way to the cafeteria and got a cup of steaming hot coffee. Henry had put a sign-up sheet on the wall for work that needed to be done at the farm. I saw that every slot for work had a name next to it. That was good; no one other than me was shirking responsibility today. I took my coffee to a seat out on the deck and lit a smoke, thoroughly enjoying the moment of peace. Parker and Max were working with Thomas and Harry to develop an idea for taking out the bridge. I was no demolitions expert and figured they would tell me when they worked out a plan.

I heard one of the Zodiacs fire up. I stood and walked to the railing, where I looked down on Parker and Max getting into Parker's boat.

"Where are you headed?" I shouted down to them. Max looked up and yelled back at me.

"We're going to check out the bridge from the water while the tide is in." Rather than try to carry out a shouted conversation, I just gave him a wave. I went back inside to find Lisa and Maddie sitting there, chatting over coffee.

"What's going on?" I asked.

"We were just talking about making a scavenger run. You need anything?" Lisa said. I smiled and hiked up my baggy pants and said, *"Necesito nuevos pantalones, por favor."* Lisa raised her eyebrows at Maddie.

"He said he needs new pants," Maddie translated.

"And a belt, too, but I don't know the word for belt," I said. "Size 38 ought to work for now, but at this rate I will be down to 34 in no time."

Maddie laughed. "Shedding some of that fluff, are you? We'll see if we can find something."

I left them in search of Thomas. Conner, at the coffee pot, told me he was fetching some for Thomas. I went with him to the engineering deck and found Thomas busily working on a diagram of some kind.

"What are you making?" I asked.

He looked up. "Hey Ryan, I'm working on making an improvised explosive device."

"An IED? For the bridge? What are you going to use for explosives?" I asked, looking at the diagram.

"Not sure yet, but I want to have the basic design done so I can be ready to go. Henry said he has a ton of ammonium nitrate at the farm, but that would be too bulky. We'd never be able to set the charges somewhere they could bring the whole thing down."

I thought about it for a minute, then asked, "What about the Naval Air Station? Do they have any bombs over there that we could borrow?"

"They should—when Max and Parker get back, we'll go over there and do some recon. I sent them to take some pictures of the underside of the bridge so I can figure out where to place the IED." He was being polite, but I could tell he was annoyed by my questions. I left and headed back up to the main car deck.

I found Harry in the coach listening to the radio.

"Anyone out there?" I asked

"Yeah, I've been listening to a group who have set up a camp in a shopping mall in Olympia. By the sound of it, they're building a wall around the place. I don't know what to make of it."

"Huh, that's interesting. Bring it up at the meeting, but don't make contact with them. They may be friendly, but I'd just as soon keep our presence quiet for now," I said.

"Yeah, that's what I was thinking, too," he replied. "So, are you going to come with us to Texas?"

"Yes, as you heard, Max and Lisa have decided to go with us

as well. Her husband is, or was, in Arkansas. She wants to find out if he made it or not. Max thinks it's a pipe dream, but he said he doesn't have anything better to do." That got a chuckle out of Harry.

Harry continued fiddling with the radios. My eyes were heavy, and I dozed on the couch.

I woke up to Maddie's voice.

"Hey, we're about to meet upstairs, you coming?" I hadn't realized how tired I was; I must have slept the day away.

"Yeah," I said, shaking the cobwebs from my head.

Thomas was talking to the group when Maddie and I entered.

"We found several MK81 bombs at NAS Whidbey. These warheads have about 300 pounds of composition H6 explosives. One of them will be sufficient to blow up the bridge."

Max spoke up, "Uh, there is no such thing as too many explosives."

Thomas smiled and shook his head.

"True, but we don't want to blow ourselves up in the bargain."

Thomas went on to explain how he would rig the IED. Most of it was over my head, but I kept nodding like I understood.

"The IED will be triggered with a walkie, so while I'm working on it we're going to have to collect all the radios, just to be safe. The finished IED will be pretty heavy, so we'll have to use a block and tackle to raise it up from the boat.

"That brings us to the next topic for discussion. We need to take the ferry to the terminal in Clinton to get the coach off," Harry added. "We'll be the last vehicle to cross the bridge." The thought of us leaving turned the group somber.

"Well, there's no reason to put off the inevitable," Thomas said, acknowledging the fact that we would be leaving in a few days. Clay brought up that he needed to make a run home to retrieve the remainder of his drugs. Parker said he would go with him in the Zodiac so that they wouldn't have to take the ferry. Doreen wanted to go along, so they made plans to do that after they docked the ferry at Clinton. Harry would drive the coach back to Coupeville and help Thomas with the IED.

Harry also mentioned the group south of Seattle that he heard on the radio. He also reminded everyone of the incident that they'd had with the marauders in Olympia. Everyone agreed that we should monitor them without initiating contact. Henry gave a report on the progress at the farm; it looked like there would be a good crop of squash this year, and with the help of the rest of the group, they should have enough food to make it through the winter. He went on to talk about planting a variety of crops next spring. The plan was to scavenge seeds from the surrounding farms' seed banks. The overall outlook for the group was a positive one. They talked about the need to start hunting the Shriekers/Freaks/Vectors once the bridge was taken out. It would be a slow process, but they figured they could eventually reclaim the island.

A chirp from Clay's radio interrupted the discussion. Conner's voice came across the airwaves.

"Hey guys, we've got company."

I turned my radio on.

"What exactly does that mean, Conner?"

"There's a boat headed toward us. It isn't coming fast and all its lights are on, so they aren't being sneaky, but they are definitely headed our direction."

We had drilled for this possibility earlier and everyone went to their posts. I retrieved one of the M4s with an ACOG scope and went to the bridge on the end of the ship facing the channel. Max, Thomas, Henry, and Merle went to the main car deck to repel boarders. Harry and Maddie went to the coach and tried the VHF radio to hail the boat on channel 16, the emergency maritime channel. Clay turned off all the lights on the ferry and Conner manned the search light on the flying bridge, where I was.

"Don't turn that thing on unless I tell you to," I said, and he gave me a thumbs up to show that he understood.

Harry came over the walkie.

"Hey Ryan, this guy says his name is Josh and he's looking for his Uncle Ryan."

"I'll be damned," I said to Conner, "it's your Uncle Josh."

I replied to Harry over the radio. "Ask who's with him." I hoped that Barb and the rest of her clan was onboard the boat.

"He says it's just him and two other survivors," Harry replied.

"Okay," I said over the radio. "Everyone stand down, and someone find Carla and tell her that her brother is here."

Clay turned the lights back on and we all made for the main deck to welcome our new arrivals.

The main deck actually sat eight feet above the water. Parker and Max had stolen a floating dock and had tied it off at the rescue boat davit, giving us a place to dock our small boats. They had two extension ladders tied together side-by-side for getting personnel onboard, and the davit worked for anything that had to be hauled up onto the deck.

Josh tossed the line across and Parker tied him off. A blonde woman and a young girl stood in the back of the boat.

I waited on the main deck. It was several minutes before I saw Josh's head pop up the ladder. I went over and greeted him as he got his feet firmly on the ferry deck.

"Hey Josh," I said, giving him a hug.

"Hey Uncle Ryan, I wish I had better news for you, but..." I just held him in the hug.

"Don't worry about that right now. Let's get you guys settled and then we can talk."

Josh introduced everyone to Liv and Stacey. People were saying hello and greeting them with hugs when Carla came running across the deck with Conner in tow.

"Josh! Oh my God, Josh." She encompassed him in a flurry of hugs and kisses, then stopped and looked around.

"Mom? Dad? Hope?" Josh just shook his head and wouldn't look her in the eye.

"Josh, where is everyone else?" Her voice now became a little shrill as the panic set in. "Josh, did you leave them somewhere safe, are they coming behind you... where are they, Josh?"

"None of them made it, Carla," Josh stated. "They are all gone, except for Denise; she's still in San Diego."

It was a crushing blow to Carla's already fragile psyche. She fell to the ground; Conner just caught her. Maddie stepped in and tried to bring her around, but she was out.

"Get a stokes-litter, and then take her to the crew quarters." Meg and Jean jumped into action.

"We'll get her an IV and keep her comfortable, that's about all we can do." Conner was visibly shaken himself.

"What's wrong with her?" he asked Maddie.

"I don't know," she replied. "She's probably in shock and her body just shut down. She should be okay, but we need to keep an eye on her." They hustled around getting Carla taken care of. Josh just stood there staring.

I went to him. "Hey man, don't worry. She's just a little overwhelmed. She lost Jake and then Lauren, so she's been through a lot." I took our three new people up to the passenger cabin and got them some coffee. I asked the girl if she wanted cocoa and she seemed miffed.

"No, I'll have coffee too." And after a stare from her mother, she added, "Please."

Josh filled us in on what had happened to Barb's group and how everything went to shit pretty much that first night. He explained where he and Liv had met and how good Stacey was with a rolling pin. They had spent the last two days searching the island, looking for us. They went to Maxwelton Beach first, as Josh remembered that was where the last family reunion had been held. When they found no one there, they went to the old homestead in Langley. Josh said he vaguely remembered that one of his Mom's cousins had a farm in Coupeville. He wasn't even sure where it was, so they had just stayed close to the beaches, looking for signs of life. When they rounded the point and saw the ferry, Josh said he knew he'd found us.

"Only the damn Brant family would think to steal a ferry," were his exact words. I pointed out that it was actually the pirate Clay Hansen and his sister Maddie who had acquired the ferry.

We set them up in their own little area, which consisted of two big booths in the passenger cabin.

"We are talking about building walls for some privacy, but we haven't gotten that far yet," Doreen said. She was the acting captain's wife and was taking a lead role in the logistics of the group while on the ferry. No one seemed to mind, and it was a job that needed doing. I left them to get situated and went to the crew's quarters to check on Carla. I found Meg sitting with her.

"Hey, how is she?" I asked.

"She's stable; I think it was just the breaking point for her," Meg responded.

I sat down and kicked my feet up onto an empty bunk.

"So, how are you doing?"

"I'm fine," she said.

"Any more messages from the freaks?" I asked.

"All the time, but I am getting much more adept at closing off the seemingly endless chatter. It's nice during the day, when they're sleeping. I can sense them, but it's just a presence, not actual thought pictures," she said.

"Well, it will be nice to have someone that can track them down and find their hiding places," I said.

"You know, they're not evil," she said.

"What do you mean by that?" I asked.

"It's like everyone thinks the freaks are evil, demons or something. The truth is they are more like mentally challenged teenagers with an unquenchable need to feed. They aren't killing for fun—they're killing to survive."

"So, what you're saying is we shouldn't be killing them?" I asked, remembering the people I'd seen that had been eaten by these mentally challenged teenagers.

"No, it's us or them at this point. I'm not saying that; I'm just saying I don't like it that I'm going to be used to track down their lairs, so that we can slaughter them in their sleep." She seemed to be on the verge of tears.

"What about the smart ones?" I asked. "Do they think of us as anything but a food source?"

"They know we are smarter than the four-legged ones: dogs, cats, horses, and cows; but no, they don't think of us as being like them. They are learning to not come running when they hear weapons fire." Meg seemed almost proud of them. "But even the smart ones are not really smart; they're just more aware of what's going on, I think."

"I'd offer to take you with us, but I don't think that it's going to be any different for us, actually; we'll have to deal with it more on a daily basis than you will." I said.

"No, this is my home. I have Sarah and the kids here and I will be fine. I just don't like all the killing. I know it's necessary, but I don't have to like it," she said, and smiled at me. "Now, why don't you treat yourself to a shower? That wound is healed enough that you can, and you smell pretty awful."

"Thanks, sister dear," I said, and headed to the shower room. Maddie and Lisa had been true to their word and found me some new clothes while I slept; a brand new pair of Carhartt cargo pants and some heavy-duty T-shirts, and best of all, some new underwear. I felt like a new man after my shower. I stuck my head back into the crew's quarters.

"Hey, are you going to be all right, Meg?" I asked.

"Yeah, little brother, I'll be okay. Thanks for letting me vent. It helped."

"No problem. And just so you know, I love you!" That got a big smile.

"I love you too, Ryan. Now go get some more rest, you goofball."

The next morning I awoke with the sun and felt pretty good. My side still hurt, but it was no longer debilitating. I went in search of Clay to see when he planned to haul anchor.

I found him on the bridge going over the charts with Parker.

"Hey guys, anything I can do to assist?"

"Yeah, go down to the operations center and help Conner. Thomas is already onshore working on the bomb, and he gave Conner a checklist of stuff that has to be done prior to us getting underway," Clay said. "Do what he says, but keep an eye on him and make sure he's okay."

"Got it," I said, and left to go below.

I found Conner checking and rechecking all the switches and controls in the operation center. He looked like he had it under control, so I just let him know I was there to help him however he needed it.

"Thanks, Uncle Ryan. Thomas taught me all this stuff, but it's a lot to remember, ya know?"

"I know; you want me to read the checklist to you for startup?" I asked.

"Could you? That would be a big help."

I ran through the checklist and he double-checked all his work.

"I think we're ready to go," he said. He grabbed the intercom handset and called up to Clay.

"Ready to fire, main one and main two."

"Standby, we're clearing the small boats and Josh is towing

the dock to shore," Clay came back over the speaker. A few minutes passed before he returned to the intercom.

"Okay, kick the tires and light the fires!"

Conner looked at me, his finger poised over the green start button. I gave him a confident nod, and he pressed it. The number one main came to life. He began checking all the gauges and then came back over to the control console. He didn't even look at me this time, he just mashed the start button and the number two main spun up and chugged away happily. He ran down the tower of gauges and monitors and then picked up the mic,

"Number one and number two mains are running within normal parameters." His accomplishment was almost as big as the shit-eating grin on his face.

Clay came back over the intercom, "Good job, mate. Stay on station and monitor those gauges and let me know if any red lights start blinking."

"Roger that, captain," Conner shot back.

I smiled and slapped him on the back as I made my way back upstairs. He had this under control.

The ship's whistle blew two long blasts as we weighed anchor and headed for the ferry terminal on the south end of the island. I walked to what was the bow for this part of the trip and enjoyed the wind blowing in my hair as we pulled out of Penn Cove.

Josh and Parker pulled up next to the bow of the ferry and waved from the cabin of the 26-foot Duckworth. Then Josh pushed the throttles forward and sped off to scout the ferry terminal for any potential problems.

I loved being at sea. The smell of the ocean, the sound of the wind as you pushed through it. I leaned on the gunnel and stared into the water.

"Hey Cuz," Maddie said as she walked up behind me.

"Hey," I replied.

She leaned over the rail next to me. "I was talking with Clay last night. He told me that he doesn't expect to last much longer than the six months of drugs he has stored at the house. I think he's just trying to make me feel better. I want to try and find some more of the drugs he needs."

I looked up from the water and over at her. "What does Doreen think?"

"She thinks he won't last another six months, period, but she also said he's proven her wrong about everything else." Maddie looked torn.

"Do we even have a clue where to find the type of drugs he needs?" I asked.

"Yes, but you won't like it." She told me about the medical warehouse in Renton.

"You're right, I don't like it."

We held an impromptu meeting and discussed the possibility of making a run on the warehouse. Clay was against it, Doreen was for it.

"Clay, you won't last a week without those drugs, and right now that week starts exactly one hundred and seventy-two days from today. It's all I think about." Doreen was in tears by the end of her rant.

"It would only be a temporary reprieve, honey," Clay said. "I don't want anyone risking their life to give me another month."

"Look, we don't have to decide this right now," I said. "We'll go ahead with the plan as it stands today. We dock at the Clinton ferry terminal and unload the coach. Then Maddie can go with you, Parker, and Josh to get the drugs that are still at Clay's house. On your way back, you can scout out the medical warehouse. If it looks doable, we will hit it after we blow the bridge. Josh can pick up the team in Renton, and we can leave for Texas from there." Everyone stood there for a minute, looking at each other.

"Fine," Doreen said, and left the bridge.

"Clay, are you okay with that plan?" Maddie asked.

"No, but it is better than going off half-cocked," he said. "If it looks like anything but a cakewalk, I'm not going to allow it."

"Good. Now let's get this thing to Clinton and go from there," I said.

Forty-five minutes later, Harry and I drove off the ferry in the coach.

"What do you think is going to happen?" Harry asked me.

"I think Maddie will storm the gates of hell to save her brother. I'm just glad I'm not going to be there when she does; he's going to be pissed."

We were halfway up the island, headed for the farm, when we heard Maddie on the radio.

"Harry, can you hear me?"

Harry pulled the coach to the side of the road and went to the radio. She was calling on the VHF.

"This is Harry, go ahead."

"We are headed south on Josh's boat. We left Clay on the ferry. Doreen, Josh, Parker, and I are going to make the run on the warehouse to get Clay's medicine. We'll check in with you when we get back to the boat."

Harry looked at me; I just shrugged.

"Okay, Maddie. Please be careful and let us know that you are safe as soon as you can." He looked at me as if to say something. I held up my hands.

"Don't even say it, Harry. We both knew this was coming."

He put down the radio mic and went back to the driver's seat, started the coach, and pulled back onto Highway 20.

Maddie had a map of Seattle and the surrounding area out on the table, and she was going over their route to the medical warehouse.

"I think it would make more sense to dock down here near Burien, find a vehicle, and head straight to the warehouse, and then head to the house if we strike out," she said, pointing to area just west of Renton on the map.

"That is, *if* we can find a vehicle," Parker added. "This point is about nine miles from the warehouse, so if we have to hoof it we're looking at three hours in and three hours back, at least."

"Josh, how long do you think it will take us to get here?" she said, still pointing to Burien on the map.

"Well, it's pretty calm today and we're making good time; I'd say an hour and half."

"That doesn't give us much time at the warehouse if we want to make it back to the boat before dark on foot, but let's play it by ear. Hopefully we can find transportation," Parker said.

An hour and ten minutes later, they were approaching the area where they planned to disembark.

"Head toward that dock at your two o'clock, Josh," Maddie directed. Josh corrected his heading and aimed for the floating dock that she pointed out.

They were all a little keyed up. Although it was daylight, they felt the pressure of the task ahead of them and the possibility of running into trouble. Parker double-checked his M4. It had a suppressor on it and an ACOG scope. He had a utility vest with several magazines for both the M4 and the suppressed Sig Sauer Mosquito he carried. The Mosquito was only a twenty-two, but the sound it made was just barely louder than someone spitting—he liked that. Doreen carried the other Mosquito and one of the Wilson Combat shotguns. Josh carried his CHP .40-caliber automatic and one of the M4s with no suppressor. Maddie had her trusty AR on a single-point sling and the Judge strapped to her leg.

They pulled up to the dock. Parker stepped off the boat and tied off the lines. They checked their comms and headed out.

The dock was attached to a small boathouse with a set of stairs that reached up the hillside to a stone terrace. Parker took the lead and poked his head up over the top of the stairs to find the terrace was a hundred feet deep with a guesthouse nestled into the bank behind it. He knew it was a guesthouse because of the fancy sign on it that said *Guesthouse.*

They had already discussed the fact that they didn't want to get bogged down searching every house they came to, so Parker lead the group around the side of the guesthouse to a gravel pathway that lead up through the beautifully landscaped hillside. The sun penetrated the canopy of evergreens in bright beams that lit the cultivated forest, giving it a surreal appearance. The main house loomed ahead a few hundred feet to the east.

"I imagine that would set you back a million or so," Josh remarked.

"Yeah, a couple of weeks ago; now, not so much," Parker said as he motioned to Maddie. "It doesn't look like the garage is attached to the house. What do you think?"

She surveyed the layout. "Let's move straight to the garage and see what's in it."

They moved as stealthily as possible toward the garage. When they got close to the house, Maddie signaled Parker that she would cover him while he checked it out. He nodded his understanding and moved to the back of the garage.

The garage was small and it appeared to be much older than the house. It emptied straight on to the road that bordered the property. He glanced back at Maddie and then went to the side door. Inside, he could see the form of a car under a cover. He banged on the door twice with the palm of his hand, then listened and watched. Nothing moved or shrieked at him, so he tried the knob. It turned freely in his hand, but the door wouldn't budge; the deadbolt was thrown. Without much thought, he broke out the windowpane with the butt of the M4, reached in, and turned the deadbolt.

The doorframe next to his head exploded. In the next second, he wondered what was happening when the windowpane next to his ear shattered. Then he heard Maddie open up with her AR, sending rounds toward the house. The next thing he realized, he was inside the garage with his back against wall. The right side of his face stung and he reached up to find a splinter of wood sticking out of his cheek. He removed it with a quick jerk and then rolled over and peeked out the door. He couldn't see anyone, and the gunfire had ceased.

Maddie called out. "You in the house, we aren't looking for trouble, we're just passing through." The reply came in the form of several more shots fired.

Parker kept clear of the door and went over to the car. He pulled the cover off to find a 1960 Porsche 356b convertible. The fact that he kept on finding classic cars was not lost on him, but right now, he wished it was a minivan instead of a hundred thousand dollar Porsche. He radioed the others.

"I'll lay down some cover fire and you guys beat feet to the garage." He didn't wait for an answer. He stepped to the door and loosed a dozen rounds at the second story of the house.

Josh came first, sliding around the corner and diving into the doorway. Parker shot a few more rounds at the house and then Doreen popped out from behind a tree fifteen feet away and sprinted to him. Several more shots came from the house, and Doreen fell. Maddie began pumping more fire at the house, and Josh darted back out, grabbed Doreen, and dragged her into the garage. He searched her all over but couldn't find where she'd been hit. She rolled over and gave him an embarrassed shrug.

"I tripped."

Josh didn't say anything; he went to the front garage door and peeked out the row of windows. He unlocked the door and rolled it up, then looked around the corner back at the house.

Maddie came over the radio.

"I think there is only one. I need you to distract him again and I'll get up against the house where he can't get an angle on me."

"Then what are you going to do? Don't be stupid," Parker said. "Give me a minute."

He walked over to the Porsche and looked it over. It had a tiny backseat, but with the roof down, they could make it work. There were no keys, but the 356b didn't have any antitheft locks, so hotwiring it would be a breeze. Parker clicked the transmit button.

"Maddie, when we start shooting, make for the garage."

"Okay" she replied.

"Josh, shoot at the house when I start shooting; Doreen, be ready to help Maddie if she needs it." They both nodded their understanding.

Parker aimed at the second-story window and began firing. Josh joined in from the front of the garage. Maddie ran from tree to tree until she was fifteen feet from the garage, then sprinted for the door. When she ran through the door, Doreen caught her in a hug and stopped her progress after a few backward steps. Parker swung the door shut and turned toward Maddie.

"We're going to steal his Porsche and ride out of here," he said. Maddie looked at him, then at the Porsche, then back at him.

"In that little thing?"

"Yep!" he said as he went around the car and opened the door. He got under the dash and pulled the ignition wires free. He stripped and twisted them together, and then touched the power wire to them. The Porsche's starter whirred and the engine fired right up.

"I got movement at the back of the house," Josh said, as he began firing a few rounds off in that direction.

"Everybody on board as best you can!" Parker said as he slid in behind the wheel. Maddie jumped in the passenger seat and Doreen sat on the folded-up ragtop with her feet in the backseat.

"Come on, Josh!" she yelled at him as Parker got the car moving. Josh fired a couple more rounds, then jumped on the back of the car as it pulled out of the garage, with both Maddie and Doreen grabbing onto him.

Parker swung the car left onto Maplewild Street, and Josh slid precariously close to the right fender, his left foot just catching the bumper in time to stop him from flying off. Bullets zipped past them like angry bees as Parker tried to push the accelerator through the floor. A few hundred yards away, the road took a right turn. By the time they hit the corner, Josh had his head stuck down behind Maddie's seat, his ass in the air and his legs dangling off the back, with Doreen hugging both as tight as she could. Parker downshifted and made the turn without losing either of them.

They drove for a couple of minutes and then pulled to a stop next to an empty field. It took both Maddie and Doreen to pull Josh back out of his spot, but everyone had come out unscathed. Parker had parked the car sideways across the road.

"Everybody out, and be ready in case they're following us," he said.

They all got behind the car and crouched down, pointing the weapons back down the road. They listened but heard no sound of anyone following.

Maddie stood up and slung her rifle onto her back.

"Okay, I hate to split us up, but Josh, we have to get the boat moved before they think to go look for it. Head straight to the waterfront from here and then work your way back to the dock. If they have found it, or are down by the water, don't risk it. If they aren't around, get the boat and bring it north a couple of miles and wait for us. Doreen, you go with him; Parker and I will go to the warehouse."

"No, you may run into more trouble and you'll need as much firepower with you as you can," Josh said. "I'll get the boat; you guys get Clay's meds." Then, without waiting, he started off at a trot across the field to the west.

They squeezed back into the Porsche. With Doreen sitting sideways, she could actually fit into the backseat with her feet up behind the driver's seat. They sped off in search of the warehouse.

Twenty minutes later, they pulled up in front of what Maddie said was the warehouse.

"How did you know about this place?" Parker asked her.

"Liv, Josh's girlfriend, told me about it. She'd been here with her brother a couple of times."

"Will they have the drugs Clay needs?" Doreen asked as she climbed out of the backseat.

"They should; they supply all the hospitals in Seattle. The real question is, will we be able to find them?"

The radio sounded off. It was laced with static, but understandable.

"Hey guys... the boat and I'm... our rendezvous... no contact... anyone." Well, that was good news.

"Roger that, we are at our destination and are starting the search. We'll be in touch every half-hour," Maddie answered. They heard a couple of clicks in response.

They headed toward the buildings, looking for the main office. Parker held up his hand and stopped.

"You hear that?" he said in response to the audible sound of a generator running in the distance.

"Yeah, they must have a pretty big fuel tank in order for that to still be running," Maddie said. "Either that or there is still someone here."

They cautiously made their way around the buildings, following the sound. After walking a couple of blocks, they came to the source of the sound. There were several industrial Caterpillar diesel generators chugging away behind a fence. To the right was a massive storage tank.

"Well, that answers that question—or does it?" Parker said.

The building closest to the generators looked like office

space, accompanied by a parking lot full of vehicles. Some looked like company cars, but many, if not most, looked like private vehicles that belonged to the warehouse workers.

"That is not a good sign," Maddie said. "That means there were a bunch of people here when the shit hit the fan."

Parker nodded. "Yeah, we need to be really careful. Let's check out the offices to see if we can figure out where they have the stuff we need. We'll never find it just looking around; this place is huge."

The front doors were intact, which they took to be a good sign. The places that had freaks in them usually had busted-up entryways. The building was too big to scout out, though, so there could be other, less obvious ways inside. Maddie and Doreen positioned themselves behind two different cars as Parker approached the doors.

He stood to one side and banged on the doors with his fist a few times, then waited. No people, nor freaks, moved inside, from what he could see. He tried the door... locked. He pulled the Sig Mosquito from its holster and aimed it at the lock. The first shot did no damage—the bullet just ricocheted off—so he holstered the .22 and blasted the damn thing with the M4. They could all hear the shrieking loud and clear as soon as the sound of the gunshots ebbed. Parker peeked around the edge of the door. The lights were on, but he could see no one at home. He waved the girls forward and stepped into the office.

He immediately noted the temperature and the smell. It was pleasantly cool, but still smelled like a dead man's ass. The A/C was apparently still working, but that had not saved the office workers, several of whom were now deceased and littering the floor in front of him. Doreen came up behind him.

"Good golly, the smell is enough to gag a maggot." There were no maggots present, which was a relief, but Doreen caught sight of the carnage and immediately backed away and started throwing up. It was her first exposure to the results of an attack. Maddie understood and consoled her as Doreen regained her composure.

Parker cleared the front room to make sure there weren't any freaks lurking in a dark closet or hallway. Although it was obvious they had been here, it appeared that they came in through the back of the office, which connected to one of the warehouses. There was no immediate threat that he could see.

The power from the generators supplied the office as well as the warehouses, and several computer workstations sat idle, their desktops mutely staring back at Parker.

"Maddie, come here," he called from the front of the building. She stuck her head in the door.

"What'd you find?" He pointed at one of the monitors.

"Looks like Bill Gates wins a few points; his damn operating system is still running on a couple of the PCs in here."

Maddie came in, yelling back at Doreen to stay put. Parker pulled the dead office worker away from the desk and pulled a chair up to the keyboard. Maddie sat down and moved the mouse.

"Damn, screen saver password." She began opening the desk drawers, checking to see if the worker had written down the password. She remembered Ryan telling her that by requiring stronger passwords that contained multiple letters, symbols, and minimum lengths, companies were inadvertently weakening their security. Most people ended up just writing the password down on a sticky note and storing it close to their computer. After going through the desk and not finding it, Maddie was about to try another workstation when she flipped the keyboard over, and there it was. She moved the cursor to the password field, typed it in, and hit enter. It came back with "wrong username or password." Ryan had also told her that instead of constantly changing the entire password, a lot of people just added a number to the end of the previous password to make it easier to remember. She tried the password again and added a 1 at the end. Still no luck.

Look for clues within your immediate area, Ryan's voice in her head reminded her. She scanned the cubical and saw a calendar with the 14th of the month circled. She tried the password again with a 14 tacked to the end of it, and the computer's desktop popped up.

"I'm in!" she announced.

She began to look at the most recently loaded spreadsheets and after twenty minutes, she found what she was looking for. She sent the page she needed to the printer in the hope that it was still working as well.

Parker heard the printer next to him whir to life. He pretended that it hadn't startled him, and retrieved the paper from it. "Inventory Building Sixteen," he read at the top of the page.

"Okay, let's go see if we can find this," he said as he handed it to her. "Good work, Maddie."

It was two o'clock in the afternoon and we hadn't heard a peep over the radio. Harry was pacing like a father waiting for his daughter to return from the prom.

"Why the hell haven't they called us?" He'd been out to the coach every fifteen minutes trying to raise them on the radio.

"Look, Harry, the warehouse is fifty miles from the island. They're probably out of range." It was a weak argument, but it was the best I had. He left us in the building that Thomas had set up as his bomb factory at the farm and went back to the coach.

"I wish he would just stay the hell out there," Thomas said. "He's making me nervous, and that isn't a good thing for me to be." I could tell he was serious.

"I'll go sit with him and wait for some info," I said, and got up to leave.

"Ryan," Thomas said.

I turned around. "Yeah?"

"Have Harry move the coach down to the other side of the barn, and gather everyone that's working. I am getting to a critical place here, and if I fuck up I don't want to take anyone out with me."

"Yes sir," I said and went to do as he asked.

I gathered the crews working the farm and had Harry move the coach. We were all sitting on pins and needles waiting for a loud boom and a mushroom cloud to appear on the other side of the farm. After what seemed like forever, Thomas came around the end of the barn.

"Well, it didn't go off when I connected the wires, so that's a good thing. Now I'm just wondering if the damn thing will go off when we want it to." A nervous laughter rippled across the group.

"Okay, I need three of you to help me load this thing onto the pickup, and then we'll move it down to the pier." Merle, Henry, and Derek got up and followed him, and the rest of us sat there wondering what to do.

"Why don't we all head back down to the farmhouse and fix some dinner? I'm sure everyone will be hungry soon," I said, and Molly started giving out orders to folks to keep them busy.

Forty-five minutes later, the radio came to life.

"Harry, you got a copy?" It was Maddie, and I'd never seen someone look as relieved as Harry looked right then.

"Hey sweetie, I copy!" he replied.

"Sorry for the long wait. Everyone is fine, we are back on Josh's boat and headed for the ferry now. The mission was a success." The news was good, and Harry could finally relax.

"Okay baby, we'll see you back at the cove, over."

The sun was setting by the time the ferry returned, and we hurriedly shuttled everyone back onboard. Thomas oversaw the loading of the IED onto Josh's boat, and with that, everything was set for the big day.

It was a clear night, and we all gathered on the open car

deck. Conner and Carla, with the help of Trish and her mom, had procured three picnic tables from the Clinton ferry terminal and had set them up on one end of the ferry. Everyone else had brought various beach and camping chairs from shore. Henry had found a nice size fire pit that he'd somehow gotten back to the ferry. We sat around the fire, Derek playing the guitar and the rest of us singing every song that we knew and some that we obviously didn't. I sang out of tune but loved the sound of my own voice. Parker got most of the lyrics to "Bad Moon Rising" right, but got the verses mixed up. Maddie sang "Evangelina," an old Hoyt Axton tune; and by the time she finished, I'd tears welling up in my eyes, thinking of J.

We heard the rumbling of thunder in the distance, so we broke up the party and all headed for bed. As I walked by Clay, he waved me over.

"You know, there isn't a thunderstorm within a hundred miles of us tonight," he said.

"Huh," I said, not sure what to make of the comment. Max overheard and stopped next to us.

"I didn't want to say anything, but that wasn't thunder—that was artillery, or something like it. At Fort Lewis, we used to sit around listening to it when we were out in the field on maneuvers."

"So, you think there are still some army grunts out there shooting off artillery?" I asked.

"Either that or someone is trying to eliminate some of the freaks," Max said.

"Could be the group Harry heard over the radio, or the ones that attacked Maddie's group," I said. It worried me, but there wasn't a lot we could do about it. Probably just a storm Clay hadn't seen on the radar. We broke it up and headed for our racks.

I was the first one up the next morning. I made the coffee,

and when it finished brewing, I took a cup up to the sundeck. I looked across Penn Cove and marveled at its beauty. It seemed so peaceful that for a few minutes I forgot about what the world had become. A couple of otters floated nearby, busy having breakfast. They would set a shellfish on their stomach and bash it with a rock, eat it, then disappear below the water for another. The sun peeked out over the mountains to the east, the smoke from the fires there creating a picture worthy of Galen Rowell.

My thoughts were interrupted by the sound of a rooster crowing somewhere onshore. The rest of the world didn't care about the drastic turn our human lives had taken—it just kept going. The sun rose, the rooster crowed.

Hmmm, chicken and biscuits... I miss chicken and biscuits. I laughed to myself and went to find out who else was up.

After a breakfast of two hotdogs and a couple more cups of coffee, I was ready to go. We spent the better part of an hour saying our goodbyes, but high tide was approaching and we had to cut it short. Max, Lisa, Harry, Maddie, Thomas, and Parker went ashore with me in Parker's Zodiac. Josh and Conner set out for the pass in the Duckworth carrying the IED. Parker had rigged climbing ropes and harnesses for him and Thomas. It was decided that they would climb out and tie off under the bridge's catwalk, then lower the block and tackle to Conner and Josh in the boat.

The IED itself would be detonated using a walkie-talkie. It was risky, because any signal on the designated channel would set the bomb off once it was armed. Thomas had designed the IED with the walkie-talkie in place, and left it turned off and without a battery. He used the cheapest set of radios he could find with a range of one mile. I asked him why he wasn't using the higher quality radios for the bomb. He said the limited range was the main reason. If a stray signal from some other radio on that channel was floating around out there, he didn't want our bomb's radio to hear it. It made sense to me. He also pointed out, with a smile, that the radio wouldn't survive the operation.

Before setting off on their part of the mission, Josh and Conner had been fully briefed on their role. They would deliver the IED, and once that was accomplished, they were to go radio silent and return to the ferry.

Thomas had inventoried all the walkie-talkies, and spent the morning collecting them from everyone on the ferry. He systematically removed the batteries from each of them and put them in a locker with orders that they were not to be touched until he returned. Our group took our radios and did the same with all but one, which we would use up until the time that the IED was to be activated.

Harry stopped the coach about halfway across the southern span of the bridge and let us out. He then kept driving until the coach was back on the mainland and far enough away to be safe from the blast. Max and Lisa pulled the Humvee past us and stopped. Parker and Thomas drove the F250 with all the equipment in the bed.

Thomas went over to the railing separating the road from the sidewalk, nimbly climbed over it, and leaned over the outside rail. Josh and Conner waited in the Duckworth, tied off to the stanchions directly below us.

"Okay guys, give us a few minutes to get organized and we'll send down the line," Thomas said over the radio.

"10-4," Josh replied.

Parker laid out the block and tackle and simulated how it would hang below the bridge. He used zip ties to bundle the ropes at the block so they wouldn't move while he was getting it in place. The deck of the bridge sat 180 feet above the water. The area Thomas had chosen to attach the IED was a little less than that. Having arranged the ropes they would use to raise the bomb, Parker began to work on the rigging that would secure him and Thomas. He tied an additional line to the top of the block and tackle rig and secured the other end to his harness. Then he attached another line at the same place and handed the other end to me.

"When we get down there, you guys will lower the block and its rigging over the side. When it gets down to me, I will pull it over with my line. Once we have the IED in place, we'll signal you to pull all the rigging back up here." I nodded my understanding.

"You ready to do this, Thomas?" he said.

Thomas did not look overly excited about the whole prospect, but put on a brave front.

"Hell yes, let's get this done. Remember, once I tell you to disable the radio, we will have no comms, so if you have any questions, ask them before that. Under no circumstances are you to use the radio after I tell you to disable it. Turn it off, take out the battery, and set it in the vehicle. Are we clear?" he said, looking directly at me.

"Yes," I replied.

Parker double-checked his rigging, then his harness, and did the same on Thomas.

"Well, nothing left but to do it."

With that, he climbed over the rail and stood waiting for Thomas to do the same. Thomas climbed over, and it was obvious that he was nowhere near as confident as Parker. His hands shook just enough to be noticeable.

Max and Lisa each held the belay lines for them, and Parker was the first to lean back.

"On belay?" he said.

"On belay," Lisa answered.

He stepped down the side of the bridge. Thomas had rappelled before, but never at such height.

"I'm having a moment here," he said with a nervous smile.

"Take your time," Parker said from below him.

Thomas took a couple of deep breaths and then leaned out away from the bridge.

"On belay?" he said in a bit of a squeaky voice.

"On belay," Max answered confidently.

The worst thing you can do when rappelling is lean into the structure or rock you are going down. It puts your entire weight on the line and you lose your footing. And that's exactly what Thomas did.

"Oh shit!" he said, not out of fear this time, but out of embarrassment for his mistake.

He struggled for a minute, then, with Parker's assistance, he got his feet secured and regained control. I watched as they inched down the side of the bridge to the latticework of steel girders that made up the support. Now that they were at that level, they would be climbing across, not down.

"Okay, give us some slack," Parker called over the radio.

"Roger," I said as Max and Lisa played out a few feet of line.

I could no longer see them, and the only way to determine their progress was the line playing out as they crossed to the predetermined spot under the bridge.

"Okay, have Max and Lisa play out another six feet of line and tie them off. Double-check each other's knots; it's our lifeline," Parker said over the radio.

It was not time for messing around, so we did exactly what he said without giving him any of our normal brotherly chitchat.

"Done. You're secured with about six feet of play," I radioed.

"Send down the block and tackle," was the next thing we heard.

We all pitched in and successfully lowered the rig over the side. It was pretty damn heavy, but with all of us on the line that Parker had given to me, we were able to let it down slowly.

"That's good," Parker said, and we could feel the tug as he pulled it back under the bridge.

We listened to the progress over the radio as we hung over the rail to watch as much as possible. Josh and Conner had the IED hooked up about an hour into the whole project, and were now hoisting it up a foot at a time.

They had to pull down on one line while still holding the tether attached to the bomb so the wind wouldn't swing it too much. It took them another twenty minutes to get the IED up to where Thomas and Parker waited patiently.

"Looks like we got the easy part," I said to Maddie.

Parker and Thomas had debated the best way to secure the IED to the spot they had chosen. Thomas designed the device so the blast would be directed at the supporting structure, but he admitted it was just a mathematical equation and we would have to wait to see if it was going to act as we hoped. The final decision was simple: duct tape, lots of duct tape. They wedged the IED in between a vertical and horizontal support, and spent thirty minutes wrapping it with duct tape.

"That's not going anywhere," Thomas told Parker.

While they wrapped the IED in duct tape, we hauled the block and tackle rig back up and onto the deck of the bridge. We got it all loaded into the back of the F250 about the same time we heard the radio squelch.

"We are almost done. Anybody got anything to say before we shut down comms?" Thomas asked.

"Yeah." It was Josh in the Duckworth. "We are going to stick around down here until you get back on top of the bridge safely, just in case."

"Okay, but if this thing goes off prematurely, there won't be anything to retrieve," Parker answered.

"Roger," Josh said somberly.

"Anybody else?" Thomas asked. "No? Okay, disable the radios now."

I turned off the walkie and removed the battery, which I put in my pocket. I laid the radio in the Humvee, as Thomas had requested.

The next thirty minutes dragged by for those of us on the bridge. Knowing that we were sitting right above a 300-pound bomb that was now being armed was nerve-racking. We retreated to Pass Island, which was a couple hundred yards away. I sat on the side of the road and watched through the binoculars. I couldn't see much, just glimpses of them as they worked.

"Hey Parker, why don't you go ahead and climb on up while I arm this thing?" Thomas said.

"We're in this together. Just don't fuck up... no pressure," Parker answered.

"Okay, here goes nothing."

Thomas dried his hands on his pants and took the battery out of his shirt pocket. With his left leg wrapped around the girder that held the bomb and his right foot on the horizontal support, he leaned over the IED and looked at the radio. He reached out to put the battery in and his foot slipped off the support. He swung out wildly and his left foot caught in between the girder and the bomb. Parker reached out and grabbed him and stopped him from breaking his ankle. The battery landed a second later in the water, about twenty feet from where Josh looked up at them in angst.

"I got you!" Parker said as he pulled him back to the support. "Now aren't you glad I stuck around?"

"I'm going to need to change my underwear when we're done here," Thomas replied.

Parker gave Josh a thumbs up and added, "I think we all will; please tell me you have another battery."

"Yeah, I have a backup here somewhere." He searched his pants and produced a second battery.

Thomas repositioned himself over the IED and slid the battery into the radio.

"Here is where we find out if I did this part correctly." He reached over to the radio controls and paused just an instant before turning the switch to the "on" position.

"Well, we're still breathing," he said, smiling at Parker.

I saw Parker waving at us. He was back to the edge of the supporting structure below the bridge. We drove back to his position, got out, went to the railing, and looked down.

"Get those belays untied and take up the slack," he yelled up. Max and Lisa did as directed and were ready on belay.

"Ready on belay?" I shouted down to them.

"On belay," Parker shouted back up.

Max and Lisa gave me a nod.

"On belay," I shouted, and Parker and Thomas began climbing back up.

When they got their feet on the bridge deck, I felt much better.

"How did it go?" Maddie asked Thomas.

"I don't know," he said. "I expect we will all find out together when it either goes 'kaboom' or 'psst.'"

That got a laugh out of everyone, even Parker. We stood around for a couple of minutes while Parker got all the lines put away in the truck, and then it was kind of awkward. What do you say to someone you may never see again?

I held out my hand to Thomas. He shook it and gave me the typical halfway man hug.

"Take care of Maddie and Harry. They need someone to watch their backs," he said. I nodded, and turned to Parker.

"Going to miss you, brother; hopefully we will meet again someday," I said as I gave him a full-on bear hug.

"Yeah, I never was able to keep either of you from tagging along. I'm sure you'll show up again eventually," he said, stepping from my hug into one from Max.

With all our farewells said, there was nothing to do but retreat. I handed the walkie to Thomas and then the battery from my pocket.

"Wait until we get to the other side before you put that back together, okay?"

He chuckled. "Why, ya scared?"

"No, just don't want to be around when your bomb does work," I said, smiling.

Max, Lisa, Maddie, Harry, and I got into the Humvee and headed for the other end of the bridge.

Parker and Thomas climbed into the F250 and backed it up past the end of the bridge, turned around, and drove to a safe distance. I looked down to the water and saw Josh waving goodbye from the boat. I gave him a wave back.

Thomas waited until Josh had gone a good distance back out of the channel and then put the radio on the hood of the truck. He put the battery back in, turned it over, then flicked the power on. He looked over at Parker.

"You want the honors?" he said.

"Nah; it's all you, Thomas."

*****

We stood on the overlook north of the pass. I felt the blast in my chest before I heard the *Whump!* Then I felt the ground tremble under my feet. The bridge deck, where we had been standing just moments before, heaved into the air before breaking to pieces. It was quickly obscured in a cloud of debris. What followed was a sound of screeching metal as the structure tore itself apart. It sounded like giant swords colliding, with cracks and pops thrown in for good measure. Pieces fell to the channel below, sending geysers of water fifty feet into the air. A wide chasm was left, with tendrils of metal girders hanging from each side.

We stood there slack-jawed for a full minute after the last of the debris had settled. In the stillness that followed, I was lost in my own thoughts for that brief moment.

We were leaving the family we'd just found. Meg, Sarah and the kids, Jean, Lynn and her grandkids, Henry and Molly, Parker, Carla and Conner... their faces passed through my mind's eye. We were all leaving someone here we cared about with the hope that others we loved were still hanging on, waiting for us.

Hang on just a little longer, we're coming!

About the Author

Mark has always been a bit of a vagabond. Born in Washington, raised in California he joined the Coast Guard after high school. During his Coast Guard career, he was an Admiral's driver in San Francisco, a deckhand on a cutter in the Bering Sea, and an Aviation Electrician in North Carolina, Texas, and Southern Florida. After he left the Coast Guard he worked security, first guarding MX nuclear missiles, then at a nuclear power plant in California. Eventually he went to college in Wisconsin, only to drop out after meeting his future wife. He went on to finish college at 36 and owned a Miracle Ear franchise for a while. He went into publishing for a short time before becoming an Information Systems Specialist. He currently splits his time between West (by God) Virginia and Surfside Beach, SC.

http://www.pmarkdebryan.com

Facebook
https://www.facebook.com/P.MarkDeBryan

E-mail
pmdebryan@gmail.com

Acknowledgements

To John O'Brien, thanks for encouraging me to write, for showing me the ropes, and for giving me so much help.

To Sara Jones, an excellent writer and my editor, I send heartfelt thanks for her encouragement and hard work. She has had faith in this book from the start and is the best. To my beta readers Lisa, Rebecca, Bobby, Larry, Kara, Lee, John, and my sister Lori, thank you for test-driving this book and for your help in the story's development. A special thanks to Carlton Keith Parsons for his technical assistance.

To Miki at Marathon Coach, thank you for chasing down your engineers and getting all my technical questions answered. I hope your entire company enjoys the story.

To Justin McCormick for the awesome cover.

To my daughter, Lori, who edited the very first draft of my short story, I love you and am so proud of the woman you have become. To my son, Brad, thanks for coming over and watching football with me; it is the best respite.

Last but certainly not least, to my wife of 28 years, Jonie. Thank you for not shooting me, and for letting the dogs in and out four million times while I wrote this... I love you!

John O'Brien's series is the best thing out there, give him a read. Here is a link to his first book in the series *A New World*

http://www.amazon.com/gp/product/B004W0CL2Y

Diagram of the Marathon Coach

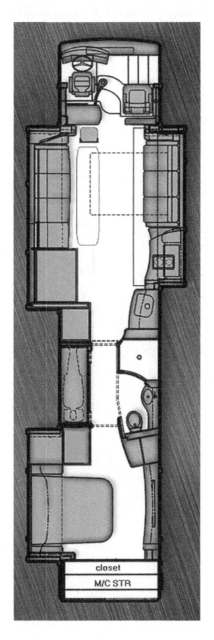

closet

M/C STR

Diagram of the Tokitae

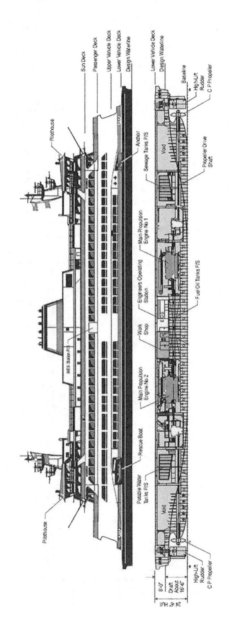

Made in the USA
Coppell, TX
15 April 2022

76612917R00194